in a jam

kate canterbary

vesper press

copyright

Editing provided by Julia Ganis of Julia Edits.
Editing provided by Erica Russikoff of Erica Edits.
Proofreading provided by Marla Esposito of Proofing Style.
Proofreading provided by Jodi Duggan.

For the meatballs.

about in a jam

When Shay Zucconi's step-grandmother died, she left Shay a tulip farm —under two conditions.

First, Shay has to move home to the small town of Friendship, Rhode Island. Second—and most problematic since her fiancé just called off the wedding—Shay must be married within one year.

Marriage is the last thing in the world Shay wants but she'll do anything to save the only real home she's ever known.
Noah Barden loved Shay Zucconi back in high school. Not that he ever told her. He was too shy, too awkward, too painfully uncool to ask out the beautiful, popular girl.

A lifetime later, Noah is a single dad to his niece and has his hands full running the family business. That old crush is the farthest thing from his mind.

Until Shay returns to their hometown and turns his life upside down.

CW/TW: absentee parent(s), brief mention of parent death, brief mention of parent chronic illness, mention of incarceration, mention of temporary foster care placement, reference to teenage teasing/bullying (not detailed, not explicit), incidence of fat-shaming, living with a neurodivergent child.

prologue

Shay

Today's learning objective:
Students will be able to know when it's time for an axe.

I WAS in my wedding dress when he called. Dress, veil, shoes, and an industrial-strength corset to smooth down my squish. It was a great cupcake of a gown too, heavy and poufy and impractical for a July wedding but it looked perfect nonetheless. Everything was perfect.

He said, "This isn't going to work out, Shay."

I knew what he meant and I knew it before my name left his lips. He wasn't talking about the raw bar or the dogwood branches canopying the aisle or the band. And I wasn't surprised.

I should've been surprised. I should've been shocked. But the spots where those emotions should've lived were filled with a dry, brittle emptiness that cackled back at me. And that cackle said I should've known better.

All I could do was rip the veil from my head and fling it to the hotel suite's plush carpet while a quartet of bridesmaids cried out in horror. The veil meant something, and they knew it. A hair out of place wasn't a risk I'd take, not minutes before moving outside for pre-ceremony photos.

The photographer lowered her camera as I said to my ex-fiancé, "Okay."

Okay, apparently this doesn't warrant an in-person conversation.

The photographer took a step backward. Then another.

Okay, we're not getting married in three hours.

My maid of honor Jaime moved toward me, a hand outstretched and her eyes wide.

Okay, a year and a half of planning, right out the window.

My bridesmaids Emme and Grace exchanged a glance that seemed to ask *What the hell?*

Okay, all the things I thought I'd done right, wasted.

Audrey smoothed the skirt of her navy bridesmaid's dress and ushered the hair and makeup artists toward the door.

Okay. Okay.

"Did…did you hear me?" he asked. "Do you get what I'm saying?"

I wish I could say this sort of thing didn't happen to me. Not that I'd ever been left at the altar before—or damn close to the altar—but that I'd been left *somewhere.*

"You're ending it," I said, hating the quiver in my voice. He didn't get to destroy me like this and listen while I broke down. I yanked at the suffocating bodice of my dress. I was going to throw up if I didn't get this thing off me. "You'll make this announcement to the guests?"

He didn't respond immediately, and in that silence I heard a ticking that sounded very much like a turn signal. "I can't be the one to do that," he said, "because I'm not there."

I hadn't completely understood what it meant to turn on a dime until my ex-fiancé dumped me and refused to clean up that mess, all within the span of five minutes. I'd loved him, and I'd loved him for *years*, yet he destroyed our wedding day and I wasn't even surprised. I couldn't access any of the affection I'd once felt for him right now. All the good and kind things I'd once attached to him turned bitter. They shriveled on the spot. As much as I had loved him, I discovered I could now despise and resent and loathe him. It came to me rather easily.

And that did surprise me.

"What do you mean you're not here?" I asked, kicking off the fuchsia heels that perfectly matched my bouquet. "Don't you think you should say something to your family?"

He cleared his throat. "They won't be coming. They already know. I told them last night." Another throat clearing. Another turn signal. "After the rehearsal dinner."

A shocked noise shot out of me, something between a laugh and a gut punch groan. Now I was certain I was going to vomit. But before I sprinted to the bathroom, I was going to—for the first time in three years—tell this man precisely what I was thinking. No more editing. No more putting on a good face.

"*Last night*—what? No. To hell with that. And to hell with you. I can't imagine why you'd tell your family last night but wait, like, eighteen hours to tell me. The person you were supposed to marry today. And I don't care. I don't want an explanation. It doesn't matter. We are finished." I pulled at the bodice until a satisfying rip filled the room. Then my friends were there, surrounding me, untying, unzipping, unhooking until that gorgeous whipped cream dream of a gown—the one I'd planned the entire wedding around, the one I'd hunted down, the one I'd starved myself for—pooled at my feet. "Never speak to me again. *Never*."

I threw my phone with the intention of it smashing into the wall and crumbling into a million pieces but my aim was terrible and it landed on the bed, its dark face glaring back at me in the sea of crisp white linen.

"What do you need?" Jaime asked.

I shook my head. Three hundred of our closest friends and family members would be arriving within the hour. Save for the ones the ex had already warned off. There was no fixing this.

"Do you want me to get your mom?" Emme asked.

"No," Jaime and I said in unison. I admired my mother but *maternal* or *comforting* were not words anyone would use to describe her.

"Do you want a giant bowl of liquor and an axe?" Grace asked.

"How about a giant bowl of liquor and a quick exit?" Audrey asked.

"Something like that," I whispered.

"We've got you," Emme said.

I sobbed then, loud and hysterical and shattered.

My friends closed in around me, one wrapping a robe around my shoulders, another pushing a bottle into my hand and saying "Drink" with a firmness that wouldn't be swayed, a third plucking the pins from my hair while another gathered up the gown and got it out of sight. Not that I could see much through this uncontrollable downpour of tears.

"He can fuck right off." That was Emme.

"He never deserved her." Audrey.

"He'd better hope I don't get my hands on him." Grace, ever feral.

"While you plot his dismemberment, I'm going downstairs to—to handle everything. I'll talk to your mom and stepdad too."

Something about Jaime's carefully worded announcement, about *handling* my ruination, tore through me harder than anything the ex said this afternoon. I brought the bottle to my mouth and tipped my head back, not caring whether the vodka burned my throat or dribbled down my chin or smudged my lipstick.

None of it mattered.

I didn't have to be perfect anymore, and that came as a strange sort of parting gift. A gift I hadn't asked for and didn't want. But I'd been fond of perfect. I'd liked that look for me. And I'd played by the rules of perfect. I'd done everything right.

And none of it mattered.

chapter one

Shay

Students will be able to do battle with attorneys, cow trucks, and pirates.

"YOU HAVE TO SIGN FOR A LETTER."

I blinked up at Jaime from my cocoon on her sofa, day drunk and dressed in three-day-old pajamas. Two weeks after being left at the altar, I was at least slightly drunk most of the time but I didn't cry constantly, which seemed like an improvement.

That, or evidence of dehydration. I wasn't sure.

"But why?" I asked.

She scooped her long, silky brown hair up and tied it in a ponytail. "I don't know, doll. I tried to do it for you but the dude asked for ID."

It took me a minute to scrape myself off the sofa. The door was quite the journey for me. I'd only ventured outside the warehouse-turned-loft apartment Jaime shared with three other women a handful of times since everything fell apart on my wedding day.

The first time I pulled myself together enough to leave the apartment was to chop off six inches of hair—hair I'd spent nearly two years growing out for the perfect wedding look—and then take my natural blonde to rose gold.

I had no specific reason for wanting shoulder-length pink hair. I couldn't explain it. All I knew was I didn't want to see the old version of me in the mirror anymore.

That was what led me to the tattoo. Much more permanent than changing up my hair but I'd wanted it for years, and now I needed a visible reminder that whoever I had been before this disaster wasn't the me of today.

Then, I sold everything touched by my former relationship. Dresses of every kind. Engagement photo dresses, engagement party dresses, bridal shower dresses, bachelorette dresses. The after-party and the next-day brunch outfits, the honeymoon looks. Those fabulous magenta shoes and the veil. Anything I'd worn with the ex. All the random bits of wedding kitsch I'd carefully collected. Even two-ish years of bridal magazines.

And that damn gown. As it turned out, I hadn't ripped it in any significant way. Just a tear along the side seam, nothing a tailor couldn't handle. Seeing as that designer hardly ever made anything to fit a size sixteen gal like myself, there were dozens of brides lined up to buy it from me.

There wasn't much left after that. The clothes I wore to teach kindergarten. A collection of yoga pants in assorted shades of fading black. A shoebox filled with wacky earrings I loved but my ex-fiancé had hated.

So, here I was with new hair and fresh ink, guzzling liquor while bingeing mindless reality television on my best friend's couch in days-old pajamas as the ex enjoyed the honeymoon I'd planned and paid for as a wedding gift to him. That was my prize for following the rules.

That, and whatever the hell I had to sign for at the door.

I shuffled across the apartment, a blanket draped over my shoulders and clutched tight to my chest because this tank top could not be trusted to contain me. One wrong move and it was tits out.

Jaime leaned against the wall while I handed over my identification and signed for the letter. "What is this?" I asked the courier.

"Not my job to know," he said. "Just my job to serve the papers and you didn't make this one easy on me."

"Cryptic, much?" Jaime said as he took off down the hall.

I turned the envelope over in my hands. "Whatever it is, I don't think I care," I said, trudging back to the couch. I tossed the envelope to Jaime. "Just tell me what it says."

I stared at the television, blanket pooled at my waist as I slurped up the last of a truly heinous blend of red wine, ice, and Diet Coke. Heinous. A crime against wine. Also delicious.

Jaime tore into the envelope and I appreciated—not for the first time—the complete absence of judgment from her. Some people wouldn't abide this much wallowing. They wouldn't debate tattoo designs or cheer when the first locks of hair hit the salon floor. Jaime didn't judge, she embraced, and that was only one of the best things about her.

"It's about your step-grandmother," she said as she flipped through the pages. "The one who died."

I rattled the ice in my cup. Grandma Lollie died a couple of months ago, quiet and happy in her bed at a Florida retirement community she'd insisted on describing as "a *swinging* good time." She'd been ninety-seven years old though that never stopped her from tearing it up on salsa night. I'd lived with her for a time during high school when things were complicated for me and I loved her dearly.

She was one of the only family members that I considered true *family*. I'd believed with my whole heart that not having Grandma Lollie at my wedding was the worst thing that could happen to me.

That was a cool way to tease fate.

"This doesn't make any sense," Jaime murmured, shuffling the pages. "It sounds like she left you a—a *farm*. In *Rhode Island*."

My gaze fell to the laundry baskets, trash bags, and mismatched boxes assembled along the wall. This haphazard, ramshackle mess loudly and proudly proclaimed that some combination of my sweet, amazing, crazy friends went to the luxury high-rise condo in the Back Bay of Boston I'd shared with the ex and snatched everything they believed to be mine.

Everything, right down to a nearly empty bottle of olive oil and a broom I'd never seen before.

They were the best friends anyone could ever ask for and the closest thing I had to family here in Boston. They kept asking if there was anything I needed, if I was okay. And the truth was, I wasn't all right. Not even close.

But I didn't say that.

I glanced back to Jaime, asking, "What?"

She shook her head, pointing to the cover page. "We need to call your step-grandmother's attorney because I don't understand this stuff and there are a whole bunch of dates and requirements in here that seem really important."

I wandered into the kitchen to insult another glass of wine with ice and soda. "That doesn't make sense. It's probably a mistake. Lollie wouldn't have left me the farm. It's been in her family for hundreds of years and she had four actual grandkids, you know, from my stepdad's first marriage. She would've left it to them. Or my stepdad. Or anyone else."

Jaime pointed to the document. "We need to call this guy."

"I don't have a phone," I said. "You took it away. Remember?"

She'd pried the phone from my hands at some point. Between her and the others, they held me off in the moments I wanted to scream at the ex for waiting until the last possible seconds of our wedding day to end our relationship, and in the moments when I wanted him to explain what happened, to tell me what went wrong, what *I* did wrong. Why he'd chosen to make a fool of me.

The explanation wouldn't help. I knew that. But there were bits of time when I was tired of being drunk and sad and numb, and I wanted to stand inside the rage of being wronged in such a careless manner. I wanted that rage to exhaust me. To drain me to the extent that I was too tired to cry, too tired to even feel the numbness.

That rage was the truest thing I could feel, and even then it was little more than charbroiled disappointment. I'd planned that wedding down to the last inch and then—poof. It was gone, like none of it had ever existed at all. Like everything the wedding had represented—everything it had meant for me—never existed.

"We'll use mine," she said, pulling the device from the back pocket of her jean shorts.

I held up my glass in salute. "I'm telling you, it's a mistake. She didn't leave the farm to me."

"But what if she did?" Jaime shot me an impatient stare before dialing the number listed on the papers. I returned to the sofa, half listening while she explained our situation to someone on the other end of the line. A moment later, she handed me the phone, saying, "They're putting us through to the attorney now."

I switched over to speaker as the line rang. Then, "Hello, this is Frank Silber."

"Um, yeah, hi, this is Shay Zucconi," I said.

"Miss Zucconi! We've been trying to track you down for a month," he said, a laugh ringing through his words.

I turned over the envelope. No need to explain that he had my old-old address, the apartment where I'd lived before moving in with the ex. "Yeah, I recently moved."

"Well, now that I have you," he said, still with that jovial laugh, "I'll explain the terms of your inheritance."

"About that," I said, ignoring Jaime's arched brows. "I don't think you have the right person. Lollie's son, maybe, or her grandkids? I really don't think I was supposed to get anything."

"Your step-grandmother was very clear about her wishes," he said.

"She reviewed her will with me about three months prior to her passing. This is what she wanted."

"Okay, but—" I didn't know what else to say and Frank took my silence as an opening.

"Your step-grandmother's estate names you, Shaylene Marie Zucconi, as the sole recipient of the residence, farm buildings, and agricultural land known as Thomas Twins Farm, commonly referred to as Twin Tulip, located at eighty-one Old Windmill Hill Road in Friendship, Rhode Island."

"That's insane," I said. "I—I don't understand why she'd leave the farm to *me*."

"I can't speak for Lollie but I do remember her saying on several occasions that you'd know what to do with the farm," Frank said.

I glanced down at my sleep shorts and tank top. "Frank, I don't even know what to do with myself. Acres of land seems like a lot of responsibility for me."

He responded with a deep chuckle, as if I wasn't being completely honest, and pressed on. "There are two important requirements that I have to explain. First, you must live at the property at least fifty percent of the year and—"

"But I work in Boston," I interrupted. "I can't commute from Rhode Island."

"If you're not willing or able to meet both requirements established by the trust, the property will be turned over to the town of Friendship," he said.

Why would Lollie do this to me?

I met Jaime's gaze, giving her a slow shake of my head.

She held up her hands, shrugged. "You could always return it to the Native Americans it was mostly likely stolen from."

I muted the call while Frank went on about the town taking the farm. "She did that about forty years ago. Gave back a ton of land." I paused as Frank shouted to his assistant. "It pissed off her family in a big way but she didn't care."

"I like this lady," Jaime replied.

"And the second requirement," Frank continued, "was most important to Lollie. Her family has lived and worked that land since the early 1700s and she wanted that family presence to continue. In order for you to fully inherit the property at the end of the provisional year, you must submit proof of marriage or domestic partnership to the estate within that year."

"So," I started, pausing for a gulp of my shameful sangria, "I have to move to Rhode Island, live on a farm, *and* get married? And I'm the only one who can do this? Not my stepdad's kids or literally anyone else?"

It sounded like Frank was shuffling papers on his end. "That was Lollie's choice. However, you're welcome to cede the property to the town. It would end a three-hundred-year-old tradition of a single family working that farm, though I understand not every tradition was meant to continue for perpetuity. I'm sure Lollie understood that too."

"I wasn't even her real family." It sounded like a pathetic excuse coming out of my mouth. It felt that way too. Grandma Lollie had been as real as it got for me. I'd never been close with my mother or stepdad. If I'd been anything for them, it was a logistical nightmare. I'd only met his kids a few times but they all had ten or fifteen years on me, and their lives were in different places. "She was my *step*-grandmother."

"As I mentioned, Lollie believed you'd know what was best for the farm." Frank made a loud nasally, gargly sound. "If I understand correctly, Lollie's other grandchildren have expressed limited interest in even visiting the family land."

"I mean, we could check in with them again, right? Maybe they've changed their minds."

Frank laughed. "I'm afraid estates don't work that way, Miss Zucconi."

"Okay. Since I'm not getting married and I can't move to Rhode Island, I guess I can't accept this inheritance," I said, and those words stung. I hadn't been to the farm in years, since shortly before Grandma Lollie moved down to Florida and leased it out to a young couple to manage the tulip growing, but it existed in my mind as a place that would always be there for me.

Until now.

"Don't make any decisions today," Frank said. "It's yours for the next year. Give it some time. There's no need to turn over the property to a municipality any sooner than necessary. Take the year. In the meantime, I'll have my assistant overnight express the keys and paperwork to you."

After I provided Frank with Jaime's address, he ended the call, and my gaze landed on the overflowing boxes and baskets lining the wall. Everything I owned was packed into those containers, There was a time when I'd promised myself I was finished living out of a suitcase. That my life wouldn't be about portability anymore. That I wouldn't be halfway here or there. That I wouldn't live like this anymore.

And here I was, thirty-two years old and right back in another temporary situation with no clue what came next.

Except…I could decide what came next.

My life didn't have to revolve around anyone else. Not anymore.

I could do whatever I wanted.

Jaime peered at me. "How are we doing?"

I shrugged. "Okay."

"Is this it? Are we getting married?" Jaime asked.

I shook my head. "I wouldn't do that to you."

"I'll do it *for* you," she repeated.

"We're not getting married. I'll get struck by lightning if I think about marriage for more than a few seconds and you'll probably lose all your chaos bi credibility, not to mention. Everyone knows your stance on monogamy and legally binding unions."

"We could have an open marriage," she said.

I really could not ask for anyone better than Jaime. "You're too good to me. And you're kind to offer. But everything I know about farming could fit into this glass." I held up my drink. "I don't know. This whole thing is ridiculous. I can't…I mean, I never actually liked living in that town. But I was kinda happy on the farm and it's not like—well. Hmm."

I counted the containers. It wasn't that many. If I organized it just right, I could fit everything into my car. I could pick up and go. I could go right now if I wanted. I didn't need to wait for the keys. I knew where Lollie hid all the spares.

Aside from the fact I could leave, it seemed like I *should*. Grandma Lollie's farm was the only place that ever felt like home to me and I had this narrow bit of time before I'd lose it. I had to go there while it was still mine.

"What are we thinking?" Jaime asked. "I know that look. You got that same look when you decided to completely overhaul the apples and pumpkins unit two days before the start of school a few years ago. It's your crazy scheme look."

I tore my gaze away from the boxes and smiled at Jaime. She taught first grade next door to my kindergarten classroom. "No crazy schemes," I replied. "Good news for you though."

"And what would that be?"

"I'm getting off your couch for good."

"And where will you be going, doll?"

I drained the contents of my glass. "I'm moving to Rhode Island tomorrow."

She flopped back against the cushions. "This is it, isn't it?"

"What?"

"The start of your villain era," she said. "The 'no fucks given, ask me if I care, throw out your whole life and start over just because you feel like it' era."

I thought about that for a second. It was true, I didn't have any fucks left. And if my shameful sangria and midday pajamas were any indication, I did not care. All I had left to do was throw out the remnants of my life. And the idea of that felt like the first breath of fresh air in far too long. "Yeah. Maybe."

"I WANT TO SUPPORT YOU," Jaime said as I shoved another box into my back seat. "I also want to make sure you're not diving headfirst into a depressive, destructive situation."

"I have a reasonable amount of depression," I said from inside the SUV. Two days after talking to Frank, I'd consolidated my things down to the essentials, taken a leave of absence from my school, and felt truly, actually alive for the first time in too long. "The appropriate amount. All things considered."

"And how about the destructive? Taking a year off from school and leaving me with god only knows who to teach with has to be a pinch destructive."

I leaned out of the SUV to catch her gaze. "I'm sorry about that," I said. "I didn't mean to screw you over in the process. I just—" I stared down the street for a moment.

"You need a break from it all," she said. "I get it. But what do we even know about Friendship? The name alone is suspicious, and just because it's a small town doesn't make it a good place to live."

"It's a sleepy little town on the Narragansett Bay. A cove cuts right through the middle," I said, using my hands to illustrate the two sides. "One side of the cove is old family farms and the other is pretty much wooded suburbia with houses and schools all built in the last century. Not much to it."

"Answer me this," she said, her hands settling on her hips. "Will there be bears?"

"What? No. At least I don't think so. No, no bears. I never heard about bears when I lived there in high school." I stared down at the sidewalk. *Shit.* Now I was wondering about bears.

"And what are you going to do on a farm?" Jaime continued. "I've known you for six years and not once in that time did you give me the impression that you know anything about tulips or how to grow them."

I laughed. "I don't. I have no clue what I'm going to do with the tulips or the land or anything. But I'll substitute in the local school district and—I don't know." The upside to living with my ex in a condo he owned for the past two years was I had a comfortable amount of savings. I could be a little reckless right now. The engagement ring tucked into my wallet's coin purse promised I could be slightly more reckless if necessary. "I'll figure it out as I go."

The only plan was that I didn't have a plan, and that wasn't going to slow me down. It was senseless but so was the rest of my life right now. Might as well stop trying to fight it.

She handed me the last laundry basket, one filled with bedsheets, a cast iron Dutch oven, three boxes of Cheez-Its, and a tangled mess of charger cables. "I expect regular check-ins with you. I'm not talking about a few texts here and there. You'll video call me, understand? Don't make me introduce myself to the Friendship Police Department and send them out on a wellness check."

"I'll call," I said. "We haven't gone more than a few days without talking in years. You think I'm going to start now?"

She waved her arms at my SUV. "You're starting a lot of things that you don't usually do. I just want to be clear about the ground rules. And don't eat a whole box of Cheez-Its on the drive. You'll get a stomachache and then you'll be in a terrible mood."

"Okay, Mom," I teased.

"You joke but I'm completely serious," she replied. "I know how you get when you binge the Cheez-Its."

"I'll call you when I get there," I said, stepping forward to pull her into a hug. "Thank you for Mommying all over me."

"You're welcome," she said against my shoulder. "I'm only one call away. Say the word and I'll be there."

"You don't have a car, James. And you don't drive," I said.

"I'd make Audrey drive," she said. "Better yet, Grace. She doesn't care about speed limits. The point is, you're less than two hours south and I'll be there any time you need me. Or any of us. Or *all* of us."

I nodded. "I know."

"As soon as you've settled in and I can wrangle everyone, we'll come down for a weekend visit," she said. "If you aren't bored to death living in the country and back on my couch by then."

I wanted to tell her I wouldn't be back on her couch but I wasn't convinced that was true. For all I knew, I'd get there, remember all the things I'd hated about Friendship, and turn right back around.

But I had one year with my step-grandmother's family farm before I lost it forever. I wanted to squeeze as much life out of that time as I could before I had to forfeit this unexpected gift from Grandma Lollie.

I DIDN'T HATE Friendship upon arrival but I did have a big problem with the four cow trucks parked in Grandma Lollie's driveway.

Seriously. Trucks painted like cows. Black with white spots and thick eyelashes around the headlights. Little name emblems on the driver's side doors reading *Buttercup*, *Clarabelle*, *Rosieroo*, and *Gingerlou*. And they were blocking my access to the house. I could barely see the old Victorian or its wide, gracious porch that meandered around the front of the house. The twin turrets—as everything came in pairs around here—reached up into the cloudless sky over the tops of the trucks, which gave off a circus-y vibe that annoyed the hell out of me.

Thomas House was whimsical to its core, the gingerbread-styled exterior painted in shades of green with trim in vibrant pink and purple. A heart-shaped wildflower garden swayed in the breeze. I knew I'd find a fairy garden behind the sunflower yellow barn. If memory served, there was a flagstone path lined with an uprising of rosemary and anise that led straight into the side of the barn. On the other side of a pair of enormous beech trees with thick, low-slung branches meant for sitting and reading on a summer day lived a rosebush that had completely engulfed an old wrought iron bedframe, forming a literal bed of roses. And there were acres of tulips planted in swirling, meandering lanes. Everything here was intentionally wacky.

Cow trucks were not part of the whimsy and wacky.

I rolled down my window to get a better look at the closest truck. "What even the fuck," I muttered.

The sides were scrawled with *Little Star Farms* in a light blue-gray, vintage-styled script with a quartet of hand-drawn stars above the words.

I didn't remember a farm by that name in the area, but even if I did, why would their trucks be parked here? My first and only explanation was not a charitable one. I assumed this farm was using Lollie's land as their junkyard. I grabbed my phone and searched for Little Star Farms. There had to be a phone number for this place and I'd tell them to move their cow trucks to other pastures.

My thumb hovered over the phone number when I zeroed in on the address. Old Windmill Hill Road. This farm was just up the street.

"Even better," I said, backing up the gravel lane to the road. "We'll get to the bottom of these cows in person."

I didn't remember every farm and family around here but I did remember Lollie's neighbors and they weren't dairy farmers. Those people had orchards. Apples and berries and stuff like that. I'd helped Lollie around the farm while I lived here, mostly in the form of working the cash register at the far end of the pick-your-own fields in April and May, but I didn't know enough about farming to tell whether an orchard could transform into dairy land. Couldn't really see how that would work out but who knew?

I sped up Old Windmill Hill toward the parcel of land now known as

Little Star Farms, as determined to right this wrong as anyone in all of human history.

When I reached the top of Old Windmill Hill—with the namesake four-hundred-year-old windmill on one side—I turned down the lane marked with a large sign announcing Little Star Farms. A series of smaller signs hung beneath, reading *Fresh Baked Bread*, *Local Blueberries*, and *Homemade Jam and Wildflower Honey*.

The place was bustling with workers. Trucks lined either side of the gravel lane and several greenhouses and large outbuildings stood in the distance, their tall doors flung wide-open. The old farmhouse was still where I remembered it but it was different now, the footprint expanded and styled into a storefront.

I made sloppy work of parking, half on the gravel, half on the heavily trod grass leading to the greenhouses. It was the best I could do, seeing as the parking area was packed. Discovering a line to get into the store only fueled my frustration. The need to bring bread and jam to the community wasn't so great that these people could leave their moo mobiles wherever they wanted. And where the hell did all these people come from anyway?

Instead of waiting in line to speak with someone inside the store, I headed toward the greenhouses. I passed an outbuilding stocked with machinery and all-terrain vehicles and then another building filled entirely with baled hay. I tried to get the attention of the workers but they were busy unloading supplies with a forklift or carrying a large section of fencing or barking orders and jabs at each other. They didn't seem to notice me at all.

If I'd been feeling determined before, I was angry now and that anger was odd. It was an *odd* sensation. The longer I stood there, baking in the late afternoon sun and half listening as the workers called back and forth to each other, the clearer it became I wasn't completely numb. I'd felt alive since the moment I'd hatched this non-plan to come here, but that was like coming out of a shame-induced coma.

It was that realization that distracted me from registering the man walking up the lane and the little girl stomping beside him. It distracted me hard enough that I missed the girl's eye patch and the plastic sword she waved with gusto.

It wasn't until I heard "Ahoy! Land ho!" that I snapped out of my thoughts to take in a pirate girl and the great, bearded mountain of a man holding her small hand. He had a pink backpack slung over his shoulder and a soft lunch box dangling from his fingers. A hat with the Little Star Farms insignia and dark sunglasses shielded his eyes, and in that moment, it seemed he was going to walk right by and ignore me the way everyone else had.

"Yo ho ho," the girl called, sliding the eye patch to her forehead. Decorative, not functional.

It seemed he hadn't noticed me until the girl pointed her sword in my direction but then he dropped the lunch box, a cloud of dust rising up around it as he muttered something to himself. Then, "What are you doing here?"

"I am here," I started, high on my newfound anger, "because trucks belonging to this farm are blocking the entrance to *my* farm and I've been trying to find someone who can get them moved. As quickly as possible."

"Thar she blows," the girl shouted.

I gave her an encouraging smile and nod because kids just wanted to be acknowledged and she was putting a ton of energy into this pirate bit. Then I turned my attention to the man beside her. "Do you know who is in charge here?"

"Do I know who is in charge," he repeated slowly, as if I was the one doing the bit. "Yeah, I think I do."

I flung my arms out. "Can you tell me where to find them?"

He gave a small shake of his head and bent to retrieve the fallen lunch box. He handed it to the girl before crossing his arms over his chest. "Right here," he said. "You found me."

chapter two

Noah

Students will be able to repress everything.

SHAY FUCKING ZUCCONI.

In my town. On my farm.

And she didn't remember me.

That only seemed appropriate. All things considered.

"Are you wearing a onesie?" Gennie asked, finally dropping the pirate's brogue for a moment. She circled around Shay, giving her clothes a close study. "It looks like a onesie. How do you go to the bathroom?"

Shay gave Gennie a smile that held no hint of annoyance. That surprised me. I figured she would have no use for the six-year-old who'd never once kept a thought to herself. Or she'd offer some curt remark and then ignore the child.

After all, Shay Zucconi was too good for all of this. For all of us.

"It's called a romper," Shay said. She sounded like she was talking to a friend. "If you want to talk about real grown-up onesies, that's a body-suit, and those are a lot easier in the bathroom. These things"—she gave a half turn, gesturing to the zipper down her back—"are a little bit of a nightmare." She held out her hand to Gennie. "I'm Shay. What's your name?"

She ducked behind me, suddenly shy. I felt her fingers balled in my t-shirt. "Gennie," she whispered.

Shay waved, saying, "It's so nice to meet you, Gennie."

I really wanted to hate her, and for a million different reasons, but most of all, she'd showed up here after all these years and she didn't remember me. Not that I wanted anyone to be rude or dismissive to Gennie—the kid had been through enough—but I would've appreciated it if I could walk away from this exchange resenting Shay. That would really help me out.

Instead, she gestured to Gennie's striped skirt, the one with the ragged hems because the kid was not to be trusted with scissors, and said, "Tell me about this look you've put together. It's fabulous."

"I like black and white," Gennie said, abandoning me altogether and dancing off to give a little twirl. "It's my favorite but Noah says I should try other colors."

Shay reached for the diamond pendant resting at the base of her throat, zipped it back and forth several times while she blinked at Gennie. It took her a second but then her gaze snapped to me. *Zip zip zip.* "Noah?" she whispered, finally abandoning the necklace to push her sunglasses to her head and gape at me. Heat crawled up my neck. "Noah *Barden*? What? Why didn't you say so sooner? You are the last person I expected to find in Friendship."

Wasn't that the damn truth.

"I could say the same to you," I replied.

She glanced out at the rolling hills around us, her gaze far off and the shake of her head slow. "Yeah. I mean, this was not on my bingo card."

We stared at each other while Gennie twirled around us, sword aloft. If Shay intended to offer an explanation as to why the hell she was here after fourteen years and a teenage vow to get the hell out, this would've been a fine time to do it. Would've been a fine time for me to do the same.

But the moment passed and Gennie stopped beside Shay to toy with the bracelet on her wrist. "Your hair is really pretty," she said.

"Thank you. It's new," Shay said, lifting a hand to her strawberry-blonde hair. "I'm still getting used to it."

"You look great, Shay. Time's been good to you," I said, which was stupid because we weren't the same kids we used to be and the last thing I needed was a problem like Shay again. Even if the years had taken that unforgettable girl with those cat eyes and that curtain of long blonde hair and transformed her into an unforgettable woman with pink hair and curves too luscious to contemplate in this heat. She still stood on the short side of average and her skin was still peachy and clear, not even a freckle daring to interrupt all that perfection.

"You're kind to say it but that's hardly the case," she said, making an up-and-down gesture in my direction. That was when I realized the compound nature of my stupidity. I couldn't call attention to her appearance without making mine free game. If there was anyone who knew what it was for their body to be a constant source of public comment, it was me. "You, on the other hand, are barely recognizable." She did the up-and-down thing again. "You grew, like, a whole foot."

"Noah's a hundred feet tall," Gennie said, still fixated on Shay's bracelet.

"Only eight inches." I shoved my hands into my pockets, waiting for the rest. Ever since moving back to Friendship, the first things anyone said to me were about losing the weight and my skin clearing up. Once they were finished recapping my history as a fat kid with enough acne for it to be memorable, they promptly moved on to whatever they needed from me. Sponsor the softball team, buy a booth at this upcoming event, donate a basket for that charity auction, join this new committee, rescue that family's farm before it hit the auction block.

But all she said was, "It's really good to see you, Noah," and I was sixteen all over again. Sixteen and awkward as fuck and in absolute awe of this girl.

And that could not, under any circumstance, continue.

"Yeah, you too. So, about those trucks down at Twin Tulip," I said, rubbing a hand along the back of my neck. As usual, it felt like concrete. "The guys kept seeing trespassers parking there and hiking down to that little cut-through in the woods, the one that leads to the cove. We stationed a few out-of-commission delivery trucks down there to make it difficult for anyone to park." I lifted a shoulder, the one with the pink backpack Gennie threw at me the minute she got off the bus. Hated the pink backpack but loved Shay's pink hair. Of course. Made sense. "We didn't know anyone was coming."

Her brows creased and she made a face I didn't really understand. "I didn't know I was coming either."

"Your earrings don't match," Gennie announced. "Aren't they supposed to match?"

"Don't see why they should," Shay replied. "If I can't have fun with my earrings, why even wear them?"

I reached into my back pocket for my phone. "I'll get someone to take care of those trucks now."

"Wait a second," she said with a laugh, her hands fluttering while I shot off a text message. "What's with the cow delivery trucks? And the *dairy*? What happened here? What about the orchard?" She pointed to my hat. "And that. Little Star Farms? What's *that* all about?"

I held her gaze, my heart in my throat. I was certain she had me nailed right then and there and I'd have an eternity of explaining to do while she handed my ass to me but—

"So much has changed," she cried, waving at the greenhouses and the farm stand. "I can't believe it. Didn't that used to be a row of berry bushes? Something weird, right? Like fraggleberries."

"Fraggleberries aren't a thing. You're thinking of gooseberries," I said.

"Fraggleberries should be a thing," Gennie murmured.

"Yes! That's it. Gooseberries," she said. "The gooseberries are gone!"

"No one bought the gooseberries. They were a terrible use of resources," I said. "Anyway. About the dairy. My dad didn't know how to say no when neighboring farms asked if he wanted to buy them out but he never knew what to do with all those assets either. When I took over, I consolidated the operations, including the old McIntyre dairy, into one. We distribute across the region and offer home delivery. Milk, produce, breads. It's not a big deal."

Gennie took that moment to stab her sword at the ground and announce, "I'm bored as a motherfucker."

To her credit, Shay had no reaction to Gennie's outburst. She only blinked and glanced up at me.

"Imogen," I snapped. "This is why they gave you the boot from summer school. We've been talking about this. You can't—"

"But that's how bored I am." Turning to Shay, she grabbed her hand and said, "Can I show you the goats? They're so funny."

"I think," she started with a glance toward me, "Noah's trying to talk to you about that adult word you just used. What do you think about giving him your attention before we make plans to visit the goats?"

Gennie bobbed her head and turned to me with an expectant pout as if she'd endure the minor inconvenience of listening but only because Shay liked the idea too.

Now that I had an audience, I couldn't remember the first thing about how to set limits with a rogue of a child. "You can't use that word," I said. "We've talked about this. You can't use any variation of that word."

Gennie dragged the toe of one of her sneakers in the dirt. With a shrug, she said, "I'll try."

I stared at her for a long moment. I knew that promise was as flimsy as they came and she wanted nothing more than to end this conversation and introduce Shay to our goats. I knew she was already halfway in love with Shay.

That was how it went with Shay. One minute of gazing into those feline eyes and it was all over.

If I was smart, I'd end this now. I'd start Gennie on her chores and send Shay on her way.

But I wasn't smart when it came to Shay. I'd never been smart.

"I'd like you to do more than try," I said. "And Shay is not your prisoner, Gen. She probably has things to do"—I cut a glance toward the last woman on earth I expected to find on my land today—"or something like that."

Gennie stamped her foot once. "I promise I won't use the m-word for the rest of the day." Beaming up at Shay, all trace of rebellion gone, she asked, "Do you want to see the goats or do you have things to do?"

With a shrug, Shay replied, "I could meet a goat."

Gennie grabbed her hand and damn near sprinted down the path between the greenhouses. I followed at a more measured pace, watching them laugh together and listening in as Gennie introduced Shay to the farm.

"I'm not allowed in that field," Gennie said, pointing her sword toward the white boxes in the distance. "It's for the bees and Noah says bees are too busy making honey to be nice to me."

"He's right about that," Shay said, tossing a smile over her shoulder.

Shay had always had one of those faces meant for smiling. Not every face was meant for smiling but Shay's was one of them. The corners of her lips were always tipped up as if she was waiting for a reason to smile.

And when she aimed those smiles in my direction…well, the adolescent version of me had lived and died by those smiles.

I stared out at the bees. I wanted a few of them to come sting some sense into me.

"That's the greenhouse Noah uses for his secret projects," Gennie said, sword angled toward the glass building set apart from the other hothouses. "I'm not allowed in there."

"No one's allowed in there," I called. "And they're not secret projects. They're just things I don't want anyone interfering with until they're ready."

"Sounds like a secret project," Shay teased.

They jogged down a gentle hill, still hand in hand, crossing into land formerly belonging to the McIntyres. It was quiet down here, insulated by trees from the wind that screamed in from the bay. The goats seemed to like it well enough.

"And that one, with the big white dot near her eye, is Dottie. I named her Dottie. Because of the big dot," Gennie explained.

"Makes sense," Shay said.

She glanced back at me, several paces removed from the enclosure and my arms folded over my chest as if I could fortify myself against this woman. I stared off into the distance.

"People come here and do yoga with the goats," Gennie continued. "Someone always screams when a goat climbs on them."

"Goat yoga," Shay said. "Wow. This place has really changed."

"The yoga studio in town approached us and—" I held out a hand, wishing for a simple way to explain that *yeah, this place has fucking changed in the past decade and a half* and *if you hadn't left and forgotten all about me, you'd know that*. "Their students clean out the farm stand after every class. It's good for business."

"Good for business," Shay repeated as she looked me over. "Okay."

I would've responded to that loaded look, would've said something about how *someone* had to pay attention to the business. But Gennie scaled the fence and dropped into the goat pen, sword and all, and yelled, "I named this one Lacey. See? This one. She doesn't have any lace though. It's just a cool name. And that one's Cagney. Noah said I had to name her Cagney even if I think it's a dumb name."

"Just because you don't like it doesn't mean it's dumb," I called.

"Is she allowed to be in there?" Shay asked me.

"They're harmless. Worst they'll do is knock her over and she'd just enjoy that." I shrugged. "Anyway, do you get the impression that I could stop her?"

"Fair," Shay murmured. After a few minutes of listening to Gennie's explanation of each goat's name and watching her attempt to pick up the smallest of the group only for that goat to lick her face until she fell down giggling, Shay glanced over at me again. "I can't believe you're here. With goats and a greenhouse with secret projects and a *kid*."

There were so many things I wanted to say to her and most of them were not kind. But more than any of that, I wanted to tell her that I couldn't believe *she* was here. I hated that. I didn't appreciate her draining me of all the resentment and contempt I'd built up over the years with little more than a smile from her.

Instead, I called, "Gennie. You're gonna lose that sword if you're not careful."

"Okay," she replied, wrestling the sword away from Dottie. "We have to see the puppies now. Shay wants to meet the puppies."

I glanced over at Shay, a brow raised. "She'll keep you here all night if you're not careful."

"You have that many puppies?" she asked with a laugh. "You're good to worry but you don't have to rescue me. Not from your little girl. She's a real sweetheart, Noah."

I could've corrected her. Could've mentioned that Gennie was my niece and I was her legal guardian and I didn't have a wife waiting at home for me. That none of this had happened the ordinary way.

But once again, all I could do was watch while Gennie skipped off toward the dog run with Shay at her side. Here I was, thinking I'd beaten the worst of my shyness out of me years ago only for Shay to bring it roaring back.

With an annoyed shake of my head, I studied the goats. "Would it have killed any of you to be rude or offensive? You have no problem doing that during yoga. You ate that woman's hat the other day, Lacey, but now you're playing nice? That's some very convenient bullshit."

The goats bleated their outrage back at me.

I yanked off my hat, ran the flat of my hand over my forehead, and marched across the field. I was fully aware that I could've gone back to work and left Gennie and Shay to visit with the dogs. I didn't have to hover. I didn't have to supervise. Gennie knew her way around the farm, and Shay—well, I didn't give a fuck about Shay.

That wasn't true but I preferred it to the alternative.

When I reached the dog run, it was the sound of Gennie's laughter that hit me first. It was deep and infectious, the kind that came from the belly and forced a smile to my face every time I heard it. She didn't laugh like that often. She didn't laugh much at all.

I found her up against the fence, a pair of old golden retrievers nosing at her pockets. Odds were high she had food stowed in there. It was a wonder the goats hadn't gotten there first.

"Can dogs eat bagels?" she asked through her laughter.

"Just a little bit," I told her.

Shay watched while Gennie broke the bagel she'd been saving since fuck if I knew when into crumbs and fed the dogs from the palm of her hand. Some of the other dogs circled, sniffing at the newcomer and accepting the head scratches she doled out. Most of them were content to laze in the sun, others peeked out from inside the kennels. Not a lot of running took place in this dog run.

"Noah," Shay started, gesturing to the old-timer leaning against her leg, "when did you get all these animals? I don't remember you guys having"—she waved at the dozen or so dogs—"anything like this before."

"We have them so they don't die," Gennie replied, still focused on distributing bits of bagel.

Shay gave me a *what the hell does that mean* grimace.

I peered at the bunkhouses where some of the farm crew lived.

Easier than making eye contact with Shay. "We take in elderly dogs that have trouble finding homes. Give 'em a comfortable place to live out their days." I tipped my chin toward the bunkhouse. "The guys like having dogs around."

"And we have chickens too," Gennie said, "but they're dumb bitches."

"Imogen," I cried. "We just talked about calling things dumb and you know that other word is not acceptable."

Gennie cut a glance toward Shay. Her voice lowered, she said, "But they're not smart."

Shay pressed her knuckles to her mouth and choked down a laugh which triggered a laugh in me. I had to turn away, clear my throat, and mentally flip through this month's expenditures to pull it back in.

When I shifted back, Gennie was on the other side of the run, trying to coax an ancient basset hound from inside the kennel. Unless she had a pork chop in one of those pockets, I knew that dog wasn't going anywhere.

Then again, it wasn't completely impossible that Gennie didn't have a pork chop on hand.

"What don't you do?" Shay asked. "When do you sleep?"

"Infrequently." I nodded toward Gennie. "Less since she came along."

"I'll bet," Shay murmured.

Another silent moment settled between us as we watched Gennie playing with the dogs and it frustrated me to no end that Shay could still go quiet and watch the world. It would've made my fucking day for her to experience an ounce of my awkwardness. After all this time, I felt like I deserved that much. I couldn't be the only one struggling to string words together here. Couldn't be the only one with flashes of heat climbing up my neck and around the tips of my ears. It couldn't just be me suffering.

"This really is amazing, Noah," she said.

I nodded and called to Gennie. "It's getting late. You still have chores to do."

"With the stupid chickens," she muttered to the basset.

"I heard that," I said.

"But I didn't say dumb *or* bitches," she replied.

Shay smothered a laugh, saying, "She's a firecracker. Oh my god."

I pushed away from the fence and stepped toward the path leading up to the house. "Those trucks should be gone by now," I said. "Sorry about the inconvenience."

"Oh. Thank you." She lifted a hand to her face, toyed with one of her earrings. "It makes so much sense now—and thank you for helping with that. I should've known there would be a good explanation. After that drive, and I ate too many Cheez-Its, and I just—the name on the trucks was unfamiliar and—"

"Yeah, I get it. Things change and you haven't been around in a while."

Shay took a step backward, grabbed the pendant at the base of her neck again. She zipped it back and forth as she peered at me. "I'm shocked you're here at all. This place wasn't kind to you and—"

"Come on!" Gennie ran up and saved me from having to survive the rest of that comment on my own. She took hold of Shay's hand, saying, "The chicken house is a mini version of our house. It has a mailbox too but it's only big enough to hold one egg."

"Only one egg?" Shay asked. The disbelief in her words made Gennie's eyes sparkle, the girl's answering nod coming as a whole-body quiver. "You have to show me that."

Again, I followed them because what the fuck else was I going to do? Pink backpack high on my shoulder, I climbed the gentle hill while Gennie regaled Shay with stories of the chickens' misdeeds.

When they reached the coop, Gennie went right to work collecting eggs. As was her habit, she insulted the chickens as she opened each box. "Don't peck me, you nasty old wench!"

Shay turned to me, her eyes wide. I realized she looked tired, the type of tired that edged into weariness. She hid it well. All those bright smiles and the boundless enthusiasm she had for Gennie. You'd have to really look to see it. "Just wait. It gets more colorful."

"Get away from me," Gennie grumbled. "Stupid asshat."

I motioned to the henhouse. "Like that."

"Gimme the egg, shithead."

I nodded while Shay clapped a hand over her mouth. "And that."

"Fucking chores. Hate this dumb shit."

I rocked back on my heels. "Mmm. That one too."

"Noah," Shay whispered. "What is going on right now?"

Gennie emerged, the basket full of fresh eggs and her expression murderous as usual. "Here," she said, setting the basket down halfway between us. That was her way of making it clear how much she hated coop patrol. "I'm going to find my kitties."

I snapped my fingers, pointing to the house. "Not before you wash your hands."

Gennie trudged toward the white farmhouse on the other side of the gravel drive, still muttering about the chickens. Once the door banged shut behind her, I said to Shay, "She's working through some stuff. She's had a tough few years."

"I'm sorry to hear that." She tucked her hair over her ear.

"She's my sister's kid," I said because I was fully incapable of keeping anything to myself when I had Shay's attention trained on me. "Eva is Gennie's mother but Gennie lives here now. With me. I adopted her last fall."

Shay gave a slow nod. She didn't ask any of the follow-up questions that everyone else liked to harp on, like where was Gennie's mom and why wasn't she with her child and what about the father? She just met my gaze without an ounce of judgment and asked, "Is she okay? Eva?"

My shoulders sagged before I could stop myself. "No. She's not. But

Gennie's here now and things are getting better. Slowly. If you ignore everything you just heard from her."

My sister was a little more than two years older than me and Shay, and she'd already left home when Shay came to town. If it was possible, Eva had been even more motivated to get the hell out of Friendship than anyone else.

Shay gave another slow nod. "That's a lot of stuff. For both of you."

The problem with Shay was there was no way to resist her. Even with all the resentment in the world fortifying me, I was defenseless against a few kind words and a sympathetic smile. She'd always had an ability to make people feel special. More than special—*chosen.* For once, I knew better than to fall into that trap.

"Yeah," I managed. "The profanity is part of the package."

She gave a quick bob of her head as if this was completely expected. "Is Gennie getting help to work through it?"

I barked out a laugh. "Oh, yeah. Tons of therapy. We go to Providence twice a week to see a therapist and she works with some specialists during school hours too." Despite my better judgment, I added, "School is difficult for her. She missed a lot during"—I glanced at the house, shrugged—"everything that happened. You've seen how she behaves so it hasn't been easy. They want her to repeat kindergarten."

"Oh, shit," she said under her breath.

"Yeah, that was Gennie's take on it too."

"The emotional impact would be worse than any academic deficits," Shay said. "You can't let that happen, Noah."

"Trust me, I'm working on it," I snapped, now regretting that I'd shared so much. I didn't need input from anyone else on this. I already had more than enough.

"Is there any possibility of her being promoted or is this a done deal?"

I lifted the shoulder carrying Gennie's backpack. "Summer school was the last-ditch effort. She was kicked out after asking the teacher if they'd be doing boring shit again today."

Gennie barreled out of the house then and sprinted toward the barn while screaming, "Goin' to get the kitties now!"

"Only if they want you to get them," I called after her. "You will not win a fight with barn cats." We watched her streak by, dust and gravel flying behind her. I glanced over at Shay. "When she first came here, she wouldn't go anywhere near the animals. Cried her head off when she got within fifty feet of a goat. Now she'll grab frogs right out of the pond. Bare hands."

Gennie emerged from the barn, her arms overflowing with annoyed cat. "This one is Brownie," she announced, "because she's brown. I couldn't find the other but that's okay because she's a hunter and yesterday she had pieces of—"

"Let's not tell Shay that story," I interrupted. "Not everyone needs the details of the barn cat's catch of the day."

Shay gave me a small smile and mouthed "Thanks."

"Just a few minutes with Brownie," I said, watching the cat squirming in Gennie's hold. "You've been all over the farm this afternoon, kid, but we need to get you fed and washed and ready for bed."

"Bedtimes are bullshit," she murmured to the cat. "'Specially in the summer."

"And I should head back to Twin Tulip," Shay said, taking a step away from us. "I haven't unpacked yet and—wait, where am I?"

"This is our new house," Gennie said. "It's away from the farm stand and the old house because Noah values his privacy."

Shay swallowed a laugh. "Hmm. Yeah."

"We'll walk you back," I offered.

"Shay can have dinner with us," Gennie said.

My gaze met Shay's and the quick shake of her head came as a relief. I couldn't manage a meal with her. I'd barely processed her reappearance in Friendship and the power she still held over me. I couldn't bring her into my house and sit next to her at my kitchen table too.

"That is so sweet of you, Gennie," she said, "though I just moved to this town and there's nothing in my house, so—"

"So you probably don't have anything to cook," she said. "But we always cook so much that we have lots of leftovers." Gennie turned her big brown eyes on me. "Remember how you said I could have a playdate this week?"

"That was before you were expelled from summer school," I said, trying to keep my voice low. "And I don't think you can have a playdate with an adult. Playdates are for kids."

"Then it's just a date?" Gennie asked. "Can I have a date with Shay?" My life was coming full circle in strange, unpleasant ways, and I didn't get a chance to respond before Gennie added, "I can show you my room and we can go on the swings and we'll have so much fun!" She set Brownie on the ground and ran toward me, her hands pressed together like she was praying. "Please, Noah. *Please.* No one ever wants to come over for a playdate with me."

And that basically broke me.

I glanced at Shay, trying as best I could to silently release her from all involvement here. As kind as she'd been to Gennie—and me too, I had to admit—I knew this was the last place in the world she wanted to be. She could leave the way she always did and we'd be fine without her. Gennie would take it hard but as soon as I pressed play on *Pirates of the Caribbean*, she'd lapse back into character and get over the total infatuation that came with meeting Shay. And I'd get over it too—all over again.

We'd be fine. We had to be.

Then Shay said, "I'd love to stay, Gennie. Thanks so much for inviting me."

My niece and the love of my stupid teenage heart walked into my house hand in hand and I felt a hard knot of pressure form deep in the center of my chest. I rubbed my knuckles against my sternum but it didn't help.

DINNER WAS a death march to the end of my endurance when it came to Shay Zucconi.

I barely remembered eating or negotiating with Gennie over finishing her vegetables. I must've done both, seeing as Shay and Gennie were busy carrying dishes to the sink and loading the dishwasher. And that left me standing in the middle of the kitchen while the entire universe tilted beneath my feet.

This couldn't continue. It just could not. I wanted the sanctity of my house back but more than that I wanted the freedom that came from believing Shay was long gone from my life. If she was out of reach, I was okay.

"Can we have another playdate? Tomorrow?" Gennie asked her. "We can play at your house this time."

"It's almost time for your bath," I said to my niece. She frowned at the clock on the stove. She wasn't great with telling time but she knew this was at least an hour before her usual bath time. "Say good night to Shay and thank her for spending the afternoon with you."

Gennie looked up at Shay, her dark eyes wide. "Thank you for spending the afternoon with me," she said. "I don't have to go to summer school anymore so we can play tomorrow if you want. I can help you. I'm a really good helper. I put things away all the time. And, Noah, you said we had to go down to the tulip farm because there's a lot of poison ivy all over the place. So, we can do that tomorrow."

Fuck.

Now I remembered what I'd forgotten when parking those trucks down at Twin Tulip.

"There's poison ivy?" Shay yelped. "Where?"

"Yeah," I said with a sigh. "On the beech trees along the main drive. Especially around the trunk of the one with the tire swings." I met Gennie's hopeful gaze. "I guess we'll come down with the goats at some point this week."

Shay laughed and I had to work at not smiling in response. "You'd like to inflict that upon the goats?"

"No. They'll eat it," I said, dropping a hand to Gennie's shoulder. I steered her toward the stairs. "Get ready for that bath. I'll be up in a minute."

"Good night, Shay," Gennie called as she climbed the stairs at a glacial pace. "I'll tell Dottie and Lacey about our playdate."

"Thank you, my new friend," Shay said. "It was so much fun to visit with you."

Once Gennie was out of sight and I heard her bedroom door creak open, I said, "Thanks for indulging her. Don't worry about those playdate plans. She'll forget about it tomorrow."

Shay wiped her hands on a dish towel and busied herself with straightening everything on the countertop. Tiny touches and nudges. The smallest possible imprint. And now it was everywhere. She was everywhere. And I'd never be able to forget it.

"But…goats?"

"Yeah." I yanked off my hat, shoved it back on. "It's nothing. I'll send someone down to handle it. We've been doing it as long as we've had the goats. Just slipped my mind this summer."

She nodded once and that seemed like the end of this discussion, the end of this horror show of a day. Then she said, "It really is good to see you, Noah."

That was not what I needed to hear from her.

"Yeah. Well." I ripped the hat off again. "We've kept you long enough."

"Thanks for rolling with it," she said with a laugh. "Oh—but how do I get back to the farm stand?"

For fuck's sake. What the hell was wrong with me? "Let me grab Gennie. We'll drive you back over in the four-wheeler."

"No, no. I'm fine walking. I'll find my way. Just point me in the right direction."

Halfway between slamming the damn hat back on my head, I stiffened and turned to glare at her. Really glare. Beyond the entry-level glaring I'd given her all afternoon. This was an executive glare, the kind born from a toxic blend of *what the hell is wrong with you* and *have you met me?* "You're not wandering through an orchard after sunset. That's not an option." I called up the stairs, "Gen, get down here. We need to drive your friend down the hill."

"I'm naked!" she cried.

"Put your clothes back on."

"They're in the hamper," she replied.

"Take them out." I was going to need some hard liquor to close out this evening. Liquor and some serious alone time.

"Really, I'm fine to walk," Shay said, heading toward the door. "You have enough going on here. I'll just use my phone for directions."

The fuck you will.

"You said I'm not allowed to wear clothes out of the hamper," Gennie shouted.

"Put the clothes on that you just took off," I said. "That's not the same as wearing something to school that you dug out of the laundry."

"I'm gonna go," Shay said, hand on the doorknob. "Thank you again for dinner—and a bit of catching up."

I pointed at Shay as I climbed the stairs. "You're not going anywhere." To Gennie, I said, "Kid, just put something on. We're only going for a quick ride in the four-wheeler."

"Can I drive?" she asked.

"No," I shouted. To Shay, I added, "I don't let her drive. I let her steer *once* and now she thinks she's training for Formula One."

Gennie met me halfway up the stairs and she was dressed in entirely new clothes. She simply said, "I couldn't find the stuff I was wearing today."

"Awesome. Whatever. Shoes, now, please."

When we returned to the kitchen, Shay gave me a glance that repeated her assertion of not needing an escort back to her car. And that was tough shit.

We headed toward the barn where I kept the ATV I used around the farm, Gennie once again glued to Shay's side. She asked about Shay's bracelet and her nail polish, and what she thought of the *Pirates of the Caribbean* franchise. I didn't hear Shay's response but it seemed to satisfy my niece.

Gennie settled into the second row of seats and directed Shay to sit in the front, beside me. This kid wasn't doing me any favors today. I pulled out of the barn and worked hard at keeping my gaze on the trail. It was all I could do to prevent myself from staring at Shay's legs, bare from the mid-thigh down. Not that it mattered what she was wearing. She could be decked out in a snowsuit and I'd still be at my max.

Gennie babbled on about the dogs and the goats, and asked Shay about the animals at her house—none—and why that was—apparently Shay had her hands full taking care of herself and couldn't possibly look after another living thing, not even a houseplant.

That I nearly stopped the four-wheeler there in the Macoun trees and demanded an explanation for that comment was proof I could not spend any amount of time near Shay. I could not exist in this proximity to her again. I couldn't stop myself from going overboard in obsessing over her while she barely noticed anyone else. And I resented her for dragging me down this far in a matter of hours.

We cleared the apple trees and then the greenhouses, and came into the parking lot, now dark and empty save for one high-end SUV. Ahhh, yes. That was the Shay Zucconi I remembered. "Here we are," I said, circling around to the driver's side.

"Ducks!" Gennie screamed as she shot off the seat and sprinted across the lot.

"There's a nest over there," I said by way of explanation.

"So, she loves everything except the chickens," Shay said.

"More or less." I tightened my grip on the steering wheel.

Shay turned to face me. She stared while I looked everywhere but at her. Eventually, she said, "Let me help you with Gennie."

"We have plenty of help."

"I don't doubt that you do but Gennie is still going to be held back if you don't change it up. Let me help her. I have a good idea of what she needs. I've taught kindergarten for nine years—"

"You're a teacher? When did that happen?" The last thing in the world I could imagine for Shay was a job as intense and hands-on as teaching.

"As I'm sure you're aware, things change." She gave me a salty look. "I can tutor her before school starts and catch her up while working on some of the behavioral issues too."

That was exactly what Gennie needed and what I'd begged the school to provide, and my hostility toward this woman was almost great enough to flat-out refuse. "Why do you want to do that?"

"Because I hate seeing kids held back," she said immediately. "And Gennie is a quick kid. She's bright. I bet she's behind in a lot of basic skills and that leads to frustration and other big feelings, and that probably triggers some of the behavioral stuff."

"What's in it for you?"

She gave a rueful laugh. "What's ever in it for teachers?" When I only stared ahead, she added, "I need something to do to keep me distracted from my life before school starts, at which point I'll be too exhausted to think about my life."

That...didn't sound right.

"And what are you looking for in return?"

"What am I—*what*?" She frowned at me like she couldn't believe I'd ask that. "I'm looking to prevent a good kid from repeating a grade level and adding another helping of childhood trauma to her life. Get rid of that poison ivy for me and we'll call it even."

Gennie appeared in the beam of the headlights, yelling, "There are three eggs!"

"Do not go near that nest unless you want a duck chasing you." To myself, I muttered, "She's gonna get chased by a duck."

Again, I was reminded I was not qualified for parenting.

Finally, I glanced over at Shay. Goddamn, she was pretty. But that was only the outside. The girl I'd known wasn't selfless. She didn't go above and beyond simply because it was right. She didn't go looking for the good in others. I had to ask, "Why?"

She pulled her keys from her pocket, rubbing the pad of her thumb over a fob. "Because you'd do it for me." She motioned to the four-wheeler like it could prove her point. "And you wouldn't take no for an answer."

chapter three

Shay

Students will be able to handle marriage proposals with the grace of a squawking goose.

NOAH BARDEN ROLLED up two days later with a trailer full of goats and a six-year-old waving her sword out of the truck's back seat window.

I spotted them from my spot on the floor of the left parlor—two of everything in this house—where I was enjoying a pudding cup for breakfast. The floor because there wasn't much furniture, and the pudding because I was done with dieting for the dress. Or any other reason.

I went in search of shoes and grabbed my water bottle before meeting Noah and Gennie outside. I was proud to report there was water in that bottle. I'd debated spicing it up with something stronger but day drinking alone in an empty house felt like an altogether different level of drunkenness. It was a plateau I didn't want to hit.

I'd polished off a bottle of wine and a block of cheese last night but that was different. Totally different.

From the shelter of the porch, I watched Noah release the goats while

Gennie used his leg for sparring practice. If he noticed her attack, it didn't show on his face.

Kinda like how all memory of our friendship didn't show on his face.

Of all the people I'd guessed I'd run across here in Friendship, Noah Barden hadn't even made the list. That boy's singular mission had been getting the fuck out of this town. He'd hated farming and farm life and the entirety of this place—and I'd shared a lot of those sentiments with him. We'd been united in our desire to hit the road and never look back.

Funny how that worked out for us.

But the part I really couldn't reconcile was that my old friend seemed angry with me. Not only was he *not* happy to see me, I had the distinct impression he didn't want to see me at all.

That was strange, right?

And yet here he was, leading a dozen goats into my poison ivy patch.

Also strange.

Then again, people changed. This sleepy town had changed in hundreds of little ways. It was still sleepy, farmland and ancient windmills dotting the landscape with old stone walls slowly sinking into the earth, but now there were quaint shopping centers, coffee shops with strung-light patios, and signs announcing high school football games and upcoming festivals.

My memories of this place weren't cozy. I'd managed through the years my mother and stepfather had left me in Lollie's care and some of that time had been happy though I barely remembered who I was in high school. Hell, I couldn't remember who I was before falling down the wedding rabbit hole to hell. Shit happened and it made people different in the process.

If Noah was a grouchy, glarey man now, who was I to judge? Not me. That was not in my job description.

"Shay!" Gennie yelled. She abandoned Noah's leg and ran toward the porch, her dark, tangled hair flying behind her and the sword scraping along the brick walkway. "We brought all the good goats. We left the naughty ones in the pen."

"You have naughty goats?"

She barreled into me, her little arms locking around my waist and her face pressed to the squish of my belly. "Two of them," she mumbled into my shirt. "They learned how to get out and they went to the dog run and made all the dogs angry. And they did it at four-fucking-thirty in the morning. That's what Noah said. He said the bad word. Not me. I didn't say fucking. He did."

"And you've repeated it fifteen times since then," he said from the walkway. He didn't come any closer, instead shoving his hands into his jean pockets and watching the goats.

Maybe he didn't like people. He'd always been far on the introverted side.

I still couldn't get over his physical transformation. It was like he'd traded in his body for a much taller, more muscular version. His hair was still dark, and his eyes—when not hidden behind sunglasses and under the shadow of caps—were still hazel, but I had to go looking for those familiar pieces of him. His skin was tanned and freckled from his time outdoors, and confidence blared from the sharp cut of his scruffy jaw and those broad shoulders. This was no self-conscious kid. He was in control and he knew it.

"You're welcome to stop saying it any time," Noah explained.

"I said fuck because I was telling the story," she replied.

He sighed. "You could say something else. Like fudge."

"Why fudge? That's dumb."

I smiled at Gennie. "Have you ever seen the fairy garden?" I pointed toward the barn. "It's around that way. Follow the stones painted red with white dots, like toadstools."

She gave me a serious stare. "Are there real fairies there?"

"You'll have to look for yourself."

She considered this for a second before handing her sword to Noah.

"I don't want to scare them," she explained. "They might think I'm trying to conquer their land if I'm armed."

"Smart thinking," I said.

Gennie ran off, leaving me and Noah alone. I tipped my water bottle in the direction of the goats. They were penned in with flexible fencing and busy munching everything in sight. "They get right down to business," I said, unscrewing the cap on my bottle. "Do you lease them out? Is that another one of your new ventures, goat landscaping?"

He shrugged, still watching the animals. "Sometimes."

"When did you come back?"

There was a long, long moment where Noah didn't respond. Then, "Five years ago."

"Where were you before that?"

"Manhattan."

"Oh, really? Where?" New York was my hometown, even though I hadn't lived there in nearly twenty years, and I loved talking about the city with anyone who knew it well. It was like discovering you had a mutual friend who was always involved in the drama. There was always so much ground to cover.

"Lived in Brooklyn. Worked on Wall Street."

I marched down the steps. "You worked on *Wall Street*?"

"Yeah. Worked on the legal side of mergers and acquisitions."

I wanted to take a sample of his tone and study it under a microscope because I couldn't see how someone could be both bored and confrontational inside a handful of words. It was art.

Before I could gamble on another question, he waved at the expanse of Thomas land fanned out before us. "What are you going to do with all this?"

I gave him the best answer I could cobble together. "Not a clue." I wandered down the path leading toward the huge heart of wildflowers. "I had no idea Twin Tulip would be mine. Lollie never said anything."

"I'm sorry," he said from several paces behind me. "About Lollie."

I glanced over my shoulder at him. "Thank you. She always liked you."

"You don't need to bless me with the approval of people no longer living," he said. "I get too much of that as it is."

"She always liked you," I repeated. "You know she liked you."

After a pause, he said, "She was one of the good ones. I tolerated her."

We walked in silence for several minutes, circling the wildflowers and starting toward the tulip fields.

"Are you getting bulbs in the ground come November?" he asked.

I stared at the field, now nothing more than topsy-turvy rows of weeds and the occasional patch of wildflowers. "I don't know. Maybe? I wouldn't even know where to start with that."

"I can—" He stopped, scratched the back of his neck. "I can send some guys down here to help you when things slow down for the season."

Since I couldn't think more than a few days ahead at a time, I didn't jump on his offer. I didn't say anything at all. We looped back toward the kitchen garden and the yellow barn, silent for several minutes. I gestured to the gentle hillside leading down to the cove. "This is the very best spot on the whole farm. Isn't it beautiful up here?"

"Yeah," he murmured.

I glanced over and found him nodding at me, his cap pulled low and his eyes shadowed.

"No, not up here. Not this part. The cove," I said, pointing again. "I always told Lollie this would be the perfect spot for weddings. Can't you see a little arbor here and seats there? The photos would be amazing." I took a sip of water. "You know what would be even better? A space for wedding receptions too. And gardens. More gardens. Three seasons of gardens. Not just five minutes of tulips in the spring. It's so unique and charming here. I just know there would be massive demand."

"Then you should do that," he said.

I laughed. "Build a wedding venue? No. I should not be anywhere near weddings right now, and that sort of project takes time, which isn't something I have. I'm only here until next summer. I can't keep Twin Tulip after that."

Even through the shadow of his hat, I could read his scowl. "What?"

I went for my water again, buying myself a second before unloading this story on him. "I have a year to move here permanently and get married. If I don't do both, the Thomas land is handed over to the town's historic trust."

Noah folded his arms over his chest. "Says who?"

"Lollie's will."

"That won't hold up in court," he said. "I want to see this will. None of that sounds right."

"That was my reaction too," I said, "but it's what Lollie wanted." I shook my head. "Since I can't keep Twin Tulip, I'm just taking this year to enjoy it while I can. I'll go back to Boston next summer."

"I want to see that will," he repeated. "I can't imagine the town has the interest or resources to fight you for the land. If you contested it, they'd probably fold. Litigating a matter like this isn't in their best interest."

"So, you're a real big-time lawyer," I mused, taking in the man wearing the hell out of jeans and a t-shirt. "Just like you'd always planned."

"Why don't you want to fight this?"

"Because what am I going to do with this place?"

"You'll build the wedding thing," he said. "It's a good idea. I get so many inquiries about renting out our barns and sheds for weddings and events but we need all the space we have. We don't have an inch to rent and I've looked. You're right. The interest is there."

"But my life is in Boston. My friends and my job are in Boston. I'm taking a break from everything right now but I can't stay here forever—

and then there's the issue of getting married. I'm not optimistic about my prospects, Noah."

"I'll marry you."

I barked out a stunned laugh. "You'll *what*?"

He looked away, muttering something under his breath that I didn't understand. Then, "This will, the completely unenforceable one with the ridiculous clauses—it grants a one-year intermediary period?"

"Yes. In order to fully inherit the land, I have to live here and be married by next July."

"I'll marry you," he repeated. "You don't want to fight a frivolous will? Fine. Then meet the terms of the will, build the venue, close the estate next July, dissolve the marriage next August."

"You're joking," I said. When he didn't respond, I continued. "It's not that simple."

"It can be," he replied. "Just choose to be unemotional about it."

I gazed at him, this fully grown man who barely resembled my old friend. He was different now. Hard and calculating in a way I didn't understand. He was indifferent and that was the last thing I'd ever imagined he'd be.

"What's in it for you?" I asked, throwing his words from the other day back at him.

He met my eyes and I recognized him for a split second before he stared out at the shimmering blue of the cove. "The land, obviously. If you go through with this wedding business, you still have a surplus of acreage. Everything from here"—he pointed to the far side of the property, beyond the barn—"up to the top of the hill. If you're not cultivating it, I can put it to work. There's a good spot for a pollinator garden. Or a summertime cutting garden, pick-your-own style, that's close enough to the farm stand for us to carve out a path through the orchard. That's a light lift for a big impact."

"You want…the land."

Still staring at the cove, he asked, "Why else would I offer? It's a business deal, Shay. I'll take a stake in your venue and help get it off the ground, and put some of your land to work in the process. You'll inherit the farm. What else is there?"

The acid in my throat tasted like chocolate pudding. The water wasn't helping. Too much talk of weddings today. One hundred percent more marriage proposals than I could stomach.

"That's—wow. That's a lot of things packed into a few sentences, Noah. Okay. You should know I just got out of a—um, well, a situationship. So, I can't really talk about the future or marriage without wanting to barricade myself under a blanket. Not even a fake marriage."

He folded his arms over his chest again and I noticed his thick, corded forearms. This was an objective observation. Scientific, really. Not at all based on attraction or interest. It was more a study in contrasts: this strong, sun-kissed man versus the boy I'd known all those years ago. More and more, it seemed the Venn diagram comparing the two was a pair of circles overlapping only in name and origin. The past fourteen years had pushed the rest apart until the edges only kissed each other.

"What happened?" he asked.

"Not something I feel like discussing," I said.

We stared at each other for a heavy minute. Then, "I can secure financing for this kind of project. You might run into issues with the title being tied up but I can work around that."

"Because you want a summertime cutting garden."

He shifted, taking in the land, mostly flat with slight hills, and all the whimsical weirdness contained in its borders. "The only square of earth I don't own on the hill is this one. There's an opportunity to increase my holdings and give me access to the one thing I don't have the right space for, which is an event center I can rent out year-round. A summertime cutting garden is a simple revenue generator. The costs would be next to nothing and it would fill the pick-your-own gap between blueberry and apple seasons. Would you like me to continue? Should I explain the rest of the ways your land can be better utilized?"

No, this new, grumpy vibe had nothing to do with me. This was Noah, all grown-up and freed of his teenage ideals. He cared about revenue generators and land holdings now. I didn't know whether it was college or Wall Street or coming home to Friendship that had changed him but I didn't like it.

"It's just about the land," I said.

He watched me for a moment. "It doesn't have to be emotional, Shay. Things get a lot easier when you stop making everything about your feelings."

"How can you say that?" I asked. "You used to—"

"Noah!" Gennie hollered. "I caught a grasshopper and it's brown."

"We can both get what we want. It doesn't have to mean anything," he said to me before turning his attention to Gennie. "That's probably a cricket. Don't crush it, okay?"

"I won't," she said, jogging closer. "I'm not going to bring it home. It lives here with the Twin Tulip grasshoppers."

"Yeah," Noah agreed. "Little Star would be like a foreign country."

"Like Connecticut," she said.

Noah gave a quick shake of his head that said he wasn't getting into geography with Gennie right now. "Let me see," he said to her, bending low to look into her cupped hands. "You must've been wicked fast to catch him."

"Fast like this," she said, sprinting a few yards toward the wildflowers and back again. She did this several times before announcing that she needed to see the goats and show them the cricket.

When she was out of earshot, I asked, "When should I come by to work with her?"

"Therapy is on Tuesday and Thursday afternoons," he said, suddenly occupied with his phone. "Afternoons are best. She's a little more chill, if you can believe that."

"So then, Monday, Wednesday, Friday? We only have a few weeks until school starts and I want to give her a fighting chance and—"

"Yeah. That's fine."

"Okay." I tried to catch his eye but he was very interested in his phone. "I'll see you tomorrow, then. At your place, right?"

He nodded, still thumbing out a message. "There's a turnoff leading to the house. It's about half a mile past the main entrance. There's a mailbox. If the apple trees stop and cows start, you've gone too far."

"Noah, Bootsie got out of the pen," Gennie called.

"Goddammit." He shoved his phone in his back pocket and spared me a quick glance. "Figure out if I'm marrying you, okay? Good."

I watched as he headed in the direction of the goats with his new body and new personality.

And his marriage proposal.

chapter four

Noah

Students will be able to deflect like their life depends on it.

THE FIRST TIME I saw Shay Zucconi, I was driving my mother's beat-up old SUV on my way to school for the first day of junior year. I had a daily countdown to graduation going and that day was a turning point. It was the start of the last half of the horror show that was my high school experience. I was close enough to the end to see life after this town and I wanted nothing more than to reach out and grab it.

She waited on the corner of Old Windmill Hill Road, long honey-gold hair falling down her back and clothes that looked very, very expensive. She looked like she damn near owned the world. She was beautiful in a way that overwhelmed me, though it wasn't just her face, her body. She was a sunbeam through a storm cloud.

Even to this day, I couldn't explain why I pulled over but I knew I had to stop for her. It struck me like a physical necessity.

I rolled down my window and asked if she wanted a ride to school rather than waiting on the bus. I knew she was Lollie Thomas's granddaughter because everyone knew everyone's business in the farm community, and my parents had been loudly curious about the circumstances that brought this girl to our neighbor's home. I was curious too.

I worshipped her from the minute she slid in beside me, smelling like heaven and looking at me with those cat eyes. I believed then that she saw me, the real me. She didn't do anything miraculous and that was helpful because I didn't think I could tolerate any miracle beyond being with a beautiful girl who chose to ride with me.

She captivated everyone like that. The first school day was barely through before Shay had been inducted into the popular crowd and the guys who always got the girls had called dibs. But I picked her up every morning and I drove her home when she wasn't busy with the cool kids, and she sat with me, gorgeous and made of mysteries and momentarily mine, and I let myself believe that meant something. I let myself love her, and a significant portion of me died when I was faced with the reality that it was entirely one-sided.

And then, half a lifetime later, I offered to marry her and blamed it on wanting her land, of all the asinine things.

I had too many businesses to run and an endless stream of other people's problems to handle. Plus a child pirate and all the complications that came baked in with that. I couldn't rush in and save the day for Shay. Not when Gennie was my primary concern.

So, in that sense, Shay laughing off my offer was for the best. It didn't bother me. There would be nothing worse than a hollow marriage to Shay. *I didn't care.*

But what the hell had happened with her last relationship? What had gone wrong there? And why had it been necessary for her to pick up and move here to recover from it?

Not that I needed to know what that was all about. Not my problem. *She* wasn't my problem.

Unless she changed her mind about getting married to inherit Twin Tulip.

The whole thing was absurd. Every farm-related legal document I'd come across since taking over this place had some element of irresponsible absurdity to it, but the alleged terms of that will took top honors. I couldn't believe Lollie left Shay with so many unnecessary complications.

None of it would hold up in court.

Instead of volunteering to be her husband, I should've offered to handle the matter on her behalf. One memo and she would've owned that land free and clear. I could still do that. I could explain to her how simple it would be to get rid of those terms. I could eliminate the need for a fake marriage altogether.

Instead of hashing out either of those issues, I did the one thing I should've from the start: I gave Shay the widest berth I could manage when she came to the house to work with Gennie.

I was friendly—as friendly as I knew how to be—but I kept a respectful distance. She didn't need me hovering and I didn't need to allow all of my thoughts to stampede out of my mouth. Gennie, however, was not helping. She always wanted Shay to join us for dinner after tutoring sessions. She begged and pleaded like her life depended on getting just a little more time with Shay.

Unfortunately, I knew how she felt.

Though I didn't know how she did it, Shay managed to decline all of Gennie's invitations without sending the girl into a full-blown tantrum. I appreciated that. I was complete shit when it came to winding down Gennie's tantrums.

But I appreciated Shay maintaining some limits with me too. I didn't know if it was part of her plan or the result of the most unpleasant marriage proposal in modern history but she saved me from having to spend more than a few passing minutes with her and that was a goddamn gift.

The one thing Shay could not save me from was the local gossip mill.

"It's her," Jim Wheaton, my dairy manager, said when I walked into the office that afternoon. "Isn't it?"

I settled behind my desk and woke up my computer. "I have no idea what you're talking about." I tapped a few keys. "How are today's numbers looking? Is the bottling plant up to capacity yet?"

"The one who got away rolled into town, you spent a morning on her family's spread last week, and now she's visiting with Miss Gennie. And you're pretending those are ordinary events. That's how the numbers look."

"There's nothing to say, Wheatie."

He leaned back in his chair, his long legs stretched out before him and his dark bronze fingers steepled under his chin. "You've spoken to her, I take it. That's why you needed those trucks moved ASAP."

I toggled through several screens, seeing status reports on farm stand sales, wholesale orders, and estimated apple yields for the next month. I processed none of it.

"Yes," I snapped. "You said it yourself, she's spending time with Gennie. Of course I've *spoken* to her."

He inclined his bald head. "And?"

"And I never should've told you and Bones a fucking thing about her," I replied.

Wheatie nodded like he'd expected this response. Then he unclipped the radio from his pocket, saying into the mouthpiece, "Bones, if you're in the vicinity of the main house, could you come up to the office?"

"Be there in five," came the orchard manager's response.

"You have five minutes," Wheatie said, running a hand over his head. "Seems like long enough to get the story straight, don't you think?"

"Nothing to get straight," I muttered. "She's back. Needed the trucks out of the way. End of story."

"Sure, sure. And that morning last week? You just happened to spend a few hours at her place?"

I made a serious attempt at reviewing the canning output numbers for the week but it was no use seeing as Wheatie wouldn't leave me the hell alone and I'd been up since dawn and I'd asked Shay Zucconi to marry me.

No, I'd offered to marry her. I'd never asked the question. There was a difference, and I didn't know if it made matters better or much worse.

"I'd forgotten about the poison ivy," I said, still clicking through screens. "And Gennie wanted to visit."

"Gennie wanted to visit," he boomed, clapping his hands together. "You know you're a real parent when you blame the kid. Wise. I like it."

I grimaced at my email inbox. "Gennie likes her."

"Understandable," he said. "Seeing as you also like her."

Footsteps sounded on the stairs and then Tony Bonavito stepped into the office that had once been my parents' bedroom. The marketing department worked out of my sister's old bedroom. Neither space looked anything like bedrooms now but it was still strange if I thought about it for too long.

"What's up?" Bones asked, checking the settings on his radio before placing it on the edge of my desk. Whereas Wheatie had two decades on me, Bones was a handful of years younger than me and it showed. He looked like a big kid and he got carded every time he ordered a beer.

"He's seen her," Wheatie said, staring at me, "and spoken to her. A couple of times, if my math is correct."

"All right, all right," he said, slapping his palms on his thighs. "What's the move? What's the play? Are we going straight for it, storm-the-beaches style or something low-key?" He peered at me, his eyes bright. "Do you even know how to be low-key?"

"No," Wheatie said. "He does not."

If that morning at Twin Tulip was proof of anything, it was that.

"Listen, guys," I said. "It was a high school crush. It's over. Nothing is going to happen. I have Gennie to worry about now. I don't have time for anything else. Leave it alone, okay?"

"You need to take her out to dinner. Somewhere nice," Bones said, ignoring the fuck out of me.

"No," I replied. Even if I wanted to do that, I was awkward as hell. My blurted-out proposal was fine proof of that. My general inability to form words around her was even more proof. I could not—*would not*—put any energy into wooing Shay. Not when I knew exactly how that would turn out for me.

"Yeah, one of those fancy places that buys our asparagus and turns it into broth or foam or something weird like that," Bones continued. "You'll need to eat in advance but she'll like it."

"No," I repeated. What would we even talk about without Gennie providing interference? Given ten minutes alone with Shay, I'd either offer my hand in marriage again or sit in complete silence while my ears flamed red and my heart beat loud enough for her to hear it across the table.

"You should thank her," Wheatie said. "For helping Miss Gennie. Thank her with a proper evening out."

"No," I said once again. It was a terrible plan.

"You said she was the one who got away," Wheatie continued. "You said she'd always be the one."

"Yeah, and now I have a kid who is depending on me to be stable and not hung up on some girl who will leave behind a world of hurt when she goes—which she will." I shook my head. I already knew it would hurt to see her leave again but it would kill Gennie, and I couldn't allow that. "And if we're talking about the things we said that night, you said you wanted to explore the possibilities of goat milk, and look where that's landed us. I have a herd of hooligan goats and barely enough milk to justify pursuing organic certification."

"But the price per ounce is decent," Wheatie said. "The wholesale cheese alone covers their costs."

"And the yoga is very popular," Bones said. "I'm a big supporter of that program."

"You're a supporter of the ladies in those tight pants," Wheatie said to him.

"Also that, yes," Bones replied.

"Housewives are not for you," Wheatie said.

"That's an outdated term, old man," Bones replied. "Just because they're here for yoga in the middle of the day doesn't mean they're not bossing it up."

"Remind me to never get drunk with you fools again," I muttered.

"It's part of the grieving process," Wheatie said.

At the same time, Bones asked, "What did I do?"

"Pretty sure you supplied the liquor," Wheatie said to him.

Bones shrugged, saying, "Your father only dies once if he does it right. Homemade hooch is required."

I stared at the ceiling. My father's death had been sudden and shocking, and it had come with the awareness that decisions had to be made about the farm, much sooner than I'd ever anticipated having to make them. In truth, I'd long hoped I wouldn't have to be the one making them at all.

There'd been a million things on my mind the night Wheatie and Bones had hauled me down to the edge of the cove with a bottle and wood for a bonfire, and somehow, the thing that forced its way to the surface was Shay Zucconi and the chunk of my heart she'd stolen.

We'd never spoken of that night. Not until now.

"It means nothing," I said. "Nothing has changed. Just because she's living at the Thomas place—well, it doesn't matter. Nothing is going on with us."

"Something should go on with you," Bones said. "Go for it. What's the worst that could happen?"

I could ask her to marry me.

"Dinner is the way to go," Bones added. "You'll look friendly. Thoughtful."

"Let's not be ridiculous," Wheatie said. "Friendly isn't one of his settings."

"Probably true." Bones stroked the barely-there whiskers of his beard as he peered at me across the desk. "Look. It's either ask her to dinner or carry this bullshit around with you for the rest of time, which seems terrible. I'm just saying. Your choices are take a chance or carry bullshit. I'd take the chance."

"I don't usually agree with the youngster," Wheatie started, "but in this situation, we concur."

I glanced between them. "Great, great. Thanks for sorting out my life for me. We have a freezer on the fritz at the bakehouse and six hundred pounds of blackberries waiting to be moved to the canning house and a shitshow of a goat milk operation but you two want me to take a page from my yearbook out to dinner so everything's fine. Under control. We've got it handled. Thanks."

After a long pause, Bones said, "Those blackberries went to the cannery first thing this morning. They're probably jam by now. No worries on that."

I rubbed my eyes. "At least something is going right around here."

chapter five

Shay

Students will be able to make stones speak.

"SO, based on what we've read, what would you say is the most important detail?"

Gennie dragged her tongue back and forth along her teeth as she studied the book between us. "Blackbeard was a badass," she said.

I gave her a quick nod. "Can you think of another way to say that? A school-friendly way?"

She thought about this for a minute. "Blackbeard was really good at being a ship captain and making pirate plans."

"Okay. Are there any details from the text to show this?" I handed her a stack of sticky notes. "Use these to mark the spots where you find evidence."

Last week, I'd made the mistake of arriving to our "playdate" with some early elementary storybooks. Gennie had zero interest in the classics and anything with the merest whiff of school halted our progress. When I'd told her I taught kindergarten, the betrayal was plain on her face.

I'd returned to the Friendship Public Library in search of books that would appeal to her interests. That I'd found a few titles on pirates and that they were even remotely appropriate for a six-year-old was amazing. There were several mentions of beheadings but that didn't deter Gennie. If anything, it made her more excited to read.

I watched as she flipped through the book, carefully pressing sticky notes to the passages that proved her point. Each passage required a different colored note, which was no problem since an office supply store had exploded in Noah's kitchen in the past week. Every time I visited, there were more goodies waiting on the table. Markers, pens, crayons, and every sticky note under the sun.

It was obvious Noah wanted what was best for Gennie. Colored pencils weren't going to make up for the gaps in her reading skills but they'd make the practice more fun. I gave him credit for that.

"There was a fox on the roof of the chicken house last night," Gennie said as she ran her finger over a sticky note to secure it in place.

"A *fox*," I murmured. "You'll have to tell me that story after we search for words that make the *a* sound, like in *black*."

"Like Blackbeard," she said.

"Exactly like that. Use these little sticky flags to point out those *a* sounds in the story."

"Like *cat*?" she asked. "Like my barn cats?"

"Yes, *cat* has the same *a* sound. See if there's any others in the story."

"What about *bastard*? Is that the same?"

I lifted my water bottle to my lips to drown out a laugh. Once I'd recovered, I said, "Yes, you're right, though let's keep our words school-friendly."

"School isn't friendly," she mumbled.

I leaned down to catch her eye but she looked away, suddenly interested in finding those words. "We'll work on that," I said. "It's going to get better."

"You don't know that," she said, the pout thick in her words.

"Actually, I do know it. When I was a kid, I moved and changed schools a bunch of times. It was really hard. It took me a long time to make friends and I was always the new kid. But it got better."

She kept her gaze on the pages and it was clear I had to talk to Noah about this today. She'd mentioned a few other troubling tidbits over the past week and I'd meant to share them with him but I hadn't been able to get a minute of his time. He wasn't at home when I arrived, Gennie usually in the care of Gail Castro, an eternally patient woman whose family bred and trained horses nearby. Gennie spent the day with Gail now that she wasn't in summer school anymore.

Noah typically made an appearance about halfway through our play-dates, strolling through the kitchen and then immediately disappearing into the adjoining den or back outside. I'd wanted to speak to him on Monday, but Gennie had put up a relentless fight for me to join them for dinner, and I'd made a quick exit. She invited me every time we worked together, but I couldn't maintain a cheerful face for multiple concurrent hours. Not yet.

And I really didn't want to have another conversation about Lollie's land or fake marriages or anything else. I'd done a solid job of convincing myself that Noah hadn't been serious—and I wasn't seriously considering any of it.

So, it was better that we didn't put ourselves in situations where we had to acknowledge that nonsense. I hadn't even mentioned it to Jaime. That was the level of nonsense we were playing with.

"Why did you go to different schools?" Gennie asked, her voice small as she toyed with the flags.

I gathered the other books into a pile. "It was just me and my mom for a long time," I started, "and her job moved us around a lot when I was your age. New York City; Washington, D.C.; London. Sometimes her job required her to go to other countries and I couldn't go with her. Sometimes for months or even years."

"My mom had to go away too," she said.

"It's not easy, is it? I know. It's even harder when your mom is away and you have to start at a new school and live with new people. I know."

"Did your mom come back?"

"She did," I said gently. "But she always left again. Her job is all about going to places and seeing things as they happen, and talking to people about those things. She always had to leave again."

"My mom isn't coming back," she said. "Noah takes me to visit her but she can't come back."

I didn't know what was going on with Eva and it wasn't my place to ask but my heart ached for Gennie. None of this sounded like a positive, happy situation for anyone.

"I'm sorry," I said. "That's a difficult thing to experience. You're very brave, Gennie."

"Like Blackbeard?"

"Sure," I replied.

"I don't have a dad," she went on.

"We all have a dad," I said. "But we don't always know that person. I don't know my dad."

She blinked up at me, her eyes shiny. "Really?"

I shook my head. "I've never met him. I don't know his name. It was just me and my mom until she married someone when I was a teenager. He's my stepdad now."

She bobbed her head before sliding the book across the table. "Did I get all the *a* sounds?"

I paged through the book, pointing to each flagged word and asking her to read it for me. We were almost finished when Noah came through the door, a smudge of dirt high on his cheek and his ball cap dusty. He had a milk crate tucked under his arm, and set it on the counter before glancing at us.

"How are we doing?" he asked on his way to the sink.

"Noah! Did you know Blackbeard's head was chopped off and put on a pole to warn people not to be pirates?"

He glanced to me, his eyes round. "I did not know that," he said to Gennie. "Do you approve of that form of justice? Should we implement that around here? Is that how I should warn foxes away from the henhouse?"

"No," she cried, coming up to kneel in her chair. "That's a terrible idea! And it sounds totally disgusting!"

"Good point. Right. We won't do that," he said, coming around to glance at the books piled in front of me. "Tell me if there are books or anything else you need."

"The library is good," I said, shuffling my things into my bag. "Lots of variety. We can dive into different topics every time we hang out. Makes it that much more fun."

Gennie roped her arms around my neck. "Can Shay come to dinner tonight? Please? She said her mom had to go away and she went to different schools and she doesn't have a dad. She's just like me."

I gave her back a light pat and shifted away. I was about to scoop up the books and make my exit when Noah said, "You're welcome to join us if that works with your schedule. We wouldn't want to hold you up if you have plans though. Isn't that right, Gennie?"

Gennie gave a disinterested shrug, saying, "We'll have more fun if you stay. And we can visit the dogs!"

I glanced at Noah, trying to get a read on his mood. As usual, it was hidden under his hat and behind his beard. When I hesitated, he added, "We'd love to have you but you're not obligated."

That frosted over *not obligated* was a world away from the silence I usually received. It was the Noah equivalent of a parade in my honor. "Okay, then. Can I help with anything?"

He turned away and started unpacking the milk crate. "No. It's taken care of." To Gennie, he asked, "What will you eat for a vegetable tonight?"

"Baby carrots," she replied, busy doodling on the sticky notes.

"Baby carrots are not real carrots," he said. "We've talked about this. I can cut carrots into small pieces but—"

"Baby carrots," she said, "are real and I want them."

"I cannot feed you baby carrots. They do not occur in nature. I can't sell four different colors of carrot while putting processed carrot stumps on your plate."

"*Baby carrots*," she yelled.

He looked up from the crate, a loaf of bread in one hand. "I can give you carrots in small pieces. That's the best I can do. That, or cucumbers."

She set her head on the table, her little hands fisted to her ears. "Cucumbers," she mumbled into the surface.

"Cucumbers it is," he replied, crossing to the fridge.

I swiveled a gaze between Gennie and Noah for a moment. It seemed the great baby carrot debate was settled, at least for now. After a tense minute, I said, "Gennie, why don't you pack up the supplies for today?"

"And then you can grab eggs from the henhouse," Noah added.

She lifted her head, her dark, unruly hair curtaining her face. "Do I have to?"

"If you want to visit the dogs later, yes."

"For fuck's sake," she muttered. She tossed the sticky notes and markers back in the plastic bin and carried it out of the room.

I caught Noah's exasperated gaze and offered a quick grin. He rolled his eyes. "We go a few rounds on baby carrots at least once a week."

"She has a passion. It's important."

"It's driving me mad," he said.

"Are you sure I can't do anything?" I watched as Noah started slicing a loaf of bread. "I've heard those come presliced these days."

"I don't care for the uniformity of machine slicing," he said. "Besides, this is a new recipe the bakehouse is working on. I grabbed a test loaf to try."

I stepped closer to the island where he was working. "Since when do you have a bakehouse?"

"About four years now. It started with apple crisp. We had a huge yield a few years ago and ended up turning the surplus into crisps and pies. Figured we'd break even at best. Ended up selling out. Then we tested pound cakes and shortcakes during strawberry season. Now, we have eleven year-round pies and four special pies per season. Breads were the next logical venture."

"Any other businesses I should know about?"

He glanced at the ceiling for a second, as if he had trouble recalling the details of his empire. "Summertime ice cream stand down on Old County Road, near the mouth of the cove. There's also honey and jams—"

"That's Noah's favorite." Gennie returned to the kitchen wearing her eye patch and dragging the tip of her sword along the floor. She marched toward the door. "All of his secret projects are about jam. He's like Blackbeard but for jam. But no heads cutting off."

The door closed behind her as Noah said, "I'm not the Blackbeard of —never mind."

"You did all that in the past few years?" I asked.

He returned to the task at hand, not at all concerned with responding to me. I was starting to understand this was one of his mannerisms. One of the more maddening ones.

After longer than was reasonable to keep someone waiting, he said, "It came together pretty easily. All of the pieces were already there. It was just a matter of getting it off the ground. The ice cream was a no-brainer as far as dairy surpluses are concerned."

"But the jam is your favorite."

He jerked a shoulder up as he turned toward the fridge. I was forced to notice the lovely way his jeans settled low on his hips. He looked completely different than I'd remembered him, but also, he finally looked like himself. I knew that was a lopsided sort of compliment though it was the most accurate way to explain the ways he'd changed. It was like his bad haircut had grown out and he didn't have to deal with the awkwardness of that in-between time anymore. He was taller and mature and more at ease but he looked like himself. He looked like the friend I remembered.

He came back with a cucumber in hand and I had to concentrate on keeping my gaze at eye level. "It's a smart way to reduce waste. Bruised fruit never sells but it makes great jam."

I settled onto one of the stools tucked into the island, waiting. I didn't know this version of Noah well enough to predict his next move but I had to believe he'd keep talking if I left the door open for him. And I really wanted him to keep talking.

Once the cuke was thoroughly washed and dried, he set to slicing it. I'd never noticed how long his fingers were or the number of freckles dotting his knuckles. It was kinda cute. "My mom liked canning. Loved preserves. She had a ton of recipes, most of which she stored in her head and never wrote down. It made sense to keep that going. It's good business."

"How are your parents?"

Obviously, they weren't here. I didn't want to make any assumptions but that, plus the decidedly past-tense way he spoke about his mother and the fact the family home had been converted into a market, gave me a bad feeling.

"My mother lives in North Carolina with her sister," he replied. "They have an apartment in one of those assisted living communities. She's able to get support for her MS there, which is good because she needs a lot of help these days. A lot. It's a single story, which is important with her limited mobility. Less demanding than living in an old farmhouse."

"Does that mean she's left the pulpit?"

He gave a jerky shoulder-shrug-nod. "The Reverend left before I finished college. Might've been my second year, around the end. I'm not sure. But yeah, she stepped away from the congregation when her speech issues became more prominent." Another jerky shrug. "She's probably assembled a makeshift congregation at the assisted living community. Can't keep a true theologian down."

I watched as he scooped the cukes into a blue bowl with white polka dots. His hands were huge. *Huge.* When did that happen? "And your dad?"

Noah made a noise, some sort of humming grumble. "He died. Four-wheeler accident. There's a spot on the back side of the orchard where the land gets soft when it rains every spring, and if you're not paying attention, you'll either get stuck in the mud or roll over a few times. It was dark and the conditions were stormy, and he rolled over. He went quickly but Mom had a serious relapse not long after, and she needed to move somewhere that she could get the support she required." He waved his knife at the room. "Things evolved rapidly."

"I'm so sorry, Noah."

He nodded.

"So, that's what brought you back to Friendship."

He busied himself with grabbing plates from the cupboard and utensils from the drawer before turning a fraction of his attention toward me. "Pretty much." He opened the window over the sink and called out, "Gennie, what's up with those eggs, kid? It doesn't take that long."

I couldn't make out her response but I did get the joy of watching Noah sigh with his whole body. He looked good. Better than I could've imagined.

Too bad he was such an epic grump.

Gennie clamored in, her sword tucked under her arm and making it near impossible to close the door without bobbling the basket of eggs. "Let me help you there," I said, relieving her of the basket.

"Wash your hands," Noah said to her.

"The chickens hate me," Gennie said, stomping toward the bathroom. "They want to eat my fingers."

"Your fingers would not be especially appetizing. Not enough meat on those bones," Noah called after her.

Gennie emerged from the bathroom, eye patch over her brow and hands dripping wet. "They're evil chickens. Super evil."

Noah held out the polka dot bowl. "Take your cucumbers to the table."

She accepted the bowl but stopped at my stool. "Will you sit next to me?"

"Of course. Let me help Noah with—"

"I've got it," he interrupted. "Just—go. Sit."

I spared him a quick glance but he'd already turned toward the oven, forcing me to watch the way his t-shirt stretched across his back. Yeah, these years looked good on him.

I grabbed the plates and silverware he'd set out and took a seat beside Gennie at the table. She had cucumber slices in both hands.

"I like your earrings," she said. "What are they?"

"Lobsters," I said, fingering the intricate beading. "I got these in Maine a few summers ago. A little town called Talbott's Cove. I went there with some of my friends."

"Did it hurt to get your ears pierced?"

"It's very fast. A fast pinch."

She considered this carefully. "How old do you have to be to get your ears pierced?"

Noah set two dishes in the middle of the table. "Fifteen," he said. "At least fifteen."

"But Ella has earrings and she's not fifteen."

Noah scooped chicken and roasted vegetables onto Gennie's plate. "Then that's a decision Ella's family made. We'll talk about earrings when you're"—he shook his head, passed the chicken to me—"when you're twelve. At the earliest. Okay?"

She fingered my lobsters again. "I guess so."

Noah cut Gennie's food into bite-sized pieces and handed the plate back to her before sitting down.

"How old do you have to be to make your hair pink?" she asked.

"Oh my god," he said under his breath.

I smothered a laugh, saying, "I'm thirty-two and I did this for the first time last month. There's no rush. You have all the time in the world to dye your hair and get earrings and everything like that. I promise, you're not missing anything."

She gave me a thoughtful nod. "Okay. I can wait."

Noah gazed at Gennie while she dug into her food, carefully pushing most of the vegetables to the far edge of her plate. After a moment, he blew out a breath and reached for the bread. It was abundantly clear he had his hands full with this parenting gig.

"This is incredible," I said, jabbing my fork in the direction of my plate. "When did you do all this cooking? I didn't see any of this magic happen."

He barked out a laugh. "I didn't cook. There's a meal delivery service two towns over. We supply their dairy and some produce. I've been on their roster since day one."

"This is the best meal I've had since—since the last time I was here," I said. "Probably the last actual meal too."

"Then you should come to dinner every night," Gennie replied. "Noah says I'm required to eat a real meal, so you should too."

I expected Noah to jump in and explain that wasn't possible but he just stared at me for a long beat, deep grooves dug into his forehead. When he didn't look away, I said, "Cooking for one isn't very fun. It's simpler to have Cheez-Its or a bag of popcorn or some peanut butter on crackers."

"Shay," he said, the grooves deepening.

I'd dug a ditch in his forehead. Me and my shambles.

"It's fine. Really. I'll have to look into this meal service. Sounds perfect. Especially since the school year will be starting in a few weeks and then I'll have no time."

He went on staring at me. Then, "You're going to be teaching in Friendship schools?"

"Subbing," I said. "Which is just as hectic as a regular teaching position. More, actually, since the assignments vary day-to-day. But I'm looking forward to it."

"You'll be a teacher at my school?" Gennie asked. "Fuck yeah!"

"Gennie," Noah warned, but there was no weight behind it.

"Will you still play with me after school?" she asked. "Or will you be too busy then?"

I glanced at Noah. He gave a slight nod which I interpreted to mean he was cool with us continuing our work. It could've meant any number of things but I was happy with this explanation. Gennie needed all the help she could get and I had a soft spot for this kid.

"We can still play," I told her.

She stabbed her fork into the air. "Yes!"

"You're ready for more reading and fact practice?" I asked her.

"Arrr, matey," she growled. "Me's a right good mather."

The two of us shared a laugh over that and settled into a comfortable discussion of today's reading—without the gory details. And it was comfortable, even if Noah seemed anything but happy to have me here. I wasn't into taking his vibes personally but I couldn't ignore all his drawn-out silences. And the frowning. So much frowning. Even if he'd sworn he wanted me to stay for the meal, it was obvious that wasn't the whole truth.

But I had to ask: "Is your bakehouse selling this bread at the farm stand? Can I buy this? Because I require more."

"Well, we"—Noah watched as I chose another slice—"we don't have it in production yet. Still working on the recipe."

"You didn't ask for my opinion but I think the recipe is perfect." I couldn't believe I'd ever willingly given up bread. What a tragedy. "Feel free to send me any test loaves though. I'm happy to provide additional feedback."

He stared at me a moment longer before blinking away and clearing his throat. "Yeah. Sure."

"What do you like about being a teacher?" Gennie asked.

"Lots of things," I said. "I like meeting new kiddos every year and growing a little community in our classroom. I like that we get to explore books and do experiments and learn how to treat each other with kindness and dignity. And I really like that I get to match my earrings to the things we're learning about. I have so many apple and pumpkin earrings."

"Weren't you going into public relations or something?" Noah asked.

When I glanced across the table at him, I read the surprise on his face. He hadn't meant to ask. That made it even better, as far as I was concerned.

"Yeah, that fizzled out fast. I switched over to psychology before the end of my first year and then switched to child development." Since we were finished eating, I reached for his plate, stacking it atop mine. "I didn't really have a specific plan—"

"Do you ever?"

I collected Gennie's plate and added it to my stack. "Sometimes," I replied with a laugh. "Teaching wasn't on my radar until my last year when I had an internship based in an elementary school."

"Did you stay at Boston College?"

I nodded as I gathered the utensils and consolidated the leftovers. "I did and I stayed an extra year to earn my teaching credential."

"You don't have to do that," Noah said, reaching for the dishes.

"Maybe not but I'm doing it anyway." I glanced to Gennie. "Do you think you can carry these plates to the dishwasher for me?"

She jumped up from her seat. "Aye aye, captain."

"And you stayed in Boston after that," he said.

Check out this chatty guy. I swallowed a grin. "I bounced around between districts for the first few years but then I found an independent school where I really connected with the leadership and community, and I've been there ever since."

Noah pushed away from the table and circled the island. He returned with a paper bag and dropped the remaining bread into it. "Take this with you," he said. Before I could reply, he gathered the last few dishes and set them in the sink. To Gennie, he asked, "Do you want to feed the dogs? I bet they'd like to see you."

"Of course I want to feed the dogs," she cried, jamming the last of the silverware into the dishwasher.

"You can walk Shay out and then head down there. Okay?"

That was one way to tell me I'd overstayed my welcome. It was a good thing I'd already been dumped so hard I was mostly dead inside and couldn't take offense to this man's mood.

But I had to talk to Noah about some of Gennie's more concerning comments.

"Actually," I started, gesturing toward him, "can I get a second with you? Maybe while Gennie tends to the dogs?"

He stared at me while drawing in a breath and then slowly blowing it out. It was as though I'd asked him whether I should saw off his arm with a butter knife or a rusty teaspoon.

He grabbed the paper bag and thrust it toward me. "Yeah. Sure. No problem. Lead the way."

chapter six

Noah

Students will be able to establish—and then destroy—boundaries.

ALL RIGHT. We were doing this. We were having another conversation without the buffer of my niece and I was more than likely to fuck things up. Here we go.

Gennie ran down the hill toward the dog run, yelling every step of the way, "Doggies! I'm coming for you!"

Shay watched from the edge of the gravel drive, one hand shading her eyes from the last of the day's sun.

The extremely annoying fact of the matter was that Shay was gorgeous. Just drop-dead gorgeous. The more I tried to ignore this, the more aware of it I grew. That awareness chewed at me day and night, accompanied by the lurking whisper of *you could marry her*.

I walked toward Shay, my gaze fixed on Gennie and my hat pulled low. I shoved my hands in my pockets. "Have you given any thought to our partnership?"

Shay turned to face me. "Have I—what?"

"The partnership I proposed last week. For your inheritance."

"Yeah. That." She shifted back to watch Gennie and the dogs. "To be honest, I don't—"

"I need to clear up a few things," I interrupted. "We'll draft a prenup, of course. You'll keep as much of your property as you want, we'll share ownership in the event space, and I'll keep my property. It'll be a clean agreement."

She shifted the tote bag filled with books to her other shoulder, saying, "I'm going to need a bit more time to consider all of that. Like, a lot more time. It's not just about the land for me."

"It's not just about the land for me either," I said. "I have a kid and I should've been explicit about her involvement in this from the start. I'm not letting anything hurt her. Not a single fucking thing. Gennie cannot —will not—get caught in the middle if we do this."

"I would never want that," she replied, her words sharp around the edges.

"If we do this—and I think you should know this is one of your better options if you're dead set against taking the estate to court—we have to make it safe and stable for Gennie. That means keeping it under wraps for the year, living our separate lives, and quietly dissolving the marriage once the estate is cleared. She knows nothing, not a single word. I'll negotiate anything except for Gennie." I shot a glance at her but that was a mistake. It was nearly impossible to enforce limits when instinct told me to give this woman everything in the world she wanted. "Take that with you while you're considering the matter."

"I would never do anything to hurt her," Shay said.

"Not intentionally, no. The problem is that Gen already adores you and she's going to be heartbroken when you leave."

Shay set her bag down and turned to face me. "You say that as if I'd just walk away from her without a second thought."

That's exactly what I'm saying because it's exactly what you did to me.

"No," I replied. "You're—you're good with kids. Obviously. You know what to do with kids and you know how to talk to them. I'm sure you're really great as a teacher too, even if I can't wrap my head around that career choice for you. But Gennie doesn't have room in her life for more disappointment. She can't fall in love with you over the next year and then you drop out of her life. If we do this, we protect her."

"Actually, that's a topic I've been meaning to discuss with you," she said. "It's what I wanted to talk about tonight."

I crossed my arms over my chest. I didn't like the sound of this. I didn't want to continue this conversation at all. I'd said everything I needed to say and didn't dig myself into any new holes, and now I wanted to be alone so I could properly exhale for the first time since the afternoon. "Yeah. Sure. What's up?"

"Gennie has mentioned a few things to me that I think you should hear about," she said. "There have been a bunch of comments about not having friends at school, or having a tough time with the other kids. I think her pirate persona is a defense mechanism. She uses it to manage the discomfort of these social issues."

Shit. Just...shit.

I met Shay's eyes and waited a long beat before asking, "Is there anything else?"

"She's embarrassed about her hair," Shay said. "She says it never looks nice or pretty, and my guess is that also feeds into the pirate thing."

"Why didn't she tell me? I would've—I don't know, I would've done something."

Shay shrugged. "I'm not sure but she did mention that she's worried you don't know how to do girl hair."

I ripped my hat off and rubbed my forehead. "Every time I think I'm getting a handle on this parenting thing, ear piercing and girl hair pop up and I'm right back at the start again."

"You're wrong about that. You're so far from the start, you can't even see the start."

"The start is a goalpost that moves every day," I replied. "And it's going to keep moving. Today it's girl hair. In a few years, it's going to be —I don't know—training bras and periods and Jesus Christ, I'm not equipped for this."

"I think you are," she said. "You're doing a great job with her, Noah. You'll figure it out as you go, and that's the best you can do. I mean, she eats vegetables and does chores, and—"

"And drops *fuck* into most conversations."

"Mmm. That's true. But listen. One year, on the first day of school, I was outside in the morning, greeting students as they arrived. One kid gets off the bus, walks right up to me, spits on my shoes, and says I better not be the bitch-ass cunt who's going to make him go to school. Then he runs out of the parking lot and into oncoming traffic. The day had barely started and that's where we were at."

"Oh my god." I wanted to ask what that kid's home life was like but my niece referred to the chickens as shithead bastards, so I had no legs to stand on here.

She glanced down the hill at Gennie, who was flat on the ground while one of the old dogs licked her face. "He was a handful that year. The runners always are, but he was extra special. He's starting fifth grade in a few weeks but he goes to eighth grade for math. Special children will always demand the most of us."

How did she do that? How did she make things seem infinitely possible? Not even possible but likely? As if I'd be able to reform this rogue child into a fully formed human person over the next decade despite the fact her childhood was pockmarked with trauma. As if I'd figure out how to do this *and* manage to keep my head above water.

And where did Shay get off being so—so tolerant and accepting? The girl I'd known never would've considered a career in teaching, let alone one where kids cussed her out first thing in the morning.

The girl I knew in high school—

I shoved my hat into my back pocket and shifted to stand in front of

Shay. To look at her, really look at the person I'd known all those years ago.

Was it possible she wasn't that girl anymore?

If I could change, couldn't she? And I'd *changed*. If we ignored the part where I still blushed and stumbled over my words when it came to Shay, I was nothing like my high school self. I'd projected all my insecurities onto this town, and I'd made resenting this place my entire personality.

Thank fuck I'd changed.

"Gennie had a hard time last year," I said. "When she first came here, it was rough. For both of us. It didn't occur to me she'd have trouble in school until I started getting calls."

"Being the new kid is overwhelming under the best of circumstances. I would know."

I stared at her. I wanted to know when she'd changed. Whether it was sudden or a slow shift. And I wanted to know why. What happened along the way?

"Is that why you're helping her? Because you were the new girl so many times?"

She offered a loose shrug. "A little of that. A little of knowing what it's like to feel as though you don't belong anywhere. A little of remembering what it was like to be six or seven and my mother leaving for an overseas assignment."

"Eva isn't a war correspondent. She's not embedded with a military unit or spending a year tailing a crown prince to uncover decades of corruption."

"Maybe not but the details aren't as relevant when you're a little kid being bounced from place to place. I didn't know my mother was a famous journalist at that age. I just knew a rotating cast of nannies were my only family and no one ever knew when my mom was coming home. We might have different stories but I know a lot about Gennie's. I know about fathers who donated sperm and literally nothing else, and I know about feeling like there's no one to claim you."

"Eva is serving a life sentence," I said. "She killed a federal agent while moving drugs across the Canadian border for her asshole boyfriend. Had no idea it was a sting operation or that she'd committed a dozen federal crimes in the presence of undercover agents. Didn't know how to use the gun the asshole boyfriend had given her either but she panicked and it turns out her aim is impeccable. She wounded three other agents in the process. It was an accident. A series of really fucking awful accidents and she will spend the rest of her life in prison while the asshole boyfriend has vanished into thin air." I watched this wash over Shay in waves, each worse than the one before. "Gennie was five hundred miles away when it happened. In Philly with one of Eva's friends. It took a week for social services to locate her and then three more days for them to contact my mother. By that time, Eva had already provided far too much free information to the feds without once asking for a lawyer and Gennie was already in the foster care system. The only thing Gen remembers from that time is being hungry and watching *Pirates of the Caribbean* over and over but go ahead and tell me how you know what she's been through. Tell me about how your nannies and your townhouses on the Upper East Side and in Mayfair and your Swiss boarding schools have anything in common with her. Tell me, Shay."

We stared at each other while dogs barked and Gennie giggled in the distance. The sun was low on the horizon and I could've watched the way the breeze carried Shay's hair for hours. Longer. I wanted to tuck it behind her ear and run my thumb over her cheek. Even if it cost me everything.

"I'm sorry," she said eventually. "I can't possibly know everything she's been through. I can't know what you've been through." She gave me a look that seemed to say something but I was too preoccupied with her hair to understand it. "But I wasn't wrong when I said I know what it's like when it seems as though you have no one. Like you belong to no one, no place. That *is* part of the reason why I want the best for her. No matter what happens with us, that won't change. The other part is that you're my friend—or you were the last time I was in this town and hopefully will be again—and I want what's best for you too." She reached down and hefted her bag.

I shot a hand out, saying, "Let me carry that to your car."

"No, no." She waved me off. "Carrying bags full of books is my cardio."

I stepped back and stuck my hands in my pockets. It was all I could do to stop myself from touching her.

"We cannot solve all the giant problems," she said, the bag settled on her shoulder. "But we can solve lots of little ones. I'm going to teach you how to handle girl hair. When Gennie needs hair help, come down to the house and I'll do it for her until you learn. You're welcome anytime but you should know the doorbell doesn't work and I can't hear knocking unless I'm standing right in front of the door. It's always been that way. Come in, give a shout, and we'll get to work on respectable ponytails, pigtails, and braids."

"You don't have to do that."

She nodded to herself. "That's probably true. I don't have to do anything. But that's why I'm here. I'm taking an unscheduled gap year from my life. Because it feels right. It doesn't have to make sense to anyone but me and there doesn't have to be an endgame unless I want one. That's it. I'm done with things and places and people where it's forced and it's wrong but I don't figure that out until it's too late because I was very busy forcing it to be perfect. So, I want to help with Gennie's hair and make sure she gets to the next grade and I'm going to put up with your moody bear vibe while I do it."

"What moody bear vibe?" I knew exactly which moody bear vibe she was referring to.

"The thing where you can't decide if you're my friend or not," she said, sizing me up in one swoop. "Whatever that's about isn't something

I can change but I can help your niece. Even better, I get some nice bread along the way." She patted the bag. "Thanks for that."

What the fuck was happening to me right now? How had I lost control of this situation? "Anytime."

She took another step back. "Come by the house if you need hair help. Don't bother knocking. Okay?"

I nodded, watching as she made her way to her car. She stowed the bag in the back seat and then gave me a wave. Because I couldn't help myself, not for a single minute where this woman was involved, I called, "Let me know if you need me to marry you."

She tipped her head to the side. "I'm not ready to think about that yet."

"Then let me see Lollie's will while I'm waiting."

"No need," she said. "It is what it is. No sense fighting."

She opened the driver's door and climbed into the seat. She paused as if she meant to say something but waved again. I lifted my hand in response, watching as she drove away.

This time, when I heard that reminder, it said *there goes your wife.*

chapter seven

Shay

Students will be able to play the part.

"HMM. Do these letters look right to you? Are they all standing properly?" I asked. Gennie frowned at the small whiteboard in her lap. "Any of them backward?"

Understanding hit her. "Oh. The *D*s. And the *G*s."

"You know how to make a *G*," I told her. "*G* for Gennie."

She rubbed a sock over the board, erasing the misshapen letters. "*G* for game."

I nodded slowly. We were talking about old shipwrecks up and down the Atlantic, and a few in nearby Newport Harbor. "Also that, yes."

She set to rewriting her sentence. "Do you like games? Like, sports and stuff?"

"Yeah. Sure." I bobbed my head. "Let's think about punctuation and capitalization in this sentence. Where would we do that?"

We didn't have much longer until Gennie and Noah were scheduled to meet with the school to determine whether they'd promote her to first grade. I didn't want to waste a minute of that time on side conversations.

I'd learned in the past few weeks that Gennie was really bright—and *really* struggled to stay focused. It was like she had a hundred thoughts buzzing around her head at once and it was all too easy for her to lose track of the one she needed.

She wiped the words away again and started over. She was also a perfectionist. If the work wasn't correct, everything was thrown out. If she didn't think she could do it without error, she wouldn't do it at all. Whiteboards and dry-erase markers helped cut down on the risk of being wrong but didn't eliminate it entirely.

"Like this?" she asked.

I read the words. "That's a strong statement. 'Ships wrecked because of rocks they did not see.' Nice attention to capitalization and punctuation."

"There's a football game tonight," she said, erasing the words in one dramatic swoop. "You said you like sports so you should come to the game with us."

"Hmm." I paged through the book we'd read. "Let's think about the words *wreck* and *rock*." I wrote them on her board. "What similarities do you hear in those words?"

"They both have *ck*," she replied quickly. "So, you'll come to the game? Noah says I can get a pretzel as big as my head and there's a marching band too and—"

"This is really interesting," I said. "I want to hear more about it after you look through the story and spy the other words with a *-ck* blend. Find those words and then we'll talk about giant pretzels."

I really didn't want to hear about giant pretzels.

Not that Gennie's stories weren't amazing—they were, even more than most kid stories were amazing. But we were running out of time here.

"Done." Gennie snapped the book shut. "It's the first football game. They start playing football even before school starts. Noah says everyone goes so you should go too."

"I'll have to think about it," I said. "Can you think of any other words that have the *-ck* blend?"

"Chicken. Truck." She wrote them on the board. "Fuck." She didn't write that one down, thank god. "You could come to the football game and sit with me."

Before I could respond, the side door opened and Noah entered, phone pressed to his ear and yet another crate tucked under his arm. He nodded to us, set down the crate, and stalked up the stairs.

"—and food trucks and frozen lemonade. That's my favorite. Frozen lemonade. I could have frozen lemonade every day for all of time ever."

"That would be a lot of frozen lemonade."

"You could get one too. I have money in my room."

I eyed her. "Big spender, huh?"

"Noah gives me money when I help him at the markets," she said. "I have a lot of dollars."

"It sounds like you worked hard for it."

She nodded and capped the marker. "Do you have any friends? Do you play with them at your house?"

"I do have friends," I said. "But they live in another state."

"Are you lonely without them?"

"Sometimes," I admitted.

"Then you should come to the game," she said. "You won't be lonely."

Never let it be said that Gennie wasn't determined. That girl did not give up. I grinned at her. "I will think about it. Now, why don't you help me gather all these books."

We filled my tote with the books I'd borrowed from the town library and loaded the markers and sticky notes back into the lidded container.

Noah returned to the kitchen wearing a fresh shirt, phone clutched in his hand. "Hey." After a beat, he turned his attention to his niece. "Gennie, what's the egg situation?"

"Dammit," she muttered.

"You can walk me out and then check the coops," I said.

Resigned, she shuffled toward the door. "You'll try to come to the game, right?"

Noah glanced at me but then started unpacking the crate he'd left on the countertop. A carton of cherry tomatoes, paper-wrapped herbs, several empty mason jars.

"I'll think about it." I swung my bag over my shoulder and took hold of the book tote.

I followed her outside, unsurprised when I heard her mumbling about the wicked hens. The surprise was Noah lumbering down the steps and meeting me beside the henhouse. We hadn't talked much since last week. For reasons I still didn't understand, that seemed intentional on his part.

"How's she doing?" he asked.

"She's very capable," I said.

He scowled at his phone before sliding it into his pocket. "That's good, I guess. Yesterday, the psychologist recommended having her tested for ADHD."

"Mention it to the school when you meet with them. Tell them she's being evaluated. I'm sure I don't have to tell you anything about disability law as it pertains to educational settings. I'm sure you're aware that documentation from her psychologist could be very beneficial in this matter."

He turned to face me as Gennie dashed back into the house with the eggs. "Thank you. If you hadn't shown up and yelled at me about our trucks, I don't know what I would've done."

"You would've figured it out."

"I'm not sure about that." He seemed to debate something internally before saying, "It's good to have you back."

"Is it?" I intended the question to sound teasing though I wasn't sure it landed that way. "There have been a couple of moments where I've wondered if we're still friends."

"I wouldn't ask you to marry me if we weren't." He gestured to me. "Not that I'm trying to rush you on that matter. Just making a point."

"So, you're just a bear with a pricker in his paw on a regular basis? That's your look now?" There was no way anyone could miss the teasing in my tone this time.

"Listen, don't knock it. The more people I can scare off with this look, the better. Saves me from having to mediate every damn hiccup in this town." A sigh rumbled out of him. "You disappeared, you know. You were just gone. Left town, never to be heard from again."

A moment passed where I tried to put his words in an order I could understand. I couldn't find one. "Wasn't that the plan?"

He bobbed his head but there was nothing convincing about it.

"We both wanted that. Right? We wanted to get out of here and never come back. That's why you went to that summer program at Yale. So you could leave as soon as possible." I stepped closer, my book bag brushing against his leg. I couldn't have this conversation without seeing it in his eyes. "And you left first. I spent most of the time after graduation here. Alone. I took my sweet, slow time leaving. I didn't disappear at all."

He brought his hand to the back of his neck as his lips twisted into a joyless smile that said *keep telling yourself that*.

"Am I missing something?" I asked.

"No, you have it right," he said after a pause. "I guess I figured you'd—" He pulled the hand from the back of his neck, dropped it against his thigh. "It doesn't matter."

"Noah, wait," I said, touching his forearm. He froze, staring down at my hand. "It does matter. To me."

Gennie ran out the front door, the screen banging behind her as she dashed toward me. "Did you think about it? Are you going to come to the game tonight?"

"Oh, sweetie." I glanced at Noah, hoping he'd help us both out and give me an exit from this event. No such luck. "I have to go home and do some adult chores first. I'm not sure I'll finish in time."

Gennie nodded, obviously disappointed. "Okay."

"I'll see you on Monday for sure. We'll talk about explorers. I have a really cool story about an explorer and how his ship might be one of the shipwrecks in Newport Harbor."

I opened the car door and set my things inside.

Noah called, "There's a decent food truck scene before the game. It's worth it for that alone but you should check it out. You might realize you don't hate it here."

I dropped into the driver's seat. "Is that how it went for you? You looked around one day and realized you didn't hate it here anymore?"

Noah held my gaze while warmth pressed in around me. It was a hot day. Afternoon sun. Humid too. Hot, humid, sunny. That was the only thing I was feeling.

"Check it out," he said. "See for yourself."

"THERE'S A FOOTBALL GAME TONIGHT."

Jaime frowned at the screen. She was in her classroom with the overhead lights off because she hated bright lights but I could still make out that frown. "What kind of football?"

"High school," I replied. "I think. I'm pretty sure."

"Why do we care about this?"

"The little girl I've been tutoring, she talked it up." I peered into the empty fridge. "Apparently there are food trucks. I'm guessing it's a tailgate situation. Maybe fundraising? I didn't ask a lot of questions."

"The kid you're tutoring is into food trucks? That generation has its priorities straight."

"It wasn't like that when I was in high school," I said. "Football games were as basic as you could get."

She started stapling little rainbows with her students' names and birthdays to the board. For a second, I was overcome with sadness. I didn't have a birthday board this year. I wouldn't get to celebrate birthdays or any of the other milestones of kindergarten. And I didn't have Jaime right there next to me—all because I wanted to drop out of my life and reconnect with the only place that had made me feel like I belonged.

Jaime snapped me out of my thoughts, saying, "You should go."

"Go where?"

"You should go to the football game." Still busy placing and stapling her rainbows, she didn't spare me a glance. "You can't take a year off just to sit in a big old house and drink wine and eat microwaved rice every night."

"I don't eat microwaved rice every night."

"I like how that's the part you're disputing." She gave me a quick grin. "You wanted to live in the sweet little small town, doll. You wanted to get back to your granny's farm. You're there, now you need to do it all the way. Go to the football game. Eat from the food trucks. Cheer for the home team. All of it. If you're not going to do that, you should pack up immediately and come home. You can live with me. You can sub in any district around here until you find something permanent. But you cannot stay there and do nothing."

I stamped my foot on the kitchen floor. "But Jaime—"

"But Shay," she interrupted. "I have confirmed with my own eyes that you're alive and well enough to put on a pretty shirt and go to that football game. It's time for you to get some real practice with living again, doll. Go. Get there. Do something real, even if you hate it."

I WANTED to say that nothing about Friendship High School had changed in the years since I graduated, but like everything else in this town, it had a fresh new look. The 1960s-era building with its flat roof and brown exterior had been replaced with a three-story structure, all windows and clean lines and solar panels. Where there had once been a dusty, pitted field better suited for the wanderings of geese and bunnies than any form of athletics now stood a shining sports complex.

Since coming here to Friendship, I'd had it in my head that I'd run into people from high school all over the place. People other than Noah. I figured it would happen at the grocery store or the library or maybe the coffee shop in town where I ate a balanced breakfast of iced coffee and cookies when I ran out of pudding cups. To this point, I hadn't seen another familiar face.

I guess it made sense. This wasn't the kind of small town people struggled to leave. Friendship wasn't remote or isolated, not in any true sense. Of course I hadn't bumped into anyone from high school in the produce section. They'd moved on.

Not that I was complaining.

I'd had friends in high school but it was mostly the superficial kind of relationships, the ones where I'd catch glimpses of their lives on social media now but I had to pause and remind myself how I knew them.

With that cheerful thought in mind, I strolled along the track loop, taking in the food truck options. The school's clubs and intramural sports had tables set up in the middle and the booster club was selling t-shirts.

I had to admit, it felt good to do something. Before the debacle with the ex, I went out all the time. I was an outgoing person, dammit. I was social. I liked being around people.

Now, I spent most evenings walking the Twin Tulip grounds while listening to audiobooks or podcasts and drinking wine from a stainless steel water bottle. If I could exhaust myself enough, distract myself enough, I wouldn't have to think about all the bruises and broken things. But this felt good. Strange good, like I didn't know what I was doing here but neither did anyone else.

I followed a string of students in marching band regalia into the building and asked them to point me in the direction of the restrooms. Once I was alone in a stall, I glanced at the time on my phone. Another half hour until game time.

"A healthy stream is at least ten uninterrupted seconds."

I glanced around the stall. Was this person talking to *me*?

"If you're not consistently urinating for ten uninterrupted seconds, you should consider pelvic floor therapy."

Again, I looked around as if I'd find some explanation for the woman who seemed to be speaking to me.

"Okay," I said tentatively. "Thanks?"

"Do you find you often have interruptions in your stream?"

"I—" I squeezed my eyes shut for a second. I'd had a lot of weird conversations in public restrooms. *A lot.* This was the weirdest by far and that included the time someone asked me if I'd meet their friend because they believed I was her long-lost twin who'd been separated from her at birth. Spoiler alert: I was not her twin. "I'm good. No worries."

"In my professional opinion, it doesn't sound like you're all good," she chirped.

"Are you…listening to me pee?"

She laughed. "Occupational hazard."

"Or intrusion of privacy," I muttered. I finished up, thankful for the noise of the flush for drowning out any additional comments.

Until I stepped out of the stall.

On the other side of the door stood a tall, slender woman. She aimed a huge smile at me. "Hi. I'm Christiane."

I had to scoot around her to get to the sink. "Hi," I said over the water.

"I'm a physical therapist. One of my specialties is pelvic floor dysfunction. Here's my card."

I held up my wet hands with a pointed stare. Then I moved toward the paper towels, turning my body sideways to shimmy along the stall doors because this woman was committed to standing in the most inconvenient spot possible.

"It's never too soon to tune into your pelvic floor needs," she said.

I forced a smile as I dried my hands. "Yeah. Okay. Thanks for the chat."

I grabbed the card and damn near sprinted out of there. Jaime was never going to believe this story. She'd question my sanity. My sobriety too.

By the time I made it outside, the marching band was playing an old Miley Cyrus tune and the area was rapidly filling with people. I meandered back toward the food trucks, determined to make a selection before they sold out.

I'd nearly waded through the densest part of the throng when I heard "Shay!" and a small body slammed into me from the side.

Looking down, I found Gennie, her hair tied in lopsided pigtails. "Where did you come from, my friend?"

She squeezed my waist for another moment. Then, "Come on. Noah's over here. He said I could look around but I had to be able to see him at all times but then I saw you but I don't think he'll be mad that I went far away."

Oh, god. He was going to start flipping food trucks if he couldn't find her.

"Let's get you back to where you belong." I took her hand and urged her to lead the way.

We found Noah deep in conversation with a woman at the boosters' table though he didn't look like he was enjoying it. He had his arms crossed over his chest and his jaw locked tight enough for me to notice it from several yards away. He replied with decisive nods though the deep grooves around his mouth suggested he didn't care for the discussion at hand.

The minute he spotted me and Gennie crossing the track, he held up a hand, saying, "You'll have to excuse me," and strode toward us.

"I found Shay," Gennie said.

At the same time, Noah asked, "What did I tell you about staying where I could see you?"

"But Shay almost missed us," she said. "And you told me to look for her with both eyeballs."

If I wasn't mistaken, his ears were turning a fascinating shade of red. *Fascinating.*

He glanced at me, a quick up and down that swallowed up my jeans and cute top before settling his gaze on Gennie. "There are a lot of people here. I don't want you wandering off. Okay?"

She heaved out an enormous sigh, saying, "I guess so." Then she grabbed my hand and started twirling. "I gotta dance, Shay. Watch!"

"Dance it out, girl. I'm watching." I gestured to the sports complex, saying to Noah, "When did this all go in?"

He ran his gaze over the stadium seating. "Six or seven years ago."

"Big improvement."

He nodded. "Yeah. They built the new high school on the old fields, and once it was ready, moved the kids in and demolished the old high school. Then they did all of this."

I hummed in agreement. "Is it weird being back here? At all? Or have you grown accustomed to it?"

"It's only weird when people purposely remind me of high school."

"Like I am right now?" I asked, laughing.

"No." He smiled and shifted his weight so that his shoulder brushed mine. "When they make a point of saying they remember when I was student council treasurer and that must be why I was able to keep the orchard and the dairy from going under. Yeah, a budget of five grand with extensive faculty oversight is certainly comparable. Or they ask if I remember when I was the manager of the basketball team but left the bag with all their jerseys in the locker room for the championship game up in Woonsocket. Because everyone loves that story."

"How *did* you keep the orchard and dairy from going under?"

"You asking that is a sign you've been kidnapped and are in need of rescue," he replied.

I shot an elbow at his upper arm. It felt more like a brick wall than human flesh. "I'm actually interested."

He seemed prepared to tease me a bit more but then his eyes widened and a look of complete dread crossed his face. I looked over my shoulder to follow his gaze. As I turned, he roped an arm around my waist and leaned in close enough for his beard to scrape my cheek.

What the hell?

"I know it's insane to ask this but if you can go along with me for five minutes, I will personally plow and plant your fields whenever you want it. Okay?"

I didn't respond. I couldn't. Not when those words went in one ear and landed right between my legs.

"Just follow my lead," he whispered. "Please."

I had no idea what was happening but Noah was so close and he was holding me so tight that it didn't matter. And that *please* had rumbled over his lips in the very best way, like an apology begged a moment before sinning.

Still, I was too stunned to form words. I couldn't remember the last time someone had taken me into their arms like this. But more importantly, I didn't remember it ever feeling so divine. There was a whole marching band performing on the other side of the complex, a kid dancing and twirling around me, and several hundred people nearby, though the only thing I could focus on was the hand gripping my waist.

Jaime was going to *I told you so* my ass off.

But then I heard "Hello there! Helloooo! Noah! Over here!" and I froze. I recognized that voice. The incessantness of it.

"Just go with me on this"—his words were urgent on my cheek—"and I'll do anything you ask of me. Anything at all. You name it, it's yours."

I bobbed my head as Christiane came into view, two young kids trailing behind her. Noah let out a breath and brushed his lips over my cheek. The only thing I could feel was heat, everywhere, all at once.

When was the last time someone had kissed my cheek? When was the last time I'd felt it deep in my belly? And when was the last time a kiss had been anything more than an obligation, a box ticked off in the basic affection column?

Christiane reached us with a full, glossy smile. "Noah!" she chirped. "I called last week. Did you get my message? About a playdate at the swim club? I thought I'd hear back from you. Where have you been hiding yourself these days?"

"Christiane," he replied.

Her gaze shifted toward me and with it, her smile dimmed. "And my dear new friend! I didn't catch your name." She glanced back at Noah, saying, "We met in the little girls' room. Just now."

His fingers flexed on my waist, his beard bristly as it passed over the shell of my ear. "It doesn't sound like you met if you don't know her name."

Well, shit. I mean, *holy shit*. I couldn't dissect that sentence down to its aggregate parts or explain a single reason why it worked as well as it did for me. All I knew was there hadn't been a single sexual thought in my mind for months but that tide was turning fast.

"You know how I can get carried away." She waved a hand at us. "How do you two know each other?"

"We go way back. High school sweethearts."

He shifted, hooking his thumb in my belt loop and sliding his hand into my pocket. He splayed his fingers over my belly roll and thigh crease. The only things between us were the thin lining of my pocket and some bikini briefs, and everyone for twenty feet around had to be aware of that. It was all over my face and projected above my head like a cartoon thought bubble. There was nothing covert about that move of his. I wasn't sure if neck biting would be next and, honestly, I wasn't opposed to it.

"Oh, really?" She turned a critical eye toward me. "That's so funny since I don't remember you ever mentioning a significant other. Not even once. Not one time." Her gaze turned into a frowny smile, the kind of expression people used when they wanted to meet a threshold of basic manners while also communicating that they rejected everything about the situation. "I just don't remember hearing anything about that *at all.*"

"Didn't see how it was any of your concern," he said, the words closer to a growl than anything else.

But it wasn't *just* a growl. It was predatory, almost possessive. And I knew it was ridiculous to say that because this whole moment was ridiculous but he was drawing circles on my belly roll while not so politely telling this woman he wanted none of what she was offering. If this wasn't the outer banks of possessive, I didn't know what was.

Bite my neck, honey. Just do it. Don't make me wait.

He dragged his fingers over my cheek, tucked some hair behind my ear. "Have you decided what you want to eat?" he asked, low, grumbly, perfect. I didn't know when the grumbly had transformed from mildly amusing to fully arousing but I was here now and not interested in leaving. "Hmm? I want to get you fed, sweetheart."

I wasn't proud of it but it felt like my nipples were probably visible from space.

"Not yet," I murmured.

"Then we're doing that now." He scooped up Gennie, settling her on his hip. "See you later, Christiane."

Noah steered us toward the food trucks, his hand still deep in my pocket. I was floating and melting and also buzzing with electricity.

And Noah Barden was the cause of it.

chapter eight

Noah

Students will be able to pretend.

FIVE MORE MINUTES.

That was all I needed.

If I could have five more minutes, I'd ask for nothing else in this life.

Five more minutes of Shay's body tucked close to mine, her hand flat on the small of my back. Five more minutes of knowing the feel of her skin against my lips.

Five more minutes of pretending she was mine.

But the problem with asking for five more minutes was that I'd suffer in the long run. I'd live with this knowledge and I had no doubt it would slowly ruin me.

Perhaps the ruination would come quick. Perhaps it was better that way. I'd always done well when I knew the suffering to come. My law school roommates had been a year ahead of me and they'd been an excellent resource for previewing my future misery. It'd helped set my expectations.

If someone could tap me on the shoulder or send me a text message about how much my life would suck when these five minutes were up and the pretending was over, I'd appreciate it. Always good to know the range.

I shifted, putting a bit of distance between us before this situation turned sour and Shay had to force me off her. But she trapped my hand on her waist, saying, "Don't go anywhere. Don't stop. Not yet."

Okay. Great. I'd suffer while hearing that in my head and imagining the scent of her hair for the rest of eternity. Outstanding.

"Can I have a frozen lemonade now?" Gennie asked, her arms around my neck. The beads from the bracelet she'd made last night—because Shay wore bracelets and we were obsessed with Shay—pressed against my clavicle. It was enough to remind me in loud, screaming letters that I had a kid and I couldn't fuck around just because it felt nice.

But god help me, I really wanted another minute or two of this. Of Gennie, safe and secure on one side of me, and Shay snuggled up on the other. It was like we were living a carefree life, the three of us out for a high school football game without any worries in the world.

Except none of that was true and this fantasy was seconds away from disintegrating in my hands.

"Yeah. No problem. Do you want to get it yourself?" I asked Gennie.

She shook her head against my shoulder. She didn't like me picking her up. Apparently it was too babyish and, as I'd been informed several times, she was a big girl. Forty-five pounds and toothless, but yeah. Big girl. She probably hated that I'd picked her up in front of Christiane Manning's kids too. Any minute now, she'd kick and yell for me to put her down. And I would. Just as soon as I seared every inch of this into my memory.

"Come with me," Gennie said.

And that was how I bought myself a few more minutes in line at the frozen lemonade truck with Gennie's head on my shoulder and my arm around Shay.

It was a warm night made bearable only by a steady breeze off the bay. Bearable for everyone else. I was dying. Burning up, melting down, boiling over. In all the ways I'd imagined touching Shay, I never saw it happening here at the high school or while I held Gennie in the other arm.

When it was our turn, Gennie wiggled out of my hold to place her order. She glanced back at me, saying, "Money, please."

Getting to my wallet meant releasing Shay and there was a solid moment where I blinked down at my niece and prayed for a better solution to come my way.

In the end, Shay shocked the shit out of me by reaching into my back pocket, grabbing my wallet, and passing Gennie a five. When she returned my wallet to the pocket and gave my ass a swift pat, I was toast. Just fucking done.

Shay turned her face toward me, her lips pursed in a smirk I'd always tagged as condescending. I was probably wrong about that. I needed to be wrong.

"She's still watching," Shay whispered.

She leaned in, brushed her lips over my jaw. I shuddered, my grip on her turning needlessly tight. I couldn't help it. And though I knew little about internal organs, it seemed like mine were rearranging themselves as my heart tried to break free from my ribs.

"Kiss my forehead," she said.

"What?"

"She's still watching us," Shay repeated. "Kiss my forehead. Make it believable."

Making it believable wasn't my problem.

I dipped my face, pressing my lips to her temple. Her hair smelled lovely. I remembered that scent. It had lingered in my car when we were kids. She'd stayed with me even when she wasn't.

I didn't move, my lips on her skin and her body snug against mine. Gennie was talking about frozen lemonade, and how the watermelon-flavored lemonade was superior to cherry, and her face was sticky and streaked with pink. I nodded, still holding Shay like my existence depended upon it.

The truth was, it did.

I could resist all I wanted. Fight like a motherfucker. Push her and push her and push her away.

And still, there was nothing I wanted more than this.

"What's the story?" she asked, low enough to keep it between us. "With your *friend* Christiane."

"She's not my friend," I replied. "She's just very persistent."

Shay laughed, rocking her curves against me in the most delicious way. This wasn't the time or place to be aroused, but goddamn, I was far past my limits here.

"I'm aware of that," she said. "We had a little standoff in the restroom. I didn't think I was getting out of there without scheduling a pelvic floor therapy appointment."

"A—what?"

She shook her head, her earrings swaying with the movement. They were grapes, these earrings. Bunches of purple grapes.

I didn't know why I found that absolutely charming but I did.

"Nothing you need to worry about," she said. "So, what's the deal? Did you ghost her? No, wait. You gave her a night she'll never forget and—"

"Shut up, Shay." It came out in a rumble, a rockslide of words that left her gazing up at me, her lips parted and her brows arched. There'd never been a moment where I wanted to kiss her more than I did right now, and I'd devoted two years of my life to wanting to kiss her. Yet this was different. It was so much more powerful. Truly, a rockslide.

"Wow. When did you turn into a player?" she asked. "Breaking hearts all over town, huh?"

"That's not what happened," I snapped. "She thinks—I don't know —she thinks we'd suit."

"What an old-fashioned way of saying she wants to get a piece—"

I pressed a finger to her lips. "Did I not tell you to shut up?"

She blinked at me, her brows raised as she silently commanded me to explain. Before I could think better of it, I left her lips, traced the round of her cheek, and drew my thumb over the crease of her brow. Smoothed out the curiosity gathered there. "It doesn't matter what Christiane wants because her kids have been terrible to Gen. They're twins and they're *terrible*. I know I shouldn't say that about children but, seriously, if you knew the half of it, you'd agree with me."

"What happened?"

"The boy, that little fucker, chased Gennie around the playground on her second day of school with a dead garter snake he'd found somewhere in the bushes. But she was the one who got in trouble because she elbowed him in the mouth and knocked out a few teeth when he tried to shove it down her shirt."

Her gaze dropped, her lips parted. "What the *fuck*?"

I nodded as I tucked a few pink strands over her ear again. The wind was keeping me busy here. I loved it. "That's how we met. She said the whole thing was a misunderstanding. Her boy was going through a difficult time since she and the father divorced last year. She wanted us to arrange some playdates so the kids could get to know each other. That was her solution."

"What was your solution?"

"I wrote a letter indicating I'd bring my concerns regarding student safety to the state department of education and file a lawsuit if she wasn't moved into another class."

"Was she moved?"

"The next day," I replied. "But the teacher wasn't a great fit for Gennie. Just didn't get what she was all about. They clashed from the very first minute. I'm pretty sure she retired at the end of the year and credited Gennie with that decision."

"That's not great," she murmured. "Were there any other incidents? With that boy?"

"Nothing as bad as the snake situation but lots of reports of them getting into it on the playground. And the girl, I thought she was the good seed in that bunch but that wasn't the case. Never lets Gennie play with her or the other girls. Always saying awful things about Eva when the teachers aren't around. And that's just the stuff Gennie tells me. I know there's a lot more. The issue with her hair, for example. She doesn't tell me everything."

"Have you mentioned any of this to the lady lusting after you?"

I glanced over my shoulder and spotted Christiane lingering near the bubble waffle cone vendor. She caught my eye, gave an enthusiastic wave. "Allow me to apologize right now."

"For what?"

I'd suffer for this. So much more than I'd imagined. But I couldn't care about that suffering when all this sweetness was right here, waiting for me. I tipped her chin up, slipped my fingers into her hair. Dropped my gaze to her parted lips. "This."

I brushed my lips against hers, fast enough for our surroundings yet exactly long enough to ruin my whole life.

I didn't bother glancing back at Christiane again.

"Don't apologize," Shay said, a laugh in her words. "I can be your human shield any time you need it. I'm down for that every day of the week. You should've told me that was why you were in such a hurry to fake-marry me. You had me thinking you were some kind of Scrooge McDuck, wanting to seize all the land on the rural side of the cove. You could've explained yourself better, my friend." She peered up at me, scowling. "Please tell me we're good, we're friends. I'm not sure what I did wrong, Noah, or how I gave you the impression that I—"

I kissed her again.

It wasn't a smart choice, all things considered, but that saved me from explaining my version of our history. Not that she would understand it. I had my reality and she had hers, and I had to accept that those two would never match up.

This kiss was longer and less chaste than the first. I heard Gennie say, "That's disgusting," and someone else say, "Get a load of those two," and I didn't care because Shay grabbed a handful of my shirt and made a soft noise in the back of her throat that ended me.

It didn't matter what happened next. If she disappeared from my life tomorrow. If she went back to Boston and gave up Twin Tulip. Even if she stayed though I could never touch her again.

None of it would matter because she'd kissed me back—and she'd loved every second of it.

When I pulled away, I said, "I am sorry."

Shay shook her head. "Don't be. You can use me any time you need to fend off the thirsty women of Friendship. There must be dozens of them. I'll break their hearts for you. Destroy their dreams."

"You sound…excited."

She laughed. I felt her warm breath on my neck, then her lips grazing me there. I had to work at preventing my eyes from rolling back in my head.

"When does this game start?" Gennie asked. Her lips were bright pink when she turned to face us. She looked us over as if she found Shay locked in my arms every day. I really, *really* needed this to not fuck things up for her. "Is it soon? Or can I get popcorn?"

"Did you get any change from that lemonade?"

She shrugged but slipped her hand into her pocket. Real smooth.

"You have enough for popcorn," I said. "Can you order it yourself or do you want us to go with you?"

Us.

Oh, *god*. I'd already incorporated this performance into an *us*. There were so many things wrong with me.

"You can watch me go there," she said, skipping off toward the student council's popcorn stand.

I brushed my lips over Shay's temple once more. Not because Christiane was watching or because I gave a shit about anyone's opinion. I did it because I'd wanted to do this since long before I knew what it was to kiss a woman on the forehead instead of the mouth.

"You don't have to stay," I said to her.

"Oh, but I do." She flattened her hand to my chest. "Don't forget. I've met your gal. I know her voracity. If you think she's not coming up to bat the second I leave, you're underestimating her." She laughed, adding, "And I promised Jaime I'd come out and do this small-town life thing, even if I hated it."

Who the fuck is Jaime?

"Jaime? What about me? Didn't I say the exact same thing?" I asked.

She put some time into smoothing my shirt. Like appearances really mattered on a hot August night when everyone over the age of fifteen was preoccupied with the liquor hiding in their water bottles and acting as though the bugs weren't eating us alive.

And who the fuck is Jaime? Please don't let it be the one from the situationship.

"Jaime's my best friend," she said, those precious little fingers still running over my shoulders and chest, tying concrete weights to every spot she touched before pushing me off a pier. "We've taught together for years. We talk just about every day. She's the mom of our group."

All right. We'll keep Jaime.

"What's the verdict, then?" I squeezed her hip. She was soft there, smooth and plush. My fingers could dig into her skin, cling to her, and I could leave marks if she let me. She wouldn't let me. She wouldn't because I'd never ask. "Do you hate it?"

"I don't. It's different than I remember. This whole place is different. Actually, it was pretty rude of Friendship to enter its cool phase after I left town." She laughed again, the sound pulling at my gut. She made me want to wrap myself around her. Bury myself in her. "Is it different for you?"

"Sometimes," I admitted. And that was the truth. More often than not,

I conducted business and lived my life without any of the agony from my childhood. But then there was always someone who wanted to know how I lost the weight (I had no clue; I turned twenty and everything about my body started changing) or if I could recommend the dermatologist who cleared up my skin (same as above) or if I was happy now (not in the way anyone would expect, no, but in other ways, yes). "People make weird comments. They say things that sound complimentary in their head but are like being smacked across the face with a dictionary."

"I don't like that," she said, her words low enough to make me wonder whether they were intended for me at all. Then she glanced up from my shirt, her eyes dark and the crease between her brows deep. "I'll be your human shield for that too."

Too quickly, I said, "No need. I can handle it."

"There's a ton of shit I *can* handle," she said, "and I'd still love if someone stepped in front of it for me."

"Like what?"

Her lips pulled up on one side. It was a smirky pout and I wanted to kiss it off her face so hard, my jaw clicked. "Nothing. Not relevant." She patted my chest as if she was punctuating that statement, ending it with hard finality. "I'll stay for the game. I'll give you some pointers on how to make it look like you're completely in love with me and uninterested in anyone else."

Yes. Show me what that looks like. I have no idea. "You think you can do that?"

"Here's what you don't understand about me: I'm amazing with projects. Give me a project and I'll make it happen, get it done. Like preparing Gennie for the evaluation coming up. I have a clear, measurable goal, I know how to achieve it, and nothing else matters to me until I make that check mark and cross it off my list."

"And now your goal is convincing people I'm in love with you?"

"Mmhmm. Easy peasy."

Push me right off that pier. "Just for tonight? Or longer? What's the timeline on this project?"

She paused, drummed her fingers on my chest. I had the perverse desire to grab that hand and suck on those fingers. I mean, *perverse.* "I am currently operating at a rate of one day at a time. I can give you tonight—"

My body heard something very different from what she meant. My body had ideas that went far beyond perverse. It was mortifying, really. The things I wanted were not simple or pleasant. They were demanding and intense and—and *primal*. And if Shay had even the slightest idea of the images playing in my head, she'd take her strawberry-blonde hair and her schoolteacher bags and run away from me as fast as she could. And I'd want her to run away. If she heard even a sliver of the filth in my head, she'd never look at me the same way again. Hell, *I* barely let myself think about the things I wanted.

"—and we'll see what the future brings." She drew in a breath and stared into my eyes for a long, silent minute. It seemed like I was supposed to get something out of that gaze but the only thing I could do was study the cute little bow of her upper lip and imagine biting it. Then, "If that's what you want. I wouldn't want to rub myself all over you unless you wanted it."

Fuck me.

Instead of offering that eloquent thought, I motioned to the trucks. "What do you want to eat?"

"I'm okay." She shook her head, made a scrunched-up face as if she didn't care. I didn't buy it. "I don't need anything."

"They make quesadillas that are weird and incredible." I pointed to the closest truck. "And those guys are Korean barbeque. Exceptional. Best I've ever had. Down there, that yellow truck, they do a variety of banh mi but their japchae is the hidden gem of their menu." I gestured to a few other trucks. "There's also the usual suspects. Pizza, grilled cheese, fries topped with things that don't make sense but taste good."

She stared at me, her eyes smiling and her lips pouting. It was like she was daring me to kiss her again.

"Tell me what you want."

A breath stuttered out of her. "Wh-what?"

"What do you want?" I punctuated each word with a squeeze to her hip. "From the trucks. They're going to close up and head out soon."

"Oh. Right. Oh my god, yes, the trucks." She heaved out a sigh and ran her fingers over my shoulder, down to my lower back. She drew swirls and circles as she hummed to herself and all the tension I'd stored there melted away. If she could do the exact same thing to my neck, I'd build a shrine in her honor. "I'm not sure. Is there something you'd share with me?"

Only everything in the entire world.

Since my options were split evenly between confessing that exact thing and leading her toward the closest food truck, I settled my hands on her waist and steered her in the direction of the quesadillas. "The French onion soup quesadilla is bizarrely good," I said. "Same with the pot sticker quesadilla, but you can't go wrong with the old favorite, barbeque chicken."

As she studied the menu board on the truck, I slipped both hands into her back pockets. It was an indulgence I hadn't earned and didn't deserve but we were committed to this game. She'd said so herself. Still, she cut a subtle glance in the direction of Christiane's last known location. I didn't know if she was there and I didn't much care. I was very busy twisting myself into feral knots over here.

"You should've told me about this little problem of yours," she murmured.

Instead of responding to that, I leaned close to Shay as I watched Gennie ordering popcorn. She carefully counted out her money before slapping it on the counter like she was all in on a poker game. The kid helping her came around the cart to hand her the popcorn and I appreciated the hell out of him for that because she would've upended the bag trying to reach for it.

It was also a fine distraction from the very round, very plump ass in my lap right now.

"I would've helped," she added.

The issue with this scheme of mine was that I didn't need any help shutting down advances from Christiane. I hated running into her but I could handle it. That I'd thrown Shay in front of the problem had been a selfish response. A knee-jerk reaction though still a selfish one. And now I had my hands on her ass. There was no tidy way to unwind this.

Not that I was in any rush to separate my hands from her body.

"When did you start caring so much about other people?" I asked.

"Is that your way of telling me I was a bitch in high school?" she asked, still frowning and murmuring at the menu.

"That's not what I meant," I rushed to say. See? Ending this game of make-believe only required me to be myself. Another few minutes of me being awkward as fuck and she'd never want to speak to me again. "What I meant is, you're helping Gennie, you jumped in to save me, you're—"

"I know, I know," she said with a laugh. "I was just teasing you. I had my self-absorbed moments. My shallow moments. I was a teenager who lived in a privileged bubble. I'm aware of that." She stepped up to the truck to place her order and since I was in no way prepared to stop touching her, I stepped up too. "We're going to try the barbeque chicken and…the vegetarian egg roll." She glanced over her shoulder at me. "Does that work for you?"

I nodded and pressed my lips to the crown of her head. "I'm good with whatever you want."

Gennie was busy watching the flag squad warm up while she alternated between chugging lemonade and cramming fistfuls of popcorn in her mouth.

I was free to remove my hands from Shay's pockets any time now.

Any time at all. Eventually, I would have to move. I couldn't walk around the sports complex, grabbing her ass all night. And the time would come when this charade had to end. Even if I wanted to snatch her up and take her home with me tonight, that wasn't the direction this was going.

It is never going that direction.

Obviously, I had to end this. I had to find a smooth way to put space between us and regain some semblance of control over this current predicament of mine. And do it all without tossing myself into a season of pain and misery.

All I had to do was figure out how to accomplish that.

Stepping back and shoving my hands in my pockets would work. It would be abrupt, yes, and she'd wonder what the hell was wrong with me. Nothing new there. I could also shift my hand to her lower back, maybe her elbow. Those were far less dangerous gestures than gripping her backside as if I meant to peel off these jeans and bend her over right here.

Christ almighty, I need these thoughts to leave me alone.

In the end, the choice made itself when Shay unzipped her purse.

"What are you doing?" I grabbed the card from her, shoved it back in the small bag at her hip. I hadn't noticed the thin purple strap crossed over her torso until now. "There is no way I'm letting you—no. Put your money away." I zipped the purse for her and then reached for my wallet, blindly passing some bills to the person watching this affair unfold from behind the counter. I thought I was finished. I'd put the matter down and pulled my hands from her pockets. Two birds and such. But I couldn't stop myself from adding, "Not when you're with me."

She tipped her head to the side, regarding me with a slow stare. She'd done something to her eyes, a makeup thing, and she looked more feline than usual with a thick, dark line running over her lids and past the corners. "Noah Barden," she breathed. "Get a load of you."

The images blaring behind my eyes at those words were unreal—and mortifying. "Sorry, I—"

"Don't you dare," she interrupted. "Do not stand there and apologize." She eyed me for a moment and this would've been a fine time for lightning to strike, aliens to arrive, the ground to open—whatever. Anything would be preferable to her studying me as if she could see straight through me and into the sweaty, skin-slapping visions that had overrun my mind from the second I touched her. "You're damn good at this. You've almost fooled me, and I affectionately refer to myself as a dried-up husk of a human these days, so bravo. And don't look now but your friend with the crazy eyes has a bit of steam blowing out of her ears. She just stomped off into the stadium."

I accepted a paper basket with two foil-wrapped quesadillas from the food truck window. "Why are you a dried-up husk, Shay? What happened?"

She shook her head and waved away the question as she glanced at the nearby trucks. "Nothing important. You know how I exaggerate."

It *was* important. Probably the most important piece of her showing up in this town after all these years. But I was not equipped to peel back those layers right now. It was all I could do to be this close to her and remind myself to breathe normally. I couldn't ask the right questions. I couldn't string the words together. Not tonight.

"You don't exaggerate," I said.

She lifted a shoulder, again dismissing the topic. "I've been known to overstate. The dried-up husk bit is an overstatement. I take my skincare too seriously for that."

Gennie wandered back, her cheeks crammed with popcorn and her hand buried deep in the bag. The lemonade was long gone. "It's time to go in," she mumbled. "Come on, Shay. Need to get good seats."

She took Shay's hand and towed her toward the stadium. Shay glanced back at me, held out her free hand.

I'd never moved so fast in my life.

We made our way into the stands and found a mostly empty row near the visitor's end zone. Gennie, fueled by the sugar in that lemonade, didn't want to sit. Instead, she stood next to Shay and danced in place without the benefit of music.

Shay positioned herself as close to me as she could get without sitting in my lap. Not that I would've complained about having her in my lap. She reached for one of the half-moon foil packets, saying, "We're going to talk about how much we love quesadillas now. We're going to be very cute. Sickeningly cute. At one point, I'm going to wipe a crumb off your cheek. Bonus points if you suck it off my thumb."

Suck it off my thumb.

Either she had no clue what she was doing to me or she was evil through and through. There was no in-between on this one.

"I think we'll be all right without," I managed, "the sucking. From your thumb."

I bit a huge chunk from my half of the quesadilla to prevent me from saying anything more. I didn't know whether it was chicken or egg roll or a handful of dirt smashed between a tortilla. I couldn't taste a damn thing.

Suck it off my thumb.

"Try this one," she said, handing me another wedge.

I was careful to take it without touching her. Not that it made much difference since we were pressed right up against each other and I had a distinct awareness of the side of her breast on my arm, but I required that inch of distance. I couldn't hear those words in my head without wanting her fingers in my mouth, and even if she was evil incarnate, she never asked for me to defile her in my mind. She was helping me out—or so I'd led her to believe—and I was repaying her by growing a garden of the most filthy thoughts I'd had in years. What the fuck was wrong with me?

"I think I like the egg roll best," she said, nodding to herself as she balled the foil between her palms. "You were right though. The barbeque chicken is a highly reliable choice. Always delivers. And I'd get it again. But there's something unexpected about the veggie egg roll. It checked all the boxes."

I grumbled out some noise of agreement and Shay chose that moment to twist toward me. It was no longer a simple awareness of her breast. It was as thorough a comprehension as possible without her clothes hitting the floor.

"Let me just get," she murmured, lifting her hand to my face. She ran her thumb over my top lip, to the corner of my mouth. "Perfect."

"All the boxes checked?"

"Here's what you need to do." She dropped her hand on my thigh, just high enough for me to wonder if the pressure in my chest was pleasure or the early signs of a heart attack. "Put your arm around me. Let me snuggle right into that shoulder. Yep. That's it. Your friend is a couple of rows down, a few sections over. Close to the middle. And she keeps looking this way."

"For fuck's sake, why?" I grumbled.

"Probably because you're hot."

I'd misheard. The crowd, the game. Too much noise. "What?"

"You are very attractive, Noah. I'm sorry no one's broken the news to you." She reached up, ran her knuckles along my jaw. "Hot enough that this woman has decided your kids being mortal enemies isn't even close to a disqualifier."

I pinched a few strands of her hair between my fingers, sliding down to the ends and starting over again. "Do I have to tell you to shut up again?"

"I'd rather you didn't."

I arched a brow. "Are you sure about that?"

She dropped her gaze to my lips. "Mmhmm. I'm sure. Either way, I'm just telling you the truth."

The toughest part about growing out of my teenage body was that *I* hadn't changed. The exterior looked different now but I was the same person. Getting taller, losing weight, clearing up my skin—all of that brought me confidence but those changes came to me gradually and they didn't override the fact that I'd been the furthest thing from attractive as a teenager, when it had seemed more important than anything else. And I'd lived a long time with that knowledge. It didn't go away overnight.

I shifted my hand from her hip to her waist, slipped just beneath her shirt. Her skin was warm, a bit humid from the heat. I dragged the tips of my fingers back and forth because I could, because I didn't want to keep talking about Christiane or all the ways in which our worlds had changed. And because this wasn't part of the show. Christiane couldn't see this. If the handful of people seated on the rows above us could see what I was doing, I was certain they didn't care.

This was for Shay and it was for me. No one else.

For the entirety of the first half, I divided my focus between Gennie, who realized piece by piece that high school football wasn't nearly as exciting as I'd made it out to be, and the way Shay's body relaxed into mine. It was a mess of contradictions. I hated everything about this. It was torture. It fucking hurt. And I didn't want it to stop.

There was a very significant possibility I was going to injure myself when I finally got behind closed doors tonight and gave my thoughts—and left hand—the freedom to run wild.

Gennie hit the wall not long after the halftime performance. When she shuffled over, sat down beside me, and dropped her head against my arm, I knew she was down for the count. "Had enough?" I asked.

She bobbed her head.

I carried Gennie to the parking lot, her head heavy on my shoulder. I kept a hand on Shay's waist. No one was watching us anymore but that didn't matter. I had her for tonight.

Shay gestured to the opposite end of the lot but I shook my head, steering her in the direction of my truck. "We'll drop you at your car."

"It's fine. I can—"

"We'll drop you at your car and then we're following you to Twin Tulip. No argument."

She stared at me as if she didn't understand the words. As if they truly didn't compute. Maybe it was that they didn't compute coming from me.

We reached the truck and Gennie went into her booster seat without much of a fuss. Then I opened the door for Shay.

"I'm parked just down there. I don't need a ride."

"Get in the truck."

After a second of internal debate, she climbed inside and I knew the cab would smell like her tomorrow. Part of me couldn't wait for it. The other part knew I was setting myself up for regular servings of misery.

Once I was settled in the truck, I said to her, "Thanks for everything. You owed me exactly none of it. You could've told me to go to hell and left me to deal with Christiane and it would've been deserved."

"I would not have done that and you know it."

"Thank you."

She nodded slowly, glancing around the truck. "You always did like things neat."

I jerked a shoulder up. "Some things never change."

She turned to face me. "I hope so."

Since my options were slim to none with a half-asleep six-year-old in the back seat and it wasn't like I was prepared to explain to Shay that not a single minute of this evening had been an act for me, I pulled out of the parking space and let her direct me to her vehicle.

"I'm following you," I said when she opened the door. "But keep an eye out for animals, especially when you turn onto Hog House and then Old Windmill. Loads of deer and turkeys out recently."

She waved in response. I waited for her to start the car, back out of the space. Mentally kicked myself for not offering to drive her to the game in the first place. I followed Shay out of the high school complex and down the sleepy residential streets of Friendship toward the narrow bridge that led past the white-steepled church where my mother had once preached to the hilly farmland on the other side of the cove.

"Is Shay your girlfriend?"

Gennie's little voice was thick and raspy with sleep, and she had her face turned toward the window.

"She's my friend," I said. "A very good friend." I glanced at her in the rearview. "Is that okay with you?"

"Yeah."

"Are you sure? You can tell me if it's not okay."

"Shay's my friend too," Gennie replied.

"I know."

"I thought you wanted her to be your girlfriend."

I waited behind Shay at a stop sign, staring at her, hoping to catch her eye if she glanced back at me. She didn't. "Because of…things that happened tonight?"

"No. I thought you liked her."

"I do," I admitted.

Gennie was quiet for several minutes. I assumed she'd drifted off to sleep. Then, "If she's your friend, does that mean you're going to have playdates with her too?"

I turned onto Old Windmill Hill Road, slowing as Shay approached the turn for Twin Tulip. I followed, stopping at the top of the lane to watch her park. We waited as she unlocked the front door to the house, gave us a wave, and stepped inside.

"I don't know, Gen. Maybe. If that's what she wants."

"Let's be really nice to her," Gennie said around a yawn. "Maybe she'll want to visit us more."

God, I hope so. "I'll see what I can do."

chapter nine

Shay

Students will be able to be the hostess with the most-est problems.

EXACTLY FOUR WEEKS after packing up my life, leaving the safety of Jaime's couch, and taking up residence in Lollie's home, I welcomed my first houseguests.

Jaime, Audrey, Emme, and Grace rolled down the gravel lane on Friday afternoon and they tumbled out of Audrey's hybrid SUV like they'd been trapped in the car for hours. Emme charged into the house as she yelled, "Bathroom, please," and Grace followed her, two reusable shopping bags in hand as she said, "Refrigerator, please."

Audrey pushed her sunglasses up, surveying the house and land in that quiet, all-seeing way of hers. "So this is your dowry."

"It's not a dowry," I said, rushing over to hug her.

Jaime stepped in front of her, arms outstretched. "As I live and breathe, Miss Zucconi, you are a sight for sore eyes." She crushed me in a fierce embrace, teetering from side to side as she hummed happily. "And you look alive! At least mostly alive. And you have a farm!"

We separated enough for Jaime to wave a hand at my sundress. It was too hot for anything else.

"And you're wearing clean clothes. It looks like your hair has been washed and—what's this? Do I spy a bit of bronzer?"

"That's real," I said. "Bronzer straight from the sun."

"You've been outdoors," Jaime crowed. "Who knew country air could be so good for a girl?"

Audrey elbowed her way in for a hug. "You look good, sweetheart. I'm glad you've been able to get back to yourself." She gestured to the fields and gardens beyond the house. "This is adorable."

"Yeah, we had no idea there were such cute towns around here. Especially after driving through a living history museum of the Industrial Revolution to get here," Emme said as she came down the front steps. "Sorry about the entrance. You know my bladder is ridiculous."

"It really is, Em," Grace said, joining us outside. "She was not going to make it down another bumpy old road." She tucked her silky black hair behind her ears and glanced around. "Shay, with love, where the fuck are we right now?"

"Semirural coastal Rhode Island." I waved toward the gardens. "And this is my step-grandmother's tulip farm."

"And isn't it charming." Emme leaned in close. "Do you want to come home yet? Because we can pack you up today and forget this ever happened."

I laughed, shook my head. I'd missed my people. "Is this a rescue mission?"

Jaime gave an exaggerated roll of her eyes. "What ever happened to playing it cool, y'all?" She draped an arm around my shoulders. "If you want to be rescued, we'll rescue you. If you're still cosplaying as a small-town girl, we'll play along with you for the weekend." She motioned to her overall shorts. "I came dressed for my part."

Audrey set a wide-brimmed floppy hat over her white-blonde hair. "Me too."

Grace, dressed in slim black jeans and a black tank top, crossed her arms over her chest. “I’ll be the person who spends the next three days in search of decent coffee. Thank god I brought backup cold brew.”

“And I brought blondies,” Emme added.

“They’ll go perfectly with the margarita slushies and chicken fajitas I made.” There was no need for me to add to this by noting it was the first meal I’d prepared since moving in.

“Is that a tire swing?” Jaime asked, pointing toward one of the giant old beech trees.

“And a hammock?” Audrey asked.

“Two of each,” I said. “Two of everything. Twin sisters built this place and I don’t get the impression they liked to share.”

Jaime stamped a sandalled foot on the walkway. “Yes! That’s the folksy shit I want out of this weekend.”

“Come on,” I said, laughing. “You can drop your stuff inside. I don’t want this to be a shock but the place is mostly empty. I cleared out Target’s air mattresses this morning so you won’t be roughing it too hard but my step-grandmother went through a Swedish Death Cleaning phase before she moved to Florida. She left only the bare basics. I haven’t added much.”

“Okay, so you’re sounding less alive now,” Jaime said.

“It’s all right. I promise. And I’m not rattling around here alone. There are spirits everywhere. The twins, of course. They never leave. I talk to myself all the time so it’s nice to have them listening. Also, I chat with at least three or four ghosts every night.”

They all stared at me and then each other for several seconds.

“Oh, honey.” Audrey pressed her fingers to her lips.

“Great,” Emme drawled.

“She’s fucking with us,” Grace said.

I burst out laughing.

“Too soon,” Audrey said with a sharp slice of her hand. “We are not ready for that kind of humor from you.”

Jaime gave a slow shake of her head. "Don't test me. I'm stronger than I look and I can wrestle your ass into that car. Just try me."

"No ghosts. No spirits. None that have found me interesting enough to haunt, at least," I said, still laughing. "And I told you, I see my neighbors. I'm tutoring the little girl at the farm next door."

"And this girl is alive? You're certain you aren't tutoring a ghost?" Grace asked.

"How weird is it to say the *farm next door*," Emme mused.

"Probably less weird when you haven't spent your entire life in a city," Audrey replied.

"Great, great," Emme said. "Can I have a margarita yet? I'd like that to occur soon, and if possible, I'd like it to occur while I'm on the hammock and before Shay pops off with some more concerning comments."

"AND THAT'S why I won't cut pineapple anymore," Jaime said. "That little spike from the woody part was in my finger for an entire week and I could barely wash my hair without making it worse so I didn't go out with him."

"Wait, wait, wait." I pushed my sunglasses up and craned my neck to stare at Jaime in the tire swing. "How many people are you dating now?"

"I wouldn't call it dating. It's not dating, not the way we usually think of dating." She held up one finger. "There's Andre and Honora and Sire—"

"That name," Emme said. "The volumes it speaks."

"—and sometimes Hardy."

"That's just made up," Audrey said.

"Nope, I had a Hardy at my last school," Grace said. "Hardy Woodruff. That kid had no idea what he was in for."

"—and Clara and Meena, sometimes, but I'm definitely not dating them. More like getting time with them."

"Wood-ruff," Audrey said with a snort. That was how you could tell she was tipsy. All her pristine mannerisms and polite, polished façade crumbled, and she snorted at dick jokes.

"And by 'getting time' you mean you're the little spoon in a party-sized cutlery basket," I said.

"That happened once," Jaime cried. "It's usually me and just two or three other people."

"Just two or three other people," Grace repeated. "That's all."

"I have come to accept that sex with one person is not interesting or fulfilling to me," Jaime replied. "Two is my minimum right now. I can do two if one is watching, maybe doing stuff nearby, but I prefer the two to be hands-on."

Audrey laugh-hiccupped. "Like, knitting a scarf? What do you mean, doing stuff nearby? Folding laundry? What? I know I'm outing myself as a plain vanilla Jane but you have me curious. A little confused too."

Audrey had the wonderful gift of being able to ask questions that would sound insulting or possibly aggressive coming from someone else, but she spoke with the right amount of vulnerability and authentic desire to understand others. Rare was it that anyone received one of her questions with offense, even if her phrasing was blunt. I loved that about her. Every time I tried to emulate it, I failed spectacularly.

Audrey and I were the closest in age of our group. She was another thirtysomething while the others were closer to late twenties, all of us within five years or so of each other. Jaime was the baby at twenty-eight. I'd met her six years ago when I started teaching at my school back in Boston. We clicked immediately. If I'd met her in a nail salon or at a party or any random place, I would've claimed her as a friend. That we worked together came as an added bonus.

Emme and Grace met in teachers' college. They lived together in a messy sublet situation where their rent was due in cash and had to be delivered to a little grocery store in Charlestown. But their place was really cheap and located in the heart of the North End, not far from Jaime.

If I hadn't worked across the hall from those two, I doubt we'd have found each other. They were different from me and Jaime. Their humor bit harder, their smiles were darker, their vibes were more intense. And somehow it worked for me. Grace's black-on-black style and Emme's cynicism were necessary nutrients in my daily diet.

I never would've met Audrey because she was as silent as a shadow. If it hadn't been for Emme dragging her to our group lunches around the half-moon table in Grace's classroom every day, I'd have filed her away as someone who kept to herself and preferred some distance from her colleagues. But there was a deep blue ocean underneath that quiet surface of hers. She was the strongest of us five, in every possible way, and there was more connection in ten minutes of her sitting beside you in silence than a day with anyone else.

"It's okay, honey," Jaime said. "I am the most confused. I just named six people. There's no way I can keep them all straight." She belted out a laugh. "Maybe that's the point. Nothing about us is straight."

"As long as you're happy," Audrey said, "and safe."

"All of the above," Jaime said.

"I don't think we've covered how this started," Emme said from the tire swing. "Or if we have, I forgot. When did it end with that last person?"

The day was edging into evening now and we were halfway through a second pitcher of margaritas. As I'd suspected, hanging out in the garden was the best way to catch up—and there was a lot of catching up to do. I hadn't realized how much I'd missed since going catatonic after my wedding but also the weeks (months? *years*?) leading up to it. I didn't love admitting it but the truth remained, my only focus had been preparing for the big day. Even before the final countdown, I'd been consumed with planning. It was the only thing I'd cared about. There was a month where I'd *agonized* over my nails—shape, length, polish color. That these women hadn't smothered me in my sleep ages ago was proof they were the best of friends.

"—and then, after the threesome, Keith was done. He was out and nothing was changing that. He thought he was into it. He wasn't. Fine, no problem, I have no need for Bears fans in my life. But what I learned was that I didn't want to tie myself to one person and try to make monogamy happen. It's just not for me."

"You're not missing anything by sending Keith on his way," Grace said. "That boy didn't have the stones from the start."

I wondered whether Grace knew my ex didn't have the stones—and how long she'd known that. I wondered when I'd known.

I chased that thought away with a gulp of my drink.

"What about you, Shay? Getting over the ex by getting under anyone new?" Emme asked. "It's the best medicine."

As the question floated toward me, a familiar black pickup truck rumbled down the lane. I'd thought about him and then he appeared. Like I could conjure him on command. Now that—*that* was dangerous.

"Is it normal for random people to show up at your farm?" Grace asked. "Is this what small towns are all about or is this the gruesome start of a serial killer story?"

A door slammed shut, then another, and— "Shay! Guess what Dottie did today!"

"That sounds like a student," Jaime said as she flailed, her swing twisting around and around as she turned, trapping her in the tire and preventing her from getting a look at the new arrivals. "I don't think I'm so drunk that I'm hallucinating students but you do make a strong marg, Shay."

I pushed out of my lawn chair as Gennie bounded over. "You're not hallucinating. This is my friend, Gennie. She lives up the hill. Gennie, these are some of my friends from Boston."

From the gravel drive, Noah lifted a hand in greeting. I waved back. We'd succeeded at being friendly though distant this week, and that seemed to be working well for us. Better this than debriefing our time together at the football game. Better this than explaining to myself why I'd let myself into the house last Friday night and promptly slid down the panel of the door, unable to catch my breath or make sense of the hum in my veins. Or the throb between my legs.

"I went to the dentist today," Gennie announced. Completely oblivious to the tequila fog she'd walked into. "And then the doctor, who gave me four fucking shots—"

"Hello," Emme yelped. She pushed to her feet and adjusted her bikini top. No amount of adjusting was going to help because she was busting out of that thing and she'd bust out of every bikini smaller than a two-person tent.

"And I didn't get to have a playdate with you because of all that bullshit," Gennie continued.

Jaime was still stuck in her swing and Grace edged her sunglasses down to get a look at this commotion but stayed put. I wasn't sure but it seemed like Audrey might've dozed off under that floppy hat.

"See? Four," Gennie said, inching up her shorts and pointing to the Band-Aids stuck high on her thighs.

"Now you have vaccine power," Emme said, holding out her free hand for a high five. "Makes you strong. Gives your immune system some extra fighting strength."

Noah came up behind Gennie and set a hand on her shoulder. He forced a stiff grin. "Sorry to interrupt. We didn't know you'd be—" He glanced around, cleared his throat. "That you're busy."

"It's okay," I replied. "My friends came down from the city for a visit. This is Emme Ahlborg." I motioned to her beside me and then the others. "That's Audrey Saunders under that huge hat, Grace Kilmeade over there, and Jaime Rouselle is fighting with the swing. Everyone, this is Noah Barden and my very special friend Gennie. Noah, Gennie, this is everyone."

A chorus of greetings went up. A light snore from Audrey.

"Good to meet you," Noah said.

"We've all been teaching together for the past few years," I said.

"Before she left us for this pastoral setting," Emme added.

Noah held out a paper bag. "The bakehouse did another test run. Since you liked the last one so much, we thought you'd want to give this one a try." His gaze dropped to the cocktail in my hand. His brows lifted. "We'll let you get back to it."

"Thank you," I said. "For the bread."

He swept a glance over the scene before him, a slight smirk pulling at one corner of his mouth. "If you're up for it, there's a farmers market tomorrow at Travers Point Park. There's a food truck that does bacon, egg, and cheese sandwiches. Bodega style. Top notch. Best I've had outside of Manhattan."

"I can promise you right now that I'll need two of those in order to function tomorrow," Emme said.

Noah bobbed his head. To his credit, he kept his gaze on Emme's face and away from the cleavage testing the limits of her bikini top. "There's a nitro coffee cart too."

Grace snapped her fingers. "Yes, please."

"Gennie and I will be slinging jam, cheese, and bread until noon." He reached for my cup and took a quick sip before coughing and passing it back to me. "If you're alive tomorrow morning, you should stop by."

"Please, Shay," Gennie said. "Farmers markets are really fucking boring."

Noah's gaze pinged between my face and the drink I held close to my chest. "Maybe we'll see you tomorrow." After a beat, he steered Gennie away. "Come on, captain. Set the course for the home port."

We watched as Noah and Gennie climbed into the truck, pulled through the circular end of the drive, and then turned back onto Old Windmill Hill. At some point, Jaime freed herself from the swing and strolled toward us, one hand tucked into the pocket of her overalls, the other clutching her cup.

Her dimples bookended her grin. "You failed to mention that your neighbor-girl's dad hand-delivers bread to you. Now that I think about it, I can't remember you ever mentioning Daddy Bread Baker." She glanced to Emme. "Don't you find that funny?"

"So funny," she replied.

"I'll pay you money to never call him that again," I said to them.

"It's not money I need," Emme said in a breathy starlet sort of way. "It's power."

"Ignore her. I'll take your Daddy Bread Baker money," Jaime said.

"He's just my neighbor," I said. "And he's Gennie's uncle, not her father. He's her permanent guardian."

"Let me guess," Jaime started, "there's no Mrs. Bread Baker in the picture."

I shrugged, pulling on all the ignorance I could find. "I believe he's single." Another shrug. "And I did tell you about him. I said I bumped into an old friend from high school."

"You one hundred percent omitted the part about that friend being a jacked-to-shit farmer man with arms like"—she made a whooshing sound—"and his whole 'if you're up for some naughty farmers market action, you know where to find me.'"

"That was not at all the implication," I said.

"You heard it," Jaime said to Emme.

"I heard it," the coconspirator replied.

"I heard it," Grace called.

Audrey went on snoring.

"So, he's a friend from high school," Jaime started, "one with the beard scruff I'd pay real money to feel on my ass—"

"Okay," Emme interrupted. "I think what we're trying to say is that man came here to pay you a visit and it didn't look like the first time."

I swung a glance between them before staring into my cup. "I am not drunk enough for this."

"Yes," Jaime yelled with a pump of her fist. "And she's back in the saddle, folks."

"Oh, no. There is no saddle and I am not in it," I was quick to say. "We were really close friends—nothing more—in high school but it's not the same now. Honestly, I don't even think he likes me."

"The boy brought you bread," Emme said. Jaime flailed her arms in agreement. "That's not usually how someone expresses their disinterest or apathy."

Exasperated, I said, "He just wants my land."

Jaime propped her hands on her hips. "Yeah, I'd say so."

"Your mind is lusty garbage," I replied. "No, I mean he wants this land. The farm. It's the only reason he offered to marry me. That's why he came here and brought the bread. He wants to know if I've decided."

"Now I'm up," Grace called.

"Shaylene Joann Zucconi," Jaime roared. "You've been keeping secrets, young lady."

"You know that's not my middle name."

"Yes, but it felt like a Joann moment," she replied.

"Did he actually propose?" Emme asked.

I paused. "Maybe? Sort of?" I held out my hands. "I mean, yes. In a sense. It wasn't a proposal but more like, *hey, you need to get married to inherit this place and I want some of your land so let's do this thing.*"

"How does she have two proposals under her belt and I can't get a *good morning* text?" Emme muttered.

"You didn't think we'd want to know this four seconds after it happened?" Jaime asked. "I want to know why you kept it to yourself."

"Because it's not serious," I said.

Jaime reached for my wrist and lifted the hand holding the paper bag. "The bread says otherwise."

"Only because I went crazy for it the last time I had dinner at his house."

"The last time you—" Jaime turned to Emme. "I can't. I'm out of words. Help me, Emmeline."

Emme patted Jaime's shoulder and made a shushing noise. "I think what we're trying to say is you've quietly cultivated a relationship with this guy and we are oh so very surprised by it all. Particularly the pending proposal. That's very interesting and very surprising."

"We are surprised," Jaime said, drawing out each word.

"I just—" I stopped myself, not knowing what I meant to say. "He needed some cover from this woman who listens to people while they're peeing because she's a lot, and he's not interested for valid reasons. That's the only reason anything happened between us."

"What does any of that mean?" Jaime asked.

"He needed a fake girlfriend," Grace said.

I pointed in her direction. "Yes. That."

"So, you helped him out," Emme said. "You took that one for the team."

"I did. I *helped* him," I said. "And it's the only reason he kissed me."

"Oh my goddesses," Jaime muttered.

"It was because this woman—" I continued.

"The one who listens to people while they're peeing," Emme said.

"—kept lingering and watching, and you really would not believe how persistent she is," I said. "And that's the only reason he kissed me."

"How many times?" Grace asked.

"How many times what?" I replied.

"Did he kiss you," she said.

I fiddled with the strap of my sundress. "I don't know. A few times, I guess."

"Yeah," Emme said to herself as she studied the ground. She crossed her arms over her torso. "Yeah, so, he's in love with you."

"He adores everything about you," Jaime added.

"Believe me, he's not," I replied. "He puts up with me because his niece needs help. If it weren't for that, he'd go out of his way to avoid me."

"He's in love with you," Emme repeated.

"Noooo," I said. "That's not what's happening here."

"Because it's too soon?" Jaime asked. "Because it feels like everything ended with the ex a minute ago and you're still processing it? Or because you're still burned from the ex and can't imagine getting close enough to the fire to ever feel warmth again?"

"Because you have lost your damn minds," I said. "Yes, I know the whole thing is crazy. Look around. Everything about my life is crazy right now. Noah is not—he doesn't—there isn't—no. Just no. And I am still burned, still processing. I can't—even if I wanted to, I can't. And I can't let myself believe there's anything more to the situation than him offering to help me deal with Lollie's will and me offering to be his human shield. Please don't try to convince me. Please. I don't think I can handle it."

Jaime and Emme were silent for a long moment. Then Grace asked, "Is no one going to mention the kid swearing like a pirate?"

"She'd take that as a compliment," I said. "She thinks very highly of Blackbeard."

"She's a hoot," Emme said. "She'd be a handful in the classroom but she's fun as hell."

Grace jerked her chin in my direction. "What are you going to do about the whole marriage thing?"

"I haven't decided," I admitted.

"You're considering the proposal, then." Emme said this carefully.

I shook my head. "Not really. No. It was just a silly thing. Like I said, he's only in it for the land and I"—my laugh was small and pathetic—"I am in no condition to marry anyone for any reason. It would be a disaster."

Grace, Jaime, and Emme shared a glance that loudly announced their doubts.

"Well," Jaime said, "one thing is for certain. We're going to that farmers market tomorrow."

chapter ten

Noah

Students will be able to identify and ignore the object of their deepest, darkest desires.

I SPOTTED them the minute they arrived at the park. There were two reasons for this.

First, Little Star was one of the biggest vendors at this market and that afforded us a prime location for our pop-up tent. From this position in the horseshoe-shaped assembly of vendors, I had an unobstructed view of foot traffic from the street. I couldn't miss five young women who appeared equally lost and hungover.

And second, I hadn't stopped watching for Shay since the market opened at eight this morning. I knew it was pointless, that watching for her wouldn't make her materialize any sooner—or at all. But I couldn't help myself.

I hadn't been able to stop thinking about her since leaving Twin Tulip yesterday. She'd looked…happy. Perhaps the liquor was to blame —there'd been plenty of it in that drink—or it could've been her friends. Or a combination of the two.

But she'd been happy and it looked so fucking good on her. The strappy little sundress too, the one that left her shoulders bare and dipped low over her breasts. I couldn't get it out of my head.

And I'd tried. I'd spent the whole damn night messing around with tweaks to my newest jam recipes while memories of that purple dress pushed to the front of my mind. I'd burned a batch of blueberry lemon lavender while thinking about the way the fabric settled into the valley between her breasts. I'd thought about trailing a finger from the base of her throat into that valley and then lower, until I could pull that dress up and slip a hand between her legs. The jam scorched right around the time Shay started begging me for more.

Of course, Gennie had bolted awake with the sound of the smoke detector and came downstairs, asking what the fuck was wrong and whether we needed to abandon ship.

Nope. Full steam ahead and very hard to port.

I hated myself as I thought about Shay while I was in bed last night. Hated how easy it was for these depraved thoughts to take over my days and my dreams. But at the same time—and this was the part I hated the most—I didn't hate it at all. I didn't care that I did terrible things to her in my mind. I didn't care that she'd leave again and I'd never recover. I didn't care because I knew what it felt like to hold her and kiss her and nothing else in the world mattered. Nothing fucking mattered.

Especially not when she looked happy for the first time since meeting her all over again.

The smile I'd caught yesterday, the lightness in her—I hadn't realized I'd missed it until it was there again, bright and warm and magnetic.

I was so fucked.

Shay and her friends went straight for the breakfast sandwich vendor. The woman who'd worn jean shorts and the bikini too small for any of Gennie's dolls looped an arm around Shay's waist, her head resting on Shay's shoulder. The one with the deep olive skin and dark hair—Jaime, I thought—broke out some salsa moves while the high school jazz band started their set. Salsa didn't match the tunes but I got the impression that woman cared little for matching.

The willowy blonde, the one who'd been conked out yesterday, studied the tents and banners of each vendor in the park. I saw it the moment she found me and Gennie, or, more specifically, our blue-gray tent printed with the farm's name and our iconic hand-drawn stars. The whole group turned to look in this direction. Words were spoken, and Shay gave an exaggerated shake of her head.

The blonde directed them forward when the breakfast sandwich line moved but Shay remained where she was, staring across the park at the tent with the stars for an extra few seconds.

I swallowed hard. One of these days, she was going to figure it all out and then—*then*—I'd really be fucked.

I couldn't read her expression from this distance or see her eyes behind those big sunglasses but a string connected us. It wasn't until Jaime caught her by the elbow and swung her around that I blinked away from them.

A stiff, uncomfortable breath rushed out of me. I glanced over at Lillian, my teenage cashier and Gail Castro's granddaughter. "You can take a break now. Gennie and I can hold it down for the next half hour."

Lillian wiped her hands on her jeans and grabbed her phone from her back pocket. "Okay, Mr. Barden. Thanks." She glanced around the setup. "Where is Gennie?"

I motioned toward the knife sharpening stall. "Talking weaponry with Osvaldo."

Lillian laughed. "I'll send her over." As she stepped out from behind the table, she added, "We're out of multigrain and honey herb goat cheese, and we're on the last case of strawberry jam."

I held up a hand in salute. "Thanks, Lill."

Since the morning rush had passed, I had time to organize the table while snatching glimpses of Shay and her friends. They carried their coffees and sandwiches to the far side of the park, where a pair of benches curved around a small fountain. At first, they were focused only on the food and drink but it wasn't long before the caffeine hit them and their conversation grew animated.

Gennie shuffled over, her plastic sword dragging on the grass and her eye patch worn like a necklace. "Why did I have to leave Mr. OJ?"

"Because Mr. OJ has customers, Gen. And Lillian is on her break so I need you to keep an eye on the loot."

"Oh. Right." She grabbed an empty milk crate and set it in front of the point of sale system. As much as it troubled me, she was great at running the system. Couldn't make change but the kid could ring up a sale, no problem.

I kept an eye on Shay as we sold some jam and some bread. They didn't seem to be in any hurry to leave the comfort of the shade and the benches.

The bread should've dawned on me sooner. I'd spent the whole week wondering if she was eating but the very logical solution of *bring her food* didn't hit me until the bakehouse manager asked me to check out the newest test batch.

"Noah, look! Shay's coming!" Gennie whacked the back of my arm with her sword. "And her friends too!"

"Watch the language," I said to her. "Give it a real try this time."

She held the sword across her chest. "Aye aye."

I did the only thing I could do to avoid staring at Shay as she crossed the field. I ignored her.

I focused on the kombucha and pressed juice tent beside us. They did brisk business. I didn't know much about kombucha but they'd sold out of nearly all their stock before ten this morning so they were doing something right. Where were they housed? Probably one of the refurbished mill complexes nearby. *What had happened with Shay's last relationship? The situationship, as she'd called it.* There were plenty of those complexes in this state. I'd toured some of them a few years ago when the canning operation outgrew the back room of the farm stand.

Was she here for safety? Did she need to be far away from someone? Nice spaces but they needed complete overhauls to convert into commercial kitchens. In the end, it had been cheaper to update the old cider house already standing on the orchard property. *Did that someone have a name and could I spend the rest of my life hitting him with frivolous lawsuits for the singular purpose of driving him insane?*

"Shay!" Gennie called, snapping me out of my forced distraction.

"Hello, my friend." Shay waved and Gennie wasted no time dashing out from behind the table. She threw her arms around Shay's waist and immediately launched into a recap of her visit with the knife guy.

"And he had one that was all jagged like knife teeth." Gennie clenched her jack-o'-lantern teeth to illustrate.

"That is incredible," Shay replied. She glanced up at me, her smile wide and bright. "Hi. Thanks for the tip about the food truck."

"And the coffee," Grace added. "I'd return to this rusty enclave for the coffee alone." She grinned at Shay. "You're an added bonus."

Shay beamed at her. "Aren't you a gem." To me, she asked, "Do you do this every weekend?"

"No," Gennie replied, her tone making it known she didn't enjoy market duty.

"What Gen meant to say is we cover the local markets on days when our event crew is stretched too thin. We have a crew down in Narragansett today and another in Connecticut, plus the usual at the Hope Street market on the East Side of Providence. That's always a big one. We hold it down here while everyone else has their hands full."

"I'm pretty sure I've seen y'all in Boston," the blonde said.

"Yeah, that's part of our regular circuit too." I shoved my hands deep in my pockets.

"Hear that, Shay?" Grace asked. "You can come home and still have the bread you were moaning over last night."

"I wasn't moaning," she replied. "I can appreciate good bread just the same as you appreciate good coffee."

"And you were definitely moaning over that coffee," added the one who'd thankfully traded her bikini for actual clothes.

"Markets are boring as shit," Gennie said. A beat passed before she slapped a hand over her mouth. "I didn't say anything."

"Not a peep," Shay replied.

"I didn't hear a word," Grace said.

"The dogs went crazy last night," Gennie said. "Do you want me to tell you about it?"

"Definitely," Grace replied. "Start at the beginning. Leave nothing out. What are the dogs' names?"

"Bernie Sanders, Elliot Stabler, Olivia Benson, Sandra Day O'Connor, and RuPaul were the troublemakers," Gennie said.

"Unsurprising, with that group," Grace said. "Go on."

The blonde and Bikini Top inspected the jam offerings while the others listened to Gennie's breathless story about the dogs trapping a woodchuck in the kennel and not knowing what the hell to do about it. They'd barked their heads off around midnight. Shay gave me a sympathetic face, mouthing "oh no" over Gennie's head.

"Strawberry verbena," Bikini Top said as she read one of the jam labels. "I'm not even sure I know what verbena is."

"It's a flower," the blonde replied. "Lots of tiny flowers, long, trailing stems."

"So, it tastes like flowers?"

I was ready to explain but the blonde beat me to it. "No, it's very mild. Like herby lemon or tangerine. You'd like it."

Bikini Top nodded. Then, she spotted the price sheet and her eyes flared wide. "Holy shit, it's fifteen dollars? For *jam*?"

"Emme," the blonde chided. She gave me a long-suffering smile. "We'll take two, please."

"Gennie, you have a customer," I called.

To Shay and the others, my niece said, "Watch this. I get to use the pay machine."

Gennie climbed onto her milk crate and tapped the screen. "Two strawberry verbena," I told her.

"Two…strawberry…verbena." She keyed in the order, her lower lip snared between her teeth. "Anything else?"

"Anything you'd recommend?" the blonde asked.

Gennie thought about that for a moment. "I like ginger peach on toasty bread."

"I'll have to try ginger peach, then," she replied. "You're an excellent saleswoman."

They gathered around Gennie, cooing and praising her skill on the point of sale. I stepped aside to bag the jams for the blonde. I was almost finished when I sensed someone watching me.

"Hey," I said to the one from the swing. Jaime. The best friend. "What can I get you?"

She tipped her head to the side, an order to step away from the others. "A word, if you please."

I slid the paper bag across the table and then joined Jaime in the empty space between stalls. I glanced back at Shay and Gennie but they were in the thick of a story and didn't notice.

"Hi. You don't know me. Or I'm guessing you don't since our girl has been playing fast and loose with the details these days." She held out her hand. "I'm Jaime Rouselle. I taught first grade next to Shay for six years until she embarked upon this fantastic voyage. In addition to being her best friend and coteacher, I'm also in very deep with an assortment of unsavories. You know what I'm talking about. Motorcycle gangs, mafia. And then there's the worst of them—" She leaned in close. "Private equity guys."

She was right about private equity guys being worse than any mafia on the planet but I still had to fight off a laugh. "You have my attention."

"As I imagine you're aware, our girl's birthday is coming up." She raised an eyebrow. I nodded. It hadn't crossed my mind but yeah, I knew Shay's birthday was next month. "I'm going to give you precise directions. I expect you to follow those directions without deviation. If you do not—and I'll be checking—I'll rain hell upon your bread and jam. You got me?"

Again, I had to fight off a laugh because this pocket-sized woman who could easily pass as a high schooler was threatening me with—with biker gangs? And finance bros? What was happening here?

"I think I follow, yeah. What do you need me to do for Shay's birthday?"

She stared at me for a beat, as if she wasn't convinced of my fealty. Then, "She loves vanilla cake. The cake mix kind, from the box. And chocolate buttercream frosting but not the ready-made frosting. Homemade only. Butter, sugar, cocoa. That kind. She loves family dinner birthday parties but she'll never say that out loud. She won't ask for it and if you try to find out what she wants, she'll swear up and down she wants nothing. All she has ever wanted is a family and the regular old things that come with families. Cake mix from the grocery store. Family around the kitchen table." She wagged a warning finger at me. "Do not fuck this up. Her birthday is in the middle of the week this year and there's no way I can get down here in time to pull it off. She cannot handle another disappointment so I need you to swear to me you'll get this right."

It never occurred to me that Shay wanted to belong to a family but it made complete sense. I couldn't believe I'd missed that. I guess I'd been busy assuming she had everything she could ever want. "And why are you asking *me* to do this?"

She gave me a look that must scare the shit out of her students. "You know why, Mr. Just Dropping By With a Freshly Baked Loaf of Carby Goodness."

"I really don't."

She nodded slowly. "So, that's the game? Pretend you don't care? How's it working out for you?"

I glanced over at the kombucha crew. When I didn't respond, she went on.

"Yeah. Just as I thought."

"What did you mean about Shay not being able to handle another disappointment?"

"James," Grace called. "Get over here."

Jaime held up her hand in acknowledgement. "I said what I said. Don't fuck this up. I can end you."

"I can pull off a birthday dinner and cake."

She narrowed her eyes. "Yes, you can."

"Noah," Gennie yelled. It was like a battle cry. The same one she employed when she couldn't find any socks and believed it was faster to yell than open her sock drawer. "Which bread am I supposed to give Shay?"

My niece held up the two paper-wrapped loaves I'd set aside first thing this morning while Jaime swallowed her laugh with a sip of coffee. "Don't try to be smooth," she said. "Kids will shut it down before it even starts. This munchkin will kill your game."

With a parting glance for Jaime, I moved back behind the table and relieved Gennie of the bread in question. To Shay, I said, "These are our most popular. Give 'em a try."

"Oh." She blinked at me. "Oh, thank you." She reached into her bag and retrieved her wallet. "What do I owe you?"

"What did I tell you about that? Not when you're with me." I handed over the loaves.

Her brow wrinkled as she accepted the bread. "That's really nice of you."

She held my gaze for a long moment. Her expression seemed to say she was confused and that made two of us. I shrugged because it was all I could do to keep myself from babbling and making it much worse.

"Do you need any jam to go with that?" my niece asked. "We have some apricot carmumum."

"Cardamon," I said.

Shay smiled at us and tucked her hair behind her ears. "I'm good with the bread. Thanks." She glanced back at her friends, who were very busy pretending they weren't listening. "We're going to walk around. See what's here." To Gennie, she added, "I'll see you Monday. I've got a bunch of cool shipwreck stories for us."

Gennie and I watched from behind the table as they strolled through the park, stopping occasionally to visit vendors or fall into conversation. Lillian returned, and she and Gennie were busy with a late surge of customers.

Shay and her friends left the market shortly before closing time. We usually stayed open as long as we had goods to sell and people were still buying but it was hot and humid, and a dense mass of clouds was moving in, the sure sign of an impending thunderstorm.

"Let's pack it up, Lill," I said.

It was quick work since we'd cleared almost all of our stock, and Lillian and I got the tent and table folded up just as the first rumbles of thunder started.

Once Lillian had met up with her boyfriend, Gennie and I settled into the truck. As casually as I could manage, I said, "You know, Shay's birthday is next month."

From the back seat came an unhinged screech of "What!"

"Yeah, later in the month. After school starts."

"Ugh. Fucking school."

I glanced at her in the rearview. "I have a job for you. A secret task, actually."

"Is it about Shay's birthday?"

"Yes."

"Good, because I don't want any stupid school jobs." She crossed her arms and pouted.

"What do you think about having a birthday dinner for her? Maybe after one of your playdates?

"I love it," she said. "Do we have any juice?"

I tossed her the lunch box she'd ignored all morning. "I need you to get some information from Shay but you have to use all your pirate skills to do it. She can't know that we're planning a birthday party for her."

I heard her slurp a juice box. "Then it wouldn't be a surprise."

"Right. You need to find out her favorite special meal and get some ideas for a gift."

God knew I couldn't keep forcing bread upon her. I could but that move was already obvious. If Shay didn't know it, her friends were sure to explain it any minute now.

"I can do it," Gennie replied.

"I know you can." I glanced back at her again, juice box straw clamped between her teeth and her head resting on the seat belt.

In this single moment as fat raindrops slapped against the windshield, Gennie and I understood each other. More than that, we knew we were on the same team.

It gave me a strange jolt of confidence, as if I could make it through this parenting thing without losing my mind. At the very least, I could conspire with my niece—and that was enough for me today.

chapter eleven

Shay

Students will be able to kick up their heels and lose their minds.

THE FINAL DAYS of summer break always followed a similar pattern for me. I'd expected this year to be different since I didn't have a roster of new students to meet or a curriculum to prepare. But that all changed first thing Monday morning, before I'd wandered through the old tulip beds or treated myself to coffee and cookies, when Friendship Public Schools called regarding a long-term subbing assignment. One of the second grade teachers had elected to extend her parental leave and would I mind visiting with the principal that morning for an interview?

I'd paused long enough for them to ask if I was still on the line. Then I said to myself—not the school secretary, thank god—*fuck it*.

That was it. Fuck it.

A long-term gig wasn't the plan and it changed everything I'd mentally prepared for but fuck it. Fuck the plan. Fuck the mental preparation. Fuck everything because believing I had any control over my life was an exercise in comedy.

That was how I ended up spending most of the day in room nine at

Hope Elementary with Kelli Calderon, whose baby boy had arrived very early and was doing well but she required more time at home with him before returning to school.

She showed me around her room and gave me an overview of her plans for the first two months of the year. While I was comfortable with second grade and happy to jump in, this was a huge shift for me. I wasn't just subbing anymore. This was a commitment unlike covering a few classes when a teacher was out for professional development or a personal day. Starting a school year with a group of kids was a big deal. I had to get this right because there was no way in hell I'd turn a disaster of a class over to Kelli come November.

I had to get *myself* right. I had to accept that I wasn't going to float through this year, itinerant and free from any real responsibility. I couldn't phone this in. No more lazy mornings in the garden or late-night wine-and-TV binges. I had to get back into teacher mode.

After my crash course introduction to room nine, I headed to Little Star to meet Gennie. I was feeling frazzled when I rolled up to Noah's crisp white farmhouse, partially because I'd only consumed a pudding cup and a mediocre drive-thru coffee today, but also because I'd intended to use this morning to prepare for my work with Gennie. I had a bunch of books I'd paged through but no real game plan for our time.

I didn't see Gail Castro or her horses today, which was a surprise. When I knocked on the door, no one answered. I checked my phone on the off chance Noah had canceled. No messages.

I trundled down the front steps, my book tote biting into my shoulder and my phone clutched in my hand. For several minutes I paced the gravel drive, glancing down the worn paths cutting between the rows of apple trees and back at the house. The late August heat was oppressive, even in a breezy dress, and it wasn't long before I felt frizz forming along my hairline and sweat behind my knees.

I ran the back of my hand over my forehead as I debated how long it made sense to wait here. I could go up to Little Star's central operations at the old Barden house or I could swing by the Castro ranch or—

I turned as Noah's truck thundered down the lane. Though the windows were rolled up, I caught the muffled sounds of Gennie's voice and saw Noah motioning for her to settle down.

As soon as they came to a stop, Gennie's door swung open. "—and we're late! See? She's already here and it's no fair because—"

"You will have your playdate," Noah said as he stepped out. "If you ask Shay, I'm sure she'll hang around a bit longer tonight."

"Because you made us late!" Gennie cried.

"For a good reason," he replied. He came around the front of the truck, shaking his head. "Why don't you tell Shay the news? She can decide if the delay was worth it."

He caught my eye, giving me a quick nod that said *please back me up on this*.

"What's your news?" I asked her, closing the distance between us.

Instead of putting one foot in front of the other, my shoe sank into a depression in the gravel and I teetered hard to the side. This sent my other foot kicking out which led to my shoe flying off. My bag fell from my shoulder to the crook in my elbow, which messed with my balance and sent me teetering in the opposite direction, all while I repeatedly yelped "Whoops!" and "Whoa!"

Gennie and Noah rushed toward me though I waved them off as well as I could when hopping on one foot and weighted down at the elbow. "Did anyone see where my shoe went?"

Noah took hold of my upper arm while motioning to Gennie. "Look around, okay?" He reached for my bag, saying, "Would you give me that before you face-plant in my driveway? For fuck's sake, Shay."

"I lost my footing," I argued, pointing at the gravel. Of course it looked perfectly unremarkable. "It was the ground. And the shoes. They're all wrong for this kind of surface."

Also true but not something I was prepared to announce: sweating profusely in sandals rendered them wrong for most surfaces.

He stared at me, his eyes concealed behind sunglasses. His jaw was rigid, the little muscle up near his earlobe twitching as I studied his face.

"Found it," Gennie called from the other side of the lane.

"Why are you shaking?" he asked, his fingers sliding up my arm.

"I'm not. I'm just a little jittery. I've only had coffee today." I tipped my head to the side. "And a pudding cup."

"Coffee," he repeated. "And *a pudding cup*."

"Yeah. I got a call from the school and—"

"One shoe, coming right up," Gennie sang as she jogged over. She dropped it in front of me.

"Thanks," I said to her. I slipped it on and stepped back. Noah didn't release me. "You're such a big helper."

"You kicked it really far." She sounded impressed.

"I don't even know how," I replied.

"Coffee. And a pudding cup," Noah murmured.

"Shay! Guess what?" Gennie asked.

Noah's fingers loosened on my bicep, one after the other, and then immediately tightened again. "Gen, we'll tell Shay all about it inside. We need to get her some water before she expires."

"What is expire?" she asked.

"My shoe slipped," I told him. "That's all. Nothing to get excited about."

"It means Shay forgot to fill up that big water bottle of hers today and it's very hot, so we need to get her a drink," he said. "Probably some solid food too."

"Really, you don't have to—"

"Come with me," Gennie said, taking my free hand. "I'll make some pirate juice."

"What's pirate juice?" I glanced between Gennie and Noah as they led me into the house.

He chuckled. "You'll see."

"Noah cooked some new jam last night. You can have a jam snack. Sometimes I dip my pretzels into jam."

"And that's why you have your own jar," Noah said.

"What kind of new jam?" I asked. Noah pushed open the door and a wall of cool air greeted me. It was a gorgeous relief. So much that I groaned out loud. "Oh, that's nice."

He pulled a chair from the kitchen table, deposited me in it. He shook his head like I was more problem than he'd bargained for. "Tomato."

"Tomato?" I echoed.

He dropped both hands to my shoulders and gave me a firm squeeze. "The new jam."

"That's…a jam?"

He set my bag on the counter and leaned back against the island, crossed his arms over his chest. Gennie disappeared into the pantry, soon emerging with a step stool.

"Savory jams are niche but increasingly popular. We can charge twice as much as what we would for strawberry jam and move them at greater volume, especially in restaurant and other wholesale settings," he said. "Where did you go today?"

"The elementary school. A parental leave sub position came up."

Gennie opened the freezer and started scooping ice into a cup. Noah watched her. "Shake a leg on that juice, Gen."

"I'm going, I'm going," she said, selecting ice by the individual cube.

Soon, she hustled to the table carrying a green soda bottle, a mason jar packed with something purpley-red, and the mug filled with hand-selected ice.

"What's all this?" I asked.

She tapped a finger to each item. "Cherries, rocks, rum."

"Rum?"

"Pirates love rum," Noah said with a nod to the green bottle. The label had been ripped off, and in its place, *RUM* was printed in thick black marker. "Uncles don't like rum nearly as much as they enjoy keeping their sanity."

Gennie glanced at him over her shoulder. "How many cherries?"

"Three should do it."

Gennie spooned each cherry into the mug with a chemist's precision. If only she brought that kind of focus to writing complete sentences.

After she'd finished with the fruit, I studied the jar. It didn't have any labels. Didn't look store-bought. "Do you preserve your own cherries too?"

"Yeah." He shrugged. "I don't care for the processing maraschinos go through. There's no real cherry flavor left over and it's mostly corn syrup and food coloring. Why bother if you're basically eating a gummy bear packed in juice?"

I nodded. "Why indeed."

Gennie presented the pirate juice, complete with reusable straw, saying, "This will give you big energy."

I took a sip. Ginger ale and home-preserved cherries. And we called it pirate juice. "It's wonderful. An authentic elixir of the high seas. Thank you."

She beamed. "What do you want for a snack?"

"I'm not sure," I said between sips. It was a major throwback but it was beautifully cold and the cherries offered just enough sweetness to perk me up. *Perfect.* "Do you have any Cheez-Its?"

"What? My god, no," he replied, slashing a hand as if I'd offended him. "Gen, get the cheddar Wheatie brought over last night. And the sourdough. It's in the pantry."

"Aye aye."

"The elementary school, then," he said to me.

"Yeah." I watched as Gennie set a wedge of cheese on a plate and then jabbed a knife into the heart of it. My eyes round, I blinked up at

Noah. He glanced at her and shrugged. "I'll be taking Mrs. Calderon's second grade class through November or so."

"Mrs. Calderon is the nice second grade teacher. Everyone says so." Gennie unwrapped a small round of bread and plunged a knife right into that too.

When I gave Noah *is she allowed to play with knives* eyes, he said, "Butter knives. And it's the pirate special."

"Is that what we're calling it?"

His only response was a lopsided grin. "Second grade. That's good? That's what you want?"

"Yeah, I can hang with second graders. They're fun bunnies. Not as fun as the cool cats in kindergarten, of course. I'm just a little"—I brought my hands to my temples, let my fingers wiggle—"frazzled. I thought I'd be doing the daily assignment thing. Covering whichever random classes came up. Now I'm starting the year with a class and I only have the next few days to prep. It's a big shift. Mentally and… everything else. Like I said. Frazzled."

Gennie carried the bread and cheese—and the knives protruding from each—to the table. "Can I tell you my big good thing now?" She bounced on her toes as she spoke.

"Of course. Tell me. I need to know."

"I'm not a cool cat."

I blinked. "What? Say that again?"

"You said kindergarten kids are cool cats but I get to go to first grade so I'm not cool."

She was beaming ear to ear, her whole toothy grin taking over her face and narrowing her eyes into happy slits. I jumped up, wrapped my arms around her. "You're not cool at all," I said. "Now, you're fab. Totally fabulous first grader. It's way better than cool." I turned to Noah. His arms were still crossed and that lopsided grin hadn't gone anywhere. "I thought your meeting was at the end of the week."

"It was. They called this afternoon, asking if we could come in because there was a scheduling issue." He lifted a shoulder. "I think the scheduling issue was a result of me sending some documentation from the psych about an evaluation, including specific recommendations for additional layers of special needs support."

"I showed them that I read extra good now," Gennie said. "And did some stupid word problems too."

"I am certain you were incredible," I told her. To Noah, I added, "Sounds like you did pretty well for yourself too."

He met my gaze and held it for a long moment while Gennie bounced and twirled between us. Slowly, he tipped his jaw down, and for the briefest of seconds, his stare dipped to my mouth. What was *that*?

"Are you gonna take the bus to school?" Gennie asked.

Noah met my eyes again. "Shay doesn't ride the bus. Never has."

"Because Noah takes pity on me," I replied.

"Because—" He shook his head. "Teachers don't ride the bus. Sorry, kid."

She looked up at me. "Can I go in your car? The bus sucks balls."

Noah started to reply but I held up a hand. "I brought all of those awesome explorer books I told you about but I think your news calls for a celebration. Should we visit the dogs? Or the goats? What do you think?"

Gennie sprinted to the oven and squinted at the digital clock on the panel. "Four…zero…nine." She repeated the numbers to herself a few times. Then, "Noah, is it cow time?"

He rocked back on his heels, sighed. "Yep."

"Cows," she bellowed. "The cows! They go to the milking barn! For milking! And-and-and—"

"It sounds perfect," I said. "Can we do that?"

"There are rules," Noah said.

"Don't touch anything and be nice and don't start any crazy shit and listen to all directions and leave the dairy guys alone and if I'm super best good, I can pet one cow before they go to the pasture."

Noah shot a glare between me and the untouched plate of cheese and bread. "Eat. I won't have you collapsing in the dairy barn."

I broke off a bit of bread, some cheese. Made a little sandwich out of it. "Okay? I'm eating."

He ran a hand over the back of his neck, saying, "You're sticking with me. The last thing I need is you losing a shoe in there. We keep it clean, but god, I can't have you falling over around cows. And finish that juice, would you?"

I brought the straw to my lips, smiling at him as I downed the rest of my pirate's Shirley Temple. He held my gaze for a long moment before muttering something to himself and stomping out the door.

I didn't know what I'd accomplished there but I knew it was something.

WE CLIMBED INTO THE FOUR-WHEELER, Gennie babbling about cows as she fastened her seat belt in the back seat, barely managing to stay in her skin. Noah glanced over at me, his sunglasses blocking his eyes again. Then he reached all the way across my body and settled his hand on my shoulder.

"It's a long ride," he said. His face was so close. "Think you can handle it?"

I didn't know what to do with my hands. Where were they supposed to go? Was I supposed to know that? More to the point, was I supposed to know anything or was it cool for me to sit here and let him lean into me like this?

"Yeah," I murmured. "I think so."

What are we even talking about?

"I hope you're right about that."

I didn't know what he was thinking but the way he traced the ball of my shoulder and how his breath caught just enough for me to notice gave me a good idea. Whatever I'd accomplished a few minutes ago, it was now Noah's turn to get his.

Then he yanked a seat belt across my chest and locked it into place beside my hip.

"Hold on," he snapped, hands on the wheel now. "The dairy's on the other side of the hill. I'm not stopping if you or your shoes fall out."

Noah gunned it out of the barn and down the drive while Gennie chanted "Cow time! Cow time!" from the back.

Noah was very adept at allowing me to believe that the friendship we'd once had was in the past, and the present was grudgingly knit together with Lollie's will, Gennie's academic needs, and the fragment of familiarity lingering between us, but that wasn't the truth right now. Perhaps it hadn't been the truth at all since I'd returned.

Noah had been a shy kid. He'd never talked much until I pestered him into it. Even then, he'd listened more than he spoke. Now that I thought about it, our best conversations took place in the notes we passed each other every day. Those were where he opened up the most. It was how we'd connected beyond those sleepy morning drives to school.

Was it possible this was his new version of shy? Was this what shy looked like when a man who wanted nothing more than to leave farm life behind got swept back into the family business and had to adopt his niece along the way? Were his grump and his grouch the grown-up rendition of eating lunch in the library to avoid other kids? And his use of me as a human shield against the pee-listening lady, was that just another example of rusty social skills?

"I'll do my best," I replied as he slowed at the end of the drive.

He paused, looking twice in both directions before crossing Old Windmill Hill Road. "If your best is anything like what I've seen today, I'm going to need you to do better than that." He turned, catching a narrow path running along a line of white fencing. "Pudding cup," he muttered.

"Would it help if I told you that I usually have coffee and a giant cookie at the Pink Plum in town?"

"Jesus, no. Why do you—never mind. It doesn't matter. Hey, Gennie."

"Argh," she replied.

"When we finish up at the dairy, I want you to get some eggs for Shay."

"I don't need eggs."

"Obviously you do," he said.

"I don't even like eggs for breakfast," I said.

"I don't like bare eggs," Gennie said. "But Noah mixes up the eggs with cheese and bacon and all the other good stuff, and puts it on a sandwich, and that's good shit."

The four-wheeler was loud enough to drown out my laugh. "Bare eggs," I repeated.

"The first time she said it, I thought she was saying *bear* eggs. Like grizzly bear. I tried to explain that bears don't have eggs and she told me bare eggs are real and disgusting, and, well, we got donuts that morning. Those first few weeks together were unreal."

"It must've been hard," I said, low enough that little ears wouldn't hear. "Being thrown together like that."

He nodded and shot a quick look over his shoulder. "I didn't know what I was doing. Still don't."

"Yes, you do. You're just fishing for compliments."

A smile passed over his face. "I would never."

"Are you sure about that? You weren't fishing for compliments when I tried to tell you that your friend Christiane won't stay away because you're rocking that hot uncle vibe real hard?"

"I—no." He shook his head, and if I wasn't mistaken, his ears were turning red. *Interesting.* "That's not what happened."

"Good clarification."

He reached over as if he was going to touch me but then fisted his hand and dropped it to his thigh. "I don't think I thanked you for everything. At the game."

"You did." I watched that blush climb up his neck. *Very interesting.* "Two loaves of bread is more than enough thanks."

He drove over a rise and down a gentle slope, and a long blue-gray barn came into view. Several other buildings stood nearby, along with at least twenty of the same black-and-white cow trucks I'd run across on my first day in town.

"Cows ahoy," Gennie called.

"Remember the rules," Noah said to her.

"I know. I know, I know," she sang, bouncing in her seat.

To me, he said, "You too. Wander away from me and there will be consequences."

I stared at him. I wanted to say something but no words could be found.

High school Noah was sweet. *So* sweet. Quiet, helpful to a fault. He never made growly demands or bit off orders. High school Noah would sooner break-dance naked in front of our entire graduating class than warn me about consequences for not following his directions.

And yet, I didn't mind the bossy vibe. It was like that sweet, quiet boy had found a rumbly, grumbly voice. And some seat belt snapping and an absurd insistence I couldn't be trusted in his barn.

Shy. This man was shy. While also being enormously bossy.

So very interesting.

The four-wheeler bumped onto pavement and we cut a wide loop around the parking lot before stopping at the main doors to the barn. From here, we could see the distinctive black-and-white of the cows munching on hay.

"We have a hundred and eighty-four cows," Gennie said. "And they're milked twice a day. At four and four."

Noah trailed his hand up my hip, releasing the seat belt. I glanced down, staring at the spot where his knuckles pressed against my sundress.

In the back, Gennie continued, "They're called Homesteam—"

"Holstein," Noah said.

"—and every day, they make eight billion hundred pounds of milk—"

"Eight thousand," he said.

"—and that goes into a pipe that cooks it really hot and makes eleven million bottles of milk."

"Eleven hundred," he said, still staring at me, still touching my hip.

"And in the winter, the floors are hot because they have rainbows inside them."

"Radiant heating," he murmured.

"Can we go now?" she asked. "It's going to be over, we're going to miss it!"

"We can only milk twenty cows at a time," he said. "We will not miss anything." He pulled his hand away from me and pointed at a bright white building with its garage-style doors flung wide-open. "That's the milking parlor. Come on."

Gennie ran ahead of us, saying hello to each of the cows leisurely eating their hay. She skidded to a stop in front of the white building, motioning to us with all the impatience in the world.

"She really loves this," I said.

"Sometimes." He slipped his hands into his pockets. "Mostly since meeting the calves. She didn't want anything to do with this place before."

As we approached the doors, Noah gave her a nod and she bounded inside. A member of the crew spotted her and motioned for her to join him as he tended to one of the cows.

Noah held out his arm, stopping me before I crossed into the parlor. "This is far enough for you."

"Why?"

"Because you are not wearing shoes appropriate for this setting," he said with a wave toward the interior. "And you're not dressed for"—he ran a finger along one of the dress's ruffled tiers at my thigh—"anything even loosely related to dairy farming."

I indulged in a quick scan of his blue plaid button-down shirt, sleeves rolled up to the elbow and collar open, well-worn jeans, and boots that knew every inch of this land. His fingers had raked through his dark hair a time or twenty and his short beard was freshly trimmed. He looked good and he looked good *here*. And that was a strange realization since I was still surprised to find him here.

"You were serious when you said there were rules."

"Someone has to be serious." He set his hands on his waist and cocked a hip as though he was settling in for a debate. "Might as well be me."

"Is that your way of telling me I'm not serious? Because I'll have you know, I'm plenty serious."

He gave me a look that resembled something like impatience. "No earrings today?"

"No earrings today. It was a chaotic morning. When the school called, I was still in a towel and threw on the first thing I could find. No earrings. It's a wonder I remembered underwear. And as you've already pointed out, my water bottle didn't make the cut either."

If he had a response to that, he didn't offer it. Although he did glance over my shoulder and mutter, "What the hell are you doing here?"

A Black man approached, probably in his early fifties, and pulled off his gloves. "Better question is, what the hell are you doing here?"

Noah gestured across the parlor. Gennie was talking a mile a minute and patting a cow's flank while a crew member nodded along. "The kid's been asking for a visit."

The man turned a warm smile toward me. "Jim Wheaton. I look after this little operation. Welcome to my dairy pavilion."

"Shay Zucconi," I replied. "This is much more than a little operation."

He shot a pointed look to Noah and then stared at me, his eyes round. His lips parted a few seconds before he spoke. "I've heard so much about you."

I glanced between him and Noah. "Oh, really? You knew Grandma Lollie?"

"No, I'm afraid I didn't know Lollie personally. I came here from Upstate New York not long before she moved down South. I'm sorry for your loss."

"Thank you. That's very kind of you." I paused, not sure how to ask this. "But—if you didn't know Lollie, how do you—"

"He's also responsible for the goats," Noah added.

Jim gave the pavilion a rueful glance. "That operation isn't as sophisticated as this one. Not yet. But we're getting there."

"Let's get there sooner rather than later," Noah said.

"Patience, Barden. Patience would do you good." To me, Jim asked, "Miss Gennie brought you along to meet the girls?"

"She was very enthusiastic. I couldn't miss it." I smiled, adding, "Your cows are lovely."

"They're the best of the best. We take very good care of them." He nodded at Noah. "Just how the boss likes it. He's very particular but I bet you know that."

"Shouldn't you be leaving?" Noah asked. "You've been here since first thing this morning. Go home."

Ignoring Noah entirely, Jim turned to me, asking, "Would you like a tour?"

"She doesn't want a tour," Noah replied, bringing his hand to the back of his neck.

"I'd love one," I said.

"I knew you would," Jim said. "We'll start in the bottling facility and work backward. Personally, I prefer walking through the process in reverse. Start with the package, end with the pasture. But we could also do the opposite. Just as fun."

"You're the expert," I said.

"Wheatie," Noah warned.

"Quick tour," he replied. "You stay right here but don't harass my staff unless you want them putting you to work—and they're under strict orders to do exactly that. They'll happily send you to the manure shed."

Noah glared at the other man. "Make it fast."

As we crossed the pavement toward another building, Jim pointed out overhead pipes and explained how they moved milk directly from the pumping area to a separation tank, and they avoided using trucks at this stage because the movement caused too much oxidation. He went into detail about homogenization and then pasteurization as we moved through those areas, watching from the large windows in the hall rather than going into those spaces. He led me into the bottling facility, a separate building on the compound, where I pointed to a series of windows with the manufacturer's stickers still in place.

"This looks new," I said. "Was it recently updated?"

Jim stopped at the door to the primary storage cooler. "Noah didn't tell you?" When I shook my head, he continued. "He overhauled this whole place. Energy efficiency, resource conservation, organic certification. He's been hustling this project for years."

"And it was recently completed?"

Jim gave a slow nod. "He's uncommonly good at paperwork. It frees up my time, you see. I don't have to mess with any of those details. The business is his sweet spot. He can find loopholes in the dark and has never met a grant or tax credit program he doesn't like."

"I had no idea."

Another nod. "Not much of a talker, is he?"

Go ahead and steal the thoughts out of my mind, Jim.

We were walking back to the milking parlor while Jim described his favorite sections of the one-hundred-acre property. The west pasture was especially nice come autumn.

Noah stood at the garage doors, arms crossed over his chest like always as he swung a gaze between me and Jim, and inside the parlor. He made a show of looking at his watch.

"Thank you for the tour," I said to Jim.

"The pleasure was entirely mine."

"This would make for a really fun field trip," I said. "I'm not sure where the second grade usually goes for field trips. I'll have to ask the other teachers at the grade level when they're back on campus but I'm sure they'd love everything about this."

"We'd be happy to have you. Just let the boss man know when you're coming." After a meaningful glance at Noah, Jim said, "I'll be off now."

We watched him cross the pavement and duck into the bottling facility. A minute or two passed and then Gennie jogged toward us, her cheeks red and her smile wide. "I got to help with Matildamoon and Petuniapie!" She grabbed my hand. "Do you want to help? Bonnieboo is up next."

"Bonnieboo? I'll watch you help with her, okay? I need to talk with Noah for a few minutes. Go show me your skills."

Gennie skipped back inside, satisfied with that response. Noah, on the other hand, dropped his hands to his hips and squared his shoulders. "What's wrong?" he asked.

"Nothing's wrong." It was a textbook reaction to *we have to talk* and I panted out a laugh as I rubbed my temples because I hadn't meant to set him on guard. I hadn't even meant to bring this up but—fuck it. That was the theme of this day. It would probably continue as the theme of this entire year. "I've been thinking about Twin Tulip," I started, "and this wonky little town and my whole wonky little life. I've thought about your offer too. You know, to marry me because Lollie needed me to jump through hoops to keep her farm going. Still haven't wrapped my head around that choice but whatever. Can't argue with the dead. Anyway. I have a few conditions."

A beat passed. Then, "You have—what?"

"You were right when you said Gennie can't get caught in the middle if we do this."

"If we do this," he murmured. He bobbed his head, slow and a little rusty, as if he was thinking very hard about the act of nodding and getting it all wrong in the process. "Okay." He pulled off his sunglasses and gripped the back of his neck. He stared at me, his gaze stormed over. "I thought you weren't ready to think about this. What happened? What changed your mind?"

"I don't have a good explanation for that," I admitted, and that was as close to the truth as I was willing to get. I didn't have a good explanation for anything right now. I was fumbling along. "I mean, what's the worst that could happen? All the worsts have already happened to me. It can't get worse. It just can't. So, I might as well give this a try while I still can."

The muscles in Noah's jaw pulsed. He was quiet a long time. Too long. Long enough that it occurred to me he might've changed his mind.

"If the offer still stands," I added. "It's cool if not. Totally understandable."

He stared at me, his gaze dark. "The offer stands."

I shoved my fingers through my hair, gathering it off my neck. "Okay. Great. So, my conditions."

"Your conditions."

I didn't know when he'd moved closer to me but his knuckles brushed my thigh and I couldn't remember any of the conditions I'd cobbled together. "Like I said, you were absolutely right about protecting Gennie. I don't want to do anything to hurt her or complicate her life. Or your life. So, this has to be nothing more than a legal transaction. If we do this, nothing changes. I live at my place, you live at yours, never the truth shall be revealed." His knuckles passed over my leg again but he remained silent. I hurried to add, "I'll be your human shield anytime you want, of course. You can use me as much as you want."

He turned his face to the sky, slowly shaking his head. "Shay," he grumbled. After a long beat, he dropped his gaze to me. "You're sure about this?"

I laughed. A real, true laugh that shook deep into my bones. "I am sure about nothing. Not a damn thing. I am making it up as I go along, Noah. Maybe I'll pull it off with Twin Tulip but maybe I won't. I don't know." I shrugged. "But fuck it, let's find out. Right?"

"And after the estate is finalized? What happens then?"

"Then we dissolve it," I said. "Nothing has to change."

He glanced at the cows, at Gennie. His knuckles continued their barely-there circuit across my thigh. It didn't seem as though his touch was entirely intentional. "Are you—I mean, is everything okay? You're safe here. Right? There's no stalker, no abusive ex that I should know about?"

When was the proper time to explain you'd been left at the altar less than two months ago? And really, was it necessary to explain that? I didn't think so. And I wished people would stop asking if everything was okay because there wasn't a clean mechanism for me to say no to that. The expected answer was always yes and anything else was socially toxic. "No stalker, no abusive ex. Just an avocado of a relationship. You know how it is. Perfect one day, complete trash the next. If it's all right with you, I'd rather leave it at that."

"We can do that." He bobbed his head and pressed those knuckles against my thigh too hard to be anything short of intentional. "There's no waiting period for a marriage license in Rhode Island. Any city hall can issue a license and preside over a ceremony."

"Not here, not in Friendship," I said. Really wished I had my water bottle with me today. Would've been nice to have something to fidget with while negotiating the terms of a marriage. "The town. It's too—you know. People talk. And we don't want that."

"Yeah. Agreed." He glanced inside the parlor. "Providence would be better."

Did he have this info stored in his big brain or had he gone looking for it? Had he expected me to take him up on his offer? "Right. Providence."

"Are you free tomorrow? Midday? Gen's with Gail until three, if that works for you."

Apparently, there wasn't a minute to waste. "I'm setting up the classroom and prepping for the first day but it's all on my own time. I'm not required on campus until Friday."

He frowned and rocked back on his heels. "Then I'll pick you up at the elementary school tomorrow. Eleven. I'll draft the prenup tonight."

He stalked into the milking parlor, leaving me staring after him.

chapter twelve

Shay

Students will be able to observe customs and traditions.

ON MY SECOND wedding day of the year, I skipped the gown that cost more than most compact cars and required three people to cinch me into it, and went with a hot pink romper.

An adult onesie, as Gennie would say.

It had a cute little cut-out at the small of my back that made it a touch too risqué for teaching yet a-okay for writing names on desk placards, cubby stickers, and take-home folders.

The beaded crab earrings, just kitsch enough to avoid being creepy, brushed the sides of my neck every time I moved. Those earrings screamed louder than anything I owned and they said *not perfect, not bridal, not a problem*.

I put a lot of energy into viewing this as a business arrangement rather than a marriage. I needed that insulation. It was the only way to save myself from spiraling down on memories of my first nuptial attempt. And it wasn't just the memories. It was the worst-case scenario thoughts too. *Had the ex been cheating? Had he always cheated? Was he with that person now? What did they offer that I lacked? What had I done wrong?*

Add in the trauma of my life ripping down the middle with an audience of friends and family to gasp in horror, and it was no surprise I'd spelled *Aiden* wrong five times. All the tattoos and dye jobs and binge-drinking in the world couldn't lift that mess from my memory.

But sitting in that mess wasn't going to erase it either. The ex was out there living his life. He wasn't wandering around a tulip farm, cutting his fingers while he tried to put the broken pieces of himself back in an order that made sense for this fresh, new version of his life. I knew that with more certainty than I knew anything else about him.

That was another reason for the crabby earrings. He hated those things. The lobster ones and the koi fish. The octopus too. He hated all my weird and wonderful things, and for a time he'd convinced me I didn't want them either. Shouldn't want them.

It left me wondering what else I'd lost along the way. What I'd given up. And why I'd let it happen.

Jaime's response to this business arrangement was short and direct. "This isn't a Hallmark movie," she'd said last night. "You are not allowed to forget about city life because one very fuckable farmer brings you freshly baked bread and offers to save your granny's land. You will come back to me, doll. They don't get to keep you."

"This is temporary."

"That's what they all say."

"Trust me," I said. "I'm coming back."

She snorted. "Just wait until Daddy Bread Baker gives you his baguette."

"You did not say that. I refuse to believe you said those words."

"Was it my finest moment? No. Am I a dinging toaster of anxiety because I have five big-time IEPs and three behavioral 504s in need of hands-on help? Yes. If this week doesn't end with another teaching assistant being hired, I'm gonna burn something."

"What do you mean, five IEPs? I had three and you knew each of those kiddos."

"Those three aren't on my roster. Julius's family moved, Gray's got him into a program for sensory kids, and Madgalily's decided to home-school. So, I have five new friends."

"Oh, wow. I'm sorry. I should've asked before I dumped my drama on you."

"As if I wouldn't have called a time-out and told you I needed us to prioritize *my* drama? No, doll, I'm good. I haven't been to therapy in three weeks and I'm out of laundry detergent so I'm just wearing bike shorts under dresses which isn't a problem but I feel like I'm crossing into questionable new territory of not wearing underwear here. It's possible I'm never going back. And I'm just ranty. It's fine." She heaved out a sigh. "It's fine. You're getting married! Sort of. That's fun, right?"

"It's a lot of fun," I replied. Part of me wanted to get in the car and deliver detergent to her apartment and promise everything would be all right with her class. Better than all right. Awesome, like it always was. The other part knew I had to stay here. I had to do this thing, this giant crazy thing where I grabbed the ripped fabric of my life and knotted it into some new creation that I wouldn't recognize until it was done. "And the odds are high my groom will show up this time. He wants me for my land, after all."

"More than your land."

I shook my head. "Not much more."

I couldn't nail Noah down. His thoughts hid behind a stone wall and I had yet to find the drawbridge. For every shoulder caress and every glance at my mouth, there was prolonged silence and stomping away from me with a grumble. If he wanted anything more than another business to add to his Friendship empire—and the occasional fake girlfriend—he did an excellent job of hiding it.

"Hey, so, do you want to hear about some real drama? Because there was a whole big thing at this poly meetup munch I went to the other night instead of going to therapy, like I should have."

"Definitely, yes, but I have to move first. My ass falls asleep whenever I sit on the floor too long."

"Get comfortable. It's an involved story. And maybe your new husband will buy you some furniture so you don't have to sit on the floor all the time."

MY FIRST CLUE should've been the suit.

I should've known what was coming the moment Noah stepped into room nine dressed like he'd been born for the singular and specific purpose of wearing bespoke suits. He had one hand in his pocket, the other holding a document folder. His tie was a bit loose, a bit off-center, as if he'd tugged at it on the drive over here.

I had no idea why that made me press my thighs together and I didn't want to explore it.

At that moment, with him standing in my doorway, I realized there had been a period in Noah's life when he'd worn suits and carried documents and gave his tie an irritable pull every day.

It was a wonder that New York City was still standing because I was *this close* to sliding out of my chair.

The best gift, however, came from the items he wasn't wearing. Without sunglasses or a ball cap to keep his walls high, I could see him. Still, I didn't know how to read the expression on his face. The pinch of his brows, the flat line of his lips, the dark glint of his eyes. It was a look that could mean anything from exasperated to indifferent to battle-ready.

The marker I was holding fell to the floor.

The marriage was fake. The attraction to my future husband…that was all too real.

He held up a hand in greeting and glanced around at the desks and chairs stacked to the ceiling in one corner, boxes piled in another. It was clear he'd expected a less rustic situation.

"I have time," I said, more for my benefit than his. "It looks worse than it is."

He crossed the room toward the horseshoe-shaped table I'd designated as my chaos-free corner. "Why is it," he started, gesturing with his folder, "like this? Why hasn't the furniture been set up?"

"I haven't done it yet."

"Why are *you* doing it?"

I grabbed the marker off the floor and secured the cap. "That's what teachers do, Noah. We don't have first-day-of-school fairies who make everything beautiful and organized." I pointed at the rolled-up rug perched on the windowsill. "That's part of the reason I was so frazzled yesterday. I usually work on prepping my room over the course of three weeks, not three days."

"That, and the pudding cup."

I dropped back into my chair. "Shut up about the pudding cup."

He looked around again, tapping the edge of the folder against his palm. When finished with his perusal, he said, "I brought the prenup. I want to go over it before"—he tipped his head toward the door—"we finalize anything."

I pulled my bag from the chair on the other side of the table. "Let's do it."

He studied the chair. It was second-grade-sized. "Seriously?"

"I sit in little kid chairs every day. You'll survive."

Another moment of staring passed before he dropped into the chair. His knees were level with the table. Somehow, it did nothing to dampen the power of that suit.

He opened the folder, saying, "This is a standard prenuptial agreement that states both parties will retain the assets and liabilities they bring into the union. Since I've requested use of your assets—"

Why did that sound filthy?

"—I've added language indicating I'll fairly compensate you—"

And that. Dirty as hell.

"—though both parties may agree to non-monetary compensation. In other words, we could take it out in trade."

And that. Definitely *that.*

"Prepping your fields, for example," he continued. "I have no desire to haggle with you over every inch—"

Wow. Right? I wasn't imagining this.

"—and all goods or services would be subject to your full consent, of course."

I fumbled for my water bottle. "Mmhmm."

He flipped a few pages. "Any products of this union—real estate, business ventures, offspring—"

"Offspring?"

He held up his hands and let them fall to his lap. "Obviously that's unlikely in our circumstances but it's standard for these agreements."

I toyed with my water. It was a good place to fixate. "Okay."

He traced the edge of the paper, silent a moment. "You should have your own counsel review this before signing."

"Isn't that what you're doing?"

"No, Shay, I'm telling you what's in the document but I don't represent your interests. You should have someone else."

"Like the guy in Florida who explained Lollie's crazy will to me?"

Noah rolled his eyes to the ceiling. "He definitely doesn't represent your interests. No. Not him."

"Would've been nice for him to mention that," I mumbled.

"Your mother," Noah started, "she must have—"

"Even if she does, I'm not calling her," I interrupted. "I don't have anyone. If we need to wait so I can find a lawyer, we'll wait." I motioned to the long checklist at my right. "You know where to find me."

He glanced at the list and then at me, his gaze shifting from my eyes to the crab earrings. An inkling of a smile pressed at his lips. "I cannot be objective or impartial, and I'd be lying if I said I could be, though you should know it's a fair agreement. Anything I added beyond the standard language is intended to protect and benefit you. But I won't fault you if you want to wait."

I noticed for the first time the sun-kissed highlights in his dark hair. Another thing hidden under those hats. "Do you think I need to wait?"

"No."

I flipped through the pages, reading each line and comprehending a decent amount of it. When I came to the end, I asked, "Should I sign this one? Or your copy?"

He pulled a pen from inside his suit coat, handed it to me. "Yours. You first. I'll take care of everything else."

I could not be the only one hearing this.

Then, "Nice earrings."

"Don't make fun," I replied.

"Give me some credit." He futzed with his cuffs. "I'm not about to insult my wife on our wedding day."

As impossible as it should've been, that was the first time someone had referred to me as their wife and that knowledge blindsided me. The ex never used that word. It was always girlfriend or fiancée, and I should've noticed that red flag a long, *long* time ago. Though in this moment, I hated the amount of mental energy I'd spent on the ex today. He didn't need it and he didn't deserve it from me.

When I didn't respond because I was busy rewinding the game tape on the past year of my life, Noah added, "I'm truly not teasing you. They're cute. They're"—he skimmed a gaze over my romper—"not what I would've expected." He cleared his throat. "But they're you."

We stared at each other for a moment, me with his pen clutched in my hand and him with that loosened tie I itched to straighten for him.

Then, the bubble burst.

Noah pointed at the document. "If you want to sign that today, do it now. We need to get there before they close for the lunch hour."

I uncapped the pen. Time to hurry up and get married. "Right."

THE DRIVE to Providence didn't take long and I appreciated the hell out of that. Neither of us knew what to say and I couldn't be the only one with the same questions playing on a loop in their head: *What the hell am I doing? Why the hell am I doing this? What if it's the worst decision I've ever made and I screw up everything with Twin Tulip? What if it's not the worst decision? What happens if this works out?*

Hope was such a sticky thing. And it was sneaky too. Always showing up in the moments it was least welcome.

Noah parked in an underground garage. Without looking at me, he asked, "You're sure you want to do this?"

What the hell am I doing? Why the hell am I doing this? "Are you?"

He closed his fingers around the keys, nodded. "Fair enough."

We walked out of the garage and up to the street where the sun was blinding, and thick, oppressive heat seemed trapped between the buildings without anywhere to go. Thank god I'd opted for a short romper with an air vent. I would've wilted otherwise.

Noah brought his hand to my back, steering me away from the curb. "It's up here," he said, the words tight. He must've been sweltering in that suit.

He led me down the street, that hand never far from my back, and into an old building with a gray granite façade. It was blessedly cool in here, and quiet too. As if we were the only people in the world who could think of marriage on a day like today. He pointed me toward a door at the end of a long hallway and my sandals snapped against the stone floors, fracturing the air-conditioned stillness.

Noah held the door open for me, saying, "Last chance to change your mind."

"Hardly. There are at least ten more opportunities to run out of here like my pants are on fire. This is just the first of the final chances."

"Not sure if that's supposed to reassure me"—he shifted his hand to the exposed skin where the romper cut out, his fingers sliding beneath the fabric—"or make me hold on tighter."

This guy really needed to stop with all these comments. I was not built to withstand such things, especially not while our marriage was very fake and my attraction to him was becoming very real. Not that I would ever act on that attraction. There was no way we could complicate our lives any further.

"Reassure." I said this but I didn't step away from his touch. "I swear, I won't run off. First, it's too hot to run and I wouldn't get far in these shoes, but also, I'd never do that to someone. I don't believe in walking away and leaving without an explanation. I'd have the most awful, uncomfortable conversation of my life before doing that."

"Good to know." He glanced inside the office. "Shall we?"

The paperwork was quick. Noah insisted on paying the license fee. We waited, glancing between an old painting of Providence and notices about upcoming election deadlines.

Since I had no idea what to say, I asked, "Is it blueberry season now? Or has that passed?"

At the same moment, Noah asked, "How long will it take to get the classroom ready?"

We forced brittle laughs and motioned at each other to go ahead, which resulted in another forced laugh.

"Your classroom," he said, ending this standoff.

"I'll be busy for a few days," I said. "But it will be okay. I'll get it done."

"I'd offer to send Gennie to help but I'm not sure I could talk her into going to school when it's not required. Even if it means spending time with you."

“Let’s not subject her to that.” I clasped my hands in front of me. “So, those blueberries?”

“Blueberry season is over for the year. We’re doing peaches, melons, and early season apples. And quince. Quince is big.”

“What…is quince, exactly?”

He dipped a hand into his pocket and gave a bashful grin. “It looks like a pear. Green skin, golden-yellow fruit, seeds on the inside. Tart. Super tart. No one eats it raw. Great for jams though. Exceptional for balancing sweetness and adding dimension.”

“Quince.” I said it slowly. “Sounds like a jam good time.”

Noah’s eyes creased as he chuckled. “Still want to marry me now that I’ve outed myself as a quince enthusiast?”

“Still want to marry me now that I’ve started with jam puns?”

Noah began to respond but a door opened, our names called. He gave me half a smile. “Another last chance.”

I didn’t have a single good reason as to why I was doing this. Loads of mediocre reasons, a few flat-out bad ones. Several unreasonable ones too. But I shook my head and motioned for him to follow me.

The ceremony was remarkably fast. Without the bells and whistles of a full wedding production, there wasn’t much to it. Flash some identification, answer some questions, say “I do” a few times, and that was it. That was the whole thing.

To think, I’d devoted months upon months to planning a wedding down to every picture-perfect minute and this one was said and done in fewer than five.

“Are you exchanging rings?” the alderman asked.

“Oh, I—” I grimaced up at Noah. Did fake marriages require rings? “No. I don’t know. I don’t think so?”

“Here.” Noah reached into his trouser pocket and retrieved a brown string. “It’s twine,” he said as if he was apologizing. He took my hand. “We tie it around our jam jars. I had an extra piece and”—he kept his gaze low as he looped it around my fourth finger, tied a bow—"you don't have to keep it."

"I didn't think," I started, shaking my head as if that would explain all the reasons I hadn't thought to bring something for him. "I'm sorry."

"No need," he said, still occupied with the twine.

The alderman glanced between us several times before continuing. "By the power vested in me by the state of Rhode Island, I am pleased to be the first to announce you as husband and wife. Congratulations."

Noah tore his gaze away from my hand and up to my face, his expression as cool and stony as the front side of this building. I would've given anything to know what he was thinking.

Instead, I pulled my hand from his hold and held it up in the universal high five position.

As one did upon getting fake married.

After a pause where he only blinked at my hand, Noah slapped his palm to mine. I threaded my fingers between his and pumped our joined hands like we'd just won a cutthroat game of doubles ping-pong.

Noah laughed quietly. "Come on, wife. Let's get you some lunch."

"THIS IS REALLY GOOD," I said, jabbing my fork in the direction of my plate.

"Is it good or is it that your frame of reference is limited to pudding cups and popcorn?"

I took another bite of the summer tomato salad and considered Noah's question as I chewed. "It's really good. And I don't just eat pudding and popcorn."

"Oh, right. Can't forget about the Cheez-Its."

"And rice," I said between bites. "I reheat a lot of rice."

Noah glanced out the window at the foot traffic on North Main Street while he drummed his fingers on the tablecloth. "Don't tell me that," he murmured.

I rustled in the bread basket. "Why not? It's the truth. I don't see any reason to shelter you."

He turned back to me and drew his fingers into a fist. It struck me then how right he looked in this upscale restaurant. The plaid shirts and worn jeans were deceptive but this boy knew how to order wine by the bottle and fit right in with the weekday power lunch crew. My view from this side of the table was immaculate.

"Manhattan must've loved you," I said.

He arched a brow. "In what way?"

I gestured to his suit, the still-askew tie. "Oh, you know. All the ways Manhattan loves big law and a Tom Ford suit." When his eyes narrowed, I added, "In the best ways, Noah. I swear, the best. I bet you had a lot of fun there."

He chuckled. "I didn't suffer."

"Are you telling me you were a party boy?"

Another chuckle. "Not nearly. No. But things worked out nicely for me in the city. I did my internships under the most senior partner at the firm. He'd come up from an agricultural family from Maine and hated his way through Yale the same way I did and—"

"You hated Yale? Are you kidding me? That's all you'd ever wanted."

He paused, sighed, carefully chose his words. "I didn't *hate* it but"—he shook his head, dragged his teeth over his lower lip—"dreams and realities rarely align. Anyway, this partner took me on and made a point of bringing me to all the lunches, all the dinners, all the events on yachts and at Hamptons beach houses that somehow qualified as billable hours. It was an education."

"And you signed on at that firm after you finished law school?"

"Yeah." He flattened his hand on the tablecloth, curled it into a fist again. "I had it good under that partner. A signing bonus that made a lot of problems go away. The best assignments. I didn't spend a minute on any of the usual junior associate drudgery. And he still took me on all the yachts and out to the beach houses. I didn't hate it."

"And the farm? Do you hate that?"

"I have my moments." He watched as I cut an enormous slice of tomato into quarters. "But it's a lot different now than it used to be."

Before his father passed. Before his mother moved away. Before Gennie came into his care.

He cleared his throat, shifted in his seat. "If it's good with you, I'm going to start making some calls about financing for the Twin Tulip project. In the meantime, try to put some flesh on the bones of your idea. The more detail, the better. I can have someone work it into a business plan."

"Okay." I popped a forkful of tomato, mozzarella, and basil into my mouth. "Is there anything else that you need from me now that we've"—I wiggled my shoulders which yielded a light huff of laughter from him—"officially lost our minds?"

He glanced over his shoulder, gestured to the server for our bill. "What else would I need, Shay?"

I ran my thumb over the back side of my fingers, tracing the twine. *He didn't mean that the way it sounded. He didn't mean anything by it.* "Nothing that I can think of."

I WAS BACK in room nine the next morning, a bucket-sized cup of iced coffee sweating on the horseshoe table and a plan of attack in hand when they arrived. Four of them, each bearing the unmistakable glower of teenage disinterest and grayish-blue t-shirts reading *Little Star Creamery Crew* over the heart.

"Mr. Barden told us to come here and move furniture," one of the girls said. She looked familiar but I couldn't place her face.

"Where do you want this stuff?" the tallest boy asked. His voice was somewhere down in the basement. "Do you have, like, a seating chart? We could set up the desks from that."

"I can do the bookshelves," the other girl said, holding up a hand. "I can just sit and put books on the shelves, right? I don't have to carry anything?"

"Noah. Sent you," I said. "He sent you *here*?"

"Yeah," the tall boy said. "We're not allowed to leave until it's finished so…" He motioned to the room. "What do you want us to do?"

Now that the initial shock of being gifted four teenagers had worn off somewhat, I said, "You're precious but I'm all set. Really. Thank you for checking in though."

The girl I couldn't place shook her head. "Mr. Barden said you'd say that and we're supposed to tell you it's nonnegotiable." She gestured to herself. "Like Brady said, we're not allowed to leave until it's done. I'm Lillian, that's Schultzy, and that's Camille." She slipped her hands into her jean shorts. "Where should we start?"

The tall one, Brady, popped in his earbuds. The quiet one, Schultzy, scanned the room. Camille added, "If we do this, Mr. Barden said we could have Friday night off and I haven't had a Friday off all summer." She glanced at her phone. "I really don't want to work this Friday."

I rubbed my thumb over my palm, tracing the spot where Noah had tied a scrap of twine around my finger less than twenty-four hours ago. That ring was on the windowsill in my bedroom at Thomas House now. It didn't feel right to wear it today, knowing I was going to be arranging desks and moving bookshelves. It would get snagged somewhere and I didn't want that.

Also, I didn't need to wear a wedding ring because I had no need to communicate that I was married. That was the most relevant reason. Not wanting to ruin the ring was secondary. Obviously.

Lillian pointed to the rolled-up rug. "The rug probably has to go down first. Where should that go?"

"In front of the whiteboard," I said. I couldn't rob these kids of a free Friday night, even if I didn't know what to think about Noah shipping them off to me.

It was the strangest wedding gift anyone had ever received. And it was so sweet that I couldn't wipe the smile off my face all day.

chapter thirteen

Noah

Students will be able to negotiate under less than ideal circumstances.

A SLAMMED DOOR. "I want to wear shorts!"

"Then wear shorts," I called up the stairs.

Drawers opened, banged shut. "I don't have any!"

I dropped my head against the wall. There was no way this morning could get any worse. A goat on the loose, another refrigeration problem at the bakehouse, a last-minute staffing issue at a farmers market, and now a niece stomping around in underwear and an eye patch. "You do. They're in your drawer. The bottom one."

Stomp, stomp, stomp. "I can't find them!"

"Look in the bottom drawer," I said. "Come on. We're already late. We gotta go."

"I don't want to go," Gennie shrieked. "I hate farmers markets."

"I'm sure the frozen lemonade truck will be there." I wasn't above bribery. I wasn't above lemon slush for breakfast. Not at all. "And Mr. OJ usually comes to this market. I bet he's going to have a bunch of knives to sharpen today but you won't get to see any of them unless you put some clothes on and come down here."

There was a moment of silence. I expected her to flip some furniture or push her toy box down the stairs though she opened the door and came to the landing in shorts and a t-shirt that didn't match but I didn't care. "Only if Shay can put a fancy braid in my hair."

"Shay? I don't know if she's awake, kid. It's early." And I didn't know if my wife of four days wanted me knocking on her door at seven on a Saturday morning. Hell, I didn't even know her weekend routine. Maybe she was already up and out for the day. Maybe she was still asleep, all alone in a big bed with a nightshirt rucked up to her waist and the sheets tangled around her legs and—*fuck*, no, I couldn't go there right now. I had places to be and problems to solve, once again. "I can give it a try. I think I have the hang of it since the last time Shay braided your hair."

Gennie folded her arms over her chest. "Your braids are not pretty. They're loose and ugly."

"Then a ponytail," I said. "I can do that."

"Fancy. Braid."

"Gen, we really don't have time for that." She stared at me, her dark eyes hard and her hair a tangled mess. It would take me twenty minutes to deal with that. I knew I was getting something wrong by capitulating to this little terror's demands but I didn't know what else to do. I had to cover this market and I didn't have time to fuck around. I pulled out my phone and shot a quick text to Shay telling her to expect us in five minutes. "All right. We'll visit Shay. If she doesn't come to the door, we have to leave. We can't wake her up. Okay?"

Gennie nodded. "That's fair."

I motioned her down the stairs. "Come on, then. You can put your socks and shoes on in the truck. Let's go."

Shay didn't text me back during the short ride to Twin Tulip. That left me standing on the porch, glancing between my phone and the windows bracketing the pair of front doors. I couldn't decide if I wanted to see the strawberry-blonde shimmer of her hair through the window. I mean, I wanted to see her. I always wanted to see her. But I had no idea what to do with my limbs or how to produce words when I was with her, and I couldn't repress the whisper in my head that never failed to say *that's your wife*.

When she came to the house on Wednesday to work with Gennie, I'd been stuck on the phone with an equipment supplier and only managed to wave when she left for the evening. Didn't even get a chance to haggle over her staying for dinner. Wheatie and I spent most of yesterday afternoon planning improvements to the goat operation—of which we were in desperate need if this morning's runaway was any proof—and I'd lost track of time. Shay was already packed up and heading out when I arrived. She had to talk to Emme about lesson plans for second grade or something and couldn't stick around.

So, we were married but we rarely saw each other and hardly spoke. We both wanted it this way and it had to be this way yet that didn't leave me any less off-balance. I had the definite sense that things were supposed to be different—*I* was supposed to be different—and going about my lost goats and stompy niece life as usual was like walking around all day with a pebble in my shoe.

"You're not supposed to knock," Gennie said. "We're supposed to go inside."

I cut her a glance. "I don't think that guidance applies to weekend mornings."

She gave me an eyeroll-shrug combo that spoke a preteen language I wasn't prepared to hear from her yet. "She told me I could come in whenever I wanted. That I was always welcome here and I never had to knock or ding the bell."

I motioned to the door. "Go ahead. Show me how it's done."

I assumed the door would be locked because it was too damn early for anyone other than farmers and lunatics to be up and out but Gennie turned the knob and stepped right inside. "Come on," she said, waving me forward. "Aren't we late and in a big fucking hurry?"

"Oh my god," I muttered. I followed my niece, closing the heavy oak door behind me. We stood in the entryway, glancing to the front parlors on either side of us. They were empty save for some old rugs, an antique piece of furniture or two. Shay's book bag sat at the base of the stairs, a pair of sandals on the next riser.

"Shay! Can you fix my hair?" Gennie yelled.

No response.

"Hello?" I called, stepping closer to the staircase.

"Maybe she's not home."

"Her car is outside," I replied.

"Maybe she went for a walk. She goes for walks and listens to audiobooks."

I glanced at Gennie. How did this kid know everything about my wife while all I had was a fondness for bread and wacky earrings? "If that's the case, we should—" A crash came from the back of the house and then a yelp. *What the fuck was that?* I held out a hand, saying, "Stay right here. Do not move. Not a single muscle. Do you understand?"

"Aye aye, captain."

I jogged down the hall, opening doors and glancing inside as I went. I hadn't been inside Thomas House in years, and in that time, I'd forgotten the *double the fun* chaos of this place. So many doors. So many little hallways. It was ridiculous.

When I heard another small crash, my heart buried itself deep in my gut and all I could think was *find her, find her now*. I forced open the closest door, prepared to find Shay trapped under a collapsed ceiling or a mountain of overturned boxes.

That was not how I found her.

She was bent over the lip of an old cast-iron bathtub, scrub brush in hand, ass up, and completely naked.

Shay.

Naked.

In front of me.

And it wasn't the remnant of a dream. This was entirely real. This was my reality, right now. I knew it was real because the haze of a recent shower filled the small bathroom, mingling with the sharp tinge of cleaning products. My dreams were never lemon scented.

Her hair was wrapped in a towel and her perfect heart-shaped ass stared back at me while she scrubbed the tub like she was trying to cover up a crime.

What the actual hell is happening?

I must've spoken those words because Shay hooked a glance over her shoulder and promptly screamed. She scrambled to pull the shower curtain around her while I stood there—too stunned and helpless in the face of all that plush, glorious skin to ever leave her alone again—and I aimed my gaze at the ceiling.

"I'm sorry," I said. "We knocked. We came inside and called for you. Then I heard something fall and it sounded bad and—"

"I didn't hear you," she said, still breathless. "I had my earbuds in."

"I'm so sorry. I didn't—I mean, I didn't see anything."

An unsteady laugh crackled out of her. "I seriously doubt that, Noah."

I didn't know how to respond. The truth was, the memory of her plump ass was going to haunt my descendants for the next thousand years and I had no desire to apologize for it. It was going to haunt me just the same. Worse yet, I had to spend the morning slinging jam and didn't have a single minute to devote to closing my fist around my shaft and indulging in those memories. At best, I'd have to walk around with that visual for another eighteen hours before I could get some privacy and put the memory to good use, which was a terrible, *terrible* type of torture.

I gulped down all the words rushing to the front of my mind. None of that belonged here. "Gennie wanted a fancy braid," I managed. "Obviously, this isn't a good time so—"

"Give me five minutes. Okay?"

"You don't have to do that."

"I know." Another shaky laugh. "I don't mind. Just give me five minutes. I'll meet you outside."

That was my cue to leave. I knew that yet I didn't move. Even as I stared hard at the ceiling, the shape of her remained in my peripheral vision. The shower curtain shielded her from view but now I knew the look of her bare skin and I couldn't stop thinking about it. More than that, I wanted to stay here and stand guard.

"I heard a crash," I said, "and it sounded like you were hurt."

"I knocked over all the bottles. Shampoo, conditioner, hair mask, body wash, face wash. All of it. But I'm okay. It startled me. That's all. No worries."

I nodded to the ceiling. "Got it. Okay." I couldn't stop nodding. "We'll just—we'll be outside."

I stepped into the hall, pulled the door shut behind me. Inhaled deep enough to make my ribs hurt. Blew it all out until I saw stars. None of it eased the ache pulsing inside me. Inside my jeans.

I returned to the entryway and found Gennie exactly where I'd left her. "Outside," I said, pointing to the door. "We're going to wait for Shay outside."

We sat on the porch steps, Gennie occupied with tearing the hem on her t-shirt while I stared at my hands. Shay emerged a few minutes later, her hair gathered in a wet bun and a flowery dress swirling around her ankles. I wasn't sure but it seemed like the long dress had something to do with me walking in while she was naked.

It also seemed like I could have that dress over her head and on the floor in three seconds flat but that probably wasn't her intention.

"Hello there," she called to Gennie. She kept her gaze miles away from me. "What are we doing with your hair today?"

"Noah is making me go to the market with him and I need a fancy braid for that," she replied.

Shay settled next to Gennie. "I think I can manage a fancy braid. Why don't you sit on the next step down so I can reach you?"

Gennie moved into position before asking, "Are you coming to the market?"

For a minute, Shay only brushed the snarls out of Gennie's hair. Then, "I'm not sure. I have a few things to do this morning so I might not be able to make it there in time."

"It's at a different place than the other market," Gennie explained. "This one is at an extra old farm. I'm going to have frozen lemonade for breakfast. But not the watermelon flavor. That's not for breakfast."

"Mount Hope," I murmured. "That's the farm she's talking about."

Shay nodded as she started pulling Gennie's hair into a braid. "That sounds very exciting."

"It's not," Gennie replied. "Markets are boring as fuck."

"Gennie," I warned.

"But you should come to this market and then I won't be bored," she continued. "And I can show you the sheep that live at the farm place and the little duck pond too. And there's a tent where they sell all kinds of twisty breads. Noah doesn't know how to make those yet."

"Babka," I said.

"And Dottie got out of the goat house this morning," Gennie added.

"These goats," Shay said. "Always getting into trouble." She twisted a hair tie off her wrist, fastened it around the end of the braid. "You are fancy and braided, my dear. How do you like it?"

Gennie ran her palm over the braid, her face lighting up. "I love it," she said, flinging herself at Shay. "Can I go check on the fairies? I'll be fast."

I nodded. "Go ahead." We were already late. Five more minutes didn't matter. When Gennie was out of sight, I clasped my hands between my knees, saying, "I am so sorry."

"I should probably apologize," she said, still avoiding my eyes. "I did tell you to come right in."

"I doubt any of this was what you had in mind."

"That's true," she said, laughing. "That's definitely accurate."

"May I ask," I started, as carefully as I could manage, "why you were cleaning the tub while—"

"Unclothed? Nude? Starkers? What works best for you?"

I put my head in my hands because all I could see was her bare body and I was trying to do the right thing here. Trying to be respectful. Throwing the word *nude* around didn't help. "Honestly, Shay, I have no idea."

"So, it's like this." From the corner of my eye, I saw her spread her hands out the way she did when she had a story to tell. "It never occurs to me to clean the bathroom until I'm *in* the bathroom. I decide I can't live another minute without getting to those tub stains because I see them, and the minute I leave the bathroom, they vanish from my consciousness. I finish my shower and then get right to it. No time like the present, right? And that's how I end up on my hands and knees, naked, scrubbing the tub." When I didn't respond, she added, "I'm pretty sure everyone does it that way. At least people who live alone."

"I…I don't know if that's accurate."

"Perhaps not," she said. "Have I traumatized you?" She glanced over at me. "I've traumatized you. Oh my god. I'm sorry. You've seen my asshole and now you're traumatized." She burst into laughter, leaning against me as it shook her body. "You're going to need to burn that vivid view of my ass from your memory, aren't you?"

"As your husband, I'm not allowed to be traumatized," I said. "It's the law."

"It's the law," she repeated, her laughter turning hysterical. "I guess it's a good thing we're married now. Otherwise, you'd need decades of therapy. Maybe some brief in-patient treatment." I hooked an arm around her shoulder, held her as she gasped for breath. Tears streaked down her cheeks and it took everything inside me to keep from kissing them away. "I can't believe that happened. You saw my whole ass, Noah. And god only knows what else."

I squeezed her. "I told you. I didn't see anything."

"Are you allowed to lie to your wife?"

"I'm not obligated to answer that." I brushed a loose strand over her ear. Because I was an absolute masochist, I said, "Come to the market with us. We'll forget it ever happened."

She swept her fingers under her eyes and down her cheeks. "That sounds like a terrible idea. You're going to give me the shifty eyes all day and act like you want to jump into an active volcano. All while you try to block memories of my naked tub scrub routine."

I didn't know where it came from but the laugh that burst out of me was a loud howl that seemed to trigger another round of giggle-sobs from Shay. I clutched her tight to my chest, her tears soaking through my shirt.

That was how Gennie found us and what led her to announce, "Adults are really weird."

chapter fourteen

Shay

Students will be able to sell jam and jealousy.

I SAT in my car for twenty-five minutes, switching back and forth between continuing to die of embarrassment and hoping Jaime's roommates wouldn't mind when I moved in with them again. That was the only smart solution. I had to go back to Boston. No one could get caught ass-up in a cloud of cleaning products without immediately going into hiding.

I'd start over—one more time—and do it from the safety of Jaime's cozy apartment. I'd make myself useful by doing everyone's laundry and keeping the kitchen cupboards stocked. I'd sort the mail and preview new reality TV to know which episodes were worth watching and which to fast-forward through.

Maybe I'd do that. I'd leave. No one would mind. Noah would notice, but after seeing me in the least flattering position known to humanity he'd probably appreciate my disappearance. Gennie would notice and the school too but they'd replace me within an hour or two. Someday, they'd understand that I didn't have a choice.

Though instead of screaming into pillows or preparing for my exit, I was parked outside the Mount Hope farmers market. To this point, I hadn't been able to convince myself to go in—or get the hell out of here.

After wasting another five minutes, my need for coffee won over my desire to flee.

I was out of pudding cups—Cheez-Its too—and while I had a dozen eggs from Noah and Gennie's henhouse, I didn't like eggs enough to bother with making them for breakfast. They were too much of a reminder of how I'd choked down soft-boiled eggs and flavorless turkey breast for lunch every day in the name of fitting into my wedding dress. In the name of making myself smaller and smaller and smaller until I could barely find the true threads of myself, the ones I'd abandoned in my quest to be perfect.

I could still taste the bitter hollowness that came with forcing myself to eat things I loathed because I'd convinced myself the struggle was worth it. That I could deal with it. That I deserved it.

Alas, coffee was my only hope this morning, and I could see the tents and flags of several coffee vendors to choose from at this market. Knowing that, I couldn't justify leaving now. Well, I could but I'd accomplish nothing more than making myself hangry and I was finished with being starved and salty.

The first thing I noticed when I crossed the field toward the market was the long line at the Little Star table. The blue-gray pop-up tent had at least twenty people waiting and that was substantial as far as these events went. Naturally, I based this knowledge on attending all of one previous market but I'd paid attention that day with the girls. I was observant.

I grabbed a coffee and pastry, and wandered toward Little Star. I approached from the side, playing a good game of being too preoccupied with my drink to make eye contact with anyone else.

But I noticed Noah right away. He was a blur of motion as he unpacked a crate of jam, pulled bread from baskets behind the table, reached into the cooler for cheese, tapped at the point of sale system. His hat shielded his eyes from view though a tight grimace twisted at his lips. Gennie had her eye patch on her forehead as if it was concealing a third eye. She was busy organizing the jars Noah had set on the table.

They usually had more help. And they definitely needed it now.

Without much thought, I hurried toward the table, waving to catch Noah's eye. He didn't notice. He was occupied with the tablet which didn't seem to be working the way he wanted and a customer who didn't seem happy about the shortage of seedless raspberry jam today.

I stepped behind the table, saying, "Put me to work."

He watched as I set down my coffee and pastry, wiped my hands on the skirt of my dress, and quickly scanned the setup. For a second, it looked like he was prepared to argue, to send me off into the market while he slogged it out here. But then he realized that was bananas and said, "We'll make two lines. Gennie will run the point of sale for you. Everything is labeled. It's not difficult, it's just—" He glanced at the line. "It's not usually this crazy."

Gennie bounded toward me, empty milk crate in hand. She took her place behind the second tablet, saying, "I'll show you the ropes, matey."

And with that, we plunged into the wild world of working the hottest table at the farmers market.

It didn't take long to get the line under control but the people never stopped coming. They never stopped asking for seedless raspberry or strawberry jam either. In fact, they seemed to take it as a personal offense that we'd sold out of both in the first hour of the market.

"Is it always like this?" I asked Noah between customers.

His gaze on his tablet, he said, "This one is always busy. We usually have four people working the table but there were issues this morning." He glanced up, pointed at the jam jars in front of me. "Where did all the blackberry thyme go?"

I waved at Gennie. "We sold it."

"Are you sure?"

"Yeah. I'm sure." I laughed.

"We never move much of the blackberry thyme." He narrowed his eyes, giving me a close study. "How are you doing that? What's your secret?"

I folded my arms across my chest. "No secret. Just telling everyone it's my favorite. It's easier than dealing with the raspberry rage. Speaking of which, why don't you have more raspberry if it's the fan favorite?"

"Because we only have so many raspberries, Shay." Arching a brow, he asked, "Have you tried the blackberry thyme?"

"No, but they don't need to know that." With a shrug, I added, "I'm sure you could do it too if you gave it a try."

He leaned a hip against the table. "What do you have in mind?"

I tipped my head toward the jars of blackberry thyme. "Choose your favorite underdog. I'll stick with mine. We'll see who sells the most."

"What does the winner get?" He glanced at the wave of customers heading toward the tent.

"Other than pride? Other than bragging rights?" I tapped a finger to my lips. "Winner's choice."

"Oh, that's dangerous." He scanned the crates behind the table. "I'm choosing—hmm. How about strawberry nectarine?"

"That's your dark horse?"

"Yeah. Nectarines seem—I don't know—foreign. They're not as familiar as plums or as popular as peaches. We get a lot of strawberry purists who won't even entertain a blended option. I only make it because the nectarine adds amazing dimension to the strawberry. I keep waiting for people to figure that out."

"All right." I gave a single, confident nod. "Let's do this."

At first, we were mature about our competition. We redirected requests for strawberry and raspberry with gentle efficiency and talked up our jams like they were our first-born children. But we kept it clean.

Honest. The way a jam sales sprint between people posing as husband and wife was meant to be played.

But then I took a good look at the people queued in Noah's line. The clientele there clearly skewed feminine. The couples, the families, and the people who didn't require a side of beefcake with their jam came through my section of the line. And few of them wasted their time flirting with me.

Few but not zero.

On the other side of the line, the flirting was cranked all the way up. Every time he mentioned hand-selecting the nectarines that went into every batch, or how the strawberries were his springtime babies nurtured from little shoots in his greenhouse, his customers edged in closer, touched his arm or his wrist, and sighed out laughs that said *my panties are in my pocket and I'd be happy to bend over this table right now*.

Something spicy flared in my chest when one woman leaned in so far as she examined the jars that I didn't have to guess whether she was wearing a bra.

"That's another one of my favorites," I said, sidling over to Noah. I dropped my head against his bicep and skimmed a hand down his back. His ears were burning red. "It's great with a little goat cheese too. Have you tried that? Cheese, a touch of jam, some crusty bread? It's a whole Provençal moment."

Free Boob glanced between me and Noah, stopping at the spot where I used his arm as a pillow. She straightened, saying, "Umm, no, I haven't tried that. It sounds…great."

"I'll grab some for you."

As I turned toward the cooler, Noah let his fingers trail down my arm. "Thanks," he said softly.

Once Free Boob moved along, I put more effort into keeping an eye on Noah's customers. Most batted their lashes at him and cooed over his recommendations, and I took no issue with that. He was one fine farmer and he deserved the attention, though he didn't appear to know what to do with the attention, even if it was clearing out his stock of strawberry nectarine. His ears were still burning and his cheeks were flushed from more than the heat.

It was cute. My husband, the cutie.

"Do you make the jam yourself?" my next customer asked.

I smiled at him as I showed Gennie the labels of the jars he'd selected. "I do not make the jam though I have a hand in quality assurance. No batch goes unsampled."

What was a white lie here and there when it came to jam sales? Nothing at all.

"Important job." The customer gave me a winning grin. He was a bit older than me, probably in his early forties if the lines around his eyes could be trusted. His hair was blond and wavy, and he wore an untucked blue Oxford with shorts and boat shoes. "My mom loves your products. Every time I visit her up in New Hampshire, I have to bring as much as I can carry or she doesn't give me the time of day."

"Your mom's a lucky lady," I said, bagging the nine jars—including one blackberry thyme—he'd chosen. "Hand-delivered jam is quite the treat."

"She's going to lose it when I tell her I met the beautiful jam lady who personally guarantees each batch. What should I tell her your name is?"

Laughing, I said, "You can tell her Shay is the one sampling all the—oh!"

Noah wrapped an arm around my waist and yanked me into his side. "You can tell your mother you met the guy who creates the recipes too. I'm Noah."

"Oh, yeah. That's cool," the customer replied, his eyes wide with the newfound knowledge that the beautiful jam lady belonged to the growly jam man.

"That will be one three five, period zero zero," Gennie announced.

Fumbling for his wallet, he said, "Right. Thanks. Here you go."

Gennie shoved his card into the reader as he glanced at me and Noah again. "Mom's going to be thrilled to hear I met the—uh—couple behind Little Star Farms." When Gennie returned his card and shifted the screen toward him, he added, "The whole family, even."

"Send her our best," Noah said.

It sounded like "Go fuck yourself."

He kept his arm around my waist, his fingers splayed on the round pudge of my belly, while the customer stepped away from the table. I pointed toward the jars with the deep purple gingham fabric skirting the lid, each tied with twine. "Four more blackberries."

"You have me beat by three," he said, "but we have another hour until closing time. It's anyone's game."

"Have you figured out what you're playing for?" I shifted out of his hold and shot him a cheeky grin. "I know what I'm choosing."

He ran his gaze over my long, gauzy sundress. It was like a bedsheet with straps, completely shapeless and far more comfortable than flattering. I resisted the urge to fidget or prop my hands on my hips to create the illusion of an hourglass figure hiding under the billows of fabric.

"I have a few ideas. What have you decided?"

"Well, since I've already had a quartet of ice cream scoopers in to set up my classroom, I could use some help tending to Lollie's tulip field. I don't even know where to begin." I gave in to the desire to futz with my dress. "Thanks for sending the helpers, by the way."

"Did they take care of everything? They weren't supposed to leave until it was finished."

I peered at him. "Is that legal?"

"Legal enough," he replied.

"They did a great job. Thank you. Seriously. It was a big help. I hope they got their Friday night off."

He rubbed a hand over the back of his neck. He did that a lot. I couldn't tell if it was a nervous habit or if he really needed a good rubdown. Not that I was offering anything like that. Just…an observation.

"They got their Friday night." He shot a sidelong glance in my direction. "I heard you fed them pizza."

"Of course I fed them pizza! They moved all the furniture in my classroom! The girls organized the shelves and started my bulletin boards. They were there for three full hours. And they're growing kids."

Noah laughed. "I'm glad they did a decent job but don't let Schultzy fool you. He's not growing. He's just a bottomless pit."

"The girls put away an entire pizza between them."

"Also bottomless pits. Camille will take a spoon to the empty ice cream containers and scrape out the last bites at the end of the night. She won't throw away one of those five-gallon barrels until it's scraped clean."

We shared a smile before I said, "I appreciate it, Noah. It was a huge help. Thank you."

"It was no trouble." He seemed poised to continue but then he breathed out a curse and rolled his eyes. "You're welcome to interrupt the conversation to come with goat cheese and Provence," he muttered.

I followed his gaze toward a man in outrageously bright plaid shorts and a blazing yellow polo that might've been the actual sun. The man was headed straight toward us. "Why? What's happening?"

"Regional chamber of commerce," Noah said under his breath. "He lives in Friendship too. Always has some new initiative to get off the ground or an event in need of sponsors. Never has it adequately staffed or funded. Not great at taking no for an answer." He glanced at my iced coffee. An inch of water from the melted ice sat on top of the cold brew. "Tell me you've had more than a pudding cup today."

"That's not for you to worry about." I waved him back to his end of the table as another customer approached.

I did my best to listen to Noah's conversation with the polo shirt while helping another small wave of customers. I was almost at the end of my blackberry thyme supply. Victory was in sight.

"I'm proposing a summer street fair," Sunshine Polo said. "Early in the season. June, most likely. But I need big-name involvement to get it off the ground."

"Sounds great," Noah said, his arms folded over his chest and his jaw rigid. "You can connect with my marketing crew for—"

"You can't pawn me off on the little girl who runs your social media accounts, Barden. You know that's not how your father handled things—and for damn good reason."

I was certain I heard knuckles crack though it might've been molars.

"Marina is a marketing pro. She's better at all of this stuff than I am and she has the patience for it, which is a gift I don't possess."

Sunshine Polo seemed to ignore all of this. "Now, if I could get ahold of the boys with the oysters—"

"They don't do markets."

"But this is a street fair. Completely different."

"You'll need to convince them of that," Noah replied.

Sunshine Polo slumped back as if wounded by Noah's response. "Things really have changed," he muttered.

"Probably for the better, yeah."

He slumped even more. "Well, I'll be in touch with you. Thanks for the talk."

Not even thirty seconds had passed since Sunshine Polo turned his attention on the babka vendor when a woman bustled up to the table, calling, "I don't usually see you here, Noah Barden. To what do we owe this pleasure?"

Noah reached for the back of his neck again. "Schedules change," he said. "I go wherever they send me."

"It's a good thing they sent you here today." She pulled off her mint green bucket hat and set it atop the goods in her compact wagon. "We're starting up a new program with the Narragansett Bay senior centers.

Boxed meals for the shut-ins. We wanted to run it out of Middletown or North Kingstown but we can't find a commercial kitchen big enough for the volume we need. Then I remembered you have a brand spanking new kitchen over there at Little Star. Is there a day we could come in to prep the meals? We'd need four or five hours each week. I promise, we'd clean up after ourselves. We'd be the perfect guests." When he didn't respond immediately, she went on. "It's for a good cause. Some of these seniors don't have much. No one looking after them. It's heartbreaking, really. At least the Reverend has your aunt keeping her company. Some of these folks have no one."

"I recognize that," he said, his words straining for serenity. "Though I can't commit to anything without talking to my bakehouse manager."

"Oh, we won't get in her way."

"We have an overnight production run for our breads and a full daytime production run for everything else. I can't tell you off the top of my head when—*if*—we have five hours of downtime available." He shook his head. "I'll have to take this back to the farm and talk it over with Ny before I can tell you one way or another, Winnie."

"We could probably pull it off in four hours," she said. "I might have to whip the troops into gear but we can get it done. You can count on me for that!" She dropped a hand on the table, leaned toward Noah. "Wednesdays are good for me but I can swing Fridays too."

"Winnie, I really need to talk with—"

"We can't have the seniors going hungry, Noah. You don't want that any more than I do."

I pushed a pair of jams across the table to my customer while Gennie processed the payment. Stepping toward Noah, I pressed my chest to his side and held out my hand to Winnie McGuiltTrip. "Hi. I don't think we've met. I'm Shay. It sounds like you have an amazing plan in the works. I know we'd love to be part of it though we might not be able to give you everything you need to make this program shine. And that's the most important piece, Winnie. You don't want to kick-start this and not hit the heights you have in mind. That would be devastating. For everyone." I patted Noah's chest until he nodded in agreement. "Here's what I can do for you today. Send us an email with all the details. Every last one. What you'll need—space, equipment, time, all of it—and we'll sit down with the right people to see what we can do." I reached into Noah's back pocket and pulled out his wallet. I knew he kept a few business cards in there from the last time I went pawing around. "There's the email address. I know this is going to be great, even if we aren't the ones to make it happen with you. You have a passion inside you and I can tell it's unstoppable."

She took the card while giving us a warm, appraising look. "Aren't you two something. Noah, you didn't tell me there was a leading lady in your life." Before Noah could respond, she continued. "And it's about time you have one! It's long overdue as far as I'm concerned. You're such a handsome fellow now. I remember when you were younger. What a little meatball!"

Noah seemed to deflate and turn to stone at once. For reasons I'd yet to understand, this town was all too comfortable speaking about him unkindly and having the balls to do it to his face. It had always been this way. I'd heard the meatball comment too many times to count when we were kids. That everyone felt it was acceptable to discuss his body was the strangest thing in the world to me. It would never make sense.

"You must love that he's in such good shape now," Winnie said to me.

"Bodies are extremely temporary and they're the least interesting things about us. They carry us around while we're on this earth and there's nothing more I can ask from my body than that. I certainly wouldn't spend any time worrying about the size or shape of anyone else's body. Not when I could care about their heart and their mind instead." I gave Noah's chest another pat. It was better than grabbing that ugly bucket hat and smacking some sense into her with it. "Is there anything else you might need from us today? I have an exquisite blackberry thyme jam that everyone is going crazy for, plus a special batch of strawberry nectarine that won't be around for long."

"Oh, well—" She glanced down as I gestured to the jars. "One of each. I can be a little naughty this week."

"If jam is your version of naughty," I said, the humor thick in my words, "you don't want to see mine."

"Wine doesn't count, right?" she boomed. "It's medicinal."

"You're damn right it's medicinal," I said, taking her money. "Don't worry. I won't tell on you, Winnie."

She stowed the jars in her shopping wagon. "I'll give you a shout on the email this week. So nice meeting you, Shay. You make such a handsome couple."

As Winnie rotated to the next vendor and out of earshot, Gennie said, "I do not like her."

A hearty laugh cracked out of Noah, his broad chest shaking under my palm. "She means well," he managed.

"That's the worst part," I said. "It would almost be better if she recognized the toxicity wrapped around her good deeds and so-called compliments."

His hand warm on my waist, Noah said, "You were spectacular. I don't know how you do that thing where you change their mind without telling them they're wrong but I love you." He blinked hard. "I mean, I love how you handle people. You saved me twice this morning and I don't give a shit how much jam you move today, consider your fields plowed and planted."

Once again, these words did things in my mind. Dirty, depraved things.

Things my husband couldn't possibly intend.

Instead of thinking about that for another second, I asked, "How often does that happen? The one-two punch of ambush and guilt trips?"

"All the damn time." He took a step back and shoved his hands in his pockets. "There's this expectation that I live to take on the problems of the entire community. Like I want to rescue everyone simply because my dad ran himself into the ground doing it." He shook his head and the weight of this issue seemed to clear from his eyes. "How many jars of blackberry do you have left over there?"

I grabbed a jar. "Just one. What about you?"

He ran his fingertips over the jars, sorting them into groups. "I'll be damned," he murmured. "Just one for me too."

"Then we both win."

"I've already agreed to work your fields," he said. This man. My *god.* "What else do you want from me?"

"I…don't know."

"How about I get some time on the calendar with my general contractor? You can give him all your ideas for the wedding venue and he can get that ball rolling."

I nodded as I considered this. A general contractor seemed like a very large step forward with all of this. "Yeah. Maybe? I don't know. We don't have to focus on that right now. What about you? What do you want?"

His gaze softened for a split second. I would've missed it if I hadn't been watching him. "It's okay. I don't need anything."

"Maybe there's nothing you need," I said, "but there's something you want."

His ears turned a lovely shade of tomato.

Gennie piped up then. "You said you had to do something decent for Shay to make up for running into her house like an ape and not minding your goddamn manners this morning." She adjusted her eye patch to dangle from her neck. "You said you'd have to bring her a big fucking fruit basket. You said fucking. I didn't say fucking. It was you. But I think a big fucking fruit basket is dumb. No one wants a basket of fruit."

Noah ran a hand down his face. "Oh my god."

"What would you suggest, Gennie?" I asked.

She drummed her fingertips together like she was constructing an evil plot. "The playground at the park near the library has a pirate ship."

"A—a pirate ship?" I asked.

"It's a jungle gym thing," Noah said. "The fundraising effort for that project nearly sucked the soul from my body a few years ago but Gen loves it."

"You think we should go to the playground when we finish here?" I asked her.

"That's your alternative to a fruit basket?" he asked. "How does the pirate ship help Shay?"

"I really like the pirate ship. I wish I could have a pirate ship like that just for me." She toyed with the hem of her black-and-white striped t-shirt. "The frozen lemonade truck is there a lot too."

With Noah's gaze locked on his niece, he pointed across the market. "The frozen lemonade truck is right over there. We don't have to go to the playground to get you lemonade."

"But I had to work the pay machine and there were too many people waiting for you to do it alone." She shrugged. "And maybe Shay wants to see me climb all the way to the top of the crow's nest. I'm super good at climbing and being the lookout. Noah will like it too. He can sit on a bench alone and not talk to anyone. That's his favorite."

Noah and I exchanged a glance. I lifted my brows. He jerked a shoulder up. I grinned. He managed a crooked half smile. "Okay, Gennie. I think I need to see this playground."

"Are you going to sit on the bench with me?" Noah asked.

"I don't know," I teased. "I wouldn't want to ruin the alone-and-silent thing."

He hooked an arm around my shoulders and pulled me to his side. "You couldn't if you tried."

chapter fifteen

Shay

Students will be able to drunk dial.

WHEN THE SECOND week of school rolled around, I was tired but feeling really good. My students were remembering what school was all about and I was remembering what waking up every morning and functioning like a regular person was all about. Everyone at my school was welcoming and helpful, and though I missed my girls back in Boston, it felt good to find some new teacher friends.

Still, I didn't know what to expect when the principal popped into my classroom after dismissal on Wednesday afternoon. Aside from that first morning when she'd asked me a few questions and explained the position, I hadn't spoken much to Helen Holthouse-Jones. She was outgoing and enthusiastic, and everyone called her HoJo though I couldn't form that collection of sounds without snorting.

"How's it going, Miss Z?" she called, her assorted keys and badges on her lanyard clanking as she stepped into my room. "Doesn't look like they've run you off yet."

"They haven't," I said from my spot at the horseshoe table. "Not even close."

She nodded, murmuring, "Good, good," as she glanced at the self-portraits posted on the bulletin board. She strolled toward the table, pulled out a chair. "How are you? How is this going for you?"

"It's a great group of kids," I said, setting aside my lesson plans for next week. "I think we're off to a strong start."

She crossed her legs, fiddled with her lanyard. "You know what you're doing. The children like you, the team likes you. The parents from the other second grades are already complaining that they didn't get a chance to harass me into putting their kids in your class."

"Oh. Well. Thank you," I said.

She leaned back in the chair, clasped her hands around her knee. "Here's the story, Shay. I don't want to lose you. I don't want my counterpart over at Prudence Elementary to realize I have a veteran teacher in a long-term subbing role." She gave me a conspiratorial grin. "She'll poach you right out from underneath me."

Never would I have guessed that I'd entered into the high-stakes world of teacher poaching. "Okay," I said.

"Adelma Sanzi is going out in December for a knee replacement," Helen said. "She's saying she'll be back in January but I doubt we'll see her again until February." She gave me a wide grin. "How do you feel about third grade?"

"Third grade." I blinked down at the plans. Grace could explain everything about third grade to me. It was the only year she'd ever taught and she swore she'd never move because those kids were her people. But—*December*. That felt like a million years away. And February. My god. It was like doing advanced math in my head. Did not compute. Still, I had to stay through next summer if I wanted to inherit Twin Tulip. And I was mostly certain I wanted that. "I love that age."

"Good, good." Helen nodded. She wore running shoes and wrap dresses every day, kept her hair a slightly unnatural shade of burgundy, and if I had to guess, I'd say she was somewhere between forty-five and sixty. "Hildi Lazco, down in kindergarten, will be going out for maternity leave. She hasn't announced it yet and I know she won't until June because of the screwy way we handle paid leave but she won't be back until that kid is ready for school. I know kindergarten is your sweet spot and I want you in her classroom next year."

"Next…year," I choked out.

"It's crazy to talk about the next school year when this one is still getting out of the gate. Think about it for me, okay? Good, good. We'll talk again before Kelli comes back and before Adelma goes out for the knee. And if you need me, you know where to find me." She stood, pushed in the small chair. "You don't have to make any decisions today but I don't want to lose you, Shay. Good, good. Now, get out of here while the sun's still out."

I tried to respond but it was no use. The idea of teaching in this school, in this town, next year grabbed me like a hand around the throat. I couldn't breathe, couldn't think. What had started as a low-commitment subbing gig was now leap-frogging into the future with long-term assignments and permanent placements.

And what had started as a hazy idea of living out this year at Lollie's farm had leapfrogged into a fake marriage and rough drafts of a business plan.

A small knock sounded. I glanced over and found Gennie in the doorway. She waved though cast a wary gaze at Helen. "Come on in," I said. To Helen, I explained, "Gennie and I are neighbors. She catches a ride home with me on Wednesdays and then we practice reading together."

In our second conversation in as many weeks, Noah and I decided that I'd take Gennie with me on Mondays and Wednesdays. That way, he wouldn't need Gail to meet her at the bus stop and wait until I arrived. For now, we were pausing our Friday sessions. Gennie needed that time to unwind from being back in school, even if we were cautiously optimistic about this year for her.

After a pause, Gennie scurried across the room, stopping beside the table. "Hi," she whispered, her voice tiny as she stared at her shoes.

"Oh, I didn't know that," Helen murmured. "Gennie's lucky to have you, Miss Z."

I smiled at Gennie. "It goes both ways," I replied. "I'm lucky to hang out with such a radical reader."

Helen nodded, moving toward the door. "Think about next year," she sang.

"What does she mean about next year?" Gennie asked. "What's happening?"

I forced a smile though I still felt that tightness closing in around my throat. "Nothing important. Teachery stuff."

She glanced at the papers and folders spread out on my table. "Are you going to be a teacher next year too?"

"I—I'm always going to be a teacher," I said carefully.

She ran her finger along the edge of the table. "Will you be a teacher here?"

I watched her for a minute, wishing she'd meet my eyes so I could get a sense of her feelings. She didn't allow me that. "I'm not sure," I admitted. "I'm helping out Mrs. Calderon while she's with her new baby, and I'll help out some other teachers while they are away from school. I'm not sure who will need me next year. We'll have to wait and find out."

She tipped her head to the side, her lips twisted as if she didn't like my response. Then, "Okay. Can I have a snack when we get home?"

I chuckled. "We can definitely get you a snack."

"WHERE IS MY DOOR HOLDER?" I called at the back entrance to the playground. A student waved his arms, darted forward. "Thank you, Emmanuel. All right, let's remember our walking feet as we go outside."

While the class filed past me, the gym teacher jogged over. He was a younger guy, probably late twenties, and filling in for the regular gym teacher who was recovering from a jet ski accident. It was always the gym teachers getting into accidents with their toys. You never saw an art teacher with her arm in a sling after going wild with the oil paints.

"Hey, Miss Z," he called, the whistle around his neck bouncing as he approached. "How are we doing today?"

"We had a great morning, Mr. Gagne," I said, pitching my voice in the way all teachers did when gently warning their students to keep it together. "We practiced taking turns with materials and staying inside our body bubbles. I'm sure we're going to keep doing that during gym."

"I'm sure we will. Go ahead and sit on your squares." He stationed himself beside me, his feet spread and his arms crossed over his chest as he watched the kids wandering around the numbered grid painted onto the pavement. To me, he said, "You're coming out with us for happy hour, right?"

I didn't remember Mr. Gagne's first name but I knew he coached lacrosse and a few other high school sports and covered for gym teachers across the school district as needed. He also came with the familiarity of someone who considered all of his acquaintances to be close friends.

"I haven't thought much past dismissal," I said with a laugh. It was the straight truth. Things were going well but the first weeks of school were a flat-out sprint. Most days, I walked into the house, face-planted on the closest soft surface I could find, and slept for ten solid hours.

"A bunch of us are circling up for drinks," he said. "Are you in?"

I'd never met a happy hour I didn't like and there once was a time when I was the teacher rallying everyone for a Friday afternoon gathering, but I could only manage mild enthusiasm for this one. Mostly because I wanted to flop down on my bed and stay there for the next twenty-four hours but also because Mr. Gagne seemed like the kind of guy who used the words *brewskies* and *bruh* in ordinary conversations and I knew I couldn't hang with the brewskies and bros crowd for long. Especially when sportsball was involved. We weren't meant to be companions. It went against my nature.

"—and some of the foreign language teachers are coming too," he said. "Good people. You'll like them. I'm putting you on my list, all right? You can catch a ride with me and Valdosta. She coaches girls' volleyball."

"Where does everyone go for happy hour?" I asked, trying to come up with a bar in the area and failing. There was a semi-famous oyster bar in town but that wasn't a bar in the happy hour sense. And it was much too posh for a teacher outing. "Are there bars in town? I don't know any."

He laughed. "Nah, we go a couple of towns over. Better that way. No chance of running into parents." He blew his whistle, instructed the students to do ten jumping jacks. "Come on," he teased. "We don't bite. Promise."

Even though I'd curated a list of reasons as to why this wasn't the best choice for me and I could taste the regret on my tongue, I found myself saying, "Okay. When are you heading out?"

IN CASE ANYONE WAS WONDERING, regret tasted like cheap gin and Sprite masquerading as tonic.

Regret started out sweet in cloying, unpleasant ways and the gin burned the back of my throat. And then regret was bitter, as I attempted to cover up that sweetness with vodka and cranberry juice, but the saccharine lingered.

Worse than that poor excuse for a cocktail were my surroundings.

Low ceilings, dark walls, and a constant cloud of beer-scented humidity made this bar feel like an armpit of the underworld. Even worse than that, Gagne and Valdosta and all the other people I'd met tonight left while I was in the restroom.

I circled the bar twice, passing the now-empty table where a dozen or so teachers had been gathered for the past few hours and pausing at each shadowed booth and axe-throwing lane. I ducked into both bathrooms and checked the parking lot. Gagne's Honda was nowhere to be found.

Everyone was gone and they'd forgotten about me.

I refused to consider the possibility that they'd intentionally left me there. I couldn't do that. Not while gin and vodka made my thoughts slow and squishy.

I plopped myself down at the bar, resting my arms on the surface for a second before noticing it was sticky. The bartender approached and set a coaster in front of me. He was cute in a skinny guy, long beard kind of way. "What'll it be?"

Motioning to the table littered with beer pitchers, glasses, and decimated plates of chicken wings, I asked, "Do you know where that group went?"

He shot a quick glance over my shoulder and shook his head. "I just got here a few minutes ago."

"No worries," I replied, though I had many worries. "Could I get a vodka cranberry?"

I didn't need another drink. I didn't need the last two but the conversation had been flowing and it was easy enough to order another round, and then another. Though the group wasn't exactly my speed—heavy on the brewskies, bros, and sportsball, as I'd predicted—it was fun being with people and sharing in the struggles of back-to-school.

Tears stung my eyes as I thought about talking and laughing with the group all night only for them to pay the tab and walk out while I was away from the table. Of all the ridiculous things that had happened to me in bathrooms in the past month, from the pee-listening lady to Noah learning the topography of my ass, this one hit the hardest. I didn't want to cry over casual acquaintances but I knew I'd never let this happen to any casual acquaintance of mine.

The bartender set the drink in front of me but I didn't touch it. Instead, I pulled out my phone and logged into a car service app. I ended up opening and closing the app five times, assuming this sticky little corner of hell didn't have the best internet service, before realizing the shortage of cars on my screen wasn't a glitch.

No, there was only one car available in the area and it wouldn't arrive for forty-five to sixty minutes. I requested the car and stared at the screen for a moment, waiting for confirmation. It didn't come.

"I could've been in bed," I grumbled to myself. "Instead of talking about the freshest drama in girls' volleyball all night."

I opened my text messages, scrolled past Jaime, Audrey, Grace, and Emme. Even if they wanted to help me, they were more than forty-five to sixty minutes away. I stopped at Noah. We didn't text each other often. Hell, we didn't speak to each other often. Part of that was changing Gennie's schedule and the start of school. The other part was we hadn't figured out our relationship yet.

Not that we had a relationship.

We were married but only as a technicality.

And we were friends but more like old friends who didn't know how to pick up where they'd left off. There were moments when we slipped right into old familiarity and they were the best moments. It felt like I had my friend back. But there were moments when we stumbled over each other and we couldn't find our way through time and misunderstandings.

I tapped his name and read the last message he'd sent. It was from Wednesday, saying he was running a few minutes late at the dairy and would I mind hanging with Gennie a bit longer? Of course I didn't mind.

I started typing.

Shay: Why is it that car services are nonexistent in this part of the world?
Shay: I just think it's really rude that I have to wait 45–60 minutes for a ride.
Shay: You're always telling me that this town has changed but where the hell are the car services? What about food delivery? We are still in the backwoods as far as the important things are concerned.
Noah: Where are you right now?
Shay: I don't know.
Noah: I need you to do better than that. Where the hell are you?
Shay: I'm at a bar with sticky surfaces and axe throwing.
Noah: Have you been drinking?
Shay: Only a little bit.
Noah: Define little bit.
Shay: I started with a gin and tonic but that was heinous so I switched over to vodka cranberries because even the grossest bars have to be able to get that right.
Noah: And you don't know where you are?
Shay: Not a clue.
Noah: How did you get there?
Shay: With a lacrosse coach.
Noah: Can you ask someone the name of the bar? Or look around for a sign?

I WAVED TO THE BARTENDER. "What is the name of this place?"

He smiled as he ran a glance over my maple leaf earrings and down my navy t-shirt dress. "Billy's," he said. "That's what everyone calls it. Officially, it's Woodchuckers." He pointed toward the axe-throwing lanes. "Are you up for a round?"

"Hmm." I shook my head. "Maybe later."

"Holler if you change your mind," he said, stepping away. "I'll set you up."

Shay: The cute bartender said it's Billy's but also Woodchuckers.
Shay: He says I can throw some axes if I want. He'll set me up.
Noah: Tell the cute bartender you're married.
Shay: I'm only a little married.
Noah: Like you're only a little drunk?
Shay: Now it says my car won't be here for 75 minutes. This is bullshit.
Shay: It only takes 75 minutes to get somewhere in Rhode Island if you're coming from Massachusetts.
Noah: Cancel the car. I'll be there in 20 minutes.
Shay: You don't have to come get me.
Noah: That doesn't change the fact that I am.
Noah: Stay where you are. Drink some water. Don't touch any axes.
Noah: Or bartenders.

chapter sixteen

Noah

Students will be able to enforce limits and issue ultimatums.

I COULD HEAR my blood pressure in my ears when I pulled into the parking lot.

My wife.

At a bar.

With a lacrosse coach.

And a cute bartender.

Plus some motherfucking axes.

My headlights cut across a shabby building that was hardly more than a hole-in-the-wall, and not for the first—or fortieth—time tonight I wondered why the hell Shay was here. I killed the engine and stomped inside, damn near ripping the door off its hinges as I went. I didn't care if I was being a bear. I really did not.

Shay was seated at the bar, her head propped on her upturned palm and a half-empty tumbler of something pink in front of her. Her jean jacket was on inside out and her lips were pressed together in a deep frown that made it look like she was seconds away from bursting into tears.

I wanted to gather her up and hold her close and promise to make everything better.

I also wanted to wring her pretty little neck.

Stepping up beside her stool, I said, "I figured you were exaggerating." I swept a glance around the interior. "I was wrong."

She turned her face up to me, her eyes red and glassy, her makeup smudged onto her cheeks. "How did you get here so fast?" She picked up her phone, peered at the time. "That was only fifteen minutes. Wait. Sixteen."

Because my wife was alone and upset in a strange bar and speed limits don't apply in those situations.

"You forget I know all the shortcuts here in the backwoods." She watched as I waved down the so-called cute bartender and handed him some cash. "Does that cover it?" I asked him.

He arched a brow at the two twenties. "Yeah. We're good."

I wrapped an arm around Shay's waist, eased her off the stool. "Let's go," I said. "You're going to explain this situation to me in the truck."

"There's nothing to *explain*," she drawled as we stepped into the cool night air. "This part of the world doesn't know how to make a decent gin and tonic and everyone forgets me. I guess I'm not worth remembering."

I steered her away from the curb. "That's bullshit and you know it."

She wobbled on flat ground, leaving me no choice but to hook an arm behind her knees and carry her to the truck. She yelped, ringing her arms around my neck and saying, "Oh my god, Noah. What are you doing?"

"Quiet down. We're almost there," I said.

"Don't tell me to quiet down," she snapped. "You're going to hurt yourself. I'm not light."

"I know my strength, sweetheart. Don't you worry about me." I crossed the lot, stopping at the passenger side. "Still feeling woozy?"

"I'm not woozy," she replied, indignant as all hell. "It was my shoe."

"You use that excuse a lot. I have yet to believe it." I bent, setting her on her feet so I could open the door. "Did you eat anything tonight or are you running entirely on cheap liquor?"

I held her hand as she climbed inside. "I'm not answering that."

"Fantastic," I muttered, closing her door. I really wanted to understand this woman's thought process. Anything to explain why she was all the way out here in the diviest dive bar in the whole state with—what was it?—a lacrosse coach.

I settled into the truck, flipped on the heated seats because that short dress was no match for tonight's damp, chilly weather.

"Everyone forgets about me," she said in a sad, small voice.

I pulled out of the lot and headed toward the main road. "That's not true."

"If I wasn't forgettable, people wouldn't be able to leave me so easily and go on with their lives like nothing was different. And it just keeps happening. That's how I know it's true."

I was helpless here. I still wanted to wring her neck. I wanted her to apologize for shaving several years off my life. And I wanted to take her in my arms and let her cry it out because she didn't deserve this. She didn't deserve any of it.

"I don't think you're forgettable," I said. "Believe me. I know. I've tried to forget you. I couldn't. Nothing I did chased those memories away."

She sniffled. I reached into the back seat and blindly handed her the box of tissues I kept back there. Tissues, baby wipes, and emergency snacks were essential to my survival these days.

"Why did you want to forget me?"

"I wanted to forget everything about this town." That wasn't the whole truth but I didn't have the capacity to articulate any of it after getting texts from my lost, drunk wife and sprinting out of the house at ten o'clock. "And I did, I forgot most of it. Except you. You are entirely unforgettable."

"Then you're the only one," she said from behind a fistful of tissues.

My heart twisted and thudded in my chest. "Who forgot you, sweetheart?"

"Other than everyone?" she cried. "Because it's everyone, Noah. Everyone leaves. Everyone walks away. Take my mother. Even when she wasn't on assignment, I lived with nannies and never saw her. After the nannies, it was boarding school. When I got booted out of boarding school, Lollie was the last resort and she was the first and only actual parent I ever had. Why did my mother bother having me if she didn't want a kid? I have wondered that my whole life and I still don't know the answer."

"I know," I said, and I did. The last time I'd heard a version of this story, it was a few days before our high school graduation. That was when her mother announced she'd left early for an assignment and wouldn't be attending the event. If memory served, Shay didn't see her mother once in the two years she lived in Friendship. "I know."

"And, of course, the ex. He just fucking ended it and then he was gone. It was over and I don't even know why. I thought if I could be perfect, he'd stay. If I did everything right, it wouldn't fall apart on me. I wouldn't get left behind again. But it was over and everything we had collapsed around me. It was like an explosion. Like a bomb went off in the middle of my life and I couldn't recognize the pieces that were left. I couldn't recognize myself. I still don't and I don't know what I did wrong."

"You did nothing wrong," I said. I didn't know who this guy was or what he did but I was prepared to make it my life's work to ruin him.

"There had to be something," she sob-yelled. "No one walks away from the people they want in their lives. No one walks away from happy and fulfilling relationships."

"Have you considered that he could be a miserable bastard incapable of experiencing happiness or fulfillment? Because that's a real thing. I know a lot of attorneys with that problem. Bankers too."

"Then why am I the one being abandoned, Noah? Why is it me? If everyone else has the problem, why am I punished for it?"

"Sweetheart." I sighed. "What happened tonight? How did you even end up there?"

"The lacrosse coach was covering gym classes today and he invited me out with some teachers and coaches," she started, tears clogging her words, "and I didn't want to go because he seemed like a sportsball bro and I don't know how to talk to those people but I went because I used to love happy hours with my school friends and I never do fun things anymore. And it was fine and they were nice but then I went to the bathroom and everyone left."

The worst thing about loving Shay in high school had been watching her go out with worthless guys and promptly get her heart trashed. Even if it was just for fun and she wasn't taking it too seriously, her feelings took a beating when those guys showed themselves as juvenile jackasses.

Experiencing it again—*while married to her*—lit a fire in my stomach. I was right back to wanting my hands around her neck and requiring some apologies from her, preferably while on her knees, for the torture of this evening.

The knots in my shoulders were climbing up my neck and turning into a headache. "Who the hell is this lacrosse guy?"

She held up her hands, tissues balled in each palm. "I don't know. Something Gagne."

"I'm going to fuckin' find out who he is," I muttered. Little Star would not be sponsoring that team this season. I turned toward a shopping plaza and headed for the fast food drive-thru. "We're getting you something to eat."

"I'm not hungry."

"Fries it is," I replied. "What do you want to drink?"

"Anything but Sprite," she said through a shuddering breath.

I pulled through the lane and placed the order. Waiting on the car ahead of us, I glanced at Shay. She wasn't crying anymore, which reduced my murderous urges, but she looked miserable. Like this night had well and fully crushed her. "Are you warmed up?"

"I think so," she said. It was about as believable as saying she wasn't hungry.

I twisted around, knowing I had a sweatshirt or something in there from earlier in the week. September days were hot but the mornings carried the early whispers of winter. "Here. Take this." I handed her a hoodie with the farm's logo across the chest. "You're going to need a real coat soon enough."

She arranged the hoodie over her legs like a blanket and slipped her hands inside the neck. "I have real coats," she said. "Several of them. I've been in Boston, Noah. Not Barbados."

I rolled toward the pickup window and passed the fries and soda to Shay. When I was back on the main road, I said, "I need you to stop choosing inadequate people, Shay."

"Don't you think I'm trying?"

"Sweetheart, I don't have a single clue what you're trying to do here but I know you need to stop spending all your time wondering what you did wrong when these half-assed people leave you. Stop giving yourself to people who have no hope of ever playing on your level. Stop chasing people who don't know how to show up for you. It's a waste of your time and so are they. Let them go. Let the door hit them on the ass on the way out. They're the ones who fucked up. Not you."

"Then I'm going to be alone."

"How the fuck did you get that from what I just said?"

She rustled in the bag of fries as she spoke. "You said I choose people who don't play at my level. If that's true—and I don't think it is —there's no one here."

I'm here. I am right here. All I need you to do is notice me.

"And I don't think I'm on any different level," she continued. "I'm… I don't know what I am but it's not something that people want. They wouldn't keep leaving if they wanted me."

"Have you run this theory past Jaime? Because I can't believe she'd tolerate one minute of this bullshit. And you need to know I'm not standing for it either. Don't mourn the loss of people who don't deserve you."

Shay didn't respond. She sipped her drink and stared out the window as I drove through the silent streets of Friendship.

Then, "Where's Gennie?"

"She's asleep. Mrs. Castro is at the house with her. She plays poker with the orchard crew on Friday nights. I caught her before she headed home." I paused, trying to find the calm to speak without unleashing the mess of worry and anger and fresh jealousy gathered inside me. "We probably should've discussed this up front but I don't want my wife driving around with people she doesn't know and getting stranded in dive bars on the other end of the bay. Don't do that again."

"We should've discussed this up front but I don't want my husband telling me what to do with my Friday evenings."

"As long as you're my wife, I won't have you making careless decisions."

"As long as you're my husband, I won't have you telling me how to make my decisions."

A rasp sounded in the back of my throat as I rolled down the lane to Twin Tulip. "As long as you're my wife, I won't have you dating lacrosse coaches."

"As long as you're my husband," she shouted, "I won't have you restricting my social life." She reached for the door handle. "And it wasn't a date. It was a bunch of teachers and coaches. It was your basic buck-a-beer happy hour."

I pointed at the door handle. "You've already proven that you can't walk on your own. Stay there. The last thing I need is you falling in the wildflower garden."

She crossed her arms over her chest and pouted at me with her whole face as I rounded the hood. She was fucking adorable and I would've laughed if I wasn't busy being furious at her. I opened the door, held her hand, and looped an arm around her waist to keep her steady. The restraint it took to keep from throwing her over my shoulder was considerable.

As we climbed the porch steps, she said, "And just so you know, I don't currently possess the interpersonal skills necessary to date." She glanced over at me, her eyes weary. "I just want to go places and have fun once in a while. I want to feel like myself again."

"What part of you doesn't feel like yourself?"

She opened the front door and kicked off her shoes but didn't bother switching on any lights. "The part that sits alone in this house every night and tries to figure out who I am now. The part that wants to know why I'm so easy to leave behind."

"Then you're finished sitting here alone," I said. "You know where to find me and Gennie. Get your ass up the hill unless you want us parking ourselves down here. Don't think we won't."

"You say that now but just wait until you're scowling at me across the table and then hustling me out the door when you've had enough of me," she said. "And he's with the girls' volleyball coach, I think. It *wasn't* a date."

I brought both hands to her waist as I followed her up the main staircase. I was guilty of the scowling. That one was on me. I hadn't realized I was so transparent when it came to my inability to be that close to her for that long without wanting to drag her into the pantry and shove my hand between her legs.

"You don't have to worry about me dating anyone," she added. "That won't be happening for a long time. If ever again. I mean, I know we're not *really* married but—"

"I still don't want my wife getting stranded in dive bars," I interrupted. "I don't want you in situations where your safety and security are in the hands of a lacrosse coach."

"I was perfectly safe and secure," she said, pushing open a door at the far end of the hallway. "I mean, we're in the middle of nowhere. What's the worst that could happen to me at some no-name bar with a bunch of teachers?"

I pressed my fingers to my brow with a groan. "Don't make me answer that."

Again, she left the lights off but moonlight spilled over an old, heavy bed, revealing a tangle of sheets and blankets. She shrugged out of the jean jacket and tossed it in the general direction of a wingback chair in the corner.

"You're saying I'm not allowed to go out with some teachers after school? Is that really your bottom line?"

Shuffling toward an antique bureau, she tipped her head to the side as she removed her earrings. Though they were just earrings, there was something profoundly intimate about watching her peel back these layers of her day. It was a ritual I'd never before considered and now I knew it, right down to the way she rubbed each lobe between the pads of her thumb and forefinger once the earrings were stowed away.

As if I needed more intimacy than standing in her bedroom with her late at night. I closed my hands around the footboard of the bed to keep from taking her into my arms. She'd be flat on the mattress within ten seconds if I did that. Moaning in a minute. Hanging on to that headboard and crying out to the heavens in five.

"I'm saying surround yourself with better people," I ground out. This headache was going to crack my skull right down the middle. "You knew this coach was all wrong and you went anyway. Stop doing that shit."

Shay stepped behind an open closet door and returned a moment later in loose sweatpants and a tank top that gave me more information about the shape and texture of her nipples than I was equipped to receive.

“You’ll call me the next time you need a night on the town.” I gripped the footboard harder. She stared at me, her hands on her hips. I pointed to the messy bed. “Let’s go. Under the covers. I’ll pick you up and put you there myself if I have to.”

She blinked at me for a second. Then, “Don’t you dare.”

The only thing I heard was an invitation. I strode forward, locked my arms around her thighs, and tossed her over my shoulder. “I provided you with adequate warning.”

“What are you doing?” she yelled.

I tossed her on the bed and pinned my hands on either side of her head. Leaning in close, I said, “Allow me to make myself clear. I don’t give a pickled fuck how or why we came to be married. You are my wife. If you need some fun, you’ll call me. I’ll be the one taking care of you. I’ll give you anything you want, including a properly prepared gin and tonic. If you can’t accept that, you’re welcome to divorce me now.”

She reached up and ran her fingers through my beard. I felt her touch in every inch of my body. “When did you get so bossy?” she whispered. “When did that happen? And it’s not just tonight although you are slathering it on extra thick.”

If that hand moved even an inch, nothing could stop me from kissing her. If she gave me that tiny sign, it was all over. “Right around the time I became the boss.”

She gave several slow, heavy blinks, her lips parted and her eyes hazy. “Gail’s probably wondering where you are.”

“Gail’s probably asleep on the sofa.”

She dropped her hand, cut her gaze to the side. “I’m sorry I dragged you out so late. You should go. I’m fine. I’m not going to get into any trouble here.”

I curled my fingers around the bedsheets, allowing myself this one moment before I walked away and into an hourlong cold shower that would do absolutely nothing to block out the image of Shay tucked into her bed. I'd never forget. And how could I? Now I knew how her hair fanned out across the pillow, how the strap of her tank top slipped down her shoulder, how her eyes seemed darker when set against miles of white blankets. And I knew it not because she wanted me watching her strip away the day and settle into herself, but because some dick waffle left her at a bar.

"I don't care if it's bossy and I don't care if you like it." I stepped back and fisted my hands. "Those are my conditions. As I said, divorce me."

chapter seventeen

Shay

Students will be able to confront the throbbing consequences of their own actions.

"WAIT A SECOND. Back up. So, he picks you up from the oddball bar that you went to with the oddball people. Did he bring the kid with him?"

I glared at the screen while Jaime shook her iced coffee. That sound was scratching my brain. "No. I think he called Mrs. Castro to babysit. Or she was there? I don't remember."

Many of the details were fuzzy. One of the more shameful results of last night.

"And then you had that little conversation," she said. I didn't see any reason to share the meltdown I had over my abandonment issues. She knew. She didn't need that update. "The one where you said some snippy things and he said some snippy things."

I shifted, shoving another pillow under my head. It was noon though I wasn't prepared to leave my bed yet. "The one where he said I could divorce him if I didn't like his rules."

"Oof. You two should just bang and get it over with," Jaime replied.

I scowled at the image of her on my screen. "That is *not* the answer."

Her brows pinched together. "Pretty sure it is."

"It's not like I wanted to call him. And I didn't ask him to pick me up. He chose to do that on his own. I'd just like to know what his problem is because—"

"Because you need that information in order to bang him? Let me tell you, you're allowed to bang him without tracing those roots all the way down. And, side note, you don't need to adopt those issues, whatever they might be, because they're his issues and they're about *him*. Not you."

"I am not adopting—"

"Doll. I've heard every inch of this story. In my professional opinion, based upon the conclusive evidence I gathered with my own two eyes a couple of weeks ago, that boy adores you and he doesn't know what to do about that. Also, he's not great at speaking words. In case you haven't noticed. He needs to put all his misery to good use *and* you need to bend over and take it."

I gaped at her. "*What?*"

"Okay, I mean, maybe have a conversation about how you're both clearly very"—she waggled her eyebrows—"for each other and then bang it out. You'll feel better. Promise."

I had a hard time believing Noah saw me in any sexual sense. "I don't think that's accurate. And that's not part of our arrangement," I said, shielding my eyes from the sun slanting through the window. "And it's a damn good thing it isn't because he throws around divorce like he's already looking for a reason to end it."

Jaime pursed her lips. "Do you want to vent while I listen supportively or do you want me to offer solutions?"

"I don't know," I whined. "I'm annoyed about everything that happened last night."

"Right. Relying on your husband is so last season."

"He's not my husband."

"He *is* your husband," she replied. "You might not be doing the picket fence thing but he can give you a ride home when you're stuck in a sketchy bar without it being a great act of charity. Even if he wasn't your husband, he's your friend. You can and should expect him to be there for you when you need it." She shook her coffee again and my skull throbbed. "Remind me why you can't bang him?"

"There are so many reasons but the one I keep coming back to is he walked in while I was scrubbing the bathtub naked. No one can recover from that. Even if he was interested in me—which he isn't—he got an eyeful of asshole, James."

"You know, in some circles that's just how people get to know each other," she replied.

"In—*what*? What are you talking about?"

She waved a hand. "I'm not really into it so I can't offer much detail but I know it happens."

"Should I be concerned about you?" I asked.

"No more than usual." She shook her head. "I'm good. I've been to therapy for the past couple of weeks. I'm a week ahead on my lesson plans. I've made friends with your replacement despite resenting her existence on principle. I'm taking my vitamins, drinking my water. Having lots of sex with people I barely know. It's good. I'm good. Let's not worry about me when we have your problems to deal with. You should bang your husband."

"Oh my god, Jaime," I muttered. "That's not going to happen."

"It's the best hangover remedy I know," she said. "And I promise you will bang him eventually, at which point you'll have to come back here and admit that I told you so." She wagged a finger at me. "I'm going to add Grace to this call so she can start taking bets on when that will happen."

"I can't talk to Grace today," I grumbled. "She's going to tell me to get out of bed and get over myself, and I don't want to hear any of that."

"Then go talk to your husband," she said.

"No. I'm going to avoid him as long as possible. I did not appreciate his bearishness last night."

"You'll appreciate that bearishness later," she muttered. "If I know his type—and I think I do—it will work out nicely for you."

I slapped a hand over my eyes. "I should've called Audrey. She would've said I'm beautiful and perfect and told me how to make an anti-inflammatory smoothie to stop my skull from squeezing my brain so hard."

"She would do that because she believes she can solve most problems with the use of kitchen equipment," Jaime said. "I believe you can solve your problem with the use of your husband's equipment and I think it's nutty that you're pretending otherwise."

"He doesn't want me," I whispered, and those words pained me to articulate. There were so, so many people who didn't want me and it hurt every time I found another to add to the list. "I know you disagree and I love that you're cheering so hard but he's not attracted to me. He isn't. It took him a long time to warm up to me, and most days it seems like I get on his nerves or he can't wait to get away from me. So much scowling and jaw clenching. He's going to ruin his teeth if he keeps it up."

"We'll let his dentist worry about that."

"When he does like me, it's because we're playing a part. It's a game. And it doesn't matter how I feel because it's not going anywhere. Add to that the fact it's ridiculous to call him my husband. He's a guy I married so I could inherit a tulip farm that I don't even know how to operate and he could expand his business. Nothing is happening between us."

"You might be right," she said after a moment. "But why would he get so upset about you being stranded at a random bar? Why would he call a sitter, go and pick you up at this bar, take you home, and then give you a talking-to about what he'll allow *his wife* to do if nothing is happening? Is that how someone behaves when they can't wait to get away from you?"

I stared at her for a minute, not knowing how to respond. Then, "I thought you said this wasn't a Hallmark movie."

She lifted her shoulders, let them fall. "It won't be a Hallmark movie when you bang him. Those things never get past first base. One chaste kiss, end of story. Daddy Bread Baker won't stop until that dough rises."

"You have to stop calling him that," I said. "And I don't understand that metaphor. Am I the dough in this? Do I have to be the dough? That seems…unflattering."

"I wonder," she started, tapping a finger to her lips, "if the real issue is fully unrelated to your Daddy Bread Baker. I wonder if you've walled off everything relating to sexytimes and intimacy, and convinced yourself you're not ready."

"Of course I'm not ready," I snapped. "I just got out of a long-term relationship that ended with me left at the altar."

"Yes. He did that to you and it was awful. But when he left, he took himself away. He took a lot of important things but he didn't take you. He didn't take the best of you. I believe you're more ready than you think," Jaime said gently.

"I'm not sure," I whispered.

"You will be," she said. "Eventually."

chapter eighteen

Noah

Students will be able to recognize and accept when they've lost.

"WHAT THE FUCK is wrong with you?" I grumbled. "Why can't you just fucking behave?"

The bowl of butter, sugar, and cocoa glared back in lumpy, petulant silence. The cake hadn't betrayed me like this. The cake had been a simple matter of following the directions on the box. This was like a secret handshake.

I grabbed my phone and tapped the number for the bakehouse. It rang twice before the manager answered. "Little Star Bake Shop, you've got Nyomi."

The offending bowl in hand, I cut a glance toward the stairs as I stepped into the pantry. "Ny, it's not working. It looks like grout. Buttery grout."

"Then add a dash of milk," she replied.

"I added milk to the last batch and it's"—I glanced at the bowl I'd hidden in here twenty minutes ago with disgust—"it's a mudslide."

"Sounds like you added more than a dash."

"What—what is a dash, Ny? Quantify that for me."

She hummed. "Probably an eighth of a cup. Not much more than that." After a pause, she asked, "How much did you use?"

"I don't know but I am out of confectioner's sugar and I'm running out of time," I said.

"I can have someone run a pound of sugar over to you but I still don't understand why you won't let me give you some frosting. I have loads of chocolate buttercream here."

"Because it needs to be homemade," I ground out.

"I can come to your home and make it there. It will take me ten minutes."

I rubbed a hand over my forehead. "I can't do that either."

Technically, I could do whatever the hell I wanted. I could ask Nyomi to bake and frost a birthday cake for Shay and I would willingly admit the bakehouse prepared it because my culinary skills didn't extend beyond canning and preserves. I didn't have to do this simply because Jaime threatened to send the mafia after me.

But I was going to do this. I was going to get it right.

"You're the boss," she sang. "Try adding a dash of milk. Start with a tablespoon. Mix for a few minutes. Add another tablespoon, mix again. And don't forget to taste it. You'll know when it's right."

"Somehow I doubt that."

Nyomi chuckled. She enjoyed laughing at me. She'd been doing it since I hired her a couple of years ago, right after she dropped out of pastry school. "Remind me again how you make jam."

"Jam is scientific," I replied.

"Baking is scientific," she countered.

"You just defined a dash of milk as *probably* an eighth of a cup."

"Sounds scientific to me," she replied with a laugh. "What is scientific about raspberry rose jam? It must take dozens of test batches to get the rose right."

"Not really."

"So, then, your first batch comes out flawless and nothing accidentally tastes like soap?"

"I don't think I've ever had a batch that tasted like soap." I rested my forehead against a shelf. "I can't discuss this right now. I have to solve my buttercream problem."

"Should I send someone over with sugar?"

I scowled at the bowl. "Yeah. Just in case. But tell them to be quiet about it."

"Do you have much history with noisy sugar deliveries?"

"You know what I'm talking about," I grumbled. "Just send the sugar. All right?"

"Sure thing, boss," she said. "And if a pint of chocolate buttercream disappears from my kitchen with that extra-quiet sugar, no one will be the wiser."

I didn't argue with her because there was a strong possibility I'd need that assist.

Exiting the pantry, I listened closely for any sound of Gennie or Shay. Gennie had promised to keep Shay upstairs for today's tutoring session, and while I trusted my niece, I knew there were limits to the child's persuasive powers. Also, her attention span.

Back at the counter, I measured out a precise tablespoon of milk and mixed it into the frosting. Though I doubted it would do anything, the consistency loosened up. It was still uneven but I let the mixer run, gradually adding small amounts of milk. It was thicker than frosting ought to be and some of the sugar wasn't completely incorporated but it wasn't grout and it wasn't a mudslide either. Progress, possibly.

One of the baking assistants arrived with the sugar as I switched off the mixer. Dante waved through the kitchen window but said nothing, which meant Nyomi had put the fear of god in him. And that was why she was the best baker in the state. Fear—and kickass pies.

I opened the door, spoonful of frosting in hand. "Taste this," I said.

"Tastes like chocolate," Dante said around the spoon. "It's good. Whip it a little longer. Needs a dash of vanilla too."

"So that's an eighth of a cup of vanilla, right?"

"Hell no." He handed the spoon back. "More like an eighth of a teaspoon."

"Nothing makes sense," I muttered to myself. I took the sugar and the backup buttercream stored in an ice cream pint container. "Thanks for this. And thank Ny for me."

He jogged down the steps toward the four-wheeler he'd driven over here, saying, "She says she wants to be thanked in the form of Ceylon cinnamon."

"Fantastic." I closed the door behind me, abandoned the sugar and frosting, and went hunting for vanilla.

I didn't have much time. Even if Gennie kept to the plan, they were bound to finish within the next fifteen minutes. I needed everything to be as close to perfect as I could get it by then.

Shay and I hadn't spoken much since Friday night. I told myself she was busy with school. I didn't want to consider that she was busy taking me up on my offer to end our marriage. One of these days, I was going to have a conversation with this woman without choking on my words or being a damn fool. Probably not today. That seemed like too much to hope for.

I added the vanilla and mixed the frosting a little longer, and it slowly took on a familiar consistency. I knew I'd stepped over some lines with Shay, and I'd been aggressive with her in ways I hadn't before. It was possible she'd come downstairs in a few minutes, take one look at this party, and walk right out the door. If she did stay, it would be purely for Gennie's benefit. I was the guy who yelled at her about choosing terrible friends and threw her into bed and dared her to file for divorce. She wouldn't stay for me.

With one eye glued to the clock and both ears listening for the creak of the staircase, I spread frosting over the cake. I couldn't get it even to save my life but the cake was fully covered. Maybe Shay would assume this was Gennie's handiwork. That would help. This could pass as the work of a six-year-old.

As I shoved every single measuring cup and spatula I owned into the dishwasher, I heard Gennie loudly say, "We should go downstairs now, Shay. Maybe you can stay for dinner. That would be lots of fun."

I had to press a hand to my mouth to swallow some hysterical laughter at her mechanical tone. If Shay didn't already know what was going on, the jig was definitely up now.

"That's very sweet of you," Shay replied, a laugh ringing in her words. She knew. She totally knew. "Let's talk with Noah first. Okay?"

"Noah will say yes," Gennie said, confident as could be. "Promise."

Gennie crouched down on the step so I could see her face and flashed me a thumbs-up. I braced both hands on the countertop and went along with this ruse, asking, "Finished already? What did you work on today?"

"We read about a shipwreck in Newport Harbor," Gennie said as they cleared the final stairs, "and it might be the ship from a famous exploration and then we did some—happy birthday, Shay!"

Gennie bounced and danced as Shay blinked from the Happy Birthday banner on the wall to my haphazard attempt at a cake to the bouquet of sunflowers on the table. I wasn't sure whether they were still Shay's favorite flowers. We had a ton of late-season sunflowers out near the bee colonies and grabbing a few had seemed like a safe gamble this morning.

Now I wasn't too sure.

"Happy, happy birthday," Gennie said, still holding Shay's hand, still bouncing like the floor was a trampoline. "I made the banner and all the letters are right. See? And I made special placemats too. Noah helped me spell your name. And there's cake and we got you a present and—"

Shay stared at me, her eyes narrowed as if she didn't understand what was happening here. "You did all this?"

I shrugged. "It's your birthday." I hooked a thumb over my shoulder, toward the oven, adding, "Gen and I have dinner, if you can stay. The meal delivery people threw together something"—*don't say special, don't tell her you're hanging on by a goddamn thread here, don't say special, don't put more pressure on this than you already have, do not say special*—"different. For us. For you."

Yeah, no pressure whatsoever.

Her lips parted, her expression softened even more. "Oh." She blinked quickly. Her eyes were shiny. "Oh my goodness." The words were clogged with emotion. She swallowed hard, pinched the tiny diamond pendant on her necklace and dragged it along the chain. *Zip zip zip.* "That's—that's so sweet of you." She glanced down at Gennie, who hadn't stopped bouncing yet. "So sweet of both of you to think of me."

"Will you stay? Please, please, please?" Gennie pressed her hands together. "You have to stay. Say yes. Say yes!"

Shay ran a hand over Gennie's hair as she met my gaze. "I'd love to."

I clapped my hands together, saying, "Gen, give the coops a quick check. Then I need you to work your salad magic."

I opened a cupboard to keep from staring at Shay. To stop myself from asking why this brought tears to her eyes. To prevent a flash flood of apologies from flying out of me.

"Salad magic." Gennie sang this like a jazzy jingle.

"What can I do?" Shay asked.

Still concealed behind the cupboard door, I heaved out a sigh. When I couldn't hide in there any longer, I grabbed a bowl I didn't need and set it on the countertop. "Take Shay outside and show her around the coop."

Gennie reached for Shay's hand, saying, "Stay with me. I won't let them peck you."

The coop didn't need to be checked. The egg boxes were empty. I knew this because I checked them before Gennie and Shay arrived from school this afternoon. But I needed a minute because I couldn't breathe with the pressure of getting this right for Shay. I would've been fine with any reaction other than this one. Even if she'd declined the invitation and walked out the door, I would've handled that without issue.

This…was different.

While they were outside, I pulled several dishes from the oven and did my best to make them presentable. I owed Fig and Fennel, the meal delivery people, a fuck-ton of fresh basil for this special order.

Shay and Gennie returned when I was popping the cork on a bottle of white wine.

"No eggs," Gennie announced, turning the basket upside down as proof.

"They were perfectly behaved," Shay added.

Gennie bobbed her head. "I threw them a cookie."

"Where did you get a cookie?" I asked her.

"I don't know. I had it in my pocket."

"That's just great." I shared an exasperated glance with Shay. "Time to work your salad magic."

Shay settled onto one of the stools on the other side of the island, her hands clasped under her chin as she watched Gennie climb up her stepladder and get to work. "I have to see this," she said.

"It's magic," Gennie started, "because I throw these ugly things into a bowl and mix it up, and then it's not ugly anymore. And it tastes good. Magic."

The ugly things in question were salad greens, slivered apple, nuts. A light vinaigrette. A bit of cheese. But I didn't mind the theatrical production of it all if it resulted in Gennie consuming a salad without first drowning it in ranch dressing.

I held up the uncorked bottle. "Wine?" I asked Shay.

She waved it off. "No. Thank you. I—I'm abstaining this week." She laughed to herself, glancing away. "I had more than enough last weekend. As you might recall."

"It happens to the best of us." We couldn't talk about *any* of the things I recalled from that night. Couldn't do that. Couldn't go there because it was impossible to fall asleep without thinking about her in bed and I couldn't look at raspberries without comparing them to her nipples —and I'd yet to find a raspberry I liked better. "Water? Soda? Pirate juice?"

"Pirate juice," Gennie repeated in her jazzy jingle voice.

"Water would be great," Shay replied. "Are you sure there's nothing I can do? I'm feeling useless over here."

"You just spent the past two hours tutoring my niece out of the goodness of your heart," I said, filling a glass of water for her. "Don't feel too guilty about sitting." I set the glass in front of her, avoiding her outstretched hand because I couldn't touch her right now. Not even a light brush of the fingers. It would kill me and I had to keep it together for at least another hour. To Gennie, I asked, "How's the magic coming?"

"Almost done." She frowned at the salad bowl. "It's time for the apples."

Shay watched as I carried several dishes to the table. "What have you cooked up tonight?"

"I have reheated. Gennie's doing all the cooking here." I motioned to the dish. "It's not much. Some macaroni and cheese, a veggie gratin, and the Fig and Fennel spin on pot roast."

"And apple salad," Gennie called.

"An updated version of apple and carrot slaw," I said.

Shay started to respond but stopped herself. "That's—*no*." She gave a slight shake of her head, the corners of her eyes creasing. "Is that Lollie's special occasion menu?"

"As much of it as I could remember," I said. "The veggie dish was hazy to me. I hope this is okay."

"You—" She pressed her fingers to her lips, held them there as her eyes glistened over again. It was very important to my continued existence that she not shed those tears. I would not be able to keep my hands to myself if she cried. "I can't believe you did this. I can't believe you remembered. Thank you."

"It was Gennie's idea."

When in doubt, throw the kid in front of the problem. Excellent distraction; worked every time.

"Remember how I asked you all those questions about your favorite things? And you told me about your Grammy's parties when good things happened?" Gennie asked, deviousness sparkling in her eyes. "It was my secret project for your birthday." She held up the salad bowl. "Magic all mixed in."

I took the bowl from her and motioned for Shay to take a seat. "You're an excellent spy," she said to Gennie. "And look at these place-mats. Wow. This is amazing."

Gennie beamed as she settled into her seat beside Shay. "We did a good job?"

"You did a *great* job," Shay replied. She glanced across the table at me. "Thank you."

I shrugged as if my grip on the fake side of this marriage arrangement wasn't precarious at best. "No problem."

For several minutes, the meal served as an adequate distraction for everyone. Gennie was busy deconstructing everything on her plate and picking out the bits she deemed palatable while Shay kept up a running chorus of murmurs and quiet groans. I did my damnedest to exist without making anything awkward.

It was unproductive to admit this but I'd harbored a slight hope that Shay would've walked downstairs and reacted to this little celebration by rushing over and throwing her arms around me and demanding I reciprocate. These were the hopes I'd always harbored, the ones that always went unfulfilled. And this was a problem I created for myself. Over and over and over I expected an outcome that would never materialize.

Hell, I'd *married* her on the off chance the playing field would shift and that outcome would move into my reach. But nothing had changed.

Not really. I could throw all the birthday parties I wanted and pick her up at all the dive bars along the Narragansett Bay and give her everything she needed but none of it would change anything for us. It wouldn't change anything for her.

And that was okay. I could live with that. I could shove the truth aside one more time, a thousand more times, if it meant she had what she needed. A birthday party, a ride home, a husband in name only. We were here now, we were in this, and it didn't matter whether I'd vowed to save myself from falling down the same old hole for Shay Zucconi again. I had to accept that those fantasies of her running into my arms—and falling apart in my bed—were fully unattainable.

That wasn't going to happen. Not to me, not in this lifetime.

It was time for me to accept that, even if parts of me died in the process.

"Have you heard about the Harvest Festival?" Gennie asked as she picked the breadcrumbs off her mac and cheese.

"Not too much, no," Shay replied. "Do you want to tell me about it?"

"It's this weekend. There's a carnival and games and music, and a market too. Noah said I can have money to play the games. And there's a face-painting booth too and you can get anything you want. Butterflies, stars, tigers, monkeys. Anything," Gennie said, sounding very authoritative. "And a football game too but I don't care about that."

"It's new," I said, "in the past few years. It's a community event but the high school boosters group organizes it." He shook his head with a sigh. "Though I wouldn't call anything they do *organized*."

"Everyone expects Noah to solve the world's problems," Gennie said.

Obviously, I had to be careful what I complained about around her.

Shay met my eyes with an amused expression.

I shrugged, adding, "It comes together in the end. It's not bad. Farmers market, food trucks, art fair, plus everything else. It raises some money for class trips and grad night events so that's positive."

"And Noah got other people to work at the farm tent so I don't have to do the pay machine." Gennie aimed very wide, very hopeful eyes at Shay and I knew what she had up her sleeve. "Will you come with us? We could go on the rides together and play games and get frozen lemonades and—"

"Slow down," I said to my niece. "You need to take at least five more bites if you want to have cake tonight."

Shay fought off a smile as Gennie counted out exactly five bites and then announced, "Done. Now can we talk about the Harvest Festival?"

"It sounds like a lot of fun," Shay said to her in a measured tone. "Maybe I can meet you there?"

There it was. The distance. The boundaries. I hated it but there was nothing I could do. This was my reality. Shay didn't want any of the things I wanted and it didn't matter how many times I kissed her in front of the entire town. None of it was real.

"I guess so." Gennie pushed her plate away. "Can we open presents now?"

"Presents? No, no, no. This was all the gift I could possibly need," Shay replied. She started gathering our plates, and when I tried to take them from her, she pinned me with a sharp stare. "I'm doing this. Be quiet."

"You could ride in our car so Noah doesn't have to drive you around the parking lot," Gennie said. "Like he did after the other football game."

Shay ducked her head, a smile pressing at her lips. "That is an excellent point."

I glanced at Gennie while Shay was busy organizing the plates and dishes, and pointed to the gift-wrapped package on the island. Gennie got the hint and sprang up from her seat to retrieve it. "We picked this out special for you."

Shay stared at me and gave a swift shake of her head. "You shouldn't have."

Before I could respond, Gennie tore the ribbon from the top of the package. "I'll show you how to do this."

"Thank you," Shay replied, grinning as Gennie shredded the wrapping. "You're very helpful."

Gennie handed her the small white box. "Open it," she urged.

Shay removed the lid and gasped softly. She glanced up at me and seemed poised to say something but Gennie was quick to steal her attention.

"Cows," Gennie cried. "It's cows!"

Shay lifted the black-and-white beaded earrings from the box and held them up. "I have never seen anything more perfect in my whole life," she said, a grin splitting her face. "And they're wearing little flower crowns. I can't believe how adorable this is."

Gennie ran a finger over the beads. She was proud of herself and I loved that. The hours we'd dedicated to hunting down the right gift had been worth it.

She asked, "Remember when I asked if you only liked fruit and fish for earrings?"

"Suddenly it makes sense," Shay said, laughing. She met my gaze, her eyes soft yet serious. "Thank you. This has been the best birthday. I can't believe you did all of this for me."

"You deserve it," I said.

She deserved everything, even if I couldn't be the one to give it to her.

chapter nineteen

Shay

Students will be able to study the geopolitics of pantries.

I DIDN'T WANT to leave and I couldn't figure out why.

I had lesson plans to write for next week and a call from my mother to return but none of that was enough to get me moving. Any time in the past hour would've been great to make my exit. We'd shared hefty wedges of a truly delightful birthday cake while Gennie worked at charming me into attending the Harvest Festival with her and Noah this weekend. Now she was tucked away in bed after a hard-fought bath and Noah was busy insisting I wasn't to help him with the dinner dishes.

Though I knew Gennie had been hiding something this afternoon, I hadn't expected this wonderful little event. My heart was still overflowing from the pure joy of it. I couldn't remember the last time I felt so many good things all at once.

Birthdays were strange occasions for me. As a young kid, I'd had a few typical parties—as typical as anything was within my mother's Upper East Side set or London's in-crowd—but those events had always been far divorced from any emotional significance. By the time I landed in my first boarding school, I had expected nothing from a birthday. Maybe a call from my mother if she wasn't in a remote war zone.

Later, when I came to live with Lollie, my relationship with this day turned sour. I was suddenly aware that birthdays were family events loaded with traditions and customs I'd never known. It was more comfortable to distance myself from such things than embrace them.

It drove Jaime crazy, of course. Jaime loved throwing parties of all sort. But I never let her throw me a birthday party. The idea made me squirm and I always talked her down to something simpler, something smaller. Dinner out with the girls. Cocktails at one of the posh new spots. That was enough.

Now, after this evening with Noah and Gennie, with my chest bursting from all these precious little touches, I wasn't so sour. And I wasn't ready to leave.

There was often a gravity associated with my visits to Noah and Gennie's house. There was always a moment when the energy shifted—either within me or from Noah or some other source—and it was time to go. It made sense.

What goes up must come down.

I couldn't get my hands around that moment tonight. It wasn't there.

So, I lingered. I tidied the kitchen table while Noah packed away the leftovers. I organized his refrigerator, including the full shelf of jam experiments, while he repeatedly muttered, "You really don't have to do that." I wiped down the island despite the grumbly growls coming from him. And now, I felt it necessary to towel-dry the dishes after he washed them.

We hadn't talked much since that incident at the bar last weekend. Once the initial saltiness passed, the embarrassment hit and I didn't know what to say to him. I wanted to apologize for being a pain in the ass and crying all over his truck. He hadn't signed up for that.

That left me back in that weird spot where it seemed as though we were shouting at each other from across a canyon, close enough to misunderstand everything yet too far apart to make the jump and close the gap.

"Where does this go?" I asked, holding up the salad bowl.

"Put it down," he replied. "It's your birthday and my house. For fuck's sake, Shay, you're not doing the dishes."

"I want to help." I set the bowl on the island and started drying another dish. "Thank you. Again. This was amazing. And very unexpected."

"I can't very well forget my wife's birthday, can I?"

Noah did not want me to rattle off a bullet-pointed list of the reasons why this was far more than remembering my birthday. He'd sooner pick me up and toss me in my car than allow me to acknowledge that he recreated the meal Lollie prepared for most special days or Jaime's signature birthday cake. And I couldn't even start on the earrings. My god. I was absolutely tickled.

"You didn't have to do this," I said easily.

He shrugged. "It was no problem."

I went on drying the dishes while Noah washed, setting each item on the island since he wouldn't direct me to their proper homes. "This Harvest Festival sounds like a big deal."

"You haven't seen the signs?" he asked. "They're all over town. I'm sure there's one out front at the elementary school."

"You're probably right. I don't know. It's been so hot, I can't get into a harvest-y mood."

"That's fair," he murmured.

"I think I know where this one goes," I said to myself, stepping toward the pantry with the cake platter. The leftovers were already packed up and ready for me to take home. Noah refused to keep any on account of his concern that Gennie would cram her pockets with cake and feed it to the farm animals.

I set the platter down and reached for one of the mixing bowls crammed on the countertop. The contents looked like chocolate pudding. I grabbed another. This one looked like dry, chocolatey paste. There were three others, each in various states of preparation though it was clear all of them were attempts at homemade frosting.

I'd assumed Noah outsourced the birthday cake as he had with the meal. And why wouldn't he? He was terribly busy running this farm and raising a child. I didn't expect him to make frosting from scratch.

My cheeks flushed as I stared at these bowls. Pressure built behind my sternum. He did this for me. He suffered through at least six batches of buttercream and didn't bother to mention he'd whipped it up himself.

But it wasn't about buttercream.

It was cow earrings and poison ivy and loaves of bread every time I turned around. It was picking me up and forcing me to eat french fries when I was drunk and sad and petulant and it was sending ice cream scoopers to set up my classroom. It was my friend, the one who had changed so much but not in any of the ways that mattered.

It was my husband.

"Where the hell did you wander off—*oh*." He stood in the pantry doorway, staring at the bowl in my hands as he ran a hand over his jaw. "That's nothing. Just—don't worry about it."

The pressure in my chest swelled so big that I had to put the bowl down, wrap my arms around his neck, and press my lips to his.

He smelled like dish soap and he tasted like cake and even if this was the worst idea I'd ever had, it felt completely right.

Seconds ticked by while he stood there, his arms at his sides and his body frozen against mine. Then, like a switch flipped inside him, a growl sounded in his throat and he locked his arms around my torso. He let loose, his teeth scraping over my lips, his tongue in my mouth, his beard rasping my chin as he slanted his lips over mine. It was a wild scramble to touch and taste and hold and it wasn't enough. Nothing was nearly enough.

I dragged my fingers up the back of his neck and into his hair. He groaned into my shoulder, deep and loud, and it freed something inside me. "Come here," I whispered, tightening my hold on his hair to bring him back to my mouth.

His laugh was quiet and dark. "I don't think so, wife."

"What—" Before I could finish that thought, he picked me up, set me on the edge of the counter, and stepped between my legs. He skated his hands over my thighs, pushing my dress up as he went. He drew circles on the inside of my thigh, just above my knee, and if asked, I'd have to say that was the singular source of all pleasure in my body. Stunned, I watched my legs shaking under his touch.

"That's better," he rumbled.

No one had ever handled me with such authority. With such audacity.

He kept one hand on my thigh and brought the other to my face, running it along my jaw and into my hair. He leaned in, nipped at my lips before sealing his mouth to mine. This felt new and wild but it also felt like we'd always done this.

I pried my hands off the edge of the countertop and ran them along his shoulders, up the corded slope of his neck. Again, he groaned but this time he matched it with a hard thrust between my legs and I saw stars. I dropped my head against the shelving as a breath shuddered out of me.

Noah dipped his face to my neck, raining kisses and licks and bites there. Pressing into the crook of my shoulder, tasting the spot behind my ear, inhaling as if he could swallow the scent from my skin. All the while, rocking steadily between my legs, everything about him hard.

There was no hiding it—he was aroused. Very aroused. He wanted this. He wanted *me*.

"Noah," I whispered, my fingers in his hair and my eyes hazy. My heart was pounding, shaky breaths heaving out of me. I didn't know what to say. The best I could manage was "You should've told me."

He shook his head. "I'm not going to fuck this up by speaking." He ran a thumb over my lips and stared into my eyes. For a second, it seemed like he was done, like we were finished here, but he brought his lips to mine once again and my thoughts faded away from me.

Everything I believed to be true shifted and rearranged as he trapped me between his body and those shelves. This strong, quiet man was not indifferent. He didn't need time to warm up to me. And this wasn't a performance.

I coasted my fingers along his neck because it made him growl into my skin like he was feral, and though I didn't understand why, I wanted more of that sound. He palmed my breast, his hand moving in firm circles that didn't do anything for me at first but then he swept a fingertip over my nipple and I nearly flew off the countertop.

I needed more. Something, anything. I wiggled until I could wrap my ankles around his thighs but Noah tore away from my lips with a ragged gasp. He dropped his head to my shoulder and kissed along the side of my neck. "I love your hair like this."

"Short? Or slightly pink?"

"Both," he said, gathering me in a tight embrace. "It's like you've finally stopped caring what everyone thinks and let yourself be whatever you want."

My eyes stung as I absorbed those words. "Maybe. I'm not all the way there yet."

The air was different in here. It was honest. There was no need to hide from anything.

When Noah kissed me this time, it was familiar in the best ways. I knew his lips, his tongue, his beard. I knew the taste of him. And I knew how to sink into this moment and let it feel like forever.

Eventually, he leaned back and untangled the pretzel I'd made of us, saying, "You'll get there. I know you will."

He pulled my dress down my legs and ran a hand over the fabric to smooth out the wrinkles incurred from rubbing up against each other in a pantry. Pausing, he looked me over. If I resembled even a fraction of the chaotic jumble inside me, I was a wreck. But not the same wreck I'd been for the past few months. This was a fresh, new form of wrecked. A version I didn't mind much at all. A version that felt very much alive and not dried-up or at all hollowed out.

Noah tucked my hair over my ear, saying, "I'm going to walk you out now."

"Do you have to?"

He nodded. "Yeah. One more minute in here will turn into ninety—fuck, the whole night—before we know it."

I pressed my legs together and I felt a distinct ache, a clench that nearly stole my breath. I gulped. "Oh. Okay."

"It's a school night for you," he said, as if that explained everything.

With a hand between my shoulder blades, Noah steered me into the kitchen. He grabbed my book bags and the leftover cake, and led me outside. For my part, I couldn't think beyond the heat and desire inside me, and I allowed him to file my bags in the back seat, stow the cake on the passenger side, fasten my seat belt around me. I clasped my hands in my lap to stop them from shaking.

"Do I need to follow you home?" he asked.

"No. I'm fine." I breathed a jittery laugh. "And Gennie's asleep."

"I can get someone to stay here for ten minutes," he said, a hand braced on the open car door. That stance had his t-shirt climbing up his torso, leaving a slice of skin exposed. A half-moon hung in the sky behind him and I couldn't believe how good he looked. Like an angel who knew enough of heaven and hell to walk away from both. "It's not a problem."

I shook my head. "How about I text you when I get home?"

His brows lifted as he considered this. "All right. I can live with that."

"Thank you," I said, gesturing to the cake.

"Happy birthday, wife." Noah leaned in and brushed a kiss to my lips. "I'm picking you up for the Harvest Festival. Be ready at seven."

Shay: I'm home.
Noah: Yes. It seems like you are.

chapter twenty

Shay

Students will be able to cross bridges and climb mountain-shaped husbands.

I SET my water bottle on the cafeteria's refill station and tugged at the front of my dress, a pitiful attempt at circulating the thick, stagnant air. It wasn't even midmorning yet and I was melting. September never ended without one last brutal blast of summer heat. That would've been fine, a temporary discomfort before the crisp weather promised for the weekend, but the cooling system at Hope Elementary was on its last legs today.

"Sweltering, isn't it?"

I glanced up from the stream of water into my bottle to see Helen Holthouse-Jones, who I still refused to refer to as HoJo, crossing the cafeteria toward me. Today's wrap dress was sleeveless and her merlot hair was twisted up and held with a large binder clip.

"Yes," I said emphatically. "At this rate, we might spend the afternoon spread out on the floor with the lights off."

"Good, good. That might be the only way through," she said with a chuckle. She uncapped her own water bottle and took a sip while mine continued filling. It took forever; I knew this. I liked big bottles and I couldn't lie. "While I've got you here—"

Oh god.

"I've checked in with Mrs. Sanzi and we think it would work best if you slide over to her room as soon as Kelli is back on campus. You'll have a chance to get to know her and the class and get a feel for the content." I must've pulled an expression because she gestured to me with the bottle, hurrying to add, "Unless that doesn't work for you."

"Oh, no. That's fine. It's great." I laughed through my panic. "I just—you know—I've lost track of time. Didn't realize until now that I've been with this group almost a month."

"The first month flies by, doesn't it?" She bobbed her head like she was well acquainted with fever dreaming her way through a September or two. "I'll tell Mrs. Sanzi we're ready to roll with that plan. Good stuff. Good, good. We'll deal with Mrs. Lazco later on."

I reached for my water and occupied myself with securing the cap. "Great."

Then Helen threw in a casual "Any thoughts about next year?"

I kept my gaze down. I didn't want to explain the dread associated with that question. It was too complicated—also, none of her business—and I needed time to make these decisions. In the past three months, I'd been engaged, dumped, and married, and that was on top of inheriting a farm (somewhat), leaving my job, friends, and city, and discovering I found my husband both attractive and arousing. *Very* arousing. My attempts at taking it one day at a time were laughable.

"I'm really focused on this second grade group," I said. "I haven't had a chance to think about anything else."

"Makes sense," she murmured. "If you do get a chance to think about anything else, know that it's likely I'll have a first grade opening in addition to that kindergarten class. Just something to keep in mind. All good? Good, good. All right, well, I'll let you get back to it."

I leaned against the wall as Helen exited the cafeteria, her lanyard bouncing with every step. I should've been back in my classroom, using this prep period to actually prepare for next week, but I needed another minute. The hallways were stifling and my room was at the far end of a long, poorly ventilated corridor and *next year* pressed hard against my chest.

Jaime routinely promised to drag me home to Boston after everything with Lollie's will wrapped up but there were some problems with that plan. My old school had replaced me with a very nice person named Aurora Lura, I didn't have anywhere to live aside from Jaime's sofa, and I couldn't figure out how I'd look after a wedding venue at Lollie's farm—which now had a professional business plan and initial financing approvals—while living and working ninety minutes away.

Aside from all of those very real issues was Noah and the things that happened in the pantry. I didn't know what any of that meant. He didn't leave me with a pamphlet explaining what to expect when realizing you wanted your fake husband.

Did I actually want him? Could I have casual sex with my fake husband?

The better question was whether I could have casual sex at all. I had no trouble finding people attractive and I didn't have a problem getting aroused but there were a few other bridges I had to cross before wanting to take off my clothes, be naked with them, and let that person touch me. And I couldn't always define those bridges but there was always something I needed in order for it to feel right.

Looking back now, I had no idea what it was that convinced me sex with the ex was a smart choice but the person before him had always made me feel safe. I could say anything, do anything, and it wouldn't be wrong. I knew I'd never get my vulnerabilities thrown back in my face and I'd trusted that person.

I wasn't sure if I'd ever trusted the ex that way. I'd wanted to trust him and I think I wanted it just enough to convince myself that I did. I'd convinced myself of so many things. It didn't seem possible to swallow all those lies and half-truths while telling myself I had everything I'd ever wanted.

Aside from my teenage experiences, which were the closest thing to casual I'd ever managed, my sex life fell squarely in the *serious* column. And I couldn't see how sex with Noah could be anything other than casual. There was an expiration date stamped on our marriage and also, likely, my time in this town. We could kiss in a pantry and we could snuggle at a football game but anything else would be—well, I didn't see how there could be anything else.

Even if it felt as though I'd crossed many of the bridges I needed and I did want Noah, it wasn't a good idea. It was possible he didn't feel the same way. Yes, of course, he'd been rather *intense* in the pantry but I didn't know what that meant for him. I couldn't imagine it meant anything more than one and done, get it out of the system, casual as they come.

All of those things sounded horrible to me. I didn't have sex to get it out of my system. I didn't know how to separate sex from emotions and I didn't think I wanted to try. I needed to feel something. I needed to feel like I was worth multiple failed attempts at chocolate buttercream.

But it wasn't a good idea. And Noah and I had more than enough complications between us. No need to muck things up with sex. Not when I could gift myself a fancy new vibrator for my birthday and leave those complications behind.

It was better that way. Much better. For everyone. I barely had time for such extracurriculars, considering I had to start thinking about Mrs. Sanzi's third grade class and whatever the hell those kids were supposed to learn. If I could get Grace to talk me through her curriculum, it would really help. Even if I spent a week or two embedded in Adelma Sanzi's class, I'd still have to write my own plans while she was out. Maybe I could visit with Grace and Emme for a long weekend, and Jaime and Audrey of course.

They'd understand why I couldn't have sex with my husband. They'd agree with me on this.

Regardless of anything Jaime might've said in the past.

While I was deep in my thoughts, a door banged open on the other side of the cafeteria. I was slow to shift my gaze in that direction yet quick to whisper, "*Ohhh.*"

Noah shouldered his way through the delivery entrance, two milk crates clutched in each hand, his arms taxing the limits of his t-shirt. For a moment, I did nothing more than stare. And who could blame me? His arms looked like tree trunks, and his chest, *my god*, I could make out the ripples of muscle through his shirt.

I knew what those ripples felt like, the arms too, but watching him stride across the cafeteria, his hat pulled low over his eyes and his jaw firm, was an altogether different experience.

Until he caught me staring.

A slight grin pulled at his lips as he hefted all four crates into the fridge. It was ninety-two degrees at ten in the morning, and he was carrying a whole lot of milk with those tree trunk arms and he couldn't bother to breathe heavily while doing it.

He jerked his chin up in greeting as he moved toward me, that grin twisting into a smile. I had no words. Not a single word. I wouldn't have known it until now but lugging milk crates across a cafeteria while wearing a tight t-shirt on a hot day was definitely one of the intimacy bridges I needed to cross.

"Good morning," he called.

"Mmhmm." I clutched my water bottle with both hands. "What are you doing here?"

He pulled off his hat, ran his fingers through his hair. "Nice to see you too."

"I mean—hmm." He reached for my water and took a sip. I stared at his throat as he drank. "Since when do you deliver milk to schools?"

"When the regular driver's truck overheats on the highway." He handed the bottle back, pressing it between my breasts. His index finger brushed over my nipple. The sound that whispered out of me was profane. It had no business in an elementary school cafeteria. "All part of the job."

"I-I guess so," I stammered. Was it getting hotter in here?

He traced the shell of my ear and down the side of my neck, his cheeks reddening as he glanced at my cow earrings. "Cute."

Much, much hotter.

"How many more stops do you have to make?" I asked.

He trailed a finger under my necklace, rubbed his thumb over the pendant. "This is the last."

"That's a relief," I said.

He tipped his head to the side and studied me as he ran that finger back up my neck. "And why is that?"

"Because you are a walking endorsement for an affair with the milk-man," I said.

Noah shrugged while a blush colored his cheeks and ears. "It wouldn't be an affair, seeing as we're already married." He cupped my jaw as he leaned closer. "Isn't that right, wife?"

His lips brushed mine, the fine scrape of his beard on my jaw and his minty breath warm on my skin. It was barely a kiss, just a touch, but it shot through me in a hot, flashing reminder of last night. It felt incredible —and highly inconvenient.

"I have to pick up my class in a few minutes," I said.

"Then I'm stealing this minute from you. If you want it back, you'll have to come and get it."

He looped his arm around my waist, tugged me tight against him. I grabbed his shoulder to steady myself. A growly rumble sounded in his throat as he kissed me again and that noise walked right up to all the rationalizations I'd accumulated while talking myself out of wanting Noah, and knocked them over. Those reasons and justifications, that strong, logical fortress fell like a sandcastle surrendering to high tide.

All I could do was kiss him back and wonder if I'd survive this.

From the other side of the cafeteria, a chorus of *ooohhhh* went up. I shifted out of Noah's embrace to find my class filing toward the water fountain, each little face flushed and sweaty from running around in this heat. *"Oh my god."*

"Sorry to interrupt, Miss Z," Mr. Gagne called. He tossed in a completely unnecessary wink. "Finished our kickball game early. Gotta hydrate often on days like today."

"Is that the guy?" Noah asked under his breath.

"What guy?" I knew which guy he was talking about.

"The guy who left you at the bar," he snapped, dragging a glare over the gym teacher. "The lacrosse coach. The one I'm going to kill."

"It is but we don't murder people here. It sets a terrible example for the children." I patted his shoulder. "You're doing enough to kill him with your eyes. Calm yourself. No snarling."

"Is that your boyfriend?" one of the kids asked.

"Are you getting married?" another asked.

Beside me, Noah snickered. To the students, I said, "Class, this is my friend Mr. Barden. He visited today to restock our chocolate milk supply. Say hello to Mr. Barden."

"Hello, Mr. Barden," they chorused.

Noah held up a hand. "Hey." He turned to me, saying, "You know where to find me if you want that minute back."

I watched as he strode toward the delivery door, hitting me with a small grin that landed somewhere below my belly button as he waved goodbye.

I had no idea what I was going to do about my husband.

chapter twenty-one

Noah

Students will be able to play it cool even when situations heat up.

I WAS an awkward mess the second I pulled up at Twin Tulip and climbed out of the truck on Saturday night.

Shay walked out of the house in jeans that hugged her thick hips and a sweater I wanted to get both hands under, and I couldn't speak. Her hair was different, maybe a little wavy, and the makeup she'd used on her eyes made it seem like her lashes went on forever. All I could do was stare at her for a long, long moment.

She stopped at the top of the porch steps. "What is it?" She glanced down at her sweater, her jeans. "What's wrong?"

"Nothing's wrong. You're—you're perfect."

She ran her hands down her thighs. "Then what are you looking at?"

A flashback of all the times I watched you go to festivals and dances and dates with someone else. All the times I never thought I'd get a chance to be the one taking you with me.

Instead of saying that, I jogged up the steps to meet her. "You look nice. Your sweater. It's really—nice."

"Oh. Thank you." She glanced up at me. "You're still giving me a weird face."

Yeah, well, it was weird getting all the things I'd ever wanted. Somehow, I still didn't feel like I was doing this right.

"What are you guys waiting for?" We glanced up to find Gennie leaning out the window, sword aloft. "Come *on*! We're gonna miss it!"

"No, we won't." To Shay, I said, "She's been sitting in front of the door and asking if it was time to leave yet for the past two hours."

"So, she's excited."

"You could say that."

She smiled and leaned in to bump her shoulder against mine. "Let's not keep her in suspense."

I HELD four five dollar bills just out of Gennie's reach. "This is twenty dollars," I said, "and it's more than enough for all the games and rides."

"What about lemonade?" she asked.

"That too. Make good choices. Don't spend it all in one place. And don't start any fights."

"Those fuckers better not start any fights with me."

I pulled the cash back. "What was that?"

"Nothing," she muttered. "No fights."

"Good." I handed over the money and watched as she tucked it into her fleece jacket's interior pocket. "Stay where I can see you."

I watched as Gennie ran, arms outstretched, toward the game stalls. Beside me, Shay laughed, saying, "You know she's going to win the biggest stuffed animal here and you're going to have to tie it down in the bed of your truck, right?"

"I'm betting on it. I need something new to scare foxes away from the henhouse."

She motioned to the area packed with local vendors and artisans as we strolled by. "Do you need to do anything tonight?"

"No, thank god. We scheduled crews for the entire day and cosponsored the event but I didn't have time to sign on for anything else. Something always comes up, you know? The boosters always have a last-minute emergency. They need gift basket donations for a silent auction or someone to rig up a generator or more hands to help with ticket sales. And that's just the event side. You wouldn't believe the mayhem involved in planning these things. There's always a committee or a board in need. Last year I started sending our marketing person but they're not happy unless I show up to these infernal things. Like I want to sit around someone's dining room table and talk about themes for the holiday bazaar."

Shay hit me with a long stare. "So, what's it like being the most in-demand guy in town?"

I took her hand. A smile forced its way across my face as she laced our fingers together. I wanted to do much more than hold her hand. I wanted to pick up where we'd left off in the pantry. But I'd spent the past few days obsessing over that exact thing and I didn't know if we could do it. First, because I was about as smooth as sand. But also because Gennie was never out of sight. I didn't know how to keep things stable and do right by her without forgoing my life in the process. That could not be the way this was supposed to go. It couldn't be the cost of taking her into my care.

To this point, though, it had been the cost. Not that I'd devoted much time to sex or dating since moving back to Friendship, but Gennie's arrival cut it all the way down. We were finally at the point that she could handle spending the day at the Castro ranch without panicking that I wouldn't come home. Leaving her with a babysitter in the evening—even if it was someone she trusted, like Gail—was tricky. Either I left the house after she was asleep or I accepted that she wouldn't get to bed until I was home.

None of this made for prime dating conditions, and frankly, I had no interest in going out with someone only to spend the evening loaded up with anxiety and checking my phone every three minutes.

"It's exhausting," I said with a laugh. "Popularity is not the gift anyone thinks it is."

"I'm sure," she replied. "Was it tough, taking all of this over from your parents?"

"Exhausting," I echoed. "The expectation is that I'm just like my dad. For a lot of people, he was the heart of this town and they assumed I'd simply"—I swept an arm in front of me—"step into those shoes. I can't tell you how many times people tell me how he would've handled things, or better yet, that he'd approve of what I'm doing. Or not. I get plenty of that one too."

She murmured in agreement. "You've worked wonders, you know. Regardless of what your father would've thought, you've built a little empire here."

"Fortunately for you, that empire involves fresh loaves of bread."

"I knew it was a matter of time until you figured me out."

She leaned into me as a family passed on her side and it took everything to hold in a groan.

As we walked, we ran into a bunch of her students. They all came over to say hello and tell her about their adventures this evening. There were prizes to show off and wild stories about the tilt-a-whirl ride to recount, and Shay listened to all of it with the same attentiveness she showed Gennie. It was unbelievable but I hadn't formed a clear picture of Shay as a teacher until now when she was nodding enthusiastically while a kid with all the ketchup in the world smeared across his face and shirt told her about the Ferris wheel. She did this *every day*. She entertained the nonsensical ramblings of dirty children and somehow managed to impart knowledge to them.

Most of the parents didn't even notice me. The ones who did skated a quick glance in my direction and noted my hand on her waist though they were more interested in Miss Z than anything else. That suited me just fine. I could silently stand here and let her shine all night long. It was safer too. I was never more than a second away from referring to Shay as my wife and that was the last thing she needed me saying.

The only time I had to speak was when those parents also had kids working at the creamery. They always needed me to know that Emma's clothes still smelled like waffle cones or Zeke referred to his biceps as the double scoops. Those were the ones who blinked at me and Shay like they were trying to do mental math and they were satisfied, if not a little surprised, with the result.

After we'd greeted every small child within a five-mile radius, we meandered through the food truck lane, stopping every few feet to study the menus.

"Remember the old harvest festivals?" she asked, waving a hand at the long lines waiting at every truck. "We had stale chips and orange cheese that came out of a five-gallon can, and potato sack races."

"With actual potato sacks," I added. "From the Vaudereil farm."

She peered up at me. "Did you buy that place too?"

"Yeah, but it was a clean deal. I didn't have to do anything crazy like marry their granddaughter to get it."

An elbow landed between my ribs. "I always knew it was like that," she muttered.

"It's not," I said. "And you know it." She gave me a sweet smile. "They moved away. I don't remember where. The grandkids had no interest in the land but they didn't want to sell to real estate developers. Remember Marta Vaudereil? She was the one who had the *Don't let the bastards grind you down* bumper sticker. She was cutthroat. I liked that chippy old bird."

"I do. She and Lollie were tight. They'd drink Manhattans on the porch at ten in the morning and, as they'd say, shoot the shit." She laughed. "What did you do with their potato farm?"

"We turned the old farmhouse into the bakery and we grow a ton of vegetables on that land. Asparagus, carrots, lettuce, squash. It's the reason we were able to start a community-supported agriculture box. Before that, we just didn't have enough variety to justify the price." I pointed at the bounce house in the middle of the track loop. "These kids have it good. Remember the hay bale maze on the football field? That thing was a nightmare."

"Speaking of nightmares," Shay said, "don't look now but your friend Christiane is headed this way."

Immediately, I searched the crowd to find Gennie. If Christiane Manning was here, so were her kids, and I needed to know they weren't busy tormenting my niece.

"She's at the water gun game." Shay nudged me as she tipped her chin toward the stall on the opposite side of the field. "And she's with a friend. Can you see her? That girl with the ponytail. They're playing together."

"Noah! Hello, hello! Noah, over here!"

I didn't bother repressing this groan but I did tighten my grip on Shay's waist. It was nice touching her this way, without the weight of faking it on my shoulders. I didn't have to worry whether she was gritting her teeth to get through it. Not when I knew how it felt to have her lock her legs around my waist. "Christiane."

The woman smiled at me but there was something singular about her gaze, a specificity that refused to see Shay at my side. "Would you look at this? After all those months of planning, I knew this festival would go off without a hitch. And it's so good to get everyone out in the community, don't you think?" she asked, turning and gesturing to the carnival. "I have to say, this is quite a success."

I nodded, waiting for her to acknowledge my wife's existence. When it didn't come, I said, "Yeah, Shay and I were just talking about that."

Christiane gave me a slow, deliberate blink before turning a smile toward Shay. "Hello there," she drawled. "I can't believe we haven't bumped into each other in more than a month. Where have you been hiding out?"

"I've been around," Shay replied easily. "Noah keeps me very busy. Just the other day he threw me the sweetest birthday party. All of my favorite dishes for dinner and he baked a cake for me. From scratch. Can you believe that? Homemade frosting too."

That cake came from a box but I was not about to correct her. Not when she was on a roll.

"Wow," Christiane breathed. "Happy belated birthday to you."

Shay beamed up at me. I told myself that smile was real, it was authentic. That she'd loved her birthday party—and everything after—and I didn't have to debate whether this was for Christiane's benefit. I was going to need a minute to get used to this.

"Thank you," Shay replied. "What's new with you, Christiane?"

"Oh, you know." She fluttered a hand around her neck. "Business is just booming. I am booked up for the next six months straight. I had to take the jaws of life to my schedule just to get a vacation in there."

I dropped a kiss on Shay's temple as I slipped my hand into her front pocket. Christiane tracked every inch of that move, blinking furiously the whole way.

"That's incredible," Shay said, and it sounded as though she meant it. "It's a good problem to have, right?"

"Fantastic problem," Christiane agreed. Her daughter appeared at her side, whispering something about being tired. The girl motioned to the low fence separating the track loop from the soccer fields. Her brother was sitting on the grass, against the fence, swatting at nothing with a stick. "Not all of us can be night owls, it seems. And, you know, the twins are on travel soccer teams so we are up before dawn on the weekends. That's just competitive soccer for you." She shifted her attention to me. "I've never seen Gennie going out for soccer. Does she not play? I know Francine would be happy to teach her the basics. Maybe they could get together for some girl time and—"

"Soccer isn't one of Gennie's interests," I said.

"Oh. I see." Christiane nodded. "Well, if she ever changes her mind, you know how to reach me." She waved, adding, "I'm sure I'll see you two around town."

After Christiane left with her kids, Shay said, "That was relatively painless."

"Am I supposed to put Gennie into soccer leagues?"

She shrugged. "Maybe? If she wants to? If not soccer, maybe a different sport. Activities like that can be a really good outlet for kids who don't adore school and have a hard time connecting with kids." She pointed to the rides. "What do you say? Are you up for it?"

I rubbed the back of my neck. "If you want to."

"Am I twisting your arm? Is that what's happening here?"

She wrapped both hands around my bicep and gave a playful tug. I responded by lashing her to my chest and kissing her hard. She giggled against my lips at first but then she softened, piece by piece, until she sighed into me.

"What's happening?" she asked, leaning back just enough to speak. "With us."

"I don't know," I admitted.

"Me neither."

"Do we have to know?"

She shook her head and scraped her teeth over her bottom lip. "I don't think so."

"Okay." I pressed a kiss to her forehead. "Do you want it to stop?"

Another shake of her head. "No. Not at all."

"Then twist my arm," I said. "Show me what you want, wife."

"THAT THING IS a lawsuit waiting to happen," I said as we stumbled off the tilt-a-whirl. "Too much tilting. Too much whirling. Someone is going to get vertigo and sue the shit out of this town. Thank god Gennie's too short for that ride."

Shay laughed against my chest. She was pinned tight to me because she was stumbling harder than the night I picked her up at the bar. She was also pinned tight because everything in the world felt right when she was there.

"It wasn't that bad," she said, still laughing.

"You cannot walk, wife," I said. "That's all the evidence I need."

"It wasn't that long ago that we would've ridden that thing all night."

Two things happened when she said this. First, she dropped her hand to my abdomen and let it slide down until it stopped just north of my belt buckle. Second—and most importantly—my brain took the words *ridden all night* and made that my singular requirement for survival. Food, water, rest—none of it mattered. Not until she rode me all night long.

"Let's go on the Ferris wheel next," she said.

"Tell me you're joking." I managed to walk a straight, sober line while steering Shay away from the other rides.

"Oh, come on. The Ferris wheel is like a nap in comparison." She dropped her voice, adding, "And the Hope Elementary principal is just over there, near the caramel apple cart. If she sees me, she's going to want to talk about next year."

"That's not a topic you'd like to discuss?"

She shook her head, urging me toward the Ferris wheel. "Not yet. Not tonight."

That response begged so many questions but asking them risked answers and there was a good chance I didn't want to hear them.

When we reached the short line for the Ferris wheel—which looked only slightly less rickety than the tilt-a-whirl—Shay added, "Helen already has me scheduled for long-term assignments through the end of the school year."

I ran my hand down her spine. "Are you happy with that?"

"Yeah, it's fine," she said in a tone that suggested it wasn't entirely fine. "I just—I didn't expect everything to happen so fast. But it's good. I get to know the kids instead of just popping in for a day or two. I like this. Day-to-day subbing probably would've been too chaotic for me. I need a little order in my classroom. It was the one thing Jaime and I could never agree on. She's all right with some moderate mayhem."

We stepped up to the platform and settled into a car. "Do you miss your old school?"

As the wheel started moving, Shay nodded. "Yeah. Of course. I loved that place. And all of my friends are there."

I hooked an arm around her shoulders and played with the ends of her hair. "And the happy hour situation has to be better than anything we have around here."

"That is true." She gazed out at the carnival beneath us. Gennie hadn't moved from the water gun game in at least thirty minutes. "Helen wants me for a permanent position next year."

It was too much to hope for and I could barely stop myself from begging her to take the job. "What do you want?"

She shifted beside me, her elbow grazing my flank as she shook her wrist to free her charm bracelet from inside her sleeve. The feel of her squirming, even for the most innocent of reasons, sparked something hot and urgent inside me. "That's the question I keep asking myself," she said softly. "It's kindergarten, though, and that's my one true love."

I held her wrist and drew my thumb over the charms on her bracelet. A starfish, a shamrock, an S in an artsy script, a wonky heart, and a star with a tiny diamond in the center. She always loved her stars. "Is this a decision you need to make soon?"

"No. Helen is the kind of principal who likes to clear the decks and check all the boxes as early as she can but she can't formally offer me the position until the person currently in it gives her notice. It sounds like that won't happen until June and that's on the early side." She dragged her fingertips down my leg like it was the most natural thing in the world. "But Helen still wants me to informally accept so she doesn't have to worry about it later."

The wheel slowed to a stop, and from this elevation we could see the calm waters of Friendship Cove in the distance. "So, you have time to think about it."

"Yeah." It seemed like she was finished with this topic but then she added, "It's a good school. I like the staff and the kids. The families are great. It's fun to bump into them at community events like this. I've never worked and lived in the same neighborhood, so this wasn't something that happened to me until now. There's a lot to think about. It wouldn't be terrible to stay. It's just a big change of plans."

"Hey." She glanced over, her brows lifted. I ran my fingers up the column of her neck and along her jaw. "We're in a deathtrap carnival ride. We can figure out the future if we live to see tomorrow."

When we kissed, it felt like the first time—but so much better. I sank into her, forgetting everything beyond us and this rusty car. We weren't married for the wrong reasons. We weren't faking it to get anyone off my back. And we weren't giving life to my teenage pining. This moment had nothing to do with the kids we'd once been. This was real and true, and if I worked hard enough, I could ignore all the filthy, base urges blaring from the lizard portion of my brain. The ones I hadn't been able to repress since that night in the pantry.

But I didn't want to repress them, and if the stroke of Shay's fingers on my leg was any indication, she didn't want that either.

I dropped kisses to the corners of her mouth, her chin, down the creamy line of her neck. Slipping my fingers into her hair, I met her gaze. Her cheeks were pink—could be the crisp evening air, could be making out on a Ferris wheel—and her lips were parted, her chest rising and falling with quick breaths. She was perfect.

"Do you want to come back to the house with me tonight?" I stared into her eyes, searching for a flicker of reaction. She stared back, giving me nothing.

Then the Ferris wheel started turning again and the corners of her eyes crinkled. She smiled. "Yeah. I think so."

chapter twenty-two

Shay

Students will be able to question everything they once believed to be true.

WE DROVE BACK to Noah's house in silence with Gennie conked out in the back seat. He set his hand on my thigh before pulling out of the high school parking lot and kept it there, his fingers moving in the tiniest of ways during the twelve minutes it took to cross the bridge, climb Old Windmill Hill, and turn down the gravel lane leading to his house.

Those twelve minutes were a hot, breathless eternity where I was quite certain I was a teapot on the stove, *this* close to whistling. His palm spanned the thick of my thigh while his fingers extended to the seam running up the inside of my leg. He drew his fingertips over the ridge of that seam, tracing it back and forth, which had the very pleasant effect of turning my entire body to boiling water. That my body continued to have a solid form was nothing short of shocking.

My head was the site of a hearty debate over whether I should spread my legs for him. There wasn't much room between my legs—no thigh gaps here—which meant that every time he examined that seam, the backs of his fingers blessed the inside of my other thigh with his attention. Not that I was complaining. No complaints. None whatsoever. Though I was wondering whether he meant for me to distill down to vapor right here in his truck.

In the end, I didn't move. I wanted to shift and wiggle and rock up against those fingers but I stayed exactly where I was, even when the heat spiraling through me made my legs shake. I didn't look at him when it started. I stared straight ahead while I prayed for that hand to move a few inches higher. Just a little more. I didn't need much. Just a little closer.

But if I open my legs a bit wider...

It was a fine idea and it accomplished the secondary task of announcing *Yes, I am interested in all of this.*

Maybe that was too forward. Too brazen. The problem with me—one of them—was that I didn't have much bedroom brazen. I wasn't exceptionally vocal. I didn't reveal fantasies. Sex was great but I didn't demand much from my partners. I didn't tell them I needed more attention after they finished and I didn't ask to change things up unless I was notably uncomfortable.

I didn't spread my legs in invitation.

I wanted to though. I wanted to say, clear and unashamed, that I needed the pressure of his touch deeper, harder, higher. I was boiling over here. Scalding so hot I could feel the seconds tick by in pulses between my legs.

And that was when his thumb joined the game.

Until now, it had sat stationary on the center of my thigh while his fingers caused all the trouble. But then he swept his thumb from one side to the other, drawing a band across my leg. Whether he meant it this way or not, that soft line whispered *everything from here on up is mine.*

I blinked and I rolled my lips together. I didn't want to play this game anymore. I wanted to fill the silence with my chatter and his murmurs and growls. I wanted to distract us—mostly me—from the heavy pressure building in my core. I wanted to turn the temperature down and walk this back to a place that wasn't *simmering simmering simmering*, so close to boiling over.

I never wanted this game to end.

When he hooked a right onto Old Windmill, the gravity of that turn had those fingers digging deeper into my thigh. At this point, after a silence that stretched out like a secret, I had to swallow the sigh-moan-squeak his touch twisted out of me. That was the deal, we stayed quiet. Couldn't risk breaking this moment with the coarse reality of words or heavy breathing.

Noah drove past Twin Tulip, not even slowing enough to question whether I was sure I wanted to go home with him. He traveled up the hill, past the signs for Little Star Farms, past the rows upon rows of apple trees. When we reached the driveway leading to his house, he cut a quick glance toward me. It was the only indication—other than that hand of his—that he was aware of my presence beside him. I would've given anything to know what he was thinking.

We rolled to a stop, the glow of the lights on the front porch washing the cab in brightness and casting his touch in sharp relief. Together, we stared at his hand where it rested against the dark denim, almost daring him to end the game by moving or speaking.

And he did. He ended the game when he caught my chin in his other hand, leaned over, and sealed his lips to mine. He kissed me like he'd been doing it for years, for always. Like he knew the terrain of my body and knew all of my tells too because he gave me his tongue the instant I wanted it, nipped my bottom lip when I needed something sharp, swept his thumb over my cheek before I could float out the window and off into the night sky. He gave my thigh a rough squeeze, one that seemed to gather up all the heat and desire inside me and anchor it to that spot—which happened to be within throbbing distance of my clit.

He could tip me over and pour me out.

Noah dropped one more kiss to my lips and met my eyes. "I'm going to try to get Gen into bed without waking her up all the way. Take my keys. Open the door for me."

"Okay," I said, though it didn't sound like my voice. It sounded like soapsuds floating away from the kitchen sink, empty and iridescent before they popped.

He thumbed through the key ring until he found the right one. He held it up for me, his brow arched as if he knew all about my simmering, my boiling, my kettle just waiting to whistle. As if he expected me to spread my legs, to grab his wrist and show him where I needed him.

No, that couldn't be right.

Noah was sweet and polite. He'd never—no. He wouldn't.

Then again, the other night in the pantry wasn't the textbook definition of polite.

"Go on," he said, jerking his chin toward the house.

I took the keys and reached for the door handle. He didn't release my thigh. A beat passed before I glanced down at his hand and then up, finding his eyes. "You'll have to let me go."

He swallowed. "I'd rather not."

I shot a glimpse over my shoulder at Gennie's sleeping form. "But some privacy would be nice, no?"

Slowly, he nodded. "It would be very nice."

He rocked his palm against my leg before sliding it down to my knee and closing it into a fist on the center console. I didn't move. After living entire lifetimes in the minutes it took us to get here, I needed a breath before I could rely on these legs to carry me across the driveway and up several steps.

Once I was ready, I did my best to climb out of the truck without falling on my ass. It was simple enough, though with the compounding factors of the uneven gravel and the starlit darkness—plus the painful clench of my inner muscles—I held on to the door handle until I found my balance.

I made it up the steps and unlocked the door while Noah gathered Gennie, her head pillowed on his shoulders and her arms loosely ringed around his neck. He carried her inside, one arm tucked under her bottom and the other holding her to his chest, and it struck me that Noah learned how to care for this girl within the past *year*. If I didn't know any different, I'd assume he was her father and he'd adored her since the moment she'd arrived.

He glanced at me as he moved toward the stairs. "Stay right there," he whispered.

I stared at his ass as he went and I could still feel his hand on my leg. I could measure the distance between the tip of his pinkie and the apex of my thighs from memory. For a second, I let myself dip under the surface of this heat and let it soak into my skin.

For the first time in too long, I felt all the way alive. I wasn't dried out. I wasn't a husk. I wasn't agonizing over all the things I'd lost. I wasn't planning to scream out my rage when the ball dropped at midnight on New Year's Eve rather than kiss someone.

I felt good and present and aroused, and I couldn't put my finger on the last time that'd happened with another person. I wasn't interested in digging too deep into the last time I'd been with the ex. It was buried in the past and I wanted to keep it there though I knew without much consideration that I hadn't responded this way with him. I wasn't sure I'd ever responded this way.

Rather than spend a single minute contemplating that, I assigned myself the task of straightening up Noah's kitchen. Fold some dish towels, wash a pair of cups in the sink, wipe a smudge off the refrigerator door. That was how I ended up opening the fridge—what if there were smudges on the edge of the door?—and organizing everything I found inside. I wouldn't say it was *dis*organized though I turned all the jam jars so that their labels faced forward and lined up the juice boxes in two even rows.

"Hungry?"

I jumped back at the sound of Noah's voice, low and rough enough to scrape down my spine and start a tremor behind my belly button.

"I'm organizing," I said.

"You're doing *what*?"

"Organizing," I repeated. I gestured to the open refrigerator doors. "Your juice boxes were chaotic and the jam was turned in twenty different directions."

He glanced into the fridge. "I can't have more than fifteen jars of jam in there."

"Like I said."

Nodding, he pushed the doors shut and moved toward me. Instinctively, I took a step back and then another until I hit the countertop. He followed, his eyes darker than I'd ever seen them. He dropped his hands to my waist and locked them tight there. "Can I touch you?"

A breathy laugh slipped out of me. "You've been touching me all night."

Noah pressed his forehead to mine and brought a hand between my legs. He gave me a fast, firm squeeze, jolting me upward. I yelped and grabbed onto his shoulders as he pinched and stroked me through my jeans. The way he grabbed me there, it wasn't polite. So far from polite that it bordered on degrading, as if he felt entitled to inspecting me before taking me to bed.

And…I liked it?

I mean, I did. I liked it. And I was positive he knew this because I could feel my pulse hammering in my center. I was pulsing and miserably wet from the drive here, and it was only a matter of time until my arousal soaked through my jeans. If it hadn't already.

Oh god. He's going to notice that too.

That was another thing I liked?

No one had ever handled me this way. It felt like I was tiptoeing along the razor's edge between the kind of sex I knew and understood and something else entirely. The kind that started with sweet kisses on a

Ferris wheel and cartwheeled into orgasming in the middle of the kitchen before anyone got their clothes off.

That would be a first for me.

"I want to touch you like this," he said, the words barely more than a growl. He scraped a fingernail along the seam of my jeans and I swear, it reverberated all the way into my bones. "I want—fuck, Shay, I can't even tell you half the things I want."

"Try," I whispered, nearly climbing him for more contact, more friction.

He blinked down at me, his lips parted and his breath warm on my cheek. "You'd run out of here so fast you'd leave a cloud of dust behind you."

"I'll promise on a stack of jam jars that I won't." I stared at him, my eyes pleading for more. I needed to know what he was thinking. I needed to know everything. After all that silence, all those debates about spreading my legs, I required it. "There's nothing you can say to me that will be wrong."

A blush traveled across his cheeks and over the tips of his ears. He lifted a hand to my neck and pressed his thumb to my pulse. "What if it's all wrong?"

"It's not," I said, trying to nod though his hold on me wouldn't allow much more than a shaky bob of my head.

He drummed his fingertips between my legs and I couldn't hold back a loud, needy gasp. "You like that?" he asked, a crooked smile pulling at one corner of his mouth.

"I think you know I do."

Walking his fingers up to my waistband, he was quick to flip open the button and draw down the zipper. Instead of shoving a hand into my underwear, he dragged the backs of his fingers over my belly. Somehow, this made me crazier than anything else. Forget about pinching my pussy, forget about stroking my thigh to the point of internal combustion.

This, with his fingers on the squish of my belly, had me damn close to begging.

"I want to rip this sweater off you." He leaned in close to kiss my jaw, his beard scraping over my cheek. "And these jeans. *Fuck.* Your ass looks like it belongs in my lap when you wear these jeans." Before I could respond, he added, "I'm sorry. That was—I shouldn't have said that."

I met his crinkled gaze and whispered, "More."

His eyes widened. "More?"

I made another attempt at nodding because it was obvious he didn't believe me. "Please."

He blinked away and released a heavy breath. Then, "What if I tear these jeans off you?"

"Please," I whispered.

"And I tease you through your underwear?"

"Please."

"And I lick you until your legs give out? Bite your pussy? Fuck you with my fingers? Suck your clit until you see stars?"

I balled my fingers in his shirt, yanked him closer, close enough to feel the hard shaft trapped behind his zipper. Never in my life had I begged for anything. I was prepared to end that streak tonight. *"Please."*

He set both hands on the counter, caging me there. "You have to be quiet. I can't have you waking the kid."

"I will be quiet." I pressed a hand over my mouth. "So quiet."

"And you have to tell me if you're uncomfortable," he said, his tone crisp and stern. "I don't care what it is, you'll tell me."

"Of course." I moved my hand down his chest to rest on his belt buckle but he took me by the wrist and swiftly moved me away from that area.

"Not yet," he said as he kissed my jaw and cheeks. "This is about you."

"But—"

"Shut up, Shay." With that, he grabbed the waist of my jeans and tugged them down to my knees. As he dropped down to kneel in front of me, he whispered, "Would you look at this?" He cocked his head to the side to stare at my underwear. I'd known they were soaked since getting out of the truck but without the insulation of my jeans, the damp spot felt like an ice cube against my flushed skin. "What's this all about, wife?"

He tapped my underwear and I had to layer both hands over my mouth to keep from crying out.

"I think you know," I said. "The ride back here was—"

He ran his thumb up the inside of my thigh while he grinned at me. "What was it, Shay? What had you squirming all that time?"

"I didn't squirm at all."

Noah reached for the front panel of my underwear and twisted until the fabric gathered and edged between my folds. The pressure was unreal. I covered my mouth again.

"You squirmed," he said, his focus fixed between my legs. He drew a finger up one side, down the other. His complete refusal to touch me where I needed it the most brought me back to that razor's edge and I knew nothing would be the same after this. Not for me and not for us. "That's why I held you down the whole trip."

Something inside my brain unraveled and then that looseness spilled down my back and into my belly. Something that loved him knowing what I needed and then giving it to me before I could ask or even identify it. "Is that what you were doing?"

He locked his hands around the backs of my thighs and leaned into me. He gave another tug to my underwear, pinning them against my clit as he scraped his scruffy chin along my inner thighs. My legs were ready to give out but I wasn't going to tell him that. Not until I found an outlet for the pressure building low in my belly.

"Does this pussy taste as good as I imagine?"

"I—I don't know," I admitted.

He glanced up at me, the wicked glint in his eyes the sexiest thing I'd ever seen. "I'll decide for myself."

Smiling to himself, he skimmed my underwear down, one deliberate inch after another. Instead of diving in there and solving this mystery once and for all, he traced my slit with one lazy finger until I choked out, "Noah, *please*."

"No more teasing?"

I shook my head. "No. Maybe a little. Okay, yes, tease me but also—"

He laughed. "That's what I thought."

I wanted to be offended. I wanted to be incensed by his righteous chuckling. But he bowed his head to my mound and circled his tongue around my clit, and all I could do was shove my fingers into his hair and hold him against me.

He held me open with both thumbs, baring every last inch of me to his tongue. He sucked me hard, just as he'd promised, and the stars behind my eyes were incredible. "I need," I whispered, my shoulders hunching forward as my muscles strained and softened all at once. "I need—I need—I need something. Inside me. *Please.*"

He growled against me in response, shifting one hand to my sopping core and pumping two fingers into me. Another finger rhythmically tapped my back channel and though I'd found mild interest in that before, it shot a bolt of lightning through me and coalesced all the nerves in my body to this overwhelming throb waiting to break free.

"Get there for me," he said, the words muffled as I rocked against his mouth.

I wanted to be that girl, the one who would get there simply because someone told her to, but I wasn't. I needed more, just a little more, and then I could do it. But not yet.

And Noah recognized that.

He turned his wrist, his fingers moving inside me from a different angle and adding new pressure on my back channel. He worked my clit like he was trying to suck the ghost of orgasms past from me. And then, when it seemed like we'd come this far only for it to fall apart, he tipped his head to the side and

—bit—

—his—

—way—

—down—

—my—

—labia—

These weren't the kind of bites to break skin or leave a mark. They were nips, sharp pinches between teeth. And they set me on fire. A sob gasped out of me and I notched my fist to my mouth to stay quiet and it was that requirement that forced me to feel all of the explosion. I couldn't hide from it with moans or flailing cries. I couldn't roll over and bury my face in a pillow or even snuggle into his shoulder. I had to stand here, my jeans at my knees and the scent of my arousal thick around us, and I had to surrender to an orgasm that redefined everything I knew about my body and how it could react.

When I couldn't take much more and I eased Noah away from me, he glanced up, his face shiny with my arousal. "Come here," I whispered.

He pushed to his feet as I grabbed the front of his shirt, towing him closer. "How was that?"

I laughed though I was breathing heavy and it sounded like a wheeze. "I think you know it was pretty good."

"It wasn't"—he glanced away, his brows furrowed—"too much?"

"I think I needed too much." I went for his belt buckle again but he pinned my hand behind my back. "Why not?"

"Because I'd like the next portion of this night to last longer than forty-five seconds but that's all we're going to get if you touch me."

"I don't get to touch you at all?"

He pressed a finger to my lips. "Don't pout. It makes me think about —you just can't do that to me, Shay. Not right now."

"What *can* I do?"

He blew out a breath and surveyed the swath of naked from my knees to my waist. Then he yanked my underwear and jeans back into place, not bothering with the button or zipper. I yelped at the pressure of form-fitting clothes against super sensitive skin. Noah slapped my thigh, saying, "Upstairs. Now."

"Wait." I reached for him but he gathered my hands and looped them around his neck. "What do I taste like?"

He nuzzled into the crook of my shoulder and replied with a soft growl. "My wife."

"That's not a taste."

"Mmm. It is now." He turned me around and set one hand low on my belly where my jeans gaped open, the other on my shoulder. "Remember what I said about being quiet?"

"Yeah, it's why I have a perfect impression of my teeth on either side of my thumb."

"I'll have to kiss it and make it better."

He walked me up the stairs like we couldn't risk making a single sound. The pressure to maintain this silence swelled inside me, pressing at my breastbone and pulling my shoulder blades tight. I didn't realize until we reached his bedroom, on the opposite end of the house from Gennie's, that this feeling was anticipation. It was a delicious kind of stress—just like the drive home—and I was all the way back to simmering again.

When he opened the door to his room, a breath whooshed out of me at the sight of his big bed complete with a navy and white quilt and two layers of pillows of the appropriate size and quantity.

"What was that for?" he asked, his broad chest warm against my back.

"You have pillows. *Real* pillows." I looked up at him. "Men never have real pillows."

He glanced between me and the bed as he closed and locked the door. "Yeah. That's interesting." He shifted the hand on my belly lower until his fingers cupped me between my legs. "Is this okay?"

I dropped my head back to his shoulder. "Yes."

He moved his other hand over my shoulder to my breast. He was hard against my ass. I couldn't miss the solid ridge of him or the way he rocked between my cheeks. "What about this sweater?"

I wiggled to free myself from the sweater but Noah wasn't having that. He gave my pussy a rough squeeze and whispered, "Slow down."

Motioning to the bed, I whined, "But I don't want to slow down."

He pressed his mouth to my neck, saying, "We have to discuss a few things before we take another step toward that bed, sweetheart. I need you to talk to me about protection and I need you to tell me what's off-limits for you."

Suddenly shy, I fixed my gaze on the quilt. "I had all the tests done in July after my—well, after my last situation went down in flames. Everything came back clear." I forced all memory of the ex from my mind. He wasn't entitled to destroy this too. "And I have an IUD. So."

"I haven't been with anyone in months. Since before Gennie moved in. No one since my last check-up."

"So, then," I started, forming bold words from nothing, "we can skip the condoms."

"Is that what you want?"

"I—um." I had no idea what I wanted. No, that wasn't true. I wanted to be held down again. Pinned in place in his truck, backed into the corner of the kitchen. Trapped yet completely safe. And I wanted him over me, around me, inside me. But that wasn't the question. "Yes. Is that okay with you?"

"That works." He stroked my cheek, my jaw. "What's off-limits?"

"After what happened in the kitchen"—a laugh burst out of me—"nothing."

"I don't believe that." Noah traced around my nipple, careful to never circle too close and accidentally give me what I wanted. "You'll stop me if you don't like something. Understand? I want to hear you. I don't want to hurt you or freak you out or—look, it matters to me that it's good for you, Shay. I need you to talk to me."

I could've lied to myself and said he didn't have to worry about making it good for me. I could've said this was meaningless sex. Casual. No strings. What happened tonight didn't have to matter. It didn't have to be important.

I could've lied and told Noah as much.

"Yeah. Yes. Okay." I bobbed my head. "I'll talk to you but only if I'm allowed to touch you."

"Why do you want to touch me?"

He asked this question while dragging his finger along the outer edges of my underwear, the scrap of fabric a second away from officially being declared an island since I was wet like an ocean between my legs. And he asked this question as if there was something fundamentally curious about me wanting to rub my hands all over his body.

"Because this thing you're doing, the plaid shirts with the rolled-up sleeves and the broken-in jeans, the beard, the ball caps, the growling—god, can't forget all the growling—it's impeccable. Flawless. And when you touch me and do all these things to me, I don't want to feel them alone. Does that make sense? I don't want to be alone in this. I need you with me."

His first response came in the form of him spanking—yes, *spanking*—my pussy. An open-handed slap that echoed off my clit and folded me over at the waist as a garbled cry of "Gahhhhfuck" rattled out of me.

His second response was spoken directly into my skin. "You're not alone, wife. I'm right here with you and I'm not going anywhere."

Noah tugged the sweater over my head as he walked me toward the bed. He yanked my jeans and underwear down, kicked them free from my ankles while I unclasped my bra. With a hand between my shoulder blades, he bent me over until my cheek was flat on the quilt.

I was aware of every inch of skin on display, every quiver and kick of my internal muscles, every breath puffing out of me.

A sliver of doubt shivered through me. This felt wrong. Or, more specifically, it felt like it should be wrong. I shouldn't spread my legs wider. I shouldn't press up on my toes. I shouldn't rub myself against the quilt. I shouldn't want it like this.

That shiver grew into a gasp, a throb, a shudder when I heard the rattle of his belt, the rasp of his zipper. His jeans hit the floor and then his shirt.

"I want to keep you like this," he said, skating a finger down my spine, between my cheeks. "But not this time. No, this time, I need to see you."

He moved closer, held my hips, rocked against me. He hadn't stripped off his boxers yet.

"Give me a second," he said as if he could read my mind. "Your ass is shaped like a heart and I can still taste your pussy on my tongue. I need to pull myself together, Shay."

I grabbed at the quilt, tugging it down to reveal smooth blue sheets. *Nice* sheets too. "Pull yourself together under the covers," I said. "With me."

He released me with a groan that seemed to violate all the regulations on quiet. I climbed into the bed, between the cool linen sheets, and held out my hand to him. He didn't take my hand. He prowled toward me on his hands and knees, tossing back the sheets as he came, his gaze midnight dark and jaw locked like he was seconds away from snarling.

This was my first chance to get a look at him without clothes, and *whew*. Did not disappoint. He had a glorious farmer's tan, his upper arms and shoulders pale while his forearms were sun-kissed. His chest was wide and strong, a bit of dark fuzz there and running down the center of his abs, which led me to—

Oh my god.

I reached for the erection tenting his boxers, closing my fingers around him and giving him long, thorough strokes while he dropped his head between my breasts. It felt good being the one doling out the torture for a minute.

"*Shay,*" he gasped. "Sweetheart, you're going to kill me."

"I don't think so." No one with a shaft like this could die from a few strokes. That was absurd. Almost as much as him walking around with an almighty baseball bat in his trousers and keeping it all to himself. "Have you always had this?"

He lifted his head and gave me a wry grimace. "As far back as I can remember, yeah."

I twisted my hand over his crown and back down again. A triumphant smile broke across my lips when he sighed foul curses into my breasts. "And you never thought to mention it?"

"Tell me how that conversation would go. Something like 'Hey, hi, welcome back to town, want to see if you can get your fingers all the way around my cock?' I can't see you loving that."

I pushed the boxers over his hips. He kicked them away. There was nothing else between us now, and here, beneath the sheets and the quilt, there was nothing else in the world. "Maybe not the initial conversation but definitely one we should've had within the first month or two."

He laughed and it seemed to recover some part of his resolve. He pressed my legs open with his knees, planted his hands beside my shoulders. "You have no idea how much I want you right now."

I was shaking but only on the inside. Noah couldn't see it. It was better that way. He'd stop if he knew about the simmering in my blood and all over my skin. He'd hold me close and demand an explanation. An accounting of this situation. But I didn't want that. I didn't need that. I needed him to take charge the way he did in the kitchen. In the truck. Everywhere.

I gave him a squeeze. "I have some idea."

"And what about you?" he asked, his gaze unfocused as I worked him. "What do you want?"

I dragged him through my wet heat, sliding back and forth until he bucked into my hand, until he leaned down to groan into my breast. "This," I said, notching him against my opening. "I want this. I want *you*."

He stared between us for a long moment. "I'm gonna bite that thigh when I'm done with you."

I released his shaft to draw my fingers along the crease where my leg met my ass. "Right here?"

"Right there."

He slipped his hand around the nape of my neck and his thumb settled low on my throat. It was exactly what I needed. I wasn't falling apart anymore. Wasn't floating away. I was here and I didn't have to think about anything other than the pressure building in my body, the unreal desire I felt to have him inside me.

I lifted my hands to his biceps and held tight to him as he pushed into me. We groaned together, both of us shushing the other with our eyes. My lips parted on a gasp and everything behind my eyes turned white as he stretched me. "You are…*huge*."

A noise rumbled in his throat. "You can take it." He reached behind me and grabbed a pillow. "Hold on to me," he said, pressing deeper while lifting my ass to shove the pillow under me.

That maneuver almost broke my vagina. For a second, I truly doubted whether I'd survive Noah's cock sliding all the way home like that. I'd split right down the middle and this would end poorly for everyone. I was stuffed so full I could barely breathe, let alone express to him that he was rearranging my internal organs.

But he shifted the pillow and everything changed. It made all the difference. I could breathe again. I could think past the blinding stretch inside me. And now that I wasn't at risk of choking on my gallbladder, I could focus on the steady drag of him against my clit.

"Look at you," Noah whispered, returning his hand to the back of my neck and setting the other on my waist. "Would you just look at you."

He thrust into me then, his whole body moving in a slow, deliberate snap that made me dig my nails into his skin. I wanted him to fall apart, to lose control. I wanted all those things he believed I couldn't handle. The ones that would make me run. I wanted to see what it looked like when he went wild.

"Fuck, Noah." I arched my neck back, lifted my gaze to the ceiling as he pounded into me. I couldn't believe my body could do this. I'd never felt so many good things at once—and for so long. "When you get married for real, you're going to make someone very happy."

He stilled and glared down at me, one corner of his lip curling up. "I don't want to talk about my next marriage while I'm busy consummating this one."

"I mean—"

"No." He cut me off. "You want this cock, wife, you take it without telling me about the person I'll fill up after you."

I blinked at him. "You're filthy," I said. "You're—you're a filthy, pervy beast, aren't you?" His fingers tightened around my neck. "You say these filthy things to me and then you touch me and—and it's like you're a different person. It's like you're wild on the inside and I want to know all of it."

He slammed into me so hard I lost my breath. "Don't say that," he whispered.

"Why not?"

"I shouldn't be wild with you," he said, his hand unbearably tight around my hip.

"But I want you wild," I said, arching up to meet his thrusts. "I *need* it."

His breaths came in ragged grunts as he pulled out until only his thick crown teased at my entrance. He stared down at us before rolling his hips in a hard, rough rhythm that was giving me the punishment of a lifetime. It was like an unauthorized lesson in the right way to get fucked from a man who swore it was all wrong.

"I just—I want to devour you," he said. "I want everything, all the filthy, beastly things you can think of. More. Everything."

A flash of heat spread down my belly and around my core. It weighed on the tension gathered tight behind my clit, teasing at the threads and pulling it apart as Noah's thrusts grew fast and uneven. I was so close but—again—not close enough.

"Everything," I whispered. "I want it."

His gaze locked on mine as he pumped into me. He was silent save for the breaths heaving out of him. Then, he released my hip and brought that hand between my legs, grinding his palm against my clit. "You were made for my cock. You were made to take it all. You're going to take it bent over this bed, you're going to take it on your belly and holding on to the headboard, and you are going to take it sitting on my lap while I lick those tits. And that's just what I'm taking from this sweet little cunt tonight."

Oh, yeah. That was what I needed.

Again, I was shaking on the inside though it felt like those tremors were everywhere. My breath jerked as the release hit me, all the tension and need spilling over into a flash of sated relief. It washed up to my eyelids and down to my toes, and stole all my words. The best I could do was moan and gasp as I stared up at Noah.

He flattened his hand over my mound and pressed down until I could feel every ridge of him moving inside me. A loud, profane groan slipped out of me. This was intense bordering on overwhelming. Almost too much—and yet just enough to trigger another small death in me. It was the perfect aftershock, stretching out in long, slow rumbles.

"What are you doing to me?" he asked, his eyes squeezed shut for a second. "Jesus, fuck, Shay, I can feel that."

"Made for you," I whispered, the words hoarse.

He held still, his head falling back as a dark hum sounded in his throat, and I felt it then, the pulse and spurt of his orgasm. I wrapped my hands around his arm, his shoulder, scratching and pulling to get him closer. I kissed every bit of skin I could reach. Kissed, licked, nipped. Anything. It didn't matter. I didn't care if I was wild too. If I was feral and filthy. I needed to taste him, to memorize him. I needed to gather it up and store it somewhere safe.

"Come here," I said. "Please. I need—I just—I need *this*."

He came to me, holding most of his weight on one arm but pressing his chest to mine the way I wanted. "You're okay?"

I nodded, too busy licking and kissing my way up his neck to answer. I sucked a mark into his shoulder. I couldn't explain why I needed to hold him like he might disappear at any moment. I couldn't explain why I was more desperate for him now than I was at any other point tonight. All I knew was that I needed this. I needed him.

"Let me roll you over, sweetheart," he said. "I don't want to crush you."

He pulled out and eased me to my side, tucking himself behind me. I knew I had to get up and use the bathroom but that could wait a few minutes. I had to catch my breath and confirm that my legs were still attached to my body.

Noah traced a finger over the ink on my shoulder. "When did you get this?"

"Not long ago, actually. It's new." I chewed on my lower lip. "New hair, new tattoo."

"And the same old town," he added. "Why the seedhead dandelion?"

I buried my face in the pillow. "It's silly."

"I doubt it." He touched each of the wispy seeds as they drifted toward my arm. "It's beautiful."

After a moment, I said, "You make a wish on those flowers and let the breeze carry it all away."

"You wanted a wish?"

I yawned. "Something like that."

"You're tired. Rest." Noah pressed a kiss to the dandelion and wrapped his arms around me. "Close your eyes, wife. I have you."

I laughed a little at the thought that anyone had me. I was drifting on the breeze with no idea where I'd land or put down roots—if I ever would.

"What's funny?" he asked.

"Seeds," I whispered with a grin.

"Are you all right?" I felt Noah shift behind me. "Are you sex drunk or did I fuck something loose in your head?"

"I'm fine," I said, patting his forearm. "I just need you to hold me for a minute."

chapter twenty-three

Noah

Students will be able to breathe—but just for a minute.

I KNEW everything there was to know about contentment.

This was it, right here. The woman who'd ruined me for all others tucked beside me, her clothes scattered on the floor of my bedroom, and the knowledge that I was forever changed pulsing in my chest.

Of all the times I fantasized about sex with Shay Zucconi—and there were so, *so* many times—I never gave much thought to what would come after the act. I'd always focused my hypothetical efforts on getting her into bed and making it good for her, and all the other details seemed to evaporate from my consciousness.

Now, with Shay dozing on my chest and her arm slung around my waist, I couldn't believe I'd been so shortsighted. I couldn't believe I'd ignored the subtle glory of holding a satisfied woman.

Rather, a woman I'd satisfied.

She stretched, her soft skin sliding against mine in a way that choked the air out of me and cranked my body into gear for round two.

"Hi," she whispered.

"Hi." I ran the back of my finger down her nose, over her lips. "How are you?"

A knowing smile pulled at the corners of her mouth. "I'm great." Her cheeks flushed pink. "I didn't mean to fall asleep on you."

"You can sleep on me all night," I said. *Every night. Always. Forever.*

Her hair tickled my chest when she shook her head. "I should go home."

"No. You shouldn't."

"It would be better than me trying to sneak out of here before Gennie wakes up," she said. "I can walk. It's hardly more than ten minutes."

I blinked down at her, trying to reconcile the searing need I had to sit her on my cock for the next hour with the casual implication that I'd allow her to walk down a steep hill in an area that had a considerable wildlife population in the middle of the night. *Alone.*

In the end, the only way to put these issues in order was by rolling her to her back and crawling between her legs. "That's not happening."

"Noah." She laughed as she pressed her knees together and twisted away from me.

That didn't stop me. I palmed her round ass and kissed the outside of her thighs. Hell, I'd kiss her elbow if that was what she gave me. I loved every inch of this impossible woman.

"You know I'm right. We don't want to confuse Gennie."

There was a kernel of truth in there. We did *not* need to confuse Gennie, and the last thing I wanted was to explain to my niece the nature of adult sleepovers. But I couldn't leave her alone in the house either, not even for ten minutes. God forbid she woke up and no one was here for her. It would set her progress back by ages.

"I can take an ATV," she offered. "That would work."

"That would *not* work. It's too damn dark and we take ATV safety very seriously here. We have a rule at Little Star: no driving in unsafe conditions. It's the zero rollover policy."

"I'm just going down the hill," she argued. "Paved roads all the way."

I gave her ass a rough squeeze. "Do you even know what kinds of animals are out at this hour? You've got deer and coyotes to start, and let's pretend for a second that none of them run in front of that ATV, even though they do exactly that all the damn time. Set that aside and you're left with raccoons, woodchucks, skunks. Do you really want to run across a skunk? You don't. Trust me." Another squeeze. "You're just going to have to spend the night, wife. I'll handle Gennie."

Shay stared at me, her lips pressed into a stiff pout and her gaze hazy but hard, like she was tired though annoyed enough to fight it off. As I watched her, my head on her thigh and my fingers drawing circles along her hip and the silence stretching between us, it occurred to me that I might have made an enormous error.

I wasn't holding her hostage. *Obviously.* If she insisted on leaving, I wouldn't stop her. I'd gather up Gennie, sheets and quilt and all, and we'd drive Shay down to Twin Tulip. If she really wanted to go, I'd make that happen in the safest way possible.

But I didn't believe she really wanted to go.

For starters, she was still in my bed. Still naked, still tolerant of the hands I couldn't keep off her. She wasn't circling the room in search of her underwear or shrugging off my touch. And second, she hadn't said a word. I knew that could mean a hundred different things but Shay had no problem disagreeing with me. She didn't mind pushing back on me. Not now, not ever.

But most importantly, her expression wasn't one I'd associate with having insulted her. I knew because I'd done just that since her arrival and I was familiar with the way it played over her face.

This wasn't that. There was annoyance and a touch of defiance but also an edge of curiosity. Like she was waiting for me to back these claims up with action. Like she wanted me establishing some limits.

I remembered then what Jaime had said about Shay wanting a family more than anything in the world. Family didn't stop at birthday cakes and fake marriages to save the farm. Family showed up when you went out to a bar with the wrong crowd. Family hollered at you about walking alone at night. Family cared even when it was really inconvenient.

Though I didn't admit it often, I resented just about everything when it came to my family. Being stuck between an apple farmer with the biggest heart in the world and zero business sense, and a moderately progressive preacher who prioritized the appearance of a happy family over the reality still bothered me.

Leaving my law practice to move home and untangle the financial sinkhole that was Barden Orchards swallowed up several years of my life with boiled-over resentment.

Watching while my sister was sentenced to life in prison was an enormous source of my hostility. That she hadn't bargained away information on that boyfriend of hers woke me up in a cold sweat most nights.

I still wasn't free from the bitterness that came with upending my life one more time to become my niece's guardian, though Gennie wasn't the source of my anger. It was that I was always the one to shoulder these burdens. I had to step in and save the day every fucking time and I was tired of putting my life on hold to do that. I didn't want everyone to expect me to rescue them.

Though I didn't mind rescuing Shay.

It wasn't a requirement when it came to her. It was a choice.

"I want you to stay here," I said. "I'm sure you can make it down the hill on your own but you shouldn't. It's late and you are the best thing that's ever been in this bed and I want you to stay. With me."

There was a long moment where Shay eyed me carefully, as if she was searching for cracks and fissures in my words. Then, "You don't think it will be difficult for Gennie?"

I stroked a hand from the back of her knee up to her waist. "I think she'll be too happy to see you to put any pieces together. If she does, I'll deal with it. Hell, I handled it when she knocked a kid's front teeth out last year. At least they were baby teeth." I gave her ass a light slap. "I can handle this. Don't let it worry you."

"Okay." She lifted a shoulder. "I guess I'll stay."

"Yeah? If you want to leave, I'll take you home. I'm not going to keep you here against your will." I ran my thumb along the crease between her thigh and backside, and barely brushed at the wet between her legs. A shiver moved through her body and she pinned her knees together even tighter. "Unless—unless you'd like that."

The amount of wrong packed into that statement could not be minimized. No part of this felt appropriate or respectful or any of the things I wanted to be for Shay. It was filthy and primal, and *so wrong* yet unimaginably right. And I couldn't explain why it was right.

Odds were high it wasn't right at all and I'd find that out when she kneed me in the jaw.

She fidgeted with her fingers and wiggled a bit. "Maybe I would."

I stared at the smooth expanse of her thigh because I didn't trust myself to meet her eyes. I didn't trust myself to do anything other than admire the gradation of her skin from lightly sun-kissed to creamy and pale. She didn't shave her legs beyond the knee and I found strange pleasure in that realization. A strange pleasure completely removed from my wife's suggestion that she'd enjoy me defiling her.

Yeah, the fact my cockhead had a heartbeat right now had nothing to do with Shay's tentative request that I keep her—and make it rough and wild.

I dropped a hand on the flare of her thigh and held her steady, making it abundantly clear with the way each fingertip dug into her skin that I'd pin her down all night if that was what she truly wanted. She blinked at me, her lips parted and heat coloring her cheeks. Her arousal was so thick in the air between us that I could taste it on my tongue.

I ran my free hand over the knees she had pressed together. "Then that's what I'll do."

I wrenched her legs apart with more force than seemed necessary and I rocked myself along her seam, swallowing every yelp and gasp that tumbled over her lips. Her eyes were wide—startled but also *starved*. Like I could do anything right now and she'd ask for more.

"Stop me," I said, "if you don't like this."

"I will."

"If anything hurts or you're uncomfortable—"

That perfect smile of hers bloomed across her face. "I know what to do, Noah."

I set her foot on my chest and shifted it up to rest on my shoulder. I did the same with the other and banded an arm over her legs. I turned my head to scrape my teeth over her ankle. "Are you sure about that?"

"I don't know." She jerked one shoulder up and a hint of defiance curled into her smile. "Prove me wrong, then."

Rather than ruin this by attempting to string words together, I slammed into her hard. She was wet in a way that made me think of drowning, of going under and never, ever coming up again.

"Oh my god," she cried out. "Oh, *fuck*. Oh my god. Noah."

I leaned into her, pressing her knees to her chest and forcing a hoarse, desperate sigh from her. Noise like this was going to get us in trouble. "You will be quiet, wife." With a hand cupping her jaw, I stroked my thumb over her lips. "Don't think about testing me."

She nipped at the pad of my thumb and smiled about it. An uncharitable sound rattled in my chest. I responded by thrusting into her like I wanted to fuck her through the wall, which wasn't a smart approach to minimizing the noise.

The way I rocked into her was ruthless, as if I didn't care about her pleasure or anything other than using her to slake my own needs. As if I wasn't terrified that I'd actually hurt her or scare her away. That she'd quickly come to the realization I didn't know how to treat her with the tenderness she deserved, and the only thing I was capable of doing was rutting on her like a wild animal.

But this position, with her pinned beneath me and nearly folded in half, was unreal. If I wasn't a wild animal before taking her like this, there was no turning back now. I knew what it was like to see arousal fog my wife's eyes and feel the slick clench of her desire on my cock, and I'd never be able to forget.

I didn't want to forget, but more importantly I didn't want this to end. Not just this night, not just the sex. I didn't want to let her go all over again and settle back into a life where she wasn't mine.

"That's it," I said as Shay whimpered. She lashed her arms around my neck, shoved her fingers through my hair, ran her palms down my flanks. It felt like she was learning the topography, rushing to find everything she could and catalog it for safekeeping.

For the next time.

I wanted to write my name inside her. Her inner muscles tightened around me and I moved my thumb from her lips. I dropped a quick kiss there before resting my forehead against hers. I had a minute, maybe two, before I drained myself into her and then snuggled her like she was the key to preventing my soul from slipping away.

"That's my girl," I growled as she came. I collected her cries with a kiss and answered the beautiful spasms inside her with one of my own, and it wasn't until I could hear over my heartbeat again that I realized I'd been whispering *mine* into her skin the whole time.

MY PHONE WOKE ME UP. It was always the phone. No need for an alarm when I could count on something to go wrong and someone to call and tell me about it.

But before I could focus on the screen, I heard a child-sized knock at my door. Then, "Noah, some people are here to see you."

Beside me, Shay mumbled, "What's going on?"

"I have no idea," I replied, still squinting at the screen. Why would I have twenty-nine text messages on a Sunday morning? What the fresh hell? "Who is it, Gen?"

She turned the knob and pushed the door open just enough to peek in with one eyeball. "Everyone."

"Okay," I said to Gennie. "Give me just a minute and I'll come downstairs."

"Will Shay come too?"

"Oh Jesus," I muttered. "Yeah. She'll come with me. Okay?"

"Can we have pancakes?"

"Yes. We'll have anything you want. Does that work?"

Instead of responding, Gennie slammed the door and ran down the hall. Any hope of lazy Sunday morning sex just flew right out the window.

"Well. That happened." Shay patted my shoulder before climbing out of bed. "I'm going to borrow a shirt. Okay?"

Still staring at my phone, I said, "Everything I have is yours."

"That seems excessive," she said from inside my closet.

"It's not." I pulled on boxers and jeans as I scowled at text after text from folks around town saying *Congratulations!* and nothing more. What the fuck was everyone congratulating me for? Had to be a mix-up.

Shay stepped out of the closet wearing last night's jeans and one of my button-down shirts. She had it knotted at her waist and the sleeves folded up to her elbows, and I couldn't find it in me to care about whoever the fuck was at my door first thing in the damn morning.

"Come over here." I beckoned her closer but she wagged a finger at me. "I'm not joking, wife."

"We have things"—she waved both hands at the door—"to deal with. Let's do that first."

I never wanted her to wear anything but my shirts. And I wanted to rip this one off her.

She motioned to the phone in my hands. "Do you have any idea what's going on?"

"No." I sighed. "I don't know."

Shay finger-combed her hair as we descended the stairs. Gennie was parked in front of the door, sword in hand and eye patch on her wrist.

"Mr. Bones is bringing the goats up for yoga," Gennie said, pointing her sword toward the window.

I glanced outside and spotted half a dozen pickup trucks and at least ten of Little Star's four-wheelers. Regardless of the texts, this had all the markings of a farm disaster. "I really hope we don't have cows wandering the town," I said under my breath as I opened the door.

I didn't get a chance to ask about cows or downed sections of fence because most of my staff—including Bones and four goats—sent up a cheer when Gennie, Shay, and I stepped outside. Everyone was there. Nyomi, Wheatie, the farm stand crew. And they were holding bouquets of flowers and balloons. Gail Castro clutched two bottles of champagne by the neck.

Gennie ducked behind me and buried her face in my t-shirt. Shay smiled but cut a confused glance in my direction.

"Why didn't you tell us?" Nyomi shouted. When I didn't respond, she added, "That you guys got married!"

"That we—" The words evaporated off my tongue.

A strangled noise squeaked out of Shay. "Noah," she whispered. "Say something."

"Fuck."

chapter twenty-four

Shay

Students will be able to perform under pressure.

IF THERE WAS one thing small towns did with blinding efficiency, it was circulating hot gossip. I had no idea what catalyzed it from secret to gossip but there were far too many people—and goats—around to worry about that right now.

"We're just so happy for you," a woman said as she pushed a bouquet of flowers toward me.

"We were starting to think poor Noah would never find a nice girl," someone added. "He's such a sweetheart."

If only they knew that sweetheart was a feral animal in bed.

"He is a sweetheart," someone else agreed. "I was so happy when he outgrew that ugly duckling phase. I knew his moment was coming."

"Are you having a reception? You have to have a reception," another woman said, wedging a tin of cookies into the crook of my elbow.

"If you do, I'll bake the cake," a third woman said. "This is so exciting! Congratulations!"

"Thank you," I managed from behind an armload of flowers, wine, and assorted treats. "I didn't realize the news was out."

That was a delicate way of asking how the hell all these people knew about our under-the-radar marriage and why the information landed this morning, right around the time I was keyed up for another round between the sheets with Noah.

"I heard it from Jaclyn Ramos," a fourth woman said. "She wasn't sure if you kids were keeping it quiet or what but then she saw you smooching all over each other last night at the festival."

Ah, Jaclyn. This hurricane had a name. And, evidently, no concern for privacy.

"That old hen knows everything before anyone else," another woman said. "Goes to her head too."

"How long has she worked at Providence City Hall? What is it, thirty, thirty-five years? Of course she knows everything," someone said. I couldn't keep track of these people, not with all these flowers in my face. "But I'm sure these two don't mind her spreading the word."

Whyever would we mind half the town appearing at our door with the sunrise?

"Why would they?" someone chided. "These two are in love. Just look at them. Everything about them is so charming. That Ferris wheel damn near caught on fire last night. Everyone saw it."

I laughed but not for the reason any of these people expected. I laughed because they believed whatever they wanted to believe, the same way they had when I came here as a kid. They'd seen a spoiled little rich girl and they'd filled in the blanks as they saw fit. No one cared about knowing me beyond the highlights—famous mother, Swiss boarding school, Prada backpack—unless they wanted to know why I was living with Lollie, why I'd left the boarding school, why I couldn't simply live with my mother and be like any other family.

Those people didn't care to know me any more than the ones who read an entire world into the clothes my mother's personal shopper had sent from Barneys. But they wanted a piece of me just the same.

On the other side of the drive, Noah was trapped between Jim Wheaton and a younger man Gennie had introduced as Mr. Bones a few weeks back. I was only partially convinced that was his real name.

"You married her," I heard Jim say, his arms banded over his broad chest. "You *married* her."

"And you didn't tell us," Mr. Bones said. "You married her and you didn't mention a word of this."

"You married her," Jim repeated.

Noah glanced in my direction then, gave a slight shake of his head at the crowd gathered around us. I shrugged in response.

He arched his brows up as if to say *what the hell happened?*

I rolled my eyes. *Fuck if I know.*

He gave me a rueful smile. *Could be worse, right?*

I grinned back. *I don't want to know how.*

One of the goats gave a loud bleat and then they all followed suit, calling and hollering back and forth until it was too noisy to continue our conversations. The visitors started backing toward their trucks and four-wheelers, waving their goodbyes. There were hugs and well-wishes, more bottles of wine and champagne, and several not so thinly veiled comments tossed between our visitors about how they were keeping the newlyweds from our time together.

The problem wasn't that they were taking our time. It was that we'd never find our way back to the quiet bliss of lazing in bed with each other for the first time now that everything was out in the open.

"Time to move out," Mr. Bones called, motioning the goats forward. "Gotta get these gals up to yoga class."

"Why are you even here today?" Noah asked him. He motioned to Jim. "Or you? It's *Sunday*."

Jim winked. "Let's just say it's a special occasion."

As the group cleared—slowly and with several invitations to join families for dinner sometime soon—Noah and I retreated toward the farmhouse.

"What the fuck was that?" he asked as he waved to Mrs. Castro and her horse.

"It seems we have Jaclyn Ramos to thank."

"What do you mean, we have Jaclyn—*fuck*." He ran a hand down his face. "I can't believe I didn't think about that."

I handed him several of the wine bottles. "Nothing we can do about it now."

He swung a glance around the drive, concern suddenly etched on his face. "Where's Gennie?"

"I'm over here," she called. We spun around to find her in the chicken coop, egg basket hooked on her elbow and eye patch in place. "Those people were noisy and they annoyed the shit out of me." She snapped her fingers at one of the chickens. "Get away from me, dumbass."

"Hey, Gen," he said gently. "This was really hectic and surprising. I'm sorry. Can we talk, kid?"

In the chaos of this morning's breaking news, I'd lost sight of the fact that this big reveal had probably hit Gennie the hardest. All we'd ever wanted was to protect her and to insulate her from this crazy scheme of ours, but she got tossed into the deep end all the same. Any amount of resentment or hostility I felt over the unexpected announcement of our marriage was replaced with guilt. The last thing she needed was more upheaval and confusion in her life, and—

"I swear, I didn't tell anyone that you guys got married."

Noah just stared at her for a second. "What?"

"It wasn't me. I didn't do it. You don't have to get mad. Don't yell. I promise it wasn't me."

Noah and I shared yet another *what the fuck* glance.

When I could form words without sputtering out a long string of *why* and *how* and *what*, I said, "Let's go inside and talk. You said you wanted pancakes, right? I can make pancakes."

Gennie eyed me from inside the coop. "With chocolate chips?"

"Definitely," I said, enthusiasm cranked up to eleven. To Noah, I whispered, "Please tell me you haven't banned chocolate chips on account of them not occurring in nature or the disquieting uniformity of their shape."

He blinked away. "What about a bar of chocolate cut into chunks? Would that work?"

"Oh my god." I adjusted my hold on the goods in my arms, dangerously close to dropping all of it. "Everyone inside. We're making breakfast. Let's go."

NOW THAT I'D assigned myself the task of making pancakes, all I had to do was hunt down a recipe and then open each cabinet and drawer in Noah's kitchen to find everything I needed. Easy peasy. Much easier and much peasier than Noah's task of sitting Gennie down at the table and getting to the bottom of her little bombshell.

"You are not in trouble and I'm not upset," Noah said. "I am not yelling. Right? Can we agree on that?"

Instead of answering, Gennie asked, "Was it supposed to be a secret from me?"

He glanced between me and Gennie. I went looking for a mixing bowl.

"So, you see," he started, "it wasn't a secret so much as—"

"You guys would make the worst pirates," she yelled. "You'd never take over any ships or steal any loot."

Noah sighed. "Okay, well, be that as it may, I'd like to know what tipped you off and—"

"I didn't tell anyone," she insisted, her arms folded over her chest and her shoulders bunched up to her ears. "I don't suck at keeping secrets."

He dropped his arms to the table. "But how did you know?"

Gennie held up a finger. "You were looking at marriage stuff on your computer, you got dressed up in fancy clothes that one day and when I asked why you were dressed up, you said it was for adult business, and you guys are really obvious with all the love shit."

"The love shit," Noah repeated.

I whisked some eggs. I wasn't sure if that was part of the recipe but it seemed like the right thing to do.

"Yeah, you're in love and everything," Gennie said, as if she was stating the obvious. "That's why you had a sleepover with Shay last night and you're always doing nice stuff for her."

He looked up at me, his eyes wide and searching. I kept whisking.

"If you guys didn't want me to notice, you shouldn't have been kissing each other all the time."

"I guess we'll have to work on that," Noah said.

"I don't care," Gennie replied. "It's not gross anymore. I'm used to it now."

"That's a relief," he said under his breath.

"Is Shay going to move in? I think that's what married people do. They live together in the same house." She hit me with a big, expectant smile. "You can sleep in my room. I like the top bunk better but you can have it if you want."

I stared at Gennie and Noah, my fingers growing numb around the whisk. *No.* No, no, no. That wasn't an option. I was lonely in Lollie's big, empty house but it was *my* big, empty place to be lonely. It was where I wallowed in self-pity and invented wild explanations for the ex's exit from my life, where I drank wine in my underwear and ate pudding for breakfast. It was my cocoon, my safe, private space where I didn't have to pretend everything was all right and I could be as miserable or drunk or morose as I wanted. I needed Lollie's house more than I needed to maintain appearances on my fake marriage.

But if anyone figured it out—if they ever put together the terms of Lollie's estate and Noah's quest to snap up all the land on this side of the cove—it would be bad for us. Really bad.

The school wouldn't want a half-witted con artist teaching impressionable children. The town wouldn't want to buy milk and apples and raspberry jam from the farmer who defrauded an estate to grab some bargain-priced land. People around here had memories that stretched back generations. They wouldn't soon forget this and they wouldn't rush to forgive Noah either. Not to mention Gennie. God, things were hard enough on her as it was. She didn't need us piling on and making it worse with our antics.

I had to move in here. I had to leave my cocoon and my underwear wine behind. Unless I wanted to abandon everything—my teaching assignment, Lollie's farm, Noah and Gennie and everything we had going—I had to do this. I had to keep playing this game.

When I met Noah's gaze from across the room, his brows pinched and furrowed, it was clear he knew it too and he hated it as much as I did.

"I'm going to talk to my toys until the pancakes are ready," Gennie announced. "I think you guys need some alone time."

Once she was gone, Noah let out a long breath. His hands fell open on the tabletop. "I had no idea that she"—he pressed his palms to his eyes—"that she picked up on all that. When did she start reading everything on my screen? Hell, when did she start reading?"

"It doesn't matter." I shook my head, hoping to locate some levity in the midst of the wreckage I'd brought to everyone's lives. "Where would I find the"—I swirled my hands in front of me—"the thing to cook a pancake on? The flat surface thing."

Noah pushed to his feet, a scowl carving grooves around his mouth and eyes as he approached. He took stock of the aggressively beaten eggs and the other ingredients I'd lined up like brave soldiers. "This isn't how you make pancakes."

"It's not?" I tipped my head up to meet his gaze. "I don't actually have a lot of experience with pancakes. It just sounded like a good project for the moment."

He dropped his hands to my waist and backed me into the corner of the cabinets. The one from last night. The one with the biting. And... everything. With one swift movement, he picked me up, plopped my ass on the countertop, and pushed my legs wide-open. "Can we just go back to bed and pretend none of this ever happened?"

That sounded like a brilliant idea. Really and truly brilliant. But— "We can't do that again, Noah. We can't make this any more complicated."

He nuzzled into my neck and slipped a hand into my shirt. I mean, it was his shirt. Not that any of it mattered when his thumb stroked over my nipple, steady and firm and reminding me of all the things we should've been doing this morning.

"It's always been complicated, wife."

I ran my hands up his back, over his shoulders. "I'm not going to say last night was a mistake—"

"Thank god."

"—but I don't want to do that again."

He leaned back, shot me a growly frown. "Why not? It wasn't good for you?"

"It was *amazing* for me." I couldn't downplay it even if I wanted to. I was still recovering from the unbelievable high of all those orgasms. "*Everything* was amazing."

He settled between my legs, pressing tight to my center. I groaned at the feel of him, heavy and luscious against my most sensitive spots. "Tell me again about these complications."

"We don't want to make things more difficult," I ground out. "We can't sleep together anymore."

He brought his hands to my backside, shifting me to the edge of the countertop and then steering my body to slide right up against his in the most devastating ways. My inner muscles clenched hard, hard enough for a painful throb to radiate out from my core and leave all of me aching.

He scraped his teeth along the base of my neck. "Good luck with that plan."

"Maybe one more time," I said, my voice whiny and far away. "But just that *one* time."

"If that's what you want to tell yourself, go right ahead."

"But…Gennie," I said. "She thinks we're *married*."

"And I'll schedule some extra sessions with her therapist to talk it out," he replied, still occupied with my ass. "She'll be okay."

"You're sure about that? Because it wasn't long ago that you were telling me how Gennie had to stay far, far away from this mess of ours."

He growled against my neck, and for a minute it seemed like he wasn't going to respond. Eventually, he said, "Yeah. It would've been better that way. Better for *her*. But this is where we are now. Gennie and everyone else knows, and we can't change a damn thing about it."

"But what happens when this ends?"

The soft, fluffy cloud of sex hormones we'd been floating on for the past twelvish hours disintegrated with those words. Noah shifted his hands to the countertop, flat on either side of my backside, and leaned back so that only my knees pressed to his hips. "I'll handle it."

Again, I said, "But…Gennie. How are we going to protect her from that?"

He folded his arms over his chest. "I don't know." He nodded and dropped his gaze to my shirt. I knew he was staring at my nipples. Anyone within twenty feet would be staring at my nipples because they were tight, tender bullets that were testing the limits of this shirt. "Do you want Lollie's farm or not? That's the question you need to answer,

Shay. I can protect Gennie. I'll figure it out. Just don't make her any promises you don't intend to keep."

"I wouldn't."

We stared at each other for a long moment, the shadows of last night climbing up around us, pressing into every notch and groove between his body and mine. Everything was different. *We* were different. But here, it didn't feel different. It felt like we were on opposite sides of the bargaining table, every one of our unwinnable battles lined up, waiting for someone to make a concession.

"If you want Lollie's farm," he started, his words clipped, "we have to go down to Thomas House, get your things, and move you in here today." He lifted a hand, let it fall back against the arm banded over his chest. "I have an engineering crew scheduled to visit Twin Tulip this week and survey the site. Tell me now if you want me to call them off."

"I don't want you to call them off." I shoved my fingers into my hair. God, I needed a shower. I needed to sit in the shower and think for five or six hours. "But I don't want Gennie's world turning upside down. Or yours, for that matter."

"Of all the changes Gennie and I have experienced in the past year, this will be the least dramatic. It will turn your world upside down far more than it will ours."

With a petulant sigh, I said, "I can't just move in."

He eyed me, his brow arched up and those forearms just begging me to run my fingertips over the cords of muscle. I ignored that begging. "Yes, you can."

"And—and what will I do here?" I sputtered. "We can't play house, Noah. That's crazy and we already have enough crazy."

With a slow, indulgent blink, he said, "You'll do whatever you want, Shay. Come and go as you please. There's a spare room upstairs. I wouldn't force you to sleep with me, if that's what you're worried about."

"It's not what I'm worried about." A tiny, desperate part of me wanted Noah to *demand* that I sleep with him. Wanted his hand around my neck and his hips pinning me to the bed. A *very* tiny part. The rest of me knew that getting between the sheets with him again wasn't the answer to our problems. "This is your place. I don't want to intrude."

"I don't mind."

"Maybe you should," I said.

"That's tough shit because I don't." He rolled his eyes toward the ceiling, muttering something to himself I couldn't make out. "Come on, wife. I'm teaching you how to make pancakes now and then I'm breaking the news to Gen that you won't be taking the top bunk. Brace yourself for that storm." His jaw tight, he ran a glance up my legs, over my borrowed shirt, across my face. "You're not intruding. Stop thinking that. And stop pouting. You know I can't function when you do that."

"I'm not pouting."

He cupped my jaw and traced the pad of his thumb over my bottom lip. "You're pouting and I can't suck your nipples through this shirt right now because I don't want to stop at your nipples and—*oh my fucking god*, I said that out loud."

"And what else?" I whispered. "What was the next thing you were going to say?"

He dropped his hand as he stared at the floor. "Shay. Please."

"Tell me. I want to know. What would you do after you suck my nipples through this shirt I stole from you? What would come next?"

He shook his head. It seemed like this conversation was over when he blew out a ragged breath and said, "We don't have time for that this morning."

I couldn't stop pushing. Even if I pushed us all the way over the edge of a cliff, I couldn't stop. "What don't we have time for?"

He gave a dry, stuttering laugh. His cheeks were beet red. "That's enough out of you, wife. I need you to stop making that face and go find a bra unless you want me dragging you out to the barn and fucking you up against the wall."

Was it still a gasp if it came from the lusty region of France or was it just a sparkling moan? "Well—"

"No," he said. "You made me say it and I'm telling you right now, you don't want that. It's hot and dark in there, and it smells like motor oil. And I'm in no mood to be nice."

I tipped my head to the side. "You weren't nice last night."

He picked up a bowl, scowled at the aggressively beaten eggs. "That was different."

"How?"

"That was for you," he said, turning his scowl toward the items assembled on the countertop. "This…this would not be for you."

"Ohhh."

Pointing a finger in my direction, he said, "Don't. I mean it. The kid is awake and we have work to do and I can't hear that sound out of your mouth right now. I can't, Shay." He shook his head. "Five minutes ago you were telling me it was a one-time deal. You were the one who said it couldn't happen again."

"I mean, we shouldn't." The reluctance in my voice was as thick as butter.

He cut a sideways glance in my direction, his jaw rolling as he watched me. "But?"

I wasn't brazen. I was not. I didn't want to be dragged into a dark barn and pinned to a wall, my hands flat against wood and corrugated metal as Noah used me however he needed. Yet I couldn't stop myself from saying, "But it was really good." I ran my fingers over my lips, down the line of my neck. Where he'd kissed me, where he'd held me. "*Really* good."

With a rumbling growl, Noah pulled me off the countertop and marched me toward the stairs. I'd have little bruises all over my ass from this treatment tomorrow. Tiny spots of lilac and sapphire. "Up, now. Get out of here. Take a shower, find a bra, and do not come back until you can tell me what you want without changing your mind every few minutes." He delivered a smarting slap to my backside. "Do as you're told, wife."

And that was how I ended up sitting on the floor of Noah's shower and hosting a debate with myself as to whether we were the keys that unlocked some wild new desires in each other, or we were just starved for good sex and it happened to work out beautifully for both of us. Perhaps it wouldn't be like that the next time. That was probably the case. It wouldn't always be as good as last night. It couldn't.

It might be better.

"DO YOU NEED ANY HELP?"

I glanced up to find Noah leaning against the doorjamb. His eyes shadowed under another ball cap, he swept a glance at the boxes, totes, and suitcases strewn around me in his spare bedroom, the one right next door to his room. I motioned to the bed with its starched white duvet cover, now splashed with the reds and pinks and purples of several of my dresses. I hadn't bothered packing my closet at Thomas House, instead grabbing everything off the rack and tossing it in the back seat of my car for the short trip up the hill.

"Not really. Just sorting things out."

A significant portion of me hated this. I hated picking up and moving all over again, and I hated that—again—my life felt permanently temporary. I hated leaving behind the sanctuary I'd found in Lollie's home and I hated that I wouldn't be able to wander around for hours and stare at nothing anymore. Even if Noah said I was welcome to come and go as I wished, that didn't change the fact I now lived with a family and I couldn't do whatever I wanted without someone noticing.

If I parked myself on the porch, Gennie would come out to chat. Noah would check on me. Members of the farm crew would pass by. The chickens were bound to stare. I didn't have the freedom to watch the clouds and knit myself back together in peace. I was part of this place and this family now, and it didn't matter whether I wanted that or not.

Part of me resented the hell out of Lollie for backing me into a corner with this will. It didn't have to be this way and I couldn't imagine her wanting this for me or her land. But here I was, filing away one dress after another in my new closet while my fake—and devastatingly potent —husband watched.

The other side of me—a very small side that could benefit from some intensive therapy—was quivering in delight, fingers pressed to her lips to keep from squealing and a smile as big as the sun taking over her face. That side had a place to belong, a place where I was surrounded by people who not only wanted me but battled for my attention. I was the fun aunt who laughed with Gennie over the absurdity of Noah grating premium French chocolate into the pancake batter because he didn't believe in chocolate chips. I was the frisky wife who tempted her husband until his jaw was solid granite and his words sounded like rocks tumbling down a mountainside as he chased her up the stairs and out of sight.

Neither of those things were true, not true like the north or the stars, but this side of me didn't care about those details. This side would take the scraps and the crumbs, and cling to them as long as I could. It would make believe and I'd hold on until this ended the way everything ended for me.

"Let me help you with that," Noah said as I reached for one of the smaller boxes.

"It's fine." As I said this, he grabbed from the other side and we bobbled the box between us. This would not have been a problem if I'd packed like a sensible person. I had not. I'd tossed everything in without concern for where it went or whether I'd be able to find anything later, and that was how five children's storybooks, a bottle of probiotics formulated especially for women's health, and two vibrators ended up on the floor between us.

We stared at the toys for a solid minute. They were excessively veiny and blue, and completely devoid of any anatomical accuracy. One of them had a pair of uneven, asymmetrical heads. The other had circles and bumps up the shaft that called to mind an octopus.

It was a lot of information about the things I enjoyed inside me.

Eventually, Noah cleared his throat. "I know I shouldn't ask this but" —he ran a hand over his mouth—"how are those working out for you?"

"I—um." I looked anywhere but the floor. I wasn't ashamed but I was embarrassed, and that ticked something into gear for me. Something needy and insistent between my legs. Something that thrived on the unknown, the unfamiliar, the uncomfortable. "They're okay."

Noah kicked the door shut behind him. "Just okay?" He bent and picked up both vibes. He stared at them, turning them over and clicking through their settings. His ears flamed red. "Would it be wrong if I—" He paused and I knew he was forcing the words over his lips. "If I asked you to show me?"

"Not wrong," I managed, my whole body a hot, wet pool of *yes, please*. "But I don't know how." I gulped. "To show you, that is. I've never." I peered up, silently begging him to finish that sentence for himself.

"That's all right." The toy rumbled in his hand. "I've never watched."

"How do you know you want to?"

"I *know*." His gaze darkened. I swallowed hard. "Gennie is down at the goat pen. It's milking time."

The whir of the dual-headed vibrator was so loud. Like a wind turbine. Like a jet engine. "That's probably going to take an hour or two. Right?"

"At least an hour." His gaze swung between me and the toys.

After an interminably long minute, he moved toward the small desk tucked up against the wall, in front of the window. He grabbed the desk chair and positioned it backward at the foot of the bed. He set the vibes on the duvet, one of them still buzzing like a very clear, very crucial invitation. For I couldn't even begin to contemplate this without the granite-carved clarity of that invitation. I couldn't do the things I did with those toys while Noah watched unless I knew—I believed in every last cell of my body—that he wanted this without question.

He dropped into the chair and folded his arms over the back. Tipping his head to the side, he asked, "Isn't there something you'd like to show me?"

I blinked at him until I stopped thinking of all the problems with this plan. Then I dug in one of my bags until I found the item I needed. I held it out to him. "That one too."

Noah studied the deep red toy in the shape of a rose, and dark grooves of confusion immediately lined his forehead. "What does this —" He ran his thumb over the petals. "How is it—"

Before I could talk myself out of it, I stripped off my clothes and snatched up the rose. "You'll see."

He dropped his chin to his forearms and watched with a cool stare as I climbed on the bed. I didn't know where to put myself. Most of the time, I used these toys under the sheets. No thought went into positions or perspectives. I didn't care what it looked like. There was no one judging the thickness of my thighs when I spread them gratuitously wide or the way my belly jiggled as I chased an orgasm. There was no one watching and that was the precise reason I could do those things.

Suddenly I wasn't sure I could do them without the confidence that came with being alone. With knowing the only thing that mattered was making myself feel good.

"Down here," he said with a nod toward the end of the bed. "Bring the pillows with you. I want to be able to see your face while you—" He cleared his throat but didn't say anything else.

My inner thighs quivered as I settled on the bottom half of the bed, several pillows under my head and my bare feet resting on the footboard. I clutched the rose vibe hard in my hand and pinched my knees together.

This felt dirty in a weird, new way. It wasn't entirely comfortable. It was awkward and a bit unsettling. If I thought about it for any time at all, I'd convince myself I didn't want this. I didn't want to demonstrate the proper use of sex toys while my husband watched. I didn't want him to know how I touched myself when I was alone. If I thought about it, I could convince myself that I *shouldn't* want the overwhelming arousal that coursed through me like a fever.

Instead of thinking, I switched on the rose. The suction made a low, bubbling hum. It competed with the vibrator rumbling beside me and I decided that the noise was necessary. I could sink into the sound and let it drown out everything else. Let it drown out the growls and gasps from Noah. The sigh that slipped from my lips when I spread my legs and nudged the rose to my clit.

With my free hand, I held myself open as I worked the rose into the right position. It required a bit of finesse, but when I got there it was always worth it. *Always*.

"It's for—" Noah cleared his throat again. "It does something. To your clit."

"Mmmm." No longer concerned with the appearance of my thighs in this position, I let my knees fall all the way open. "It sucks me."

"Better than I do?"

I met his gaze down the length of my naked body. He held it a second before glancing between my legs and then back up, his lips pressed into a tight line. "Different."

"How? Explain it to me."

I shuddered when the toy started knotting the strings of an orgasm together. I wasn't there yet but getting close. "You're warm and soft, and you—*ohhhh, fuck*—you bite me." I trailed my fingers down to where I was wet and clenching, teasing just outside my core. "This is hard. It's aggressive. It bosses my clit around until it comes."

"Which do you like better?"

"It's not a competition," I chided. "I like this when I don't have anyone to lick my clit."

Honestly, I had no idea where these words were coming from. They weren't coming from me. I don't talk about sex or my body this way. I didn't possess the language to do this.

"It's a good thing you live here now," he said, his tone rough and strained. "I'll lick you any time you want."

He rested his cheek on his folded arms, his gaze still locked between my thighs. I reached for the vibrator beside me. A strangled noise rattled in the back of his throat. I pressed it to my opening and let my eyes shut as the sensations spiraled through me.

"How close are you?"

"Close," I whispered.

"What happens after? Are you done or do you keep playing?"

A breathy sigh burst out of me and I looked up at him. He was staring at the blue octopus vibe as I held it steady, letting it pulse and twitch inside me. I liked this toy because it required very little of me. I could slide it in, read something naughty, and let my body do the rest. "It depends what I want."

"What do you want right now?"

How was I supposed to answer that? How could anyone be expected to form words at a time like this?

"What do *you* want?" I asked.

He wheezed a humorless laugh and shoved a hand through his hair. "I want *this*."

I clicked the rose to a higher setting. It nearly stole my words. "I don't believe you."

He dropped a hand to his lap. The back of the chair obscured his movements but the agony that twisted across his face told me everything about what he was doing. "Believe it, wife."

The orgasm hit me a minute sooner than I'd expected. It came up fast and it blitzed through my muscles, leaving me shaky and uncoordinated.

I blinked at Noah but my eyes wanted to stay closed. It was like I'd accidentally popped a sleeping pill instead of a multivitamin and now each blink lasted several minutes. I couldn't get my thumb on the right button to switch off the rose, and the fingers on my other hand gave up holding on to the toy. I tried but I'd lost my depth perception along with all control over my body, and I ended up pinching at my inner thigh.

A feral sound snapped out of Noah as I went right on rolling my hips into the pulses and waves of my toys. It was mostly involuntary. Like I said, this vibe didn't require much of me and since the power button had vanished from the rose, there was no reason to stop now.

"You're so fucking beautiful." He said this as if it was an insult. As if he was more than a little angry about it. "Just so fucking—"

He didn't finish that thought because my inner muscles clenched hard and I cried out, a moany-groany jumble of swearing and sighing as another orgasm hit. This one was smaller. The first had knocked me over so this one could only kick at the rubble but that was all it took for the vibe to fall out of me and onto the floor in front of Noah.

"Oh my god," I mumbled into my hand.

Noah bent to collect the toy from the floor. He switched it off before pushing to his feet and stepping up to the footboard. Running a hand up my inner thigh, he asked, "Do you want to keep going with this one?"

He covered the hand holding the rose to my clit. I shook my head. "I can't find the button."

"Let me take care of it for you." After giving me one last lick from the toy, he pulled it away and turned it off. The hum of sex toys died. He brought a hand between my legs, gently covering me. "Is that better?"

I nodded. I felt like a child. An adorable, precious, depraved child. Maybe not an actual child but I most certainly felt precious. And so depraved. I mean, where the hell did all of *that* come from?

Though the fog of orgasm was dense, I could see his thick erection trapped under his jeans. I held out a hand to him and he took it. But rather than climbing over me or unbuttoning those jeans, he pressed his lips to my palm.

"I want to do something for you," I said.

He tapped a finger to my opening. "That was for me."

"I want to do something you'll enjoy," I argued.

"I *did* enjoy that."

"But it's your turn and—"

He kissed me, his lips hungry and insistent. "Listen to me, wife. I told you what I wanted when I asked you to show me how you use your toys. I watched you fuck yourself senseless and come until you went cross-eyed—*twice*."

With the coordination of a newborn deer, I reached for his cock. "But—"

Just then, the kitchen door slammed shut and Gennie yelled, "I got to milk two whole goats!"

"Not right now, sweetheart." He kissed my forehead, adding, "We have all the time in the world."

He gathered up the toys and set them on the desk, and returned the chair to its original position. Still quivering everywhere and incapable of moving from this splayed-open position, I watched as he glanced at the items on the desk. Books, skincare, earrings. He reached for something in the ceramic bowl I used to store my everyday jewelry. I assumed it was another wonky pair of earrings, maybe the gourds that looked a little too phallic for school use.

But then I saw the ring of twine pinched between his fingers.

He didn't have to say anything. He didn't have to make a comment about me keeping it or stowing it in a place of importance. No words necessary. He could fill in the blanks, even if I was still hazy on some of the answers.

He returned it to the bowl and shifted to adjust himself. "I should check on Gennie," he said. "You should—" He glanced around, his eyes brightening when he spotted my bathrobe. He draped it over me like a blanket and it was the nicest thing anyone had ever done for me after I'd masturbated in front of them. "I'll keep her downstairs for a few hours."

"Okay." I shrugged but it felt like a muscle spasm. "I'm going to get up. Put on some clothes. Be a human again. I just need a minute."

Stopping beside the bed, Noah ran his palm down my cheek. "I need a lot more than a minute and all I did was watch. Stay here, sweetheart. Close your eyes. You deserve it."

JAIME WAS busy folding laundry on her bed when I called late Sunday evening. Noah was negotiating the terms of a bath with Gennie, and I was still an uncoordinated, boneless wreck after the events of this afternoon. Tremors still ran up and down my inner thighs and I didn't think I'd be able to sit down for a week without thinking of Noah. It only made sense for me to skulk away to my new bedroom under the pretense of lesson planning but really to confess my sins to my best friend.

That was what everyone did when hiding from their fake husband after giving him a sex toy show.

"What's shaking, doll?"

"My legs." No point in drawing this out. "You told me so."

She pinned a towel under her chin as she brought the edges together. "I'm gonna need you to be more specific."

"Noah. And…you know."

She sifted through her basket, draping a skirt over the side and tossing smaller items to the bed. "But I *don't* know. What did your Daddy Bread Baker do and why do we love him for it?"

"We don't *love him*," I said.

"We don't love him because you are very busy remembering what actual love is all about. It will take time for you to recognize it and stop pushing it away."

"I am not pushing anything away," I argued. "As a matter of fact, I didn't push him away when he invited me to come home with him last night."

"Ohhhhh." She nodded. "I take it that dough rises."

My cheeks were hot and I couldn't suppress my grin when I said, "Something like that."

Jaime settled back against her headboard, sipping her water for a moment. Then, "Is this where you tell me it was a one-time deal and it's never happening again?"

"Well, it wasn't just the one time. There were two times. And then another—um, thing. And I moved in with him because the villagers gathered outside his house and essentially threw flowers and wine at us and then broke into song."

She closed her eyes and dragged a fingertip over her brows. "Is that small-town speak for *he rocked my world so hard that my neighbors know his name*?"

"Okay, so, he did—"

"Knew it." She gave a slow, smug nod.

"—but there were actual people at his house this morning and now I have to live with him."

"Have to live with him. Get to live with him." She held up her hands. "What's the difference?"

"We only moved me in here because—"

"The reason isn't too important," she interrupted. "I know it seems like it is but this was bound to happen. One way or another."

I glared at her. "Have you been reading tea leaves again?"

"I'm not dignifying that with a response." She sniffed. "I will only say that I hope you're cozy and comfortable shacking up with your Daddy Bread Baker."

"You really need to stop calling him that."

"I like it. I think it fits." She took another sip. "And I told you so."

chapter twenty-five

Noah

Students will be able to rebel without apology.

I GROANED out loud when my mother's name flashed across my phone Tuesday afternoon. I loved my mother. I cared about her very much. I wanted the best for her. But there were times when she was an almighty pain in my ass and I knew this would be one of them.

Letting it go to voicemail wasn't a real option. I'd have to call her back one way or another. At best, I'd delay this conversation by a day. At worst, she'd call the farm stand and ask them to track me down.

I didn't need that kind of drama in my life. Not today. It had been hours but I still hadn't recovered from running into Shay while she was dressed in nothing but a towel this morning.

Living with my wife was much more treacherous than I'd originally imagined. There couldn't be anything worse than knowing my wife was all alone down at Thomas House, right? Wrong. Knowing my wife was all alone on the other side of the wall was far worse.

She'd insisted on staying in the spare bedroom the past two nights. Something about a strict school-night routine and not being able to teach the next day if I kept her up all hours. No debate allowed. Instead, I kept myself up all hours listening for any sign she'd changed her mind.

That, of course, led to an increasingly vivid series of half-awake dreams where Shay climbed into bed with me and I found her naked beneath a silky robe. She sank down over my cock and I held those plush hips while I drove up into her. In some variations, she sucked my fingers. In others, I fisted her hair in one hand and covered her mouth with the other.

I woke up with my blood pounding hot and fast in my veins. I was needy in the most dreadful, ugly ways. Shay could barely walk by without my cock thickening in response. I'd wheezed my way through breakfast this morning, my skin too tight and my thoughts barely more than complete filth.

So, yeah, I was having a rough day.

"Hey, Mom." I pushed to my feet and stalked across my office. "How are you?"

"Noah, did you get *married*?"

I jogged down the back stairs and out the door. This would go down better for everyone if I stayed in motion, and I believed enough of that lie to march down a long, bumpy row of Cortland apple trees. "Yeah, I did."

Complete silence greeted me. I made it halfway down the row before she said, "But why?"

"Same reason everyone gets married, Mom." An unenforceable will. Access to premium land. Loving a high school crush so hard I couldn't help but throw myself on her problems.

Again, my mother was speechless. I'd expected this. She loved and accepted everyone though she couldn't comprehend anything out of me or Eva that didn't align with her inflexible vision of what was right and appropriate.

Eventually, she said, "This is the first I'm hearing of it."

"That's true." I reached the end of the Cortlands and looped back up another row. This was good. I hadn't put eyes on these trees for weeks. It was good. Time well spent. "Sorry about that. It never came up." Because I was exhausted and wrung-out from the endless circus that was well-intentioned people asking me questions about my marriage that I wasn't prepared to answer.

Are we going on a honeymoon? No, she barely wanted to go to the Harvest Festival with me. Interstate travel was a bridge too far.

Are we thinking about starting a family any time soon? Strictly rehearsals.

Are we so thrilled and over the moon to be together? Yeah, it was awesome to get everything I'd ever wanted only for my wife to remind me on a daily basis that it wasn't real and wouldn't last. Fucking awesome.

Wheatie and Bones were the worst by far. After that shitshow on Sunday morning, I assumed they'd suss out the holes in this story. Especially after previously swearing up and down that nothing was happening between me and Shay. But they skimmed right over those issues and into more meaningful topics such as the future of the Thomas land. To say they were relentless would be an understatement. If they sensed anything about this union was amiss, they ignored it to focus on the untapped potential down at Twin Tulip.

"I've had my hands full," I added when the silence stretched too thin. "We finished work on the new bottling center and Gennie just started school."

"Are you taking that girl to church on Sundays? She needs spiritual guidance, Noah."

A quiet laugh shook my chest. A lot of good that guidance did me and my sister. "Thank you for the reminder."

"It's the least you can do for her," my mother went on.

Sure. It wasn't like Gennie's therapist bumped up into a new tax bracket after taking her on as a client or I turned my life upside down or anything.

"We just don't know—" She cleared her throat several times. It took a moment for her to get the next words out. "We don't know what that child has endured."

Leaving the office was the right approach. Fresh air, sun, apples as far as the eye could see. And plenty of room to scream without anyone hearing.

"She's doing all right."

"I appreciate that you're giving her a proper family structure now," she said, "though I worry you might've gotten carried away with this marriage. And isn't she—your new bride—the troubled girl that Lollie Thomas took in, the one you tutored in math and science?"

This was the great paradox of my mother. If Shay had been a member of the congregation, she would've embraced every one of her rough edges and abrupt endings. She would've admired Shay's willingness to try again—and again and again. And she'd marvel in the woman my wife had become. She'd celebrate Shay.

But my mother couldn't extend that grace when it came to anyone who passed beyond the arm's length of the congregation and into the circle of her family. And that circle was rife with judgment and strait-jacket structure and expectations that had never made a whole hell of a lot of sense.

"Shay is a teacher," I said as calmly as I could manage. "She's teaching at Hope Elementary this year. Second grade. They love her there."

I love her here.

And for fuck's sake, my wife wasn't a stray pup from the wrong side of the tracks. It'd always bothered me when my mother eyed Shay like she was a cautionary tale on legs. Aside from the fact Shay's mother was a household name, the only portion of Shay's life not spent in a cashmere bubble was the time spent in this town.

"That's good to hear." She cleared her throat again. Talking for this long was difficult for her. We'd need to wrap this up soon. She couldn't spend all her energy for the day on a phone call. "I would've traveled there for a wedding, you know."

"I know." If I kept walking, I'd hit the old stone wall separating the orchard from Twin Tulip. Maybe I could throw rocks for an hour or two. That was a highly reliable way to process emotions. I wouldn't be able to feel my arm tomorrow but I didn't need both of them every day. "We wanted something small."

"I'm just one person, Noah. You can have a small wedding and still invite your only living parent."

I was in no mood to point out that she never went anywhere without my aunt and at least a half dozen people who fell into the mixed bag of friends, distant relatives, and people she met along the way and swept into her de facto flock.

"We did what felt right for us," I said.

She sniffed. "I'll have to live with that."

That comment brought a rueful smile to my face. Unlike my sister, rebellion wasn't my drug of choice. I found that subversive compliance worked much better for me. I was going to do whatever the hell I wanted but I'd make it look like I was toeing the line. Or better yet, I'd toe the line so hard I'd prove why the line was a fucked-up notion to begin with.

But this—marrying the *troubled girl* and refusing to apologize for doing it our way—went down with the salty satisfaction of pure, clear-eyed rebellion.

"Well. I have a team preparing Eva's appeal," I said, rounding a short row of Pink Lady apples. "I'll take Gennie to visit her next month. Any interest in traveling for that?"

I didn't have to ask to know the answer.

"That's too much for me," she replied. "It would take me a month to recover from a trip to a *penitentiary*, Noah."

There was no grace for Eva. None whatsoever. There were moments when I debated whether she was deserving of grace. She'd pulled that trigger. She'd killed that agent and wounded others. But she was still my sister. She was my mother's daughter. If we couldn't be the ones to love her through the worst, most impossible moments, what was the point of family? What was the point of any of it if we stopped giving a shit the minute those people fucked up?

"Right," I murmured. "I'll let you know when I get any news on the appeal."

"It's enough to know you're working on it. The details stress me too much." After a round of coughing, she added, "Look after my granddaughter. That's all I need."

"I hear you, Mom. That's what I'm doing."

"And extend my congratulations to your new wife. Let's hope she's a good influence for Imogen." She sniffed. "Maybe you could bring her for a visit for the holiday season."

I bent to grab an egg-shaped rock from under a Gala apple tree. I tossed it in the air once and let it thunk down into my palm. It was going to sound great splashing into the cove. "We'll see about that."

chapter twenty-six

Noah

Students will be able to confess (almost) everything.

"THEN ELLA SAID her baby brother takes baths in the kitchen sink! That is disgusting!" Gennie roared.

I met Shay's gaze across the kitchen table as she gathered plates and silverware from dinner. I gave a single shake of my head and hoped she knew that meant *does this story make any sense to you? Are babies really bathed in sinks?*

"Is it disgusting because of the baby or disgusting because of the sink?" she asked.

Gennie scrunched up her face. "All of it."

"What if you were bathed in the sink?" she asked.

"Momma isn't that wacky," Gennie muttered, clearly disappointed in our reaction to the outrage of Ella's baby brother's tub routine. "Is there any dessert for people who like dessert tonight? You said I could ask about dessert on Friday and it's Friday so I'm asking."

I shared a private grin with Shay as she stepped away from the table carrying the dishes. If there was anything I'd learned in living with her for the past two weeks it was that she *needed* to help with preparing the meal or cleaning up from it.

"Are you a person who likes desserts?" I asked my niece.

Gennie drummed her fingers on the tabletop, her lips rolled inward and her eyes sparkling. She'd launched a case for dessert early in the week and pled it every chance she got. I found it odd considering there was no shortage of sweets from the bakehouse around here but then I realized it wasn't a general request when she asked for tapioca pudding. She said Eva used to make it and tell stories about how her mother made it when she was a kid.

For the life of me I couldn't remember anything like that, but apparently Eva did and now Gennie remembered it too.

Nyomi whipped up several batches of pudding and she was halfway in love with one of the recipes and threatening to put it into production to sell at the farm stand. I didn't care about that but I was looking forward to unveiling this for Gennie tonight. It was nice being able to grant her a wish once in a while. So many of them were far outside the scope of my abilities. More than that, she deserved something good. I hadn't received a single call from school this year to report bad behavior—or language. There hadn't been any fights on the playground and the pirate talk was at a minimum during school hours.

"I'm always a person who likes dessert," Gennie said, as outraged about this oversight as she was about Ella's brother naked in the sink. "I've told you that a thousand hundred times!"

"That many?" Shay asked as she loaded the dishwasher. "And Noah still doesn't know?"

"Not so fast," I said, moving toward the fridge. "I might have something in here."

"What is it?" Gennie asked, bouncing in her seat. "What is it, what is it, I have to know!"

"Hmm. Where did I put it? Maybe I forgot it over at the bakehouse."

Shay grinned at me like I was a real pain in her ass with this ruse before turning back to the dishwasher. She had no clue how much I enjoyed being *her* pain in the ass. I wasn't sure she'd see it that way but I didn't care. I could keep it to myself the same way I always did.

"I have to know," Gennie wailed, both hands pressed to her cheeks and her mouth stretched wide in agony. "Don't make me wait, Noah!"

"Oh, look," I murmured. "Tapioca pudding."

"Fuck yeah," Gennie yelled. "Shay, my mom used to make this for me, and her mom made it for her. It's my super best favorite."

"I love that," Shay replied. "What makes it your favorite?"

"Momma used to tell me about being a little girl and how she helped her mom make jam. She'd put a little raspberry jam on my pudding and swirl it around like this"—she scribbled a hand in front of her—"but she always said the jam from the store wasn't as good as her momma's jam."

I brought the pudding to the table with a bowl and spoon, and I swallowed down the forty different reasons that story pinched at the last of my patience. Hearing about Eva's experiences with our mother from Gennie was one of the most surreal and uncomfortable parts of being her guardian. I had to bury all trace of the battles that went down between my mother and sister when she still lived at home. I had to pretend my mother hadn't turned her back on Eva after she moved out, or that Eva seemed to pride herself on refusing to be the one to reach out to the Reverend for *years*. I had to let Gennie keep her memories intact, the ones that sounded like revisionist nostalgia, and never reveal the other side of those events.

"You should make pudding with jam when you have a little girl," Gennie said to Shay.

A bunch of silverware clanked to the bottom of the dishwasher. "Sorry about that," Shay called. "I just—it slipped and—and it's fine. Everything's fine."

"When you have a baby," Gennie continued, "you should make them pudding. Even babies can eat pudding. They don't need teeth for pudding."

I glanced at Shay but she was busy fishing out forks. "Let's not worry about pudding for other people," I said. "Pick the jam you want."

Gennie bounded out of her seat and into the pantry, saying, "I already know I want mixed berry. It's the best." She slammed the jar down on the table. This child didn't know her strength—or she loved making a fuck-ton of noise. Probably a bit of both. "Ginger peach is another best. And apricot. And tangerine marmalade. And—"

"Okay," I interrupted. This could go on for hours. It was the price I paid for dragging her to all the farmers markets. "Mixed berry it is. How much do you want?"

Immediately, I recognized this to be a stupid question when Gennie replied, "Medium."

"How much is medium?"

She brought her thumb and forefinger together. "This much."

"That's height. What about circumference?"

"She wants a teaspoon of jam," Shay called from the other side of the kitchen. "Six-year-olds don't understand circumference."

"Do you think your baby will like jam or marmalade better?" Gennie asked Shay.

"Which do you like better?" Shay asked.

"I can't choose. I like them both," my niece said.

"Focus on this jam," I said to her as I spooned a dollop of mixed berry over the pudding. "How's this? Is it what you wanted?"

She took a tentative bite and gazed off into the distance like she was having an existential moment. Then, "It's the most magnificent thing I've ever eaten."

A laugh burst out of me and I leaned back in my chair. "Great. Nyomi will be thrilled."

After another bite, she added, "Mixed berry is the best jam for pudding."

I appreciated that. Mixed berry could be a beast to get right without one of the berries stealing the show. "Do you think we should put together a take-home tapioca kit? Ny's pudding and a jar of jam?"

Gennie shook her head. "No. It's a family secret. We shouldn't sell that shit."

Shay joined us at the table, a glass of white wine in hand. "Are you happy? Is this a good dessert for people who like dessert?"

"It's not good. It's *great*," Gennie replied.

Shay grinned at me. "The wonders of pudding."

"Do not interpret this as any indication you should resume your pudding breakfast lifestyle," I said. "We're not doing that here."

"Right, because it's so much better to hand-slice bread every time someone wants toast. Far more sensible."

I leaned back in my chair and crossed my arms. "It doesn't take that long."

She took a sip of her wine and I could almost hear her response gathering steam. "No, I guess you're right about that. It doesn't take long to slice bread. The process does slow down when we have to ride out to the dairy to get butter because you prefer fresh batches every few days, or when we have to go skulking around in the cheese basement—"

"It's not a cheese *basement*," I argued.

"—because you want cheese aged down to a specific day—"

"It makes a difference," I muttered.

"—or when we have fifteen different jars of jam in the fridge but we're not allowed to touch any of them because you're always in the middle of one secret project or another. Or fifteen."

"There are at least forty other jars that you are welcome to use." I gestured toward the pantry. "I believe you know where they are. You're familiar with the pantry. Aren't you, wife?"

She swallowed her smile with a sip of wine and glanced away.

Gennie loudly sucked every trace of pudding off her spoon. "These balls feel really big in my mouth."

I met Shay's gaze across the table. She gave an almost imperceptible shake of her head and rolled her lips inward to fight off a grin. "What was that?" I asked my niece.

"The balls," she replied, digging her spoon into the pudding once more. "They're really big."

"I see," I managed.

"In the pudding," she added. "They're big tapioca balls. Momma's pudding never had big balls."

Shay brought a hand to her mouth and stared down at the table. Her shoulders shook a little and I could hear the stuttering of a repressed laugh.

"I still love this pudding." Gennie sucked the spoon and stared off into the distance again. "Even if it's not the same as my memories."

"Because of the balls," Shay said, a laugh tearing through each word. I grabbed her wineglass and set it out of reach. "Hey! Give that back."

"I will when you behave yourself," I said.

"The balls feel different on my tongue," Gennie continued, ignoring both of us. "But it tastes the same."

I jabbed a finger toward Shay as she wheezed with laughter. So often, she was the one to keep a straight face but that was falling apart before my eyes. I kind of loved it. "Stop that."

"I'm trying," she said, tears welling in her eyes. "I am trying. I swear. I just—" She shot a sidelong glance at Gennie. "I can't."

"Now that I've tried it, I think I like the big balls," Gennie said. "I can bite them!"

I caught Shay's eye and we burst out laughing together.

LATER THAT NIGHT, I leaned against the doorway into Shay's room. "Hi."

She looked up from her work at the desk with a smile. "Hey."

She'd changed into a small pair of shorts and a slouchy sweater that always bared at least one shoulder in offering. No bra. I loved when she ditched the bra. Earrings too. The at-home version of Shay was one of my favorites. "Can I come in?"

We were still sorting out the rules of cohabitating while fake-married. We had no problem sneaking around and having sex in every semiprivate space we could find—pantry, barn, bathroom—but we hadn't slept together since that night after the Harvest Festival. Though no one said it out loud, sharing a bed for the purposes of sleep was one step too far. It was too far for Shay because she had her eyes on a clean exit from this town and our marriage at the end of her year here. It was too far for me because I already knew I wouldn't recover when she left. I didn't need to add memories of holding her every night to that horror show.

So, we kept to our separate rooms and treated each other to a certain amount of polite distance. She checked in with me each morning to confirm whether Gennie was getting a ride home with her or taking the bus to hang out with Gail. I checked in each afternoon to ask if she wanted to eat dinner with me and Gennie. We were so fucking polite.

I knocked on her door every night to tell her Gennie was asleep. She knocked on my door in the morning to tell me when she was getting into the shower. I knew she did this so we didn't end up competing with each other for hot water but I liked to torture myself and pretend she did it so I'd know exactly when she'd be naked.

There were moments when I thought this information served as an invitation to join her in there. Part of me *loved* the idea of barging into the bathroom, throwing back the shower curtain, climbing in there with her, and twisting her wet hair around my palm while I fucked her against the tile wall. No questions, no conversation. The other part of me knew I'd never pull off a stunt like that. I'd talk myself out of it before opening the door.

Unless Shay made it very clear that she wanted my companionship in the shower. Especially companionship of the barging-in, hair-pulling variety.

"Of course you can come in," Shay said, waving me forward.

Thank god she didn't know I was half hard and fully obsessed with her.

"Thanks." I shut the door behind me and flopped onto her bed, burying my face in the duvet. It smelled like her and now I was more than half hard. "Gen had a million things to talk about tonight. Question after question. So much to talk about. Her head is like a beehive."

"What's on her mind?"

I dug a thumb into the back of my neck to loosen the tension there. "Nothing. Everything."

"What is this about?" Shay pushed to her feet and moved toward the bed. "You're always grabbing at your neck. What's going on?"

"It's fine."

"It's obviously not." She batted my hand away and ran the backs of her fingers over my shoulders and along my neck. "You are wound tight enough to form your own diamonds, Noah."

"It's not that bad," I grumbled.

"Ha." She opened a few drawers before saying, "Take your shirt off."

I did not have to be asked twice.

"Okay, tough guy," she said, dropping her phone on the bed beside me. "I'm going to work on your knots. Is that all right?"

"You're welcome to them."

She climbed up and settled low on my back, her calves tight against my flanks. "I'm going to use some lotion. It smells a little bit like honey and almond though it's not an overpowering scent. No one is going to think you fell in a bucket of perfume. Does that work? I'm sure I can find something more neutral if you really hate it."

Honey and almond. *Fucking finally.* I'd only driven myself crazy trying to place those scents. "I don't mind," I said. "It'll wash off in the shower tomorrow morning."

Murmuring in agreement, Shay worked the lotion into my upper back, shoulders, and neck. It felt otherworldly. Her hands were strong and relentless, and I loved the way she touched me. Even better, the tension seemed a little looser.

I decided to fuck it all up by asking, "Do you want to have kids? Someday? You know, since Gennie brought it up tonight."

Her hands stilled on my shoulders. For a second I thought we were finished, massage foreplay was over, and I'd have to hobble out of here with my aching cock. But then she said, "There was a time when I thought I wanted kids. I thought I wanted the whole picture-perfect family and everything that came with it."

"What changed that?"

She moved her hands down my shoulders, squeezing as she went. "A relationship ended and I had to—to reevaluate."

"And kids didn't make the cut?"

She gave a wry laugh. "I don't know. I'm still figuring out what it is I want and what I've convinced myself to want." She squirted more lotion into her palm. "What about you?"

"In case you haven't noticed, one niece is more than enough for me."

"You never thought about marrying someone nice for reasons unrelated to expanding your empire or faking it for an estate?"

I chuckled into the duvet. "Not really, no."

Because I only thought about marrying you.

"You don't imagine yourself giving Gennie a cousin or two?"

Some version of that question came my way frequently. Everyone wanted to know if I wanted *kids of my own.* As if contributing sperm was superior and I should prefer that over a simple blood relation to Gennie. But I knew that wasn't the question Shay was asking. She wanted to know where the future would take me and whether I saw more small people who'd scream at me about baby carrots there. "I don't think so, no. I'm not going to tell you that I have an iron-clad plan because god knows all of my plans fall apart on me, but when I look five years down the road I don't see more kids there. It's hard enough caring for Gennie. She needs all of my attention."

"And she'd raise hell if you tried to bathe a baby in the kitchen sink."

"Oh my god. I know."

She drove her knuckle into the slope of my shoulder and it hurt like hell but it was a good hurt. "I'm not sure I'll believe you if you try to tell me that you weren't looking to wife someone up in Manhattan. Or Brooklyn. I bet you couldn't walk down the street without getting up close and personal with some yoga pants."

"I wasn't looking to wife anyone up," I said. "And I can't say I paid much attention to the yoga pants."

"Noah. Do not lie to me and pretend you were a monk. I've seen you in a suit and I know a thing or two about New York girlies. You had to beat them off with a lead pipe and you know it."

If there was one thing I did not want to discuss with my wife it was the sex I had before marrying her. Not because it was mind-blowing or even that great in volume but because I didn't want to think about *her* having sex before our marriage. I knew she did—and I'd known it back when we were teenagers too—but she was mine for this moment and I didn't want to make eye contact with the moments she'd belonged to someone else.

"I worked too damn much," I said. "Anything beyond that was…incidental."

"Except for all those so-called business meetings in the Hamptons where you definitely did not have any fun whatsoever because you were a good little lawyer."

"Don't forget the yachts," I said. "I was a very good lawyer on yachts too."

"You were going to live the big law bachelor life indefinitely?"

"I didn't hate the big law bachelor life," I said carefully. "It had its advantages. Not a single discussion of the size of tapioca balls, for one."

"When she's all grown up, we'll have to embarrass the shit out of her with that story. That's the kind of thing we trot out when she brings home the person she's dating for the first time or when we give a toast at the rehearsal dinner before her wedding."

It wasn't lost on me that Shay was speaking of a future where my niece brought dates home to *us* and *we* gave toasts at her wedding. Rather than fucking that up, I simply said, "You're damn right."

"Just tell me if this is too personal," she said, her thumbs working my lower back. "I was wondering if Eva is allowed visitors. Does she get to see Gennie at all?"

"Not too personal. Eva is allowed visitors. Gennie and I went to see her a couple of times. Those were—" I shook my head. "They were difficult visits."

Shay murmured. "What happened?"

"Aside from the obvious issues, we had to travel. Eva's trial was conducted in Michigan and she remained there as she awaited sentencing. It didn't occur to me until it was time to board the flight that Gennie might have trouble flying. She panicked. Complete and total meltdown. Screamed for an hour straight before falling asleep on the floor under her seat."

"Oh, shit."

"Yeah. The whole time I was sitting there thinking to myself that we'd have to do this all over again to get home. I started looking up trains and rental cars. Even private planes. There was a second where I thought we'd just live in Michigan forever." I laughed. "I called the pediatrician when we landed and she told me to load her up on antihistamines before the return flight. That succeeded in making her high as fuck. Seriously, she wore sunglasses that she might've shoplifted and sat on my lap while chain-eating M&Ms, and recited every word of *Pirates of the Caribbean* to me, complete with spot-on accents. And those were just the flights, Shay. Throw in the stress of traveling to a detention facility, going through all the security protocols, and then waiting for hours to see Eva—it was chaos. She spent four full days building up to a tantrum, experiencing a tantrum, or recovering from a tantrum. And then we repeated some version of that cycle two other times."

"I'm sorry. That must've been so hard on you."

"It was harder on Gennie," I said, though I appreciated the validation. Sometimes I forgot how much I needed it. "She remembers it being awful so she panics even more."

"It's a lot to ask of a little kid. It's a lot to ask of both of you."

"Yeah, well, we're going to have to do it all over again soon. Eva was moved to a federal facility in West Virginia upon sentencing and I promised her we'd visit. There's a long weekend coming up in November that seems like a good time to go. We'll drive this time. I think that will be better."

"Do you want any help with that?" she asked slowly. "I mean, an extra pair of hands? I can come along if it's going to make it easier for you and Gennie."

As much as it pained me to say it, I couldn't bring Shay to visit Eva. Not because Eva or Gennie would have a problem with it but because I couldn't give my niece everything she needed while also taking care of my wife. And I knew Shay would say she didn't need that from me but that didn't change the fact I wanted to take care of her and it would kill me if I couldn't.

"Not this time," I said. "I want to see if Gennie handles it better when we drive and make a lot of stops along the way so it's less overwhelming. That's what the psych suggested."

"That makes perfect sense. Just let me know if there's anything I can do to help."

After a few minutes of silence, I said, "I still can't believe she'll be behind bars for the rest of her life."

Shay hummed to herself for a second. "Can I ask how Eva got caught up in a situation like that? From everything I remember you saying when she first moved out, it seemed like she was pretty street-smart."

"She is. She was," I said. "I don't know how it happened. I'm still trying to figure it out." I groaned into the duvet when Shay kneaded a tender spot on my upper back. It seemed I was a bag of rocks covered in skin. "She spent all these years wandering around North America without a permanent address and doing everything on her terms, only for it to fall apart in a matter of months after meeting the boyfriend. How she got mixed up with the kingpin of the northern border drug trade, I'll never fully understand."

"She probably believed she knew him," she said.

"But—how?"

"It takes nothing at all to convince ourselves that we know someone's values and their intentions. That we know their heart. And it's devastating when they show us who they really are. I bet she rehashes every moment of that relationship daily."

It didn't sound like we were talking only about Eva anymore.

"Anyway." Shay gave a light slap to my flank. "I need you to stop thinking about all of this now. You're twisting yourself into knots all over again."

"You're the one asking these questions. What else do you want me to think about?"

"Think about Twin Tulip," she said, her fingers working the base of my skull. It felt weird in a very nice way. "Are the engineers and architects finished yet? When will they have designs for us to look at? And didn't you say it was almost time to plant the bulbs?"

"Bulbs will be in the ground within two weeks," I replied. "Bones has it under control. He wants to wait until it's a little colder. Something about avoiding mildew from the ground being too warm."

"Does he hate having to deal with flowers?"

"No, he loves this shit. He went through the Master Gardener program at the University of Rhode Island two years ago, mostly because he's a squirrel and needed something to do during the winter while he was planning a pollinator garden, and now all he wants to talk about is tulips. If you see him, don't ask about the flowers unless you want to smile and nod while he babbles at you for an hour or two."

She laughed. "Noted."

"The last I checked, the engineers and architects are haggling over a few things. Being as close as we are to the cove, and with the way sea levels are rising and hundred-year storms are occurring much more frequently, there are many more variables to consider."

"That sounds important. We'll let them take all the time they need to work it out. We're not in any rush."

"Are we not in any rush," I started, "or are we tolerant of the slow progress because it means we don't risk getting attached?"

She was quiet for a minute. "What does that mean?"

"It means we run headfirst into every new phase of this project but when it comes time to make the decisions, we drag it out as long as possible so that we don't have any real commitments."

"And when you say *we*, you mean *me*." Her hands stilled on my upper arms and I knew I was in dangerous territory but I couldn't turn back now. "You're saying I don't want to get attached."

"I'm already attached," I said. "I'm not going anywhere. This is home for me and Gennie. We can't pick up and move to Boston—or anywhere else. You, on the other hand, have room to walk away. You don't have to do any of this and you know it."

"You're saying I don't care?"

"No. That's not what I'm saying." It was both wonderful and awful to carry on this conversation without being able to see the expressions on her face. I had no idea how she was reacting but that granted me the freedom to continue. "You care a whole hell of a lot. You wouldn't be here, trying to give Lollie's farm a fresh new life, if you didn't care. You never would've married me and—for fuck's sake, you moved into this madhouse for the farm. You care more than anyone else I know. But there's a difference between caring and letting yourself care, and I don't think you want to let yourself."

"And why is that?"

"Shay, I have the emotional range of a rock. I'm not qualified to answer that but I will say that you shouldn't think about this place as a stop on the road back to your life in Boston. This doesn't have to be temporary."

"*What* doesn't have to be temporary?"

Everything. Your hands on my shoulders, your things in my house. The business we're building. The family we're building. Our marriage. Everything.

"Anything. All of it. Whatever you want."

"I'm going to have to think about that," she said. "Although now I realize you're going to tell me I'm dragging my feet on something else."

"I'm not going to say that." She sniffed—or was it a sniffle? I wasn't sure but now I was concerned I'd hurt her feelings. "Shay—"

"Leaving has always been the goal," she said. "Wherever I was, whatever I was doing, there's always been an end on the horizon. When I was little, I bounced between different cities, countries, schools. An endless stream of nannies. Then it was boarding schools. Then it was Lollie's farm. Don't you remember how it was back then? Getting out of this town was the only thing we could think about. It was the only thing we wanted."

"I remember." If there was anything in the world I remembered, it was conspiring with Shay about our post-Friendship lives. Those days had been a life raft for me.

"And then it was all about finishing school, finding a job, finding a —" She stopped herself to get more lotion. "The only place I'd ever stayed and put down roots was my school in Boston. Jaime is one of the only real, deep roots I have."

I couldn't stop myself from adding, "And me."

"Of course you." A small shiver moved through my shoulders as she spread the cool lotion down my spine. It was the lotion. Only the lotion. "My point is that I'm terrible at attachments. I want to be attached. I want to stay somewhere and have—god, there are so many things I want. Or I think I want them. I'm still trying to figure all of that out."

"Then stay here and figure it out," I said. "Help me build this damn event center because I have no clue what I'm doing without you."

"You'd manage just fine. And before you can argue, may I point out all the businesses you've opened without me? You built a market from your parents' old house, a bakeshop from another old house, a cannery from an abandoned cider mill, and an ice cream stand from god only knows what. And you spiced it all up with some goats and yoga. Don't pretend that you need me for this."

"Just because I can plow through by myself doesn't mean I want to," I said. "Fuck, Shay. Let me need you, okay?"

A quiet minute passed before she whispered, "Okay."

It wasn't lost on me that she hadn't agreed to stay. "You're the one who looks at Twin Tulip and sees a wedding venue. I look at it and I see the footprint of an event facility but nothing more. I can't see outdoor ceremonies at sunset or gardens designed to be the backdrop for wedding photos. Like I said, I'm a rock."

"You might be a rock but I have you beat. The only reason I can talk about beautiful, happy things like weddings is because I'm scary-good at acting like everything is fine and I'm not dead inside."

I glanced over my shoulder and shot her a sharp glare. "I've been inside you. I promise, you're not dead."

She brought her hand to the back of my head and pushed me down to the duvet. "I'm not finished yet. You can move when I tell you to."

"That's cute," I murmured. "Get it out of your system now, wife."

"Ohhhh, someone put on his bossypants."

"If you like that, you'll love it when I get these pants off."

"Look at this funny guy," she mused. "I'm old enough to remember when all you'd do was growl and glare at me."

"That was a different time."

"A time when you didn't like me very much?" she asked, laughing.

If only she knew how much I'd always liked her. That there was no one else for me. My world started and ended with her sitting beside me on those dark morning rides to school, and it started up all over again when I found her on my farm. But she wasn't ready to hear that. She was barely able to imagine a future where we didn't dispose of this marriage nine months from now and never speak of it again. I couldn't tell her that I *loved* her. Loved her so completely, so thoroughly, that no one else in the world could compare. Maybe someday I'd be able to tell her this but not yet. "A time when you didn't let me say perverted things to you or fuck you in barns."

"Was that the reason for the growling? And the glaring? You wanted to fuck me in one of your many barns? Huh. Never would've guessed that."

"It wasn't all about the barns. Sometimes you just need a glare to set you straight, sweetheart."

"What does *that* mean?"

"You know exactly what it means," I said. "Consuming nothing more than coffee and pudding all day. Going out to random bars with idiots. Telling me you're going to walk home alone—at night. You needed a good glare." *And a reminder of who you belong to.*

"You probably should've explained that from the beginning because it gave me the impression you wanted to get rid of me."

"Yeah, you're right. I didn't want anything to do with you and that's why I invited you to dinner or brought you bread all those times. And securing a line of credit forty-five minutes after you gave me a back-of-the-envelope proposal for a wedding venue was one big mixed message."

"Does it make me an idiot if I didn't realize any of that until now?"

"You're not an idiot. You're just accustomed to people failing you."

Several minutes passed as she worked my back, shoulders, and arms. Every inhale was a cloud of honey and almond. Every touch of her fingers was a lapping wave of relief. It was one of the best things I'd ever experienced.

"Where did you get all of these knots?"

"They're organic, just like everything else around here," I replied.

"It's like you've been growing them since you were born."

I laughed. "That's probably because I have been."

"Then you'll have to let me untangle them every few weeks."

I smiled. She couldn't see it but that didn't matter. "Yeah. I guess I'll have to let you do that."

Shay rubbed her hands down the length of my back and I couldn't remember feeling this light and loose ever in my life. I wanted to melt into this bed and sleep for hours. But more than that, I wanted to get my hands on my wife.

I reached back, closed my fingers around her ankle. "I have a few more knots for you to work out. Let me roll over and I'll show you."

Laughing, she leaned close to me and brushed her lips over my neck. "In a minute. I'm not done here."

Before I could respond, her phone buzzed beside me. At once, we turned our heads to look at the screen. A message flashed there.

X (DO NOT ANSWER): I need to see you.

X (DO NOT ANSWER): We have to talk.

BECAUSE I LIKED HURTING MYSELF, I asked, "Who is that?"

I heard her swallow. She was silent a moment before saying, "Well. That's my ex-fiancé."

Suddenly I was off the bed and on my feet. If the ceiling fell down around me, it wouldn't be any more surprising than this announcement. "Your—your *fiancé*?"

"Ex," she said. "Ex-fiancé."

"You were engaged." She bobbed her head while I processed this at a speed of several thousand *what the fucks* per second. "When? When were you engaged? When was this?"

She pressed her fingers to her lips. "July."

Since all I could do was repeat her words, I said, "You were engaged in July."

She stared at the floor. "I was supposed to get married in July."

"You were supposed to—okay." I nodded like it was a nervous tic. "Okay. So. That didn't happen." Running straight into the pain, I asked, "What did happen?"

A hard, bitter smile stretched across her lips though she never looked up from the floor. "He called it off."

"*He* called it off?" Who was this guy and what the fuck was wrong with him? I had the overwhelming urge to push him into oncoming traffic and then shake his hand for sending Shay back into my life with his stupidity.

"While I was in my wedding dress." The smile turned into a hard, bitter laugh. "A few hours before the wedding."

"You were—" Too many things from the past few months fell into place all at once. I understood now. I understood everything. All the comments about being empty and hollow—dead inside. Backing off when I tried to rush her into marrying me. That night at the dive bar when she broke down about no one ever choosing her. Holding me at a distance. *Everything*. "Fuck, Shay." I crossed the room, my arms open to her. "Sweetheart, why didn't you tell me?"

"I was trying to forget." She pressed her face to my chest. "And it's humiliating."

"No, it's not." I held her tight and ran my hand over her hair. "I'm so sorry he did that to you." When she linked her hands at the small of my back, I asked, "Does he contact you often?"

"No. This is the first time."

Inside my head I heard an endless loop of *she married you.* This didn't mean anything. It didn't have to mean anything. "Since July?" I asked. "The first time he's contacted you since *July*? And he thinks eleven at night on a Friday is the time to check in?"

She bumped her head against my chest. "I told him never to speak to me again, so…"

"There it is. That's my girl." I hated this guy. I fucking hated him. Later, I'd organize that hate into sections and categories, but right now he was a fucking fuckhead fucker and I wished nothing but misery upon him. "Do you want me to delete the message? Block his number?"

The amount of time it took her to form an answer should've been my first hint that this wasn't going to end the way I hoped.

"I need to find out what he wants," she said, pulling out of my hold.

She married you. She married you.

"Okay." I motioned toward her phone. "Go for it. Give 'em hell."

As she texted, I couldn't stop myself from building a mental image of this trash pile of a human who'd leave Shay on the day of their wedding. This fucker. He'd be a professional guy. Finance or business or something cushy like that. Big personality. Loud, probably, but in that *life of the party* kind of way. Expensive watch for the sake of an expensive watch. Prided himself on reading only corporate titan circle jerk memoirs and the kind of level-up nonfiction designed for businessmen who chose not to remember their anniversary. And above all else, he'd be dense enough to throw away the most incredible creature in the world.

Thinking about him was awful. It was like running my hand along a barbed-wire fence.

She married you.

"He says it's important that we talk in person as soon as possible," Shay said, frowning at her phone. "He'll meet me anywhere I want. It's funny. He's not usually that amenable."

I fisted my hands on my hips. This *fucking* fucker. "Does he know that you're here? In Friendship?"

She shook her head. "Only my friends know that and they all hate him."

"Have I mentioned how much I love your friends? I do. They're brilliant."

Shay laughed, waving off my words. "Don't worry. They love you too." She set her phone on the desk and then looked up at me, the bed between us. Her phone continued buzzing. I *hated* this guy. "I know it's probably a bad idea but—"

"Fuck," I muttered to myself.

"—I need to do this." She held her palms open, shrugged. "I just—I need an explanation."

She married you.

"And you think he'll give you one?"

She stared down at the duvet. She looked sad and vulnerable, and I wanted to do everything I could to fix that. "I'm not sure but I think I have to try."

"If you're determined to do this, I'm going with you."

"Noah, you don't have to—"

"I'm going with you," I repeated. "There's a market in Boston in two weeks. It's the last of that event for the season. It's usually a big one and I haven't been in a year or two. We'll meet him there and then you and I will have a jam sales rematch. This time you're getting a true challenge. Something like spiced cranberry orange or apricot pear jasmine." I glanced at the ceiling as I mentally paged through my calendar. "There's also a vendor up there who has been trying to meet with me for months but it's never worked for my schedule. We'll let him buy us lunch after the market. Maybe then I can get him off my back and out of my inbox."

"You really don't have to—"

"Say that again." I circled the bed, a hand unlatching my belt as I went. "Say it again and see what happens, wife. See how long it takes me to bend you over this bed and show you what I don't have to do."

For once, those words didn't make me feel like a depraved ass. I didn't question my entire belief system. I just wanted her to know that she belonged to me and I wouldn't stand idly by while she met up with her fuckhead ex. If I had to get inside her and punctuate that statement, I didn't see a problem there.

She married you.

She stared at my hands as I forced open the button-fly and let my jeans gape. She stared while I gave my cock a rough stroke through my boxer briefs. She stared and I knew exactly what she needed.

"Text him." I jerked my chin toward her phone. "Tell him you're available in two weeks. The SoWa market, South of Washington. You have a few minutes around ten in the morning and that is the only time you can spare him. Send that and then turn off your phone."

Her lower lip pinched between her teeth, she tapped out the message. I saw her pause before sending though I stopped myself from asking if this was all right for her. She'd tell me if it wasn't.

She tipped her head from side to side. Then, "Well. He read it."

"Off." I pointed at the device. "You're not going to worry about anything else he has to say tonight. He's intruded on enough of your time."

Shay responded with a quick nod though that bottom lip was still pinned between her teeth as she set the darkened phone on her desk. When she turned back to me, I grabbed a handful of that slouchy sweater and led her to the bed. I pushed her down until she was bent over, her cheek on the duvet and her backside round and lovely where I rocked against it.

I pushed her shorts down to her knees and slipped a hand between her legs. "Have you been wet this whole time?" She bobbed her head. "And you didn't think I'd want to know that while you rubbed my back?"

"I wanted you to feel better first."

I palmed her ass, my fingers digging deep into the thick softness. There'd be marks tomorrow, small ones with little more than a whisper of plum as proof that I'd held these plush cheeks apart while I fucked her hard. Finding those bruises felt like a fist of thorns twisting inside my chest. This woman was small and precious and far more fragile than anyone seemed to realize, and I struggled with bringing harm to her—even when it was enthusiastically consensual. But tending to those bruises with salves and sweet words and all the adoration I could pour into her made it better. Made me feel a bit less like a depraved beast.

"Maybe I wanted you to feel better first," I said.

"Maybe you don't always get your way."

I tapped my cock against her wet heat. "Didn't get it out of your system, did you?"

Over her shoulder, she shot me a bratty grin. "I guess I need you to do it for me."

She had no idea what I'd do to her if she truly gave me the chance.

"If that's what you want, wife, that's what you'll get."

I pushed inside her with one slow thrust and held myself there, deep and pulsing like this could be over in a minute, as she moaned into the duvet. I trailed a hand down her thigh until I reached the elastic waistband of her shorts. I twisted the band around my palm, forcing her legs together.

"What are you—*ohmygod*!" Her lips parted on a silent cry and she closed her eyes. "Noah. *Noah*."

The pressure was insane. She was a hot, unrelenting fist around my cock and I could barely stay upright. My body wanted to rut, wanted to burn itself into her. Wanted to write promises inside her. Instead, I answered by flattening my free hand low on her back and pinning her in place as I rocked into her.

"What do you need, sweetheart?"

Her mouth moved though no sound came out. She gripped the blankets and shook her head as if she couldn't bear another minute but then she rocked back against me like she could go all night.

"I just—I want you to want me," she whispered.

"That's what I've been trying to tell you, wife. I do. I want you so much it would scare you to know the half of it."

"You can't scare me," she said, the words skittering out with each thrust. She was going to need a lot of salve and snuggles after this. Probably a thorough back rub of her own. "But go ahead and try."

I focused on the elastic waistband where it cut off circulation to my fingers. I focused on the scrape of the headboard against the wall. On the cramp building in my left hamstring and the tattoo peeking out from her sweater. Anything but the coolly leveled challenge from the wife who should've been too stuffed to speak.

I couldn't tell her the truth. Not the whole of it. Not the history or the remnants of it that shimmered around us now. That truth would scare her and it would change everything. It would rob us of the thin ice of our current perfection and it would force us to walk back in time and reexamine all those moments when I'd loved her and she'd had no idea. I couldn't do it. Not while everything between us was fresh and fragile. Not when she was finally mine. Not with the man she was hours away from marrying just a few months ago closing in on us.

As her body quaked beneath me and she sobbed out her release, I said, "This is where you belong, Shay. This is the home and we are the family you've always wanted." I shook my hand free from her shorts and leaned down to press my lips to the dandelion seeds inked on her shoulder. The ones that wanted nothing more than a place to grow and bloom. "You belong here and you belong to me."

"What part of that is supposed to scare me?"

I stepped back, snarling at the throb that came when I pulled out of her. It was the only thing I could do to stop myself from confessing that I loved her in a marrow-deep way that had accompanied me around as an endless ache for as long as I could remember, and I had no intention of divorcing her at the end of this year or at any other point. "Roll over," I said, giving myself a slow stroke. "Get that sweater off. The shorts too."

She complied, her hair a rose gold mess and her eyes glassy as she fumbled with her clothes. A sliver of doubt sliced through me when I crawled between her legs and sat back on my heels. The idea of jerking off on her body sounded great in the filth library in my head but the reality of it hit differently. It felt like a new level of dirty and degrading, and I didn't know if I could take that step.

"Show me," she purred.

Not a single one of my teenage—or thirtysomething—dreams could compare with seeing her spread out before me, stripped bare, soaking wet, and staring up at me like I could do anything to her and she'd thank me for it.

I dragged my hand down my shaft. "What?"

"Show me what it looks like to belong to you."

I didn't think about tonight or tomorrow or two weeks from now when we'd deal with the fuckhead ex. I didn't think about marriage or divorce, or kids or families. I didn't think about the secrets I kept from Shay or the fact I couldn't keep them much longer.

I just came all over her belly, cleaned her up with the t-shirt I'd discarded earlier, and held her as she fell asleep.

It was then, with her even breath warm on my bicep and her hair tickling my chest, I whispered, "Love you, wife."

chapter twenty-seven

Shay

Students will be able to examine forgotten history and sunken ships.

"I NEED YOU SITTING FOR THIS," I said to Jaime.

"I'm leaning against the kitchen counter. Is that adequate?" she asked. "If not, we might have to reschedule this chat. I'm slow going today."

I opened the front door at Thomas House and then shut it behind me. "What's wrong? What's going on that you don't want to video call?" She groaned out a sigh as I settled onto the floor. I'd told Noah I needed to check on something here but I just needed a minute alone. A minute to think.

"I have a UTI. I went to the clinic last night and the meds are kicking in but I can't move or breathe very deeply right now. I can exist and that's about it."

"Oh my god, James. Is someone taking care of you?"

"Yeah, my roommates have been amazing as per usual. Don't even threaten to come up here. I'm okay. I just need to get through the next twelve hours and then I won't feel like I fell into a quarry."

"I'm not sure I know what it means to fall into a quarry."

"It's terrible. Don't try it," she said. "In other news, I will be taking a sex hiatus for at least two weeks. Probably a month."

"Is that how this happened?"

She murmured in agreement. "It's important to pee after sex, doll. Even if you can't walk or remember your name. Especially then."

"Good to know."

"So, what's going on with you?" she asked. "What do you have for me that would knock me on my ass?"

"The ex messaged me last night."

"Holy fucking shit, he did *what*?"

I nodded but then realized this wasn't video. "Yeah. He texted right after Noah and I had this big, emotional talk and he wants—"

"Wait. Wait a minute. What was the big, emotional talk about?"

I shoved my fingers through my hair because I was still processing all the ground we'd covered. Still trying to parse out what was true and what was dirty talk with feelings—and whether I should believe the dirty talk. And if any of it was true, even a single word, what did that mean for our fake marriage?

"Long story short—and it's a very long story I'll share with you on a day when you don't require a fainting couch—he wants to get moving on the renovations at Twin Tulip and he thinks I'm dragging my feet because I don't want to get attached to the project and that I want to give myself room to walk away. I said I'm—"

"Yeah, that's exactly what you're doing. I'm sorry, I can't pull off my usual love-and-hard-truths sandwich so you're getting the raw-dog truths. Daddy Bread Baker is right. You're hedging so you don't get hurt and disappointed."

"I have a lot going on," I argued. "More since the ex has resurfaced and I had to explain another one of my disasters to Noah."

"Okay. All right. Tell me what that cockwobble has done now."

I dropped my head against the panel of the door and stared up at the pair of chandeliers. "He said we need to talk immediately."

"Fuck him," she replied. "Seriously, fuck him. You don't have to answer simply because he calls."

"I'm aware of that."

"Are you though? Because it sounds like you're letting this asshole corrupt your happiness. You can—and should—block his number. Why didn't we do that to begin with? I don't know how that slipped through the cracks but do not allow the utter chaos and disrespect of that man to infiltrate your nice, stable situation. Exit him from your life, Shay."

"I just—" I stopped, pressed my lips together as a dozen justifications burned my tongue. I hated this feeling. I'd hated it last night too. It made me feel small, like I'd crawl for any crumb the ex tossed my way. At the same time, I couldn't turn him down. "I need an explanation. I need to know what happened."

"He outed himself as the pissypants bitch we always knew he was," she replied. "That's what happened. I hate it and I hate him for it but he isn't going to float in on a bubble and beg you to believe that he got cold feet. He's not going to apologize because he isn't sorry. I don't think he has the capacity to recognize the harm he did."

I uncapped my water bottle and drank deeply. Then, "When did you know?"

"Know what?"

"That he was a cockwobbling pissypants bitch."

She didn't respond for several heavy seconds. "Tell me what you want me to say here."

"Just…the truth." I took another sip. "You don't feel well enough to hold back anyway."

"I liked him when you first started dating," she said. "I mean, I liked him enough. He's a real estate developer. He's like all the other guys who make deals. Massively inflated ego, no self-awareness, and an inability to participate in a conversation without dropping a name or dollar amount for no logical reason whatsoever. It was fine."

"That doesn't sound fine," I said with a bitter laugh.

"He's funny and he could take a joke at his expense," she conceded. "I could tell him to shut the fuck up and he'd do it but he'd also laugh about him being a pain in the ass. And he'd pick up the bar tab. I had no trouble with any of that." I heard her open the fridge. "But that was it, you know? That was the whole story. There was nothing else there. Or that was all he'd let anyone see. And that didn't sit well. You know this because we talked about it a few times."

I chugged more water.

"There were a few other times when you listened to me about the strange vibes I got from him but there was a point where you decided those weren't issues for you. And there was a time right after you got engaged when I tried to tell you that I was seeing some major red flags. I remember that chat so clearly. You told me that you'd heard my concerns but you weren't breaking off the engagement because you knew him better than I did and I just didn't understand your relationship."

"We didn't talk for five days after that."

"*Five days,*" she repeated. "I thought we were broken up."

"That will never happen." I glanced from the left parlor to the right. It seemed like I hadn't been here in years. "How...how did you manage being my maid of honor?"

"I did that for you. I was *your* maid of honor. For *your* wedding. It had nothing to do with him."

"You were going to let me go through with it."

She huffed. "It wasn't my choice to make, doll. If I'd beaten you over the head with criticisms of him, you would've stopped talking to me. You would've shut me out. So, I chose to stick by you."

"I don't deserve you," I said.

"Of course you do. Don't tell yourself that sort of bullshit. You deserve me and your Daddy Bread Baker and all the other good things in this world. You don't deserve that cockwobble intruding on your time, especially if that time involves that man of yours."

"Noah said the same thing." I drew in a deep breath, blew it out. "And I know all of this but I feel like I need to do it. I need to find out what he wants and then I can set all the baggage associated with him on fire and push it out to sea."

"I don't have the energy to talk you out of this," Jaime said. "I want to. I probably should. But it feels like there's a blowtorch in my bladder and I don't have any convincing words."

We were silent for a minute. I didn't want to repeat the cycle of Jaime seeing the situation while I ignored her warnings but I needed to know. I needed an explanation.

"When are you going to do this?" she asked. "With the ex."

"Noah suggested I tag along for the next Boston farmers market. I have an outfit picked out already. Jeans, red gingham shirt knotted at the waist, strawberry earrings. Not sure about a bandana headband. Might be overkill. I'll have to test that out." I ran my index finger around the cap of my water bottle. "Noah suggested I meet the ex at the market."

"He wants to keep an eye on things," Jaime said.

"How did you know?"

She scoffed. "Have you met your husband? Really, doll. He's gonna pelt that son of a bitch with apples and run him right out of the market. Chase that motherfucker down the street."

I started to disagree but then I realized Noah would do that. He wouldn't think twice about it. He might enjoy it.

"How about we have a gathering, a get-together, a little *meet her new man* party? Something easy and low-key here at the apartment. Just a few people from school and the girls."

The girls were Jaime's roommates. Layla, Dylan, and Linnie. "I'd love that," I replied. "Noah will have to be convinced to love that. He can be a little shy."

"We'll make sure he feels right at home."

"By referring to him as Daddy Bread Baker? I don't think so. He'll throw me over his shoulder and run right out of there. I'm telling you, he's done it before."

"Why hasn't anyone thrown me over their shoulder?" she asked. "I'm down for that. Pick me up, toss me around, treat me like a rag doll. Yes, *sir*. Give me some of that."

"You're on a sex hiatus," I said.

"Oh, right."

"No one is treating you like a rag doll until next month at the earliest."

"Thankfully, I'm busy planning a party and I won't notice the shortage of sex in my life," she said. "Hey, are we all right?"

"Of course," I replied. "Why?"

"Because I couldn't give you the sandwich. Because I said your ex wasn't the one and I knew it from the start. Because I was going to let you marry him, even if it broke my heart." She made a pained sound. "You know I'm never getting married and I'm the last person in the world to end up in a committed relationship but you'll stop me if I end up with the wrong person. Right?"

Tears blurred my gaze. "What if you tell me I don't know that person or your relationship? What if you don't talk to me for five days—or longer? What should I do if it seems like you'll choose them over me?"

"I'm gonna need you to slap me," she said simply. "Just haul off and give me a head-snapping slap."

I barked out a laugh. "I'm not going to do that."

"My bad. I forgot. You were never paddled in school. God bless Louisiana." She chuckled. "You're going to have to remind me of this conversation. Or get your man to throw apples at my head. I don't know. I just need you to promise you'll try."

"I promise," I said. "I'll try."

FRIENDSHIP WAS the kind of town that took Homecoming seriously. It wasn't a simple matter of a rivalry football game with some bonus pageantry and a dance tacked on at the end. No, this town made an *event* of Homecoming weekend, packing it with all manner of barbeques, picnics, and potlucks for students and alumni alike, class reunion parties, tailgating before the game, and a big community dance. They called it Old Home Days and everyone around here always looked forward to that weekend.

Back in high school, I'd regarded the event with a fair amount of derision. It'd all seemed overwhelmingly folksy and familiar, and I couldn't figure out how to exist around that. It was like a language I didn't speak and didn't care to learn—and that was a fine summary of my youthful relationship with the place originally settled as Friendly Township.

Now, with the clarity that came from not being a self-centered teenager who was also paddling hard under the surface to keep from sinking in yet another completely new environment, I could acknowledge the charms of this event. It was all about alumni coming home and the organizers went hard at making it enjoyable for everyone. I loved that it was a community dance rather than a couple hundred high schoolers standing around and staring at each other in a dark gymnasium. And I didn't even mind dragging myself to a football game in near-freezing weather.

The only part that I didn't love was that Noah and I couldn't travel more than a few paces at a time without someone coming up to congratulate us. But my issue wasn't with all the warm wishes. It was that I felt as though everyone could see straight through me. They had to know this marriage, the one that popped up overnight and didn't add all the way up, wasn't real.

Yet they were all smiles, all kind words. Even the ones who teased me about stealing Noah away and snapping him up before anyone else could get him seemed sincere in their congratulations.

"High school sweethearts" was Noah's explanation to all their questions. It rolled right off his tongue, just the way it had with Christiane. I didn't know how he did it. "Always known she was the one." When that wasn't enough, he was quick to add, "Didn't waste a minute when she came back to town. I'd already wasted too many waiting for her to come home."

I smiled, I blushed, I leaned into him. It was exactly what I was supposed to do and I had to admit that I loved playing this part with him. He was sweet and generous, and handsy as all hell. I was lucky that my fake husband was a real beast, and we had many, many places on the farm to sneak away and explore all the filth he kept hidden behind those neat plaid shirts and simple ball caps.

The only problem was that I couldn't find the lines between fake and real anymore. They were blurry now and I'd known that would happen when we slept together but in moments like these—when we were putting on the happy couple act—I felt the need to go looking for those lines. I had to know where the boundaries of our reality were buried. Otherwise, I was liable to start believing Noah's stories and imagining a life in this town beyond my one required year.

When Gennie ran across the field to greet a friend and we were finally alone for a minute, I said, "Look at her. Look how well she's doing with her little buddy."

"I know. I can't believe it. She's a totally different kid than when she came here a year ago." He grinned down at me. "Thanks for helping with that by the way."

"No problem." I watched as they both took off a mitten and traded with each other to make mismatched pairs. "Did you spend much time with Gennie when she was a baby?"

"Eva lived near New York when she had Gennie, and I met her as a baby though I wouldn't say I spent a lot of time with her then. They moved around a fair bit. Eva didn't like staying in one spot too long. Always on one adventure or another. Van life, you know." He glanced away for a second. "She came home with Gennie when my dad died, and then again, about two years later. They stayed with me for a few months before hitting the road. So, yeah, I knew her. Somewhat."

Noah never talked much about Eva. Not now, not back in high school. I'd known she left home and ventured out on her own and that her relationship with her parents had been difficult but that was the extent of it.

Though he'd never said it explicitly, I'd always had the impression that Noah preferred that I didn't know much about his sister. Not that he was ashamed of her in any way, but so I knew him, not Eva Barden's little brother.

I'd never said it explicitly but I'd always liked that I knew Noah Barden. He'd been kind to me when I had no one other than a step-grandmother I barely knew, and he'd listened while I ranted about my lonely, privileged world.

He waved a hand at the festivities around us. "Do you remember the plan we cooked up? When we were kids?"

I laughed, my breath a white cloud in the cold air. "We had a plan? For what?"

"You don't remember any of it?" He stared at me, his brows pinched together. "Not at all?"

I shook my head. "No. Remind me."

He glanced away with an eye roll as though my Swiss cheese memory was a real problem for him. "We were going to return here and show this town what they'd lost."

"Why don't I remember this?"

"I don't know, Shay," he said, the words clipped. "But we'd always talked about coming back."

I tapped a finger to my lips as I searched through our history. "I remember that part but I didn't realize we were coming back for Old Home Days. Did I get it wrong?"

He stared at me then, his lips pulled into a flat line. His eyes were dark and yes, I'd gotten it wrong. It was clear I'd done something very wrong. "No, it was just an idea we tossed around."

"I'm not sure I believe you."

"Then don't believe me." He glanced across the field at Gennie and her friend. "Obviously it never happened so it doesn't matter."

"Isn't it happening right now? Aren't we back in Friendship for Old Home Days and showing everyone what they missed out on while we were gone? Or did you miss the part where nine thousand people have stopped to talk to us tonight?" When he didn't respond, I continued. "And the surprise marriage is only part of it. You had a big law career that involved billable hours on boats and I was left at the altar, which isn't as impressive as a yacht but it goes to show that I'm just as much of a problem as I was in high school."

After a lengthy pause, he said, "You weren't a problem in high school. Don't say that. And no one here knows about your ex."

"No one here knows I was kicked out of my Swiss boarding school because they found out I went to France one weekend to get an abortion but I still got the side-eye every day for two years."

No need to mention that the side-eye came exclusively from people like Noah's mother, who seemed to know without explanation that a girl shipped home from Europe and sent to live with a distant relative in the country was a special kind of cautionary tale.

He leaned in and brushed his lips over my temple. "It's none of their fucking business. It's not now and it wasn't then."

"Thank you," I said. He'd protected me back then, the only person aside from Lollie to know the truth of my stay in Friendship. He'd understood when I talked about accidents and mistakes, and he'd never once looked at me like I was a problem. Then, "Did you come back? For Old Home Days?"

He drew in a breath and I had my answer. He didn't have to say anything. I knew. He'd come back, expecting to find his partner in hard won redemption, and I'd forgotten. I'd escaped to Boston and into the high of pure reinvention after so many failed attempts at fitting into my newest version of perfect. I'd stripped away all of this town, leaving everything—and everyone—behind when I went.

"I never heard from you," I said, "after you left for school. I think I texted you a few times but—what happened?"

"Yeah, well." He ran a hand over the back of his neck. "I didn't have much to say. I'd spent the better part of a year telling everyone who'd listen that I got into Yale. I didn't know how to turn around and say it wasn't everything I'd built it up to be."

"You could've told me. I would've told you that going to Boston College simply because it was my mother's alma mater and they didn't care about my academic record wasn't the best choice. Not as far as existing without her shadow looming over me went."

"But you stayed there," he said.

"And you stayed at Yale."

He shrugged. "Yeah. I'd worked hard enough to get there. I could work hard enough to get through it."

"I just didn't know where else to go," I said with a laugh. "And my mother, as you know—"

"Do you talk to her much? See her?"

"She's back in London again, working on a book. She's busy. She's good." Another laugh. "She flew in for the wedding. The one that didn't happen. Jaime runs a good defense and she managed to keep her away after everything fell apart. We've played a slow game of phone tag since then." I glanced up at him. "I am sorry," I whispered. "I—I should've remembered. I should've been better for you. I should've reached out more. Stayed in touch."

"It was a long time ago," he said. "We were kids. We…we were idiots. We had no business making plans more than five minutes in the future."

Except Noah had kept those plans. He'd honored that pact. He *always* honored the pact.

"And it made sense that you might've changed your mind," he added. "There are far better things to do than roll up at Old Home Days and expect anyone to give a damn." He studied me for a moment, glancing at my eyes and then down at my lips. "Anyway. I've heard that blow jobs in the shower are better than any of this town's many, many festivals."

"Oh, you've heard that?"

"Yeah. Reputable sources too. Peer reviewed, even."

I nodded. "Of course."

"If you're determined to make amends—not that amends are necessary but if it's on your mind—I wouldn't turn down a hot shower after freezing our asses off here."

"Speaking of which, how long do we have to freeze our asses off here?" I asked.

He gave a slow shake of his head as he exhaled. "Honestly, the sooner we leave, the less likely it is that I'll get roped into doing something for the holiday tree-lighting festival."

"How does this town fund all these festivals?"

Noah waved for Gennie to join us. "I could explain it to you but you'd drop into a boredom coma before getting your mouth on my cock and I'd like to avoid that."

"I have to confess, I don't love giving blow jobs."

"Why not?"

"Because I don't like gagging, and considering"—I shot a pointed glance at his jeans—"I know I'll gag."

His grin was the most arrogant thing I'd ever seen out of him. It was adorable. I loved every egotistical bit of it. "What if I promise to play nice?"

"You don't know how to," I said, shaking my head as I smiled up at him. "You're sweet and shy now, but when the clothes come off…"

"Yes, wife? When the clothes come off?" He slipped his hand under my coat, under my sweater. Rucked up my tank top, pressed cool fingers to the small of my back. I shivered and his eyes sparkled. "Tell me what happens then."

"You know what happens."

He leaned in and brushed his lips over my ear while he drew circles along my waist. "I won't make you gag, wife. I don't want to see tears in your eyes. But I've been thinking about your tongue on the head of my cock for—well, for too long. Do you think you could handle that much?"

I bobbed my head. "Probably."

"A shower sounds nice, doesn't it? Have you noticed the detachable showerhead in there? It has nine different settings. And then there's that bench. It's a good size. Sturdy too. We could have some fun with that, yeah?"

"Yeah," I said, the word barely more than a gasp.

This was how I ended up flat on my back and stripped from the waist down in his secret project greenhouse last week. Some whispering about getting a taste of me, some light touching under the clothes, a promise that we'd enjoy ourselves. I left with lavender in my hair, dried oregano under my nails, and legs barely capable of carrying me back to the house. He'd secured me into his ATV, muttering to himself about being crazy if I thought he'd let me wander through the orchard while sex drunk. When he got me back to the house, he had me flat on my back once again and screaming into a pillow within minutes.

This was also how we'd found ourselves having sex in the pantry a few nights ago. It started out as a simple matter of asking him to help me reach one of the shelves and ended up with a bag of flour spilled all over the floor and his orgasm running down my legs. He apologized profusely for the mess—both of them—but then dragged his fingers between my thighs until my vision blurred.

And this was how we'd managed a quickie while Gennie was collecting eggs the other day. A hand over my mouth to keep me quiet while I straddled him on the chair in his bedroom. The other hand gripped my ass cheek hard enough to leave dark red marks that bruised by the next morning. When he realized this, he bent me over the bed and rubbed an herby balm he'd created into my skin. He shoved his fingers in my mouth and teased my seam with every gentle, stroking pass but he made it very clear he didn't like marking me. Unless I liked it, in which case he loved it.

"Would you like that, wife?"

Mmmm. There were moments when he whispered that word to me and I felt like the world was my heartbeat. These were the moments when I wanted to find those lines, the ones carving out the boundaries between real and fake, but these were the same moments when I wanted to cover my eyes to keep from looking. If I didn't know, I couldn't hurt myself.

"Yes," I said. I wanted to return the favor and call him *husband* but I couldn't form the word. Not out loud, not yet. It was too dangerous. I'd almost called another man my husband and that history was all too recent to ignore. Though I wanted to say it to Noah. I wanted—just for one second—for him to be my husband. And I wanted it to be real.

"Help me convince this kid it's time to go," he said as Gennie jogged over, her cheeks red and her hair disheveled.

She glanced between us. "Are we going to the football place to watch the game now?"

"Game's over," Noah said. "Yeah. They played hard. Friendship won. Time to go."

She stared at the stadium, confusion scrawled over her face. "Really?"

"Yeah. We're gonna go home, maybe have a glass of warm milk, and then watch a Civil War documentary. There were pirates back then. Probably." Noah glanced at me for confirmation. I nodded. I was still hung up on the nine-speed showerhead and the lurking awareness that I was falling hard for my husband. "Ready to go?"

Gennie gave the stadium another glance and shrugged. "Yeah. They don't have frozen lemonade tonight anyway."

"Frozen lemonade is only available in warmer weather," Noah said.

"That sucks," Gennie muttered. "I don't like football games without frozen lemonade."

"All the more reason to get out of here." Noah held out his hand to her. She took it and then grabbed for mine. "I think you're going to like this documentary."

"How many pirates are in it?"

"I'm not sure," he replied. "We'll get some blankets and heat up some milk, and then we'll talk about Civil War-era pirates."

She was asleep before the end of the opening credits.

And that was how I ended up seated on Noah's lap, the showerhead pulsing between my thighs while he pounded into me from below. I was waterlogged and wrung out from coming more times than seemed possible, my voice hoarse and my head heavy from so much—*so much*. After, he combed the tangles from my hair and apologized for letting loose, for pushing too hard.

He always thought he was too rough, too aggressive. He thought I was small and fragile despite the fact I was neither of those things, but there was something surprisingly wonderful about someone doting on me that way. I felt perfect and precious when he rubbed cream into my skin or frowned over a bite mark he'd left on my inner thigh. I felt like I'd been waiting a very long time for someone who knew how to shatter me *and* also wanted to pick up all the pieces.

And I felt an unpleasant sense of relief in discovering that person was my husband.

chapter twenty-eight

Noah

Students will be able to push back on the bastards.

"HOW DID I DO?" Shay asked. She wiggled her fingers at her sides, excited and expectant. "What do you think?"

The jam display was significantly more elaborate than anything I'd ever thrown together. "It's perfect." I reached for her and dropped a quick kiss on her lips. "You're perfect."

Really, she was. She was the cutest jam slinger I'd ever seen with her strawberry earrings, red checkered shirt, and jeans that fit like a wet dream. I wanted to snap a picture of her behind the Little Star farmers market table and slap it on our website and social media. I wanted everyone to see my adorable wife and know this was the kind of magic we were working with here.

But I didn't pull out my phone to get a picture.

If I did that, I'd probably call the farm and tell them to send someone else to cover the market because I was finished pretending that it made any sense for Shay to appear at her ex-fiancé's command. It didn't. There was no way this would end well.

"Stay close to me," I said, glancing around the market tent. I wanted to believe that I'd be able to pick him out of a crowd, that I'd know by the smug grin on his face or the overall soul-sucking demon vibe. "It's not too late to change your mind. We can leave, you know."

"We're not leaving," she said with a laugh. "Gail cleared her whole day to look after Gennie. She'll be pissed if we come home early."

"Then stay where I can see you." I gestured toward the picnic tables in the middle of the tent. "Or I can close down the table and go with you. You're worth more to me than half an hour of jam sales."

Shay batted her lashes. "Aww. I don't think anyone has ever compared me to jam sales before."

She laughed and I knew she found humor in this but I was dead serious. This guy, this dickhead douchebag guy, had been terrible to Shay. The way he ended things with her was bad enough but then he went months without once bothering to check on her until he decided it was very urgent that he see her in person.

I still couldn't believe she'd agreed to this. It was moments like these that made me want to shake her until she understood that she deserved better. That she needed to expect a lot more from people.

And there was a narrow splinter of dread inside me at the possibility of Shay seeing her ex again and realizing I was nothing more than a placeholder. I didn't expect her to go running into his open arms but I couldn't eliminate the possibility entirely. If not the ex, there was a chance she'd run into the open arms of the life she'd left behind. I knew she missed Boston and missed all her friends. Returning to Friendship after living in a busy city was tough. I knew all about it. Probably tougher than growing up in that particular snow globe and fighting your way out only to get dragged right back in.

I knew I was up against everything today but I wasn't going down easy.

THE MARKET GOT underway and I was too busy to obsess over worst-case scenarios. We sold out of all the new strawberry quince jams and Shay was selling the shit out of blueberry lemon lavender. That one required skill. Not everyone could get down with lavender. Meanwhile, I was struggling to keep up with her pace. We'd sell out of blueberry lemon lavender long before I moved even a handful of spiced pear.

We caught a break after the second hour, which was the usual time for the early birds to head out and the next wave to start trickling in. Shay turned to me with a devious smile. "You have fangirls."

"I have—what?"

"Fangirls," she repeated. "Did you not listen while all those women went on and on about how happy they are to see you again and it's been so long since you came to this market and they look for you every time they see the Little Star banner?"

I grabbed a box from under the table, busied myself restocking jars of mixed berry jam. "It's nothing."

"It's something," she countered. "You have quite the reputation."

"I was the only one," I said, "back when we started with jam. I was the only one coming to farmers markets. People associated me with the jam."

"Yes, I definitely heard mention of the Jam Man."

"They don't call me that." I inspected a jar just to avoid acknowledging her smirk. "That didn't happen."

"Oh, it happened." She dragged a finger from my wrist to my elbow. "They also love the way you roll up your sleeves. I heard more than a few whispers about forearm porn."

I shook my head. I could feel my ears turning red. "They just remember me from the early days. That's all."

"Come for the forearms, stay for the jam. That's quite the business plan." She cocked her hip and regarded me for a moment. "Is that the secret to your success?"

I returned to the box in front of me. "I'm more interested in maximizing resources and minimizing waste but sure, that works too."

"Not that I blame them," she said under her breath.

Shay looked up suddenly. She stared across the market. A man stood near the front of the tent, his gaze shifting as if he had no clue where he was and he couldn't wait to get out of here. He wore khaki pants and a polo shirt with the insignia of one of the area's most exclusive golf clubs, and he resembled every unimpressive guy I met in college and law school who'd been raised to believe everything about himself was fully impressive.

In short, I wanted to wing a jar of tangerine marmalade at his head.

He held up his hand and pointed to the picnic tables in the center of the tent.

"You don't have to do this," I said. "You don't have to go over there."

"I know. I just need to find out what he wants and maybe get a little closure." She braced her hands on my shoulders and pushed up on her toes to kiss my cheek. "I've got this. I'll be quick. I promise."

Shay

THE FIRST THING you needed to know about Xavier was that he talked for a living. He made deals all day, every day, and his phone was glued to his hand. He traveled most of the month because he knew he could close more deals in person, apply more pressure. The man knew how to string words together to get what he wanted.

Knowing that, it was bizarre when he stammered and fumbled through simple pleasantries. At the same time, everything about him seemed bizarre. He kept scanning the tent and he looked clammy, like he had a low-grade fever or a bad hangover.

"What's going on with you now?" He ran the back of his hand over his sweaty forehead as he asked this. Wiped that hand on his khakis. It was cool inside the tent and chilly outside. I didn't know why he was such a mess. "And what's with the farmers market?"

"I'm here with my—" I stopped myself, not knowing how best to explain the present shape of my life to Xavier. But did Xavier need that much information? Did it even matter to him? This was just idle chatter. He didn't care, and thus, he didn't deserve an explanation. "I tagged along with Noah today."

He glanced at his phone, asking, "You finally gave up the teaching thing?"

I couldn't nail down whether *the teaching thing* annoyed me more than *finally*. He'd never overtly criticized my job but he'd often make jokes like "Calm down, it's just kindergarten" or "It's not like the kids will care if you make a mistake" or "For fuck's sake, stop worrying about lesson plans and just show a movie."

They didn't sound like jokes anymore.

"I'm teaching in Rhode Island now." He shot a puckered frown at me, as if none of that made sense to him. That expression made his eyes look especially beady. Another detail I hadn't remembered. "So, what did you need to talk to me about?"

He reached into his pocket and retrieved some folded envelopes. "Some mail came to the condo for you."

I blinked down at the pile in front of me. Credit card offers, coupon postcards for sales long past, a mobile phone statement. Garbage, mostly. I gathered the envelopes and smoothed them out. "This cannot be the reason you asked to meet with me as soon as possible." His brows winged up and he leaned back. Before I could process that reaction, I said, "Get to the point, please."

He glared at me, his mouth twisting hard to one side. I realized then that I'd never spoken to him that way. I'd never hurried him along or given any impression that I wasn't completely satisfied with every square inch of him.

I'd never really existed in our relationship.

His throat worked as he swallowed. He swung a glance from one end of the tent to the other. Then, "I need the ring back."

"The—the ring?"

"The engagement ring," he said.

The second thing you needed to know about Xavier was that he didn't spend a dime if he didn't have to. He'd let everyone else spend the money and he'd never offer to return the favor although he wouldn't let you forget it if he spent money on you. In other words, I'd expected he'd want the ring back sooner or later.

"I'm moving on," he continued, an air of condescension heavy in his words as he ran a glance over my pink hair and gingham shirt. "With someone else. And I need to sell that ring to buy something new."

"Are you moving on or did you move on a long time ago and now is a convenient moment to make it official?" I asked.

He gave a curt shake of his head, like I was silly for asking such questions. "You don't have to be so bitter about it."

"I'm not bitter in the least," I said easily, though inside I was cracking and folding in on myself. I was such a fool. *Again*. I should've listened to Noah and Jaime. Should've known this was a mistake. For no good reason, I added, "Perhaps you could tell me why you asked me to marry you if you had other interests."

With the edge of his collar, he mopped sweat from his upper lip. "You wanted it," he said with a flippant jerk of his shoulder. "You made that very clear from the start and you never let me forget it."

I tried to remember whether he'd always been this repulsive. Why had I found this man attractive? What about him had I liked? And it wasn't all about physical appearance but everything about him was stale white bread. That was it. He was bland and boring, and righteous in his flavorlessness.

"And yet that doesn't address the question," I said. "Why propose if it wasn't what you wanted?"

He shook his head and slapped a hand on the picnic table. The people on either side of us turned to stare. "I didn't fucking care one way or the other."

A chill started at the base of my neck, swept down my torso, curled low in my belly. It felt like dread and it felt like something I'd always known but couldn't face. It was awful.

"Hooking up with you was convenient. You took care of the condo. You knew how to play along at cocktail parties and business dinners. But you were just"—he pounded his fist on the table several times and I noticed people pushing to their feet nearby—"nonstop with the marriage thing. Wouldn't let it go."

I'd always resented him for canceling the wedding with a phone call. I hated that he refused to look me in the eye as he ended it.

I knew better now. I knew that watching him form the words and giving oxygen to the dark thoughts that lingered in the mean, self-loathing corner of my mind was far, far worse.

"I figured you'd ease up once you had the ring," he went on. I was frozen all the way to my toes now. "But I was wrong about that. You just turned into a nag. It was always fucking something." He wiped his fore-head again. I didn't understand how he could be warm enough to sweat when I was as cold as a corpse. "You don't know when to give it a rest, Shay. You force it. You do it all the damn time. You invent projects and force everything to be exactly the way you want."

Jaime hadn't said it that way but there were a few similar threads. I'd made up my mind about Xavier and no one could talk me out of it. I'd barreled forward, not only in ignoring her concerns but also in ignoring his disinterest. Not to mention the white bread issue. I'd ignored every-thing. And I'd forced it, just like he said.

He ran his sneering gaze over the shirt knotted at my waist, showing a bit of skin, and my huge earrings. "And I thought you were going to drop some weight. You didn't."

My lips parted but no words came out. I went down an entire dress size for that wedding. I suffered and starved for that wedding. And he *knew* that.

He was also the same man who had given his family advance warning about calling the wedding off yet gifted me the humiliation of making that announcement while I was surrounded by photographers and makeup artists and friends.

I didn't know where I found the strength but I collected the mail and pushed to my feet. "We're finished, Xavier. Never, ever call me again."

He reached out, grabbed hold of my wrist and jerked me back down to the bench. My bracelet tightened and twisted in his grip and I could feel the charms biting into my skin. "I'm not leaving without that ring."

"Xavier," I snapped. "Stop it."

"Stop being such a bitch and give me the ring."

A shadow fell over the table and a hand yanked Xavier up by the shirt. "Let her go before I rip your fucking arm off."

"What the fuck—" Xavier dropped my hand as he scrambled to his feet, Noah still looming over him. "I don't know who the fuck you think you are but—"

"Go back to the table, Shay," Noah said through clenched teeth.

I stumbled away from them, bumping into market-goers and picnic benches as I went. As much as I wanted to, I couldn't bring myself to look back at Noah and Xavier until I'd fished the engagement ring out of the coin pocket in my wallet. I pressed it into my palm, unrelenting metal and stone, and allowed that pain to carry me back to the man who'd never wanted me, never cared for me, never respected me. The man I had to face one last time before I could drown myself in the shameful truth of his words.

When I reached the table, I found Noah glaring fire and daggers at

Xavier. For his part, Xavier stood with his arms crossed over his freshly rumpled polo shirt and his body angled toward the exit.

Noah held out his arm, barring me from getting any closer. "You're staying out of reach," he growled. "I'll handle it from here." I dropped the ring into his palm. To Xavier, he said, "You will never touch her again. If you see this woman coming, you'll turn around and walk in the opposite direction. You'll stay the fuck away from her. You will never speak to her again. Am I making myself clear? Not a call, not a text, not an email. Not a goddamn word from you."

Still staring at the exit, Xavier said, "Yeah. Fine. Whatever. It's not like I give a shit. I just want my property back."

"You're running your mouth to the wrong person," Noah replied. "As far as property law goes, an engagement ring stops belonging to you when you intend to give it as a gift and then carry out that intention, and finally when it is accepted as a gift by the recipient. Unless you have documentation proving otherwise—and I have it on good authority that you didn't draw up a prenuptial agreement—this ring belongs to Shay."

A shaky smile pushed at my lips.

"You might have had a leg to stand on if she had been the one to break off the engagement, but in this case"—Noah gave a low whistle—"you did that all by yourself, didn't you?" He held the ring between his fingers and frowned at the severe edges of the princess-cut diamond. "But if you'd rather sort this out in court, you should know I'll be representing Miss Zucconi and I have all the time in the world to fuck you over. I will find all the skeletons in all of your closets. I'll dig them up if I have to. I'll bury you in legal proceedings and court fees. I'll make it impossible for you to move more than an inch without triggering an avalanche of lawsuits. I'll end you. Do you understand me yet?"

One last thing to know about Xavier was that he didn't care whether his business dealings were aboveboard. He didn't mind taking cash under the table or claiming residency in a tax haven or fudging some of the documentation. I didn't know many of the details on these gray dealings—though I really, really should've listened to Jaime when I had the chance—but I knew enough to recognize when Noah hit him where he was most vulnerable.

Xavier took a step back and held up his hands. "Crystal clear."

Noah set the ring on the table, the ring I'd forced myself to love. It wasn't round—as I'd mentioned was my preference—and the band was yellow gold—which looked terrible next to my skin—but it was big and I'd led myself to believe that meant something. It meant nothing at all and I should've known better but I was the fool who ignored all the signs. Every last one of them.

Noah tapped a finger on the table. "Get the fuck out of here and never come back."

chapter twenty-nine

Noah

Students will be able to hover.

"IT'S FINE," Shay said when I kneeled down beside where she was seated on an ice chest behind the Little Star table and reached for her wrist. "It's just a little scrape."

"I want to see it." How I managed to say this without roaring was a mystery to me. Hell, I didn't know how I managed to function. All I could see was the moment when that asshole grabbed Shay's arm and yanked her down like he had a death wish. The precious seconds it took me to cross the market had felt like hours, days. I didn't see how I'd ever get over that. "If it's scraped, you need it cleaned. Some antibacterial cream too."

With a sigh, she leaned back and pushed up her sleeve and—that fucking bastard was going to pay in blood and bone—her entire wrist was already swollen and bruised. A thin scrape circled the base of her wrist where the chain had bitten into her skin. A number of small cuts in the shape of her charms were dotted with blood. For a moment, I could only stare at her skin while a snarling breath huffed out of me. I should've punched that guy when I had the chance. I'd never punched anyone but this seemed like a perfectly justifiable reason to start.

"Show me that you can bend your wrist," I said as I unhooked the bracelet and dropped it into her other hand. "Move it side to side."

"It's fine." She rotated her wrist though I wasn't convinced we didn't need to make a stop at the urgent care clinic. "Please don't worry."

I ripped open an alcohol swab from the first aid kit I kept with the market supplies. "This will burn but it will be quick."

She winced when the alcohol met abraded skin though she was quiet while I tended to her wrist. These injuries were minor yet that didn't make them any less enraging. The fact she was injured at all was a problem for me. I knew I should've shut down sales and accompanied her to meet that fucker. I should've been there.

"Whatever he said to you," I started with as much calm as I could find, "is bullshit. It's all bullshit and I need you to believe me about that."

She blinked at me, her eyes glassy and distant. She was somewhere else, just the way she'd been when she arrived in Friendship all those months ago. I needed her to wake up and come back to me. I *needed* her. Especially in the weeks to come when Gennie and I left to visit Eva and —with any luck—came home unscathed. I couldn't do this all on my own. Not anymore. Not now that I knew what it was like to have someone by my side.

"Wife," I said sharply, "tell me what he said."

Her lips kicked up into a sad smile. "It doesn't matter."

"It matters to me and it matters because you're trying to decide if he's right," I argued.

"Maybe he is," she whispered. She gave a small shrug. "He can be right and be an asshole at the same time."

"What did he say?"

"Just that I force things," she said. "I forced him to propose."

"Yeah, I don't buy that for one second." That guy was a lot of things but he was no doormat. He popped the question because he had something to gain and I wouldn't entertain any other explanations. And I would've said as much to Shay but I didn't want to shame her for her relationship with him. I couldn't understand how they ended up together but they did and thank god it was over.

Thank god she was mine.

"But I invent a lot of projects," she said.

"And I wouldn't have it any other way." I dabbed antibacterial cream on the cuts, adding, "Let me ask you this: Why are you willing to believe him over me?"

"It's not that I don't believe you—"

"That's what it looks like to me."

She chewed on her lower lip. Then, "What if he's right?"

I dropped my hands to her thighs and gave her a firm squeeze. "He's not. Sweetheart, I swear to you, there's nothing in the world he's right about."

She stared at my hands. "Jaime told me I shouldn't see him."

"Have I mentioned how much I like Jaime?"

A thin laugh puffed over her lips. "You told me I shouldn't see him." She opened her other hand and studied the bracelet coiled in her palm. "Why is it so obvious to everyone else and I can't—I just can't see it?"

"You came for closure and the only person to blame for what happened today is that fucking fucker." When she didn't respond, I asked, "Has he ever done anything like this before?"

"No." She gave a single shake of her head as I wrapped a measure of gauze around her wrist. "He traveled all the time. We lived together but it was like a weekends-only arrangement. We weren't together too often. He hated my earrings." She ran her finger over one beaded strawberry. "I think they set him off."

"He's never hurt you before?" I needed a reason to find him and kill him. Or slam him with frivolous lawsuits. That was more to my skill set than murder. I could litigate my ass off but I didn't know the first thing about getting rid of a body. Then again, I owned hundreds of acres of farmland. I could figure it out. "Not even once?"

"No. He just needs to sell that ring so he can buy something for the woman he was cheating on me with." She pressed her fingers to her eyes. "Or he'll just give her that ring and call it a day. Oh, god, he'd do that too. Why didn't I realize he was such an ass until now? Saying these words out loud just makes it so obvious that he was a walking red flag and I chose to ignore that because I was busy convincing him to propose."

I'd always known but it was painfully clear now that Shay aimed way too low. She carried herself with all the confidence in the world but it was only skin-deep. She didn't believe any of it and she didn't feel it. And that was how she ended up with pathetic tools like her ex and that dumbass lacrosse coach.

I closed up the first aid kit. "We'll skip this lunch. It's not important. We can head home and—"

"No, we can't cancel your lunch," she interrupted. "Not because of me. I won't add to the insanity of your inbox because my ex decided to come here and be rude. And we're meeting up with Jaime and everyone later. Really, Noah, I'm fine."

She didn't look fine. She looked like she needed a warm blanket, a stiff drink, and a steady stream of reminders that her ex was full of shit. She looked like she needed to be held and adored for days.

"You've been through a lot this morning and it's going to catch up with you sooner or later," I said. "I don't want to push you. We can skip the lunch and still see Jaime."

"We're not skipping the lunch." She paused before saying, "Thank you, Noah. For everything. What you said to him…well, thank you for being there for me."

"I'll always be here for you, Shay. Always."

She took my hands and gave me a squeeze. "I don't think anyone's ever stood up for me quite like that." She glanced to the side. "His life flashed before his eyes when you threatened to sue him."

"Good." I leaned in and kissed the corner of her mouth. "It won't be the last time I stand up for you, wife."

"We should probably—" She tipped her chin up, toward the table we'd ignored for the past half hour.

The line stretched all the way to the opposite end of the tent and it was obvious that everyone near the front had been listening to our conversation. One of the women closest to the table held up a hand and said, "No rush. We can wait."

A few people were directing the line to keep it from blocking other vendors. Someone had tasked themselves with cleaning up the jar of spiced pear I'd dropped when I saw the fucker grab Shay's wrist. Another person stood nearby with a bottle of water and a handful of tissues, ready to hand them over to Shay. People drove me fucking crazy but they also humbled the hell out of me.

I glanced down at Shay, sitting on the ice chest with her legs crossed in front of her. She looked young—and lost. A lot like that first morning when I offered her a ride to school. I held out my hand to her. "Do you feel like putting those cute earrings to work, wife?"

A touch of color warmed her cheeks as she took my hand. "I'd love to."

THE REMAINDER of the market and the lunch that followed flew by in a blur. It was good and productive but I couldn't tear my focus away from Shay for long. I kept looking for signs that the day was catching up with her though I couldn't find any. The morning had shaken her but she seemed determined to forge ahead with a smile.

I did not share that determination. All that mattered to me was keeping Shay close, which wasn't the easiest thing to do while walking through the bustling streets of Boston's North End.

"Forgive me for asking," I said after we'd ducked around a tourist group, "but how does Jaime afford an apartment in this neighborhood on a teacher's salary?"

"She has three roommates," Shay called over her shoulder as she moved in front of me to avoid a woman pushing a double stroller. "But the key detail is that one of the roommates' boss and his wife own the building and they offer it at a reasonable price."

"Are we going to meet these roommates?"

"Probably." She leaned into me as we waited to cross the street. "Dylan is the one with the boss who owns the building. Layla is in college. Linnie works somewhere in the Back Bay. Marketing or something."

"And who else will be there?"

"Emme, Grace, Audrey. Maybe a few other people from my old school. It won't be a huge group." She pointed up at a building on Prince Street. "This is it."

We climbed the stairs to the second floor of this old warehouse and traveled down a long hallway that reminded me of my first apartment in Brooklyn. It was a building just like this one but the stairwells always smelled like boiled cabbage.

We waited at the door, Shay's head lolling against my arm as I stroked her waist. "They're coming," she said after a minute.

I kissed the top of her head. "I'm in no hurry."

The door swung open to reveal Jaime, her hair pinned up in rollers and her smile contagious. "Get in here, you two. I've been bouncing around here all afternoon, just waiting to see you. Come in, come in." She leaned in close. "What happened with the ex? No, wait, don't tell me until I pour some drinks. I have a feeling we'll need drinks."

"We'll need drinks," Shay said.

I followed them into the apartment, spacious by Boston standards, and toward an industrial-style kitchen. Jaime looped back toward me, whispering, "Well done with the birthday cake."

"Then you won't be sending the mafia after me?"

She grinned. "No. I'm on your side now."

"I had to bake the perfect cake but that fuckbag ex of hers could just go around being a fuckbag without you sending the mafia after him? Is that how it goes?"

Jaime rolled her eyes toward the ceiling. "Believe me, that's not how I've wanted it to go. I wanted to get rid of him years ago."

"What the hell stopped you?"

She tipped her head toward Shay, who was busy chatting with two other women in the kitchen. "She wasn't ready for that. It sounds like she might be there now."

I hoped so. I really fucking hoped so.

chapter thirty

Shay

Students will be able to doubt everything and drive themselves crazy in the process.

I FELT like I was made of paper-thin glass. One wrong move, one faltering smile and I'd crack. I'd shatter. But that couldn't happen. I'd already shattered once. I didn't think I could do it again and live to tell the tale.

More than that, I didn't want to shatter. I didn't want Xavier's words to matter enough to make me shatter. He didn't have the right to break me twice.

Noah didn't leave my side for hours. He stayed with me as I chatted with all my friends from school, always quick to refill my drink or push a small plate of snacks into my hand or stroke my back. He was quiet, perhaps a bit more quiet than his usual, but he was pleasant to all my friends. He asked about their grade levels and how long they'd lived in Boston, and he indulged everyone's desire to know more about the idyllic town of Friendship.

Aside from questions about our storybook small town—which it was not, regardless of what Emme said—they all wanted to know if I was coming back next year. I had a really hard time answering that with Noah's hand in my back pocket.

Honestly, I was having a hard time answering anything while Xavier's words echoed in my head. I couldn't stop hearing them and I couldn't stop thinking of all the times I *had* forced it. I'd been convenient, as he'd put it, and I'd cranked up the intensity on that convenience until the only next step was an engagement.

I remembered not wanting to waste my time dating people who weren't looking for a serious commitment, and making my priorities clear from the start, but looking back, I realized I'd basically put him in a marriage headlock until he tapped out.

If I'd just dated him without all that frantic energy, I probably wouldn't be fighting to keep myself from falling apart right now. I wouldn't be examining every single moment of the past few years and wondering which were organic and which I'd dragged into existence.

If I'd just dated the ex, I wouldn't be standing here with Noah now.

I wouldn't be married to Noah now.

I wouldn't be in love with a man who'd only signed on for one year and access to my step-grandmother's land. I wouldn't have a little family with him, wonky and patched together as we were, and I wouldn't feel as though I'd gone to Rhode Island searching for the remnants of home and I'd found precisely that.

Jaime waved to me as she approached with another woman. "This is your replacement," Jaime announced. "Aurora Lura, meet Shay Zucconi. And we can't forget the Daddy Bread Baker, Noah Barden. I told her she wasn't allowed to be that girl who left the city for a small town only to run off with the first farmer she met but no one listens to me."

"I thought we were on the same side now," Noah said to Jaime.

"We are," she drawled. "But you took my bestie. I'm still allowed to be salty."

The first thing I noticed about Aurora was her funky glasses. They were an oversized cat's eye style in dark, sparkly green. They were gorgeously excessive.

"I feel like I already know you just from inheriting your classroom," she said.

"And I feel like I know you from everything Jaime has told me," I replied. "Thank you for keeping her sane, by the way. I don't know what I would've done if her new neighbor wasn't someone who could hang with her brand of nutty."

"Don't worry," Aurora said with a laugh. Her long, dark hair spilled over her shoulders. "I mean, she's nutty. There's no two ways about that. But she always has food in her classroom. I don't mind the nutty when I get a cheese stick and some crackers with it. Cold seltzer too."

"The snacks do help," I agreed.

"Oh, this is cute," Jaime mused. "It's like an ex-wives' club over here."

"You know we love you," Aurora sang.

"Yeah, yeah. I'm going to leave before one of you smothers me with all this love."

As Jaime drifted to another group, Aurora said, "I know everyone here has been hounding you about whether you're coming back next year. I don't want to be another person doing that, especially since the next school year is approximately twenty years away." She glanced at the beer bottle in her hand. "But please don't worry about me while you make that decision. I've heard there might be a fourth grade opening next year if Audrey decides to loop up with her class and I really don't mind bouncing around to different grade levels if I'm in a good school. I'll be fine either way."

Noah stiffened beside me and that subtle move shifted my glass façade. On a different day, I would've been able to bluster through this conversation. I would've been able to put Aurora at ease and avoid answering anything. But I didn't think I could do that today.

"I assumed you were coming back anyway," she went on, "since you left all your materials in the classroom."

"Don't worry about it," I said. "About the stuff. In the classroom."

Aurora's forehead creased. "But your decorations and posters and books—"

"I'll find new ones," I said. Maybe it was cavalier to walk away from the supplies I'd spent years amassing. Maybe it was as destructive as running away to Rhode Island without any form of plan or future for myself. And maybe I was just too busy holding the patched up pieces of myself together to worry about storybooks and thematic decorations.

Aurora didn't seem convinced. "There are a lot of anchor charts too. Those must've taken ages to create."

"It's okay. Really. I'll make new ones. This guy can't stop ordering markers so I have to make use of them somehow." I smiled up at Noah. "Maybe you could order some flip charts next. We have a lot of markers and sticky notes." He pinched my backside in response. "I might need you to remind me which books I used for the gingerbread unit or to send me a pic of some of the posters I made but it's your classroom now. Don't worry about me coming back to collect anything. I knew what I was leaving behind when I went."

"Here. I'll send you a text so you have my number." She pulled out her phone and keyed in the digits as I rattled them off. "Would it be okay if I called you sometime to talk about kindergarten stuff?"

"Kindergarten is my favorite topic in the whole world. Call me anytime."

"Thank you. So much," she said. "Everyone always talks about how great you are and how nothing is the same without you. To be very transparent with you, I was getting a little tired of it." She belted out a deep laugh. "It was like, 'Okay, I'll never measure up to the wonderful and magical Shay. Cool. Awesome. Great to be on board.'" She gestured to me. "And now I meet you and discover that you're exactly as great as they said."

"She's really annoying like that," Noah said.

I shifted to face him. "What?"

Still looking at Aurora, he said, "It would help if she wasn't completely perfect. I know. Trust me, I know *all* about it."

With a grin, Aurora said, "It was really good to see you tonight. Stay in touch. Call me, text me. Tell Jaime to come into my room and poke me. Whatever."

When Aurora stepped away, I asked Noah, "What was that all about?"

"You heard what I said." He shrugged. "What do you say we wrap this up and head out? I'll tell you all about the ways you're annoyingly perfect while I get your clothes off. But I'm warning you right now, wife. My heart rate hasn't gone back to normal since this morning and I'm not sure it ever will. I might just snuggle you all night. I might keep you in my bed and hold you until you're sick of me. Even on school nights."

Was I forcing this? I couldn't be. There was no way. Right? "I'm not going to get sick of you."

He swung his arm around my shoulders and tucked me close to his chest. "Let me take you home."

"Yeah," I whispered. "Take me home."

WE WERE quiet on the drive back to Friendship. It was a comfortable sort of quiet, the kind that came from knowing we didn't have to swerve around awkward silences or entertain each other. It had always been this way with us. All those early mornings driving to school together, when we were bleary-eyed and half awake, we'd barely managed more than a few words.

By the time we turned up Old Windmill Hill, I'd stopped tossing the ex's words over and over in my mind. They were still there but I could think around them now. I had to keep telling myself he was wrong, but more importantly, I didn't care what he said. He didn't matter to me. There was no reason to live or die by his words.

Convincing myself not to care when I suspected he was right was a lot like standing on the shore and trying to stay dry. Even when I thought I had a handle on it, the surf licked at my toes or a goddamn riptide curled up and crashed over me.

The real problem was that Xavier was wrong about the things that didn't matter and he'd cut me right down to the bone on the things that mattered all too much. He could hit me on my weight because he knew I struggled just enough for it to hurt but the shape and dimension of my body was nothing compared to the suggestion that I talked myself into believing people loved and wanted me.

It was one thing to hear those thoughts in my head when I was alone and mean to myself but it was another to hear them spoken directly to me. I'd barely been able to look at Noah and my friends tonight without tucking in for a lengthy internal debate as to whether I was forcing them to play along in my sad little games too.

Huh. I guess I couldn't think around Xavier's words after all.

I'd almost convinced myself of one more pathetic thing.

"What the hell?" Noah muttered when we pulled onto the gravel drive leading to his house. Several trucks were parked along the lane and Gail stood at the base of the steps, a coat clutched around her shoulders while members of the farm crew surrounded her. "Something's wrong."

He parked the truck and we rushed to join the group. When Gail caught sight of Noah, she pressed her palm to her mouth. I grabbed Noah's hand between both of mine. It was time to focus on him now. I'd fall apart over my issues later. They'd wait for me. They always did.

"What happened, Gail?" he asked.

"Gennie's missing," she said.

chapter thirty-one

Noah

Students will be able to search.

NO.

This wasn't happening.

Just—*no.*

Gennie had to be in the house somewhere. She was hiding. She was in the closet or under the bed. Curled up in the bathtub and giggling into her arm while everyone went crazy searching for her.

She wasn't gone. She couldn't be. I wouldn't accept that as reality.

But this was all my fault. I was the only person left to take care of this kid and I should've known that leaving her for the entire day was a mistake. She was still struggling through so many issues and I should've known this was too much to ask of her.

"I've looked everywhere," Gail said for the tenth time, wringing her hands. "I don't even know how she could've gotten out. I've been here all night with my crocheting. I would've heard her or—"

"It's all right," I said to her as Shay came down the staircase. "Anything?"

She shook her head. "Her backpack is gone. The sword too."

My stomach turned.

"Fuck." I ran both hands down my face. "I gotta get out there. I have to search the land."

Shay hooked a hand around my arm as I moved toward the door. "Slow down. Think. There are only a few places she'd go. Dogs, goats, maybe cows. Right?"

"Right." I blew out a breath. "But we don't know how long she's been out there, Shay, and she doesn't know the land at night. It's a three-mile walk to the dairy barn from here. One wrong turn and she falls in a stream or veers off the trail and walks into a coyote den or—"

Shay held up a finger. "Don't do that. This isn't the time to think about the worst possible outcomes. She is smart and she is capable. Keep telling yourself that. We're going to find her and we're going to bring her home." She gave me a serious nod that said I wasn't to argue with her. "Let's get everyone organized so we can split up and cover as much ground as possible."

I reached for her hand. "You're staying with me. Okay? I can't handle losing both of my girls today."

"We'll find her together. We'll bring her home."

I turned to Gail, saying, "I need you to stay here and call the chief of police. You have his home number. Wake him the fuck up, all right? And call the boys at the oyster farm. Ask them to send their boats up to this end of the cove and circle the perimeter until we find her. Tell them to get as close to the shore as they can."

She picked her phone up from the table, her hands shaking. "Okay. Okay. I'll do that." Then, "Blankets," she cried, upending the quilted bag seated on the table and pushing an armload of soft wool into my arms. "Take these. Please. I'm so sorry."

"Call the chief of police," I echoed. It was the best I could do. "And the oyster boys."

I followed Shay outside where we found a crush of four-wheelers and pickup trucks, farm crew, dairy workers, and neighbors. Gail's husband and four grandkids, all on horseback. Wheatie handed out flashlights and headlamps while Nyomi and Bones distributed walkies.

When he spotted me, Bones called, "We're hauling up the floodlights from the orchard now. They'll be here in ten."

Wheatie held up a map as he passed Shay a pair of flashlights. "We've divvied up the farm into sections. Which one do you want, boss?"

I took the map from Wheatie. As much as I tried, I couldn't focus on it. "We're going back over her favorite places. The dog run, the goat enclosure, up to the farm stand. Then over to the dairy barn. Talk to me on the radio." I slashed a hand through the air. "And no ATV accidents tonight. No rollovers. We don't have time for that."

"We know the drill," he replied with a nod.

I motioned to the Castros and their horses. "Send them over to the dairy. They can cover more ground and they know the territory—"

"We know," Wheatie interrupted. "Go. We have this."

Bones handed me a radio. "I sent trucks down to the base of the hill to block traffic. No one is getting in or out unless we allow it."

The police were going to love that. I clapped him on the shoulder. "Thanks, man."

Shay followed me into the shed, silent as I settled behind the wheel of my ATV. She fastened her seat belt and grabbed onto the overhead handle as I shot out into the night air. "We'll hit the dog run first," I said. "Shine the light on your side. There isn't much in the way of hiding places around here but if she fell or she got tired or—"

"Eyes on the trail," she said gently. "Focus on what's right in front of you."

When we reached the dog run, I drove in a wide circle to get a look at the surrounding area. "Gennie loves these dogs," I said, mostly to myself. "She would've come here."

"Let's look around. We'll get a head count."

"Of…the dogs?"

Shay aimed her light at the kennel. "Yeah. She might've taken one with her." I opened the gate for Shay and followed her inside. "How many should there be?"

"Twelve." The old pups came streaming out the kennel door, ears perked and tails wagging at the unexpected visit. "Twelve dogs, twelve goats, twelve chickens."

"Was that intentional?" She patted each head as she counted to herself.

"No. I didn't realize it until Gennie pointed it out to me a few months ago."

She turned to face me, her flashlight pointed down. "Eleven."

Shaking my head, I jogged toward the kennel. The last one had to be asleep. Too old and too tired to bother with a late-night circus. I opened the door, fully expecting to find another dog.

The kennel was empty.

A breath whooshed out of me. If she took a dog, it was because she needed a friend. Or a protector.

Or both.

I closed the kennel door, saying, "Eleven."

"We'll check out the goat pen," Shay said with more calm than anyone could possibly possess in this situation.

We didn't speak as we bumped along the trail toward the goat enclosure. This part of the farm was darker than most others, closed in by a tall stand of trees and the natural slope of the land. The goats were less enthusiastic about us visiting and only glared with their round eyes as we counted heads, finding them all accounted for and no sign of Gennie. I didn't even see any pint-sized shoe prints in the damp soil leading into the pen.

"Let's think like Gennie," Shay said when we were back in the four-wheeler. "She leaves the house because—"

"Because she thought I wasn't coming back," I said.

"She knows you'd always come back."

I shook my head as I drove toward the farm stand. I doubted she was up there but I had to see for myself. "Any time I've ever tried to leave her with a sitter at night, she's panicked. I should've known she wasn't ready for this." Before Shay could argue, I added, "When we get inside, you search the shop and back room. I'll take the second floor."

As we drove Shay called Gennie's name and shone her light on the dense line of apple trees. In the distance, we could hear other search parties and see the beams of other flashlights. There were sirens too, and the glow of floodlights brightened the night sky.

If something happened to this kid, I'd never recover. I knew that as deeply as I knew anything. And I'd never be able to look my sister in the eye again.

When we pulled up to the back door of the farm stand, I dropped my keys twice before getting the door open. Shay covered my hand with hers, saying, "We are going to find her."

I nodded because I didn't trust myself to speak. We went our separate directions, Shay ducking into the back room while I climbed the stairs. Gennie rarely came up here though she was always fascinated by the fact our marketing manager worked out of a portion of her mom's childhood bedroom. She didn't care much about the portion we'd carved out to make a storage closet.

I checked each of the offices, all the closets, and the bathroom. Gennie wasn't here.

Jogging downstairs, I found Shay waiting for me, her hands on her hips and her gaze determined. "We have to think like Gennie," she said again. "She's not going to run away just to wander the farm. She has a destination in mind and I don't think it has anything to do with the animals."

"Then where the fuck would she go?"

"What if she went to *my* farm?"

"Your—*what*? No. As I've explained to you before, this hill is dangerous at night. And what would she want with Twin Tulip? It's empty and she knows that. Why would she go there?"

"I don't know," Shay admitted. "But it's one place we haven't considered and I think she knows we wouldn't look there right away."

My gaze glued to Shay, I reached for my radio. "What's the update from the dairy?"

Wheatie responded immediately. "We're combing the pastures now. No sign of her in the barn or pavilion."

Shay twisted her fingers around the chain at her throat. The bandage at her wrist caught my attention as she said, "I have a feeling about this. We need to go down the hill."

I ran a hand over my mouth. Into the radio, I said, "We're going to check out Twin Tulip. Keep me updated."

"You got it," Wheatie said.

We headed straight for Old Windmill Hill Road, quiet as we coasted down the steep incline. "Where should we go first?" I asked.

Shay didn't answer right away. "Inside," she said eventually. "Then the front gardens and the barn. But if she's there, she's inside."

"How would she get in?"

"Aside from the fact there are at least ten doors in and out of that place, I wouldn't put it past her to jimmy open a window or break the damn thing. She believes she's a pirate, Noah."

"Yeah, I know, that's part of the problem," I yelled. "I'm sorry, I just—"

She dropped her hand to my thigh. "I get it."

"I'm going to put bars on her windows. Locks on her doors. A tracking device in her shoes."

We bounced over the turnoff to Twin Tulip, the pavement giving way to gravel. Ahead, the house was dark. I'd barely stopped the four-wheeler before Shay was out of her seat, across the driveway, up the porch. I followed, watching as she swept the flashlight over the windows, the doors. The place seemed empty and untouched but then she pushed one of the front doors and it creaked open.

She glanced up at me. "I'd say we should split up but—"

"But that's fucking creepy," I said. "If Gennie isn't here, someone is." I took her hand. "Let's do this."

Both of the front parlors were empty, the kitchens and bathrooms too. We climbed the stairs, calling out to Gennie as we went. With each step, it seemed less likely we'd find her here. And if she wasn't here, I didn't know where to go next. Deeper into the pastures? The cove? I didn't want to think about her wading through the thick salt marsh. Even a kid who was a strong swimmer would struggle in those muddy waters. And it was cold. And dark.

"Do you hear that?" Shay asked, turning her ear toward the end of the hall. "It's—I don't know what it is but it's something."

I couldn't hear anything beyond the roar of my blood pressure. "No."

"This way," she said, tugging me toward her bedroom. "I know it."

She pushed open the door and aimed her light at the bed, where Gennie was tucked under blankets and fast asleep. Bernie Sanders, a fourteen-year-old black lab gone white all over his face, greeted us with an urgent whine. He paced in front of the bed as if he knew precisely how bad it was for his young friend to be far from home this late at night.

Shay switched off the flashlight as I rushed into the room. "Gennie," I cried, peeling back the blankets and gathering her close. She startled and blinked up at me, her eyes immediately filling with tears. "What—why are you here, kid? What happened?"

"I was scared," she said as those tears spilled over.

"Of what?"

"I don't want you to go away," she sobbed.

"I know." I held her close. "I know. But I'm always going to come back."

She buried her face in my chest and shook her head. "But what if you don't?"

"I'll always come back," I repeated.

"Momma said that too."

Well, fuck. There was no clean way to walk that line. "I know it's hard to believe me but I will always come back. Nothing will ever change that."

"What if you have to go away? Like Momma did. Where will I live then?"

"I won't have to go away. I can promise you that I won't."

"But what if you decide you don't want to take care of me anymore? If you and Shay have a baby, you won't want me and I'll have to go somewhere else. Back to that scary place."

My shirt was soaked through with tears. "No, Gennie, that's not going to happen. You're my family. I'm always going to want you."

"Momma didn't want me anymore." Her words came in hiccupping jolts. "She went to jail to get away from me."

"That's not true," I said quickly. "Your mother loves you so much. She made a bad mistake and that's the only reason she went to jail. If she could be here with you now, she would be."

"What if you make a mistake? What happens to me?"

This was the most painful conversation of my entire life and that included the conversation I had with my mother about taking my father off life support. "I'll work extra hard at not making any mistakes."

"But what happens if you make a mistake and have to go away?"

"I'll take care of you," Shay said. We both looked up and found her standing at the foot of the bed, tears brimming in her eyes and Gennie's backpack in her hands. "No matter what happens, I'll always be here for you."

"You won't send me away?"

She shook her head. "Never."

Gennie stared up at me, her dark eyes swollen and red. "What if Shay makes a mistake too?"

"Teachers always follow the rules," I said. "Shay is very well-behaved. She won't make any mistakes."

"I won't," Shay added.

"What if I'm bad too many times?" she whispered.

"Gennie, you aren't bad," I said. "You're the best kid I know."

"You don't know any kids."

"I don't care. You're still the best one."

She sniffled. "That doesn't make sense."

"Neither does running away," I replied. "The whole farm is looking for you. Bones, Wheatie, Nyomi. Everyone. The Castro kids are out on their horses. Even the police."

Tears poured from her eyes and she clawed at my shirt, balling her fingers and scrambling up my chest. "Don't let the police take me."

"Fuck, no, that's not why we called them," I said, ready to punch myself in the mouth. "We called them because we needed help finding you. They're *helping* us, Gennie. They're not taking you anywhere. You're not in trouble."

In this moment, that was the truth. Later, we'd have a talk about pulling stunts like this one.

I ran a hand over her hair. "Do you want to go home now?" After a second, she bobbed her head against my chest. I picked her up and nodded at Shay to lead the way with Bernie the black lab.

We went downstairs and locked up the house using the key Gennie had lifted from Shay's room earlier today. She also had several sandwiches, two screwdrivers, a ball of twine, and my iPad in that backpack.

With Gennie bundled in Gail's blankets between us in the front seat and Bernie sniffing the night air in the cargo bed, I clicked on the radio speaker and exhaled for the first time in hours.

"We have her," I said, "and we're headed home."

chapter thirty-two

Shay

Students will be able to crash hard.

NOAH PUSHED OPEN the door and stepped into my room. His hair was a wreck, his eyes red and weary. He sat on the edge of the bed, exhaled a whole paragraph, and shook his head. "What the literal fuck happened here tonight?"

I folded a sweater, shook it out, started folding it again. I didn't need to do this. I always organized my laundry the second it was dry. Putting it away was another story and that was the story that led me to this state of uncontrollable futzing. While Noah had tucked Gennie into bed, the day's adrenaline spikes drained and I found my hands shaking. Conveniently, I noticed the shirt on the top of my laundry pile looked slightly rumpled and thus a perfect project was born. One that gave me a thread of control and just enough purpose to regain some calm too. "Are you looking for an answer to that?"

He glanced at the clock perched on a tall bureau. It was after two in the morning. Getting Gennie home was one thing, though thanking everyone for their help in searching and sending them on their way was something else altogether. They meant well, they certainly did, and I understood the desire to linger. Part of me wished they'd linger even longer than they did. I needed that crush of voices and bodies to distract me from—from *everything*.

"Not really," he grumbled. "We'll spend enough time figuring it out with her therapist this week."

"Did Gennie tell you how she got out?"

He flopped back onto the bed. "Out her bedroom window, onto the porch roof, down a pillar to the porch. Apparently she'd tested the gutters and they were too shaky."

"Perfect." I held up a jersey knit skirt, smoothed it out, folded it. "Are you okay?"

"No." He ran a hand over his face. "I am not qualified for this. I don't know how anyone could be qualified for this but I definitely am not."

I nodded. He didn't notice. "I was thinking that—I think I should go. Not right now but tomorrow. I should go back to Thomas House."

He pushed up on one elbow. "What the hell are you talking about?"

"I should move back to Thomas House. I think it would be better. For everyone but Gennie in particular."

"Please explain to me how that makes any fucking sense, wife."

"From the start, we said we'd protect Gennie. She wouldn't get caught in the middle, right?" He glared at me, his eyes narrowed to slits and his mouth cut in a sharp scowl. "She's in the middle, Noah. She thinks we're going to have a baby and abandon her."

"She also thinks her mother chose a prison sentence over her," he said, each word ice-cold. "Clearly, there are some misunderstandings rooted in the fact she's a child who has experienced multiple emotional traumas in the past year."

"Listen, I can't risk hurting your kid because we decided to get fake-married so I can inherit my grandmother's farm." I threw a bra into the basket. "And the longer I'm here, living in Gennie's house and participating in her daily life, the more it's going to hurt when I leave."

"It's going to hurt regardless. She's been attached to you from the start."

"All the more reason for me to go," I said.

"You told her you'd be there for her. You said you'd be there if anything happens to me. How do you reconcile saying that to her tonight and then moving out tomorrow?"

"You have a family here and I am intruding on that," I argued. "I can play the part of the fun aunt she visits on long weekends and summer holidays. I can be that person for her. But we can't fake our way through this when there's a real kid involved."

"You can't walk away now and pat yourself on the back. She's loved you since the day you showed up here and I think you know that."

"I know what it's like to be a kid and have people visit—never stay, just visit—in my life. I know how confusing and lonely that feels. The sooner I leave, the better it will be for everyone."

With a huge groan, Noah pushed up from the mattress and gained his feet. "Yeah, I don't buy it."

I went back to the laundry. This bra wasn't going to fold itself. "Don't buy what?"

He waved a hand. "Any of this."

"It's not a matter of whether you buy it or not," I said. "And I'm not asking for your permission."

"This story you've thrown together, the one where you save everyone by walking away, it doesn't impress me. It ignores most of the relevant facts of this situation and it fails to recognize that you will save no one and succeed only in hurting everyone." He folded his arms over his chest. "But go ahead. Tell me all about how it will be better for you to be alone at Thomas House instead of here with us."

"What do you want us to do, Noah?" I pushed my fingers through my hair. "Should we stay married forever?"

He lifted his shoulders. "And what's wrong with that?"

"What's—what's *wrong* with that?" I sputtered. The bra flew out of my hand and ended up under the bed. "Oh, I don't know. Maybe the part where I talked you into marrying me because I'm randomly sentimental about Lollie's farm and have some silly, half-formed idea about transforming it into a wedding venue. Or the part where I convinced you that I wouldn't let your niece get caught between us and I'd do everything to protect her. Or even the part where I said we could have sex and it wouldn't complicate things too much."

"I mean, yeah, that last part is pure delusion," he said.

I rolled my eyes. "We are old friends with good sexual chemistry—"

"Really good," he added.

"—but we've built this thing on a pile of empty cardboard boxes and it's about to cave in. Even if we wanted to, even if I hadn't forced this relationship from thin air, it wouldn't work."

Noah stared at me for a long moment, his arms crossed and his jaw ticking. Then, "Why not?"

"Because it's not real," I whisper-yelled. "Everything about this is fake and we're—"

"Not everything." He reached out and ran the back of his finger down the column of my neck, over the rise of my breasts. "It hasn't been fake for a long time and you know that."

"I'm living with you to cover up the fact we're only married for Lollie's estate. I wouldn't be here if it wasn't for chatty people in public records offices and you know it."

"You'd be here," he said, still drawing that finger over my sweater. "And you know it."

I closed my eyes. "The way this all started and how I convinced you—"

"Stop that," he growled. "Don't think for a minute that you convinced me to do anything I didn't want. The way I remember it, I was the one who offered to marry you and followed up on that proposal until you had to bark at me to back off."

"I didn't *bark* at you."

He moved his palm to the nape of my neck. "Get that noise from your ex out of your head. I don't want to hear another word of it."

"It's not noise." I leaned into him then, my head resting on his chest and my hands on his waist. "I forced this. If I hadn't shown up here with a problem only a fake marriage could solve, you never would've looked twice in my direction."

His fingers flexed on my neck. "That's not true."

"Yeah. Sure. I'd love to see you prove otherwise."

We were silent for a minute or two and it seemed like we'd tacitly agreed to leave this matter to the morning but then Noah said, "We can still do this. We can start over and do it better than the mess we made in the beginning."

"But Gennie—"

"Gennie is going to be all right," he said. "Tonight was awful and the things she said ripped my heart straight out of my chest but she's going to be okay. She's getting the help she needs. Would it be nice if she could've parachuted into a perfect, ready-made family? Of course, but she got stuck with me instead."

"Not a bad place to get stuck," I said.

"It's not going to ruin her life to watch while some adults figure out how to be together, okay? Be real, Shay. This is hardly a drop in the bucket compared to the shit she's seen." He huffed out a quiet laugh. "You're not going to save anyone by running away. I'm wise to your game, wife. I know you think that's going to solve all our problems but it's not. Abandoning people before they abandon you won't make anything better."

"That's not what I'm doing." It was very possible that was exactly what I was doing. It was also possible that I was feeling too many terrible things at once and the only good solution was exiting myself from the situation. "I know it isn't fair of me to fall apart right now but I can't hold it in any longer."

"You don't have to hold it in. But you don't have to leave either," he said softly. "Not yet. It's going to be hard enough dealing with our little escape artist and getting ready to visit Eva. Give me some time, wife, and if you still think you know what's best for everyone but yourself, I'll move you down the hill myself."

After a moment, I nodded. "Okay. I can do that."

"Thank god." He tucked his fingers under my sweater. "I've experienced more emotions in the past day than I have in my entire adult life and I don't like it. I'm taking you to bed, and regardless of what I said earlier I don't plan on being nice about it. Is that okay? Tell me now if it isn't."

I breathed out a laugh as he yanked my shirt over my head. Laughed as he stripped off my jeans, steered me toward the bed. Laughed when he positioned me facedown on the mattress and pushed into me with a ragged growl. Laughed as he gripped me by the hips, his fingers splayed over my belly roll, and gifted my back and shoulders hot, open-mouthed kisses. Laughed when he pounded into me, his body hard and aggressive like never before. Laughed when he hiked me up, pressed his teeth to the round of my ass, pinched my pussy, twisted my hair around his fist. I laughed when I came and when he was quick to follow.

Though at some point, those breathy, shuddering laughs had turned into breathy, shuddering sobs. It was all the same since only the mattress knew my secrets. It was the mattress that knew I had fallen for my husband today but also long before today, and this fall was quite unexpected. It was also quite irreversible, and his refusal to let me go only made it worse because I knew I'd be crushed when he realized I'd cornered him into a relationship he didn't want but couldn't leave.

That was how it would end, of course. He'd wake up one morning and blink at me through long-suffering eyes, discovering that he'd rescued me the way he rescued everyone, and in doing so, lost himself.

I knew he'd tell me I was wrong if I said any of this so I kept these secrets between me and the mattress.

chapter thirty-three

Noah

Students will be able to endure.

THE NEXT WEEK was a tiring one.

Gennie and I spent afternoons at her therapist's office working through the events of the weekend and preparing to visit Eva. There were a lot of tears and they weren't all from Gennie. This shit was hard and there was no getting around it.

It was also a quiet week. Shay stayed late at school to organize materials for a new unit she had coming up, and though I knew that was true, I also knew she was giving us a wide berth. I knew she believed it was for the best, especially for Gennie, but I missed her. I wanted to climb into Shay's bed and bury my face in the crook of her shoulder and forget all about the weight of raising a child who'd been through too much in her handful of years on this planet.

Instead, I tossed and turned all night. I couldn't close my eyes without being haunted by the visions of Shay. When she returned to Friendship and when she told me about her dream of turning Twin Tulip into a wedding venue. The day I married her and the night she kissed me and meant it.

I didn't fantasize about the girl I'd loved in high school anymore or the person I'd resented for never looking back after she left. Everything I'd felt for her then was real but it was different now—complicated and layered and sophisticated in ways I never would've understood until it thrummed in my veins. I loved her and I hoped it would be enough this time.

"GO ON," I said to Gennie. "I'll be right here the entire time."

Gennie sawed her teeth over her lower lip and kept her gaze on the linoleum floor. "Maybe she changed her mind and doesn't want to see me."

"I know she wants to see you more than anything in the world."

She nodded once. "Dr. Brianna said I'm allowed to feel lots of things at once and that's called being overwhelmed." She twisted her fingers in her black-and-white striped skirt. "Do you think my mom feels overwhelmed?"

"I'm sure she does."

She was quiet for a moment. "Are you going to come with me?"

"I am but I'm going to let you have some time alone with your mom first, like we talked about with Dr. Brianna. Is that okay? Or should we make a new plan?"

She shook her head. "That's okay." She glanced across the room to where my sister stood beside a round table, her fingers twisted together and her body shifting like she was ready to spring up from the bench. "Stay right here," she said, a hand on my shoulder, "where I can see you."

Gennie walked toward Eva, her hair in the best braids I could manage. When she was a few paces from the table, she paused. I pushed to my feet, my heart in my throat, thinking she needed me to do this with her, but then she sprinted toward her mother. She flew into Eva's arms, knocking her back a step.

Minutes went by as I stood there, watching them cling to each other, their shoulders heaving as they sobbed. Eventually, they pulled apart enough for Eva to swipe her thumbs over Gennie's wet cheeks and they smiled at each other. I sat down. My heart remained lodged in my throat.

They talked for nearly ninety minutes, most of that time consumed by words pouring out of Gennie. She didn't stop moving once, always wiggling or hopping up to dance or act out the story she was telling. Eva barely blinked, too busy absorbing every last ounce of her daughter.

When Gennie ran over to fetch me, she said, "I feel overwhelmed but it's not the bad kind of overwhelmed anymore."

"That's good. And wasn't I right? Your mom didn't change her mind about wanting to see you."

She aimed a sour scowl in my direction, shaking her head as if she couldn't believe I'd repeated her own words back to her.

Gennie led me to the table and motioned for me to sit across from Eva. My sister looked like she'd lived many years in the past one. She'd always taken after our mother, with a tall, slim build and dark hair though their similarities ended at appearances. Where my mother was a peacemaker by trade, Eva was a rebel to the core. She had the word *anarchy* tattooed down the length of her spine. My mother saw no reason to travel or go away on vacations; Eva couldn't survive without new adventures. Mom preferred constancy; Eva craved the unknown.

It was those fundamental differences—and the intolerance of them—that dug a mile-wide channel between them over the years. By the time Eva graduated, they barely spoke. Those last few years, when I was starting high school and Dad kept buying farmland he couldn't afford from our neighbors, brought out the worst in them. It was the worst for all of us.

It was no surprise Eva left home one day without saying goodbye.

She texted me often but she only called the house every few months. It stood to reason that things would've been better without Mom and Eva walking around in hostile, seething storm clouds but it wasn't. It wasn't better.

I didn't know whether Eva found what she wanted beyond the pastoral borders of Friendship, Rhode Island. I had to believe that she had found some of it. I *had* to believe that. I couldn't watch while she gazed at her daughter with awe and unmasked grief if I didn't believe she'd lived wild and free in the time between leaving home and a life sentence.

And I couldn't tell her how very much she looked like our mother.

"I have people working on the appeal," I said to my sister.

She lifted her shoulders. "I know. And I know it will take time."

"They're still working on getting you moved to Connecticut too."

Gennie crawled into Eva's lap and turned her attention to the coloring book pages and worn-down crayons on the table. "I know you're doing everything you can."

"And I'm—"

"Tell me about the girl you married," Eva interrupted. "Why am I not surprised it's Shay What's-Her-Name from high school?"

"It's not—it isn't—I mean, we aren't actually—well. Yeah. Shay Zucconi." I folded my arms on the table and leaned closer. I had no idea what I was trying to say. Where to begin? "Gennie likes her."

"I know," Eva said, laughing. "I heard *all* about Shay."

"It's not—she isn't—" This time, I knew what I was saying but I couldn't gather the right words to say it. "She's not trying to replace you."

She nodded slowly and pressed her lips together. Then, "I know that too. I'm happy there's someone in Gennie's life who can tie fancy braids and help her read about pirates and explorers." She glanced at the coloring page. "I'm really happy there's someone in your life who can do special things for you too. With everything that you do for all of us, you deserve it most of all."

I nodded. I needed that validation more than I could ever put into words. "You'd like her. She has pink hair and wears avocado earrings."

"Like, actual avocados? Or things made to look like avocados?"

I waved a finger toward my ear as if she didn't know where earrings went and said, "Beaded things that look like avocados. Beads, sequins. Embroidery, maybe? But not actual avocados, no."

"Actual avocados would be pretty badass," Eva mused. "I bet there's some kind of ancient Mesoamerican custom of wearing avocado earrings as a way of knowing the exact moment they're ripe."

In a different time, Eva would've followed that thought to the Yucatan and spent two months asking the locals about old avocado lore. Then the wind would've turned her attention in a new direction and she'd set off to hitchhike up and down Pacific Coast Highway or learn how to drive a pontoon boat down south.

"Are you doing all right?" I asked her.

With the curiosity of ancient avocados wiped from her face, Eva nodded slowly. "As good as anyone else in this place," she said. "But it hasn't been too bad. Thank you for the care packages and for keeping money on my card. That's helped." She heaved out a sigh. "There are books here. Not the best of selections and some really outdated shit but I'll take what I can get." Her eyes widened, her brows crinkled. She paused and I prepared for the worst. "I've been talking to a counselor. She suggested I think about writing to Mom."

I leaned closer, my chest nearly level with the table. "Say that again?"

She laughed though the sound was sad. Aching. "I know, right? The counselor says it might help me resolve some stuff if I reach out. If I just say hi and that I miss her and I hope she's okay. That's all." As she spoke, her eyes filled with tears and her words broke. "Even if she never responds, I'll know I tried."

"I think that's a good idea. I know it's hard for her to write. She has a tough time holding a pen or typing but there's probably someone at the facility who can help."

"I might do that," she said. "But I won't hold my breath for a response. Because she has a hard time writing."

We were silent for several minutes while Gennie colored. She told a story about pirates and submarines and how mermaids would always side with pirates. When the visiting hours ended, Gennie and Eva shared another long, tearful embrace. I gave my sister a squeeze and reminded her to let me know if there was anything she needed.

I carried Gennie out of the facility, her head heavy on my shoulder and her silent tears soaking my shirt. She didn't say much on the drive back to the hotel other than to say she wanted to visit the indoor pool again and then eat chicken fingers for dinner. All things considered, this visit was a remarkable improvement over previous attempts.

And yet it was still grueling. It was still more than I ever wanted Gennie to endure.

She splashed in the pool for three straight hours and, upon judging her five thousandth handstand of the evening, I realized she was burning off emotional energy. She needed to tell pirate and mermaid stories and race from one end of the pool to the other and handstand her ass off because it was how she worked out the stress. It was the same reason she ran off the bus every afternoon and bombed down the hill to play with the dogs. She wasn't just a hellraiser of a child. It wasn't an attack on my orderly way of life. She simply needed to do something with everything she'd experienced that day.

Gennie swam up to the edge of the pool. "Noah, am I allowed to send Momma stuff in the mail?"

"What kind of stuff?"

"I don't know. Maybe some of my good schoolwork or a letter if Shay would help me write it."

"Yeah, you can send her those things," I said. "I'm sure Shay would help you but I can help too."

"Shay's better at that stuff." She dunked under the surface and then came back up. "I was a little girl when Momma went away and I didn't really understand it," she said sagely. "Now that I'm a big girl, I know Momma still loves me and she didn't go away because she didn't like being my momma."

"You're—you're a big girl now," I repeated.

"Yeah," she replied, as if it was obvious. "And I think you need to be really nice to Shay."

I leaned forward on the lounge chair. What did this kid know that I didn't? And where was she getting her information? "I…thought I *was* nice to Shay."

"Nicer," Gennie said. "Like you *love* her."

I coughed to cover up a bitter laugh. Shay and I had exchanged a few texts this week, only the most basic check-ins from our travels and confirmation that she was well, and it was driving me fucking crazy. I couldn't wait to get home. I wanted to make things right with us and I didn't care what that cost me. I'd rip up this fake marriage and start over if that helped. I'd hire another therapist so the three of us could figure out how to do this right. Anything she wanted, I'd give her. Anything. "How do you suggest I do that?"

"You should do nice things, like take her on romantic dates," Gennie replied. "I promise I won't run away when Mrs. Castro comes to babysit this time."

Mrs. Castro was a little too busy unpacking the horror of her last babysitting gig to consider future opportunities with this flight risk. "Dates, okay. What else?"

"She liked it a lot when we had a birthday party. Maybe we should do that again."

"Another birthday?"

"I dunno. Maybe a party with cake. And presents! You should give her presents."

"Right. Okay. Anything else?"

Gennie floated on her back, her arms swishing at her sides. "You should tell her you love her. Tell her *a lot*. I think that's what you're supposed to do."

She flipped around and returned to her handstand practice.

Maybe she was right. Maybe that was exactly what I needed to do.

chapter thirty-four

Shay

Students will be able to talk themselves in and out of anything.

IT WAS strange being in Noah's house alone. It felt like someone could pull up at any minute and ask what I was doing here. If they did, I'd have to say Noah and I were married—or something like that—and I lived here now. And I'd have to make it sound like those were real, true things and not the ramblings of a deranged person who broke in and decided to call it home.

The first day, I almost packed up and headed down to Twin Tulip. Thomas House was lonely and empty but it was still *my* place. I kept that debate going for hours. I packed a bag, set it by the door, stared at the door until I decided it was crazy to move out while Noah and Gennie were away.

Then I decided it was crazy to stay here while Noah and Gennie were away.

In the end, I went to Twin Tulip, walked the land until the sky was dark, and then drove to the next town over to grab takeout. Being out like this on a weeknight, aimless and untethered without the structure of mealtimes and bathtimes and bedtimes, was just as strange as hanging around Noah's house without him. The world felt different, like a place I no longer recognized.

And it seemed as though everyone on the roads and everyone in the restaurant was aware that I was carrying on an entirely foolish debate in my head. They knew I had an overnight bag in the back seat of my car and they knew I couldn't stop arguing with myself over where to sleep tonight. Like they knew I curled in and out of believing I loved Noah—and Gennie too—and those feelings came from all the things we'd found together rather than vintage *pick me* issues. Like they knew I teased at every loose thread of our relationship until I could unravel the whole thing in less than a minute.

I returned to Twin Tulip but only paused a moment on the gravel lane before shaking my head, mentally kicking myself in the ass, and driving up the hill. "All of my things are here," I explained to the takeout bag. "I don't want to throw off my morning because I can't find any deodorant"—I scowled as Noah's crisp white farmhouse came into view—"or the right shoes."

The scowl didn't come from anger. It wasn't about resentment. It wasn't even frustration at all this pointless spiraling.

The scowl came from wanting to be here. And that was the truth, as odd and uncomfortable as it was to wrap my hands around. I wanted to be here and I wanted Noah and Gennie here with me. It wasn't the same without them.

I wasn't the same without them.

I'd never meant to fall for these people. I hadn't come here looking for a patchworked family. And I hadn't expected for any of this to start putting me back together.

I VENTURED out for a second attempt at happy hour on Friday afternoon.

This time, I met a bunch of teachers from my school at the swanky oyster bar on the water in Friendship. We were celebrating a third grade teacher who was recently selected for a prestigious program with a big tech company that would give her lots of specialized training around the country plus all kinds of hot new gadgets for her classroom.

Janita also received a hefty stipend and that was the reason she chose the swanky oyster bar on the water. The first round was on her.

Unlike that disaster at the beginning of the school year, no one ditched me while I was in the restroom. Not that I'd expect that from this group. These women reminded me of my friends back in Boston. I'd gotten to know them over the past months but there was something about seeing them outside of school, in a setting unencumbered by students and brightened by wine, that made them seem fresh and new. More themselves than they could ever be in a twenty-minute lunch period or in the hall during morning arrival duty.

Dana was bold and a little loud (just like Emme), Ingrid listened more than she spoke and was extremely thoughtful about her words when she did speak (Audrey all the way). Neveen tended toward dry wit and cynicism (Grace to be sure), while Mieke was warm and caring (not that anyone could ever compare but definitely Jaime).

They were different, of course, but there was a funny comfort in spying the things I loved most about my friends in these women. I could see myself folding right into this group, but more than that, I *wanted* to fold into this group. I wanted to hear more about Neveen's never-ending kitchen renovation headaches and I wanted Mieke to introduce me to her colorist because her plum and magenta bob was divine, and I wanted to show Ingrid around my tulip fields and I wanted wine to fly out of my nose (again) because I was laughing at Dana's outlandish takes. And that was funny in an uncomfortable way because I didn't know whether I should want it.

Putting down roots was never the plan. Not that I'd had a plan when setting out from Boston with a box of Cheez-Its and my life shattered into a million tiny pieces. If anything, the absence of a plan *was* the plan. Survive one day to the next. No sudden moves. Expect the worst. Plan for nothing.

And I'd tried to do that. I'd tried *so hard*.

But then there was a kid who needed help, and a new life for an old farm, and a fake marriage—one sudden move after another. Stepping stones from one new plan to the next. It wasn't about my survival anymore because it was all of us, me and Noah and Gennie. And Lollie's farm and a permanent teaching position next year and falling for my husband.

I didn't know whether I should want any of this or if I could trust it.

I'd meant to take this year to snatch up the last bits of home I could find at Twin Tulip and figure out who I wanted to be now. Finding a family, finding places to call my own—never part of the equation.

Yet here I was, surrounded by people who hounded me almost as frequently as Helen about whether I'd be taking next year's first grade position or the kindergarten one.

And here I was with a new and fragile marriage that we'd built on a mountain of faulty logic and old fondness for each other.

I couldn't stop asking myself whether I was forcing any part of this. Whether I'd decided along the way what I wanted this to be and then convinced myself it was. I couldn't talk myself into job offers or coworkers who insisted I join them tonight but what if I'd talked myself into loving Noah? What if I was repeating all my same old mistakes?

I didn't know how to protect myself from that.

As the evening came to a close, we parted with hugs and congratulations for Janita and promises to do this again sometime soon. When I closed out my tab at the bar, I noticed Christiane Manning a few seats down. She stared into a full martini, her chin resting on her hand.

Despite all the better judgment in the world, I said, "Hey, Christiane."

It took her a second to drag her gaze away from the glass and over to me and then another second for recognition to flicker in her eyes. Eventually, she forced a smile. "Hello there. Haven't seen you in ages."

"I've been"—I glanced out at the water and slowly shook my head—"figuring things out."

"Where's your husband tonight?"

I swallowed a sigh. I didn't mind being Noah's human shield but I was getting tired of Noah being the solitary source of conflict between me and Christiane. It was a waste of everyone's time. "He and Gennie are out of town for a few days. They'll be back tomorrow afternoon."

I waited for some sweet-edged comment but it never came. She nodded and went back to staring at her drink. I took my time adding a tip, checking my math, signing the receipt. The silence that settled wasn't awkward but it didn't feel good either. It was uneven.

"The twins are with their dad this weekend," Christiane said eventually. "I hate being in my house alone right after they've gone. All that quiet—it feels wrong." She picked up her drink but set it down before taking a sip. "A lot of the other divorced moms I know say they love the quiet and the freedom but I haven't gotten to that stage yet. I haven't figured out how to be alone yet."

I hesitated a moment before settling onto a barstool. "I can empathize with that," I said. "It's been so quiet at the house without Noah and Gennie. It's like I'm waiting for something to happen but nothing happens." I traced the grain of the hardwood bar top with my finger. "I've been ordering takeout every night because I can't remember how to cook for one."

Without looking at me, Christiane motioned to her martini. "Do you want a drink? I know you probably had enough with your friends but you're welcome to stay."

"Sure." I waved the bartender over, ordered a glass of sangria.

When my drink arrived, Christiane pinched her fingers to the stem of her glass and held it up to clink against mine. "I wasn't trying to steal your husband," she said by way of a toast. "Even though I acted like I was trying to steal your husband."

Considering this, I drank deeply. "Thank you," I started, "for that point of clarification."

"I don't like feeling empty," she said. "After my divorce, I just felt like I needed to cram that emptiness full of anything I could get my hands on."

"And…Noah seemed like someone you could get your hands on?"

She turned to me with a flat stare. "There were obvious flaws in that plan. Noah being in love with you, to start."

I wasn't going to explain the multitude of reasons her information was more than a little faulty. Nope. I had sangria to drink and no desire to hurt my own feelings tonight.

"He has a kid the same age as my twins and he's all alone, and just look at him," Christiane went on. "It seemed like we'd fit. Like we matched up in the same spots."

I gave a knowing nod. Sounded just like my approach to the ex—and nothing like my approach to Noah. "Matching up isn't all it seems to be."

"He doesn't even *look* at anyone else," Christiane continued. "Certainly doesn't notice any of us at goat yoga. And you know what? Goat yoga is not relaxing. There is nothing fun about trying to hold a pose while a goat licks your face or shoves his nose into places where goat noses do *not* belong."

"Wait. Hold on. You're going to goat yoga to catch Noah's attention?"

Christiane gestured with her glass, sending half the liquid flying at the bartender. He took most of it to the chest though some splashed across his face. He trudged away with a growl. "Why do you think anyone goes to goat yoga at Little Star?"

"I can assure you that the last thing Noah's concerned with is goat yoga." I took the glass from her, set it back on the bar. "If that was your plan—go to yoga at his farm, flirt him up at football games—you're missing the part where Noah is extremely protective of Gennie and the only reason he knows your name is because your kids have a history of pushing his niece around. You could be his dream woman—"

"Like you?"

"Stop." I gave her an impatient glare. I didn't want to play that game tonight. "You could be everything he's ever wanted, but the second someone messes with his niece, it's all over. He doesn't give a damn about his dreams if Gennie is unhappy. That's probably the reason your charms didn't work on him."

Christiane frowned at her clasped hands. "My kids can be assholes."

"All kids can be assholes. They don't usually mean it but it happens to the best of them."

"Francie can be catty and cliquey but Harold means it," she grumbled. "He's angry about the divorce. He does all kinds of outrageous shit to get attention." She shook her head. "Then his father takes him for the weekend and lets him run wild and do whatever the hell he wants. So, I'm the bad guy. I'm the mean mommy who has to take away the video games and iPad, and requires him to bathe and wear underwear."

"Listen, I don't know your son but I know a lot of kids and I know how tough it can be for them when things change in their family. Like you said, he wants your attention. It's not malicious."

The bartender returned wearing a dry shirt and a scowl etched in stone. He set a fresh martini in front of Christiane, saying, "If you throw another drink, I'm kicking you out."

"Sorry," she called after him as he walked away. She took a sip and glanced at me. "He's married."

I tipped my chin in the direction of the bartender. "That guy? Him?"

"Yeah." She bobbed her head. "I've checked."

"And you're using that information to decide whether or not to flirt with him?"

She shrugged. I didn't know how I was supposed to take that.

"Is it too much to ask for someone to worship me the way Noah worships you?"

I laughed hard. "He doesn't *worship* me, Christiane. That's a little much, don't you think?"

"Call me Christie," she said. "And it might be a little much for you but I'd give anything to have even a crumb of what you have. I mean it. I'd do anything for someone to give me the kind of attention Noah gives you. I just—I guess I want someone who notices me."

With that, I stopped seeing her as the woman who wouldn't leave Noah alone and started seeing her as someone doing her best to put the pieces back together and go forward. Someone just like me.

"You're not seeing it from where I'm standing," she continued. "That man adores you. I'd convinced myself he was stoic. Didn't wear his heart on his sleeve, you know? But then you roll into town." She blew out a breath, fanned herself. "He's not stoic at all. He was just waiting for you."

"That—" I didn't know how to disagree with her and keep the charade of our marriage alive. Was it still a charade if one person was in love with the other though she had no idea how to confess that without further trapping him in a fake marriage? Instead of stressing over those issues, I ignored them altogether. A-plus coping strategy. "Why do you want to jump into another relationship right now? What's the rush?"

She pressed her palms to her eyes. "My therapist has asked the same question every week for the past year."

"Have you figured out the answer yet?"

She groaned. "No. Maybe. I don't know. I just don't like failing at things. I want a do-over."

"You want a do-over marriage?"

"Yeah. I need another chance to get it right." Then, softer, she added,

"I don't want to do it all on my own. I can but—but I don't want to. And I deserve better than that."

"You also deserve someone who reciprocates your interest," I said carefully. It was a lesson for myself as much as it was Christiane. "If they aren't into it—"

"Oh, trust me, my therapist knows all about you and Noah," she cut in. "She's deconstructed that situation with me. I don't need the reminder that I was unhinged."

"I don't know what to say to that." I reached for my drink. "I'm glad you've worked those issues out? That you can reflect on the situation clearly? I don't know, Christie, help me here."

She chuckled. "Do you want to order some food? I forget to eat when my kids aren't around." When I didn't respond right away, she added, "Unless you already ate with your friends. It seemed like your group was having a really good time so you probably want to head home."

"Those were friends from school," I said. "They all teach at Hope Elementary." I reached across her and grabbed the menu at her elbow. "I don't have a lot of friends in this town. I could do with a few more."

After a minute, she tapped a fingertip on the menu. "Just so you know, I don't like raw fish."

"Then what are you doing at an *oyster bar*?"

She tossed up both hands. "It's the only decent place in town."

"And yet you come in here and throw drinks like you're on spring break in Daytona," the bartender muttered.

"We'll do the cheese and charcuterie," I said to him. "Thanks."

When the bartender headed toward the kitchen, Christie turned to me. "It would've been really convenient for the purposes of my internal narrative if you were horrible and heartless. I mean, it would've been great for me to be able to channel my anger onto someone other than my co-parent."

"If it helps, I've referred to you as the pee-listening lady on more than one occasion."

She steepled her fingers under her chin. "Mmm. That's good. That's helpful."

"You have to stop with that," I said. "It's no way to make friends."

"But I have picked up more than one client from public restrooms."

"What about your packed schedule? Do you really need more clients?"

She shrugged. "I'm a single parent now. A packed schedule is my safety net."

"Fair enough but don't be surprised if I won't go to the ladies' room with you."

"You've got a deal."

We polished off the cheese and charcuterie as we covered all manner of nonsense—whether we thought headbands looked good on us, the problem of trying to accumulate credit card airline miles, which barista at the Pink Plum made the best drinks, why we had no desire to go into a mall ever again—while the restaurant gradually shut down around us. Christie ordered another martini before switching to wine—none of which ended up on the staff—and I had some more sangria. I didn't trouble myself with the specific number of refills.

Being that we were still in Friendship, the car service we ordered wouldn't arrive for at least half an hour. The bartender grumbled about it but he dragged two barstools to the entryway to save us from waiting outside in the cold November rain.

"We're going to have to do this again tomorrow," I said.

"I can't drink like this two nights in a row," she said. "I'm gonna feel this for a week."

"No, I meant getting a car service." I laughed. "Because our cars are here. We're going to have to come back."

"Oh. Right." She nodded as she swiped her phone. "That's going to be a pain in the ass. Maybe I should just walk home."

"That's a stupid idea," the bartender called.

"I'm on the other side of the bridge," I said. "And up a hill. And my husband doesn't like it when I walk places at night."

"Yeah, that vibe comes across loud and clear," she said. "But then again, he does worship you. I bet he'd carry you up a hill if you asked him to."

I hugged my arms across my chest to hold in a shiver. It wasn't true. He didn't worship me. Whatever his feelings were for me, they were new and I couldn't convince myself they were here to stay. Soon enough, he'd tire of me the same way everyone else did.

chapter thirty-five

Noah

Students will be able to confess everything.

THE LAST TWO hours of our drive home were terrible. We hit miles of pointless traffic and then chased a storm through Connecticut and into Rhode Island, and Gennie was irritable the whole way. By the time we exited the highway toward Friendship, she was kicking the seat back and yell-singing an annoying theme song from a kids show.

My head was just about to split open when we finally reached Old Windmill Hill Road.

I had a difficult relationship with my family's farm and this town but I couldn't deny that I was relieved to be home. And it wasn't simply a matter of coming home after an exhausting trip with a handful of a child. I was relieved to return to *this* home, to this land, to the life I had here. The life we had together, me and Gennie and Shay.

I was going to tell Shay the truth tonight. I was going to tell her that I loved her, that I'd always loved her. All the way back to the beginning. Even if I dropped dead from admitting that I'd loved her in silence for years, I wanted her to know. And I wanted her to stay.

"I want to see the doggies," Gennie wailed as I turned down the gravel lane. "And my kitties too."

I scanned the dark clouds overhead. We were in for a downpour but this kid needed to run around. "You can visit with them until the rain starts. The minute you feel a raindrop, you come inside."

"What if I don't feel any raindrops? What if the rain doesn't drop on me?"

I glanced at her in the rearview mirror. She didn't notice. "If there are any raindrops falling near you, it's time to come inside."

"What if I don't notice because they aren't close enough for me to notice?"

"Imogen."

"Yeah?"

I turned off the ignition. "If you can't recognize when it's raining, you can't wander around the farm alone. Got it?"

She banged her feet against the passenger seat back again. "Yep."

"Go ahead," I said, "but I don't want to see you soaked to the bone in an hour."

"Aye aye." She unbuckled from her booster seat and opened the door, darting off toward the dog run at full speed.

If I was lucky, I'd get an uninterrupted half hour with Shay. I needed every minute of that time. I grabbed our bags and carted them inside. When I didn't find Shay on the first floor, I headed for her bedroom. It wouldn't be her bedroom for long. If this went the way I wanted, we'd stop pretending that we could cleave anything into hers or mine. It was all *ours*.

I pushed the door open and found her sitting on the floor, surrounded by—everything. Clothes, books, earrings, shoes. *Everything*. Then she startled, jumping a bit and scrambling back, a hand pressed to her chest. She tugged out her earbuds, saying, "I didn't expect you for another hour or two."

I reached down and offered my hand. "We hit the road early."

She stood and brushed off the seat of her jeans. "How was it? How did Gennie handle it?"

I wanted to yank her into my arms but small mountains of sweaters and books separated us. Instead, I brought my hand to the back of my neck. "Better than I could've expected."

"That's good," she said. "That's really good."

"Gennie went to visit the animals. She needed to run around after the drive."

"That makes sense."

I studied her mountains for a minute. The closet was empty and the drawers too. There was a system in place that I couldn't decipher and I had the sinking sense this was a precursor to packing. She was getting ready to leave. She'd decided this wouldn't work.

I gestured to the mountains as my stomach dropped to the floor. "What's going on here?"

"Summer is very much over." She dropped her hands to her hips. "I'm trying to get organized."

"Organized." I nodded. My stomach was in the basement. "To move back to Thomas House?"

She parted her lips to speak but stopped herself. She tapped her phone and slipped her earbuds back into their case. Then, "We did this all wrong, Noah. Maybe it was for the right reasons but—" She looked away, out the window facing the orchards. "I've fallen for you—and your niece and your farm and even this wonky town—but you married me so I could inherit Lollie's land." My heart jumped into my throat. "You rescued me like you rescue everyone."

"You are not everyone, Shay. Not even close."

Staring down at her hands, she said, "I have a lot of experience convincing myself that people love me. I don't even realize I'm doing it until those people make it painfully clear that they *don't* love me, they *never* loved me. But I can't convince myself that you would've chosen this if not for Lollie's wacky will and the land, even if you say you don't want it, and all of the things that mixed together to make this situation. And I can't convince myself that you would've chosen me."

"You're wrong about that."

"But you can't prove it, can you?" She finally met my gaze and I felt all the agony in her dark eyes. "That's what I need. *Proof.* I have all these people who give me fractions and fragments of themselves and swear it's the whole. I tell myself to believe them, to take those pathetic little pieces and make something real from them. And I do. I make relationships and promises and futures. I make everything and I make myself believe." She held up her hands and let them fall to her sides. "I don't want to do that to myself anymore."

I felt like I was being ripped apart from the inside out. "Then let me give you something better."

She layered both hands over her heart. "I can't let you rescue me again. I cannot be one more person who expects you to save the world. I have to save my own world."

We stared at each other for a long moment, the ridge of her books and clothes dividing us. Thunder rumbled in the distance and wind whipped through the trees. I brought my hand to the back of my neck again and dug a thumb into the knots there. It didn't help. I couldn't imagine anything would ever help.

"You want proof," I said. "I'll show you proof."

Shay shook her head. "Can we set this aside for tonight? I need to take a shower and finish some laundry and work on my lesson plans because this week's schedule has changed again. And you've had such a long day—a long week, really—and I'm sure you want to get Gennie back on her regular routine."

Shower. Laundry. Lesson plans. Routine. I stared, waiting for her to realize that we weren't going to *set this aside* for the night. When I couldn't stand it anymore, when the pressure was so intense the only thing I could do was hit the release valve or wait to explode, I said, "I love you. I mean, I fucking *love* you, Shay. I've loved you for years upon fucking *years* and none of the garbage leftover from your ex or your mother or anyone else is going to change that. *You* will not change that."

A breath whispered out of her and her brows fell as if she didn't understand. "Noah, I—"

"No. Don't say anything. Don't tell me I'm wrong or I don't know what I'm talking about." I took a step back and held up a hand. "You asked for proof. I'll give you proof."

I didn't wait for a response. I jogged down the stairs, across the kitchen, into the small den where I stored my books from college and law school and everything else I wanted to keep separate from farm business. On the farthest corner of the highest shelf sat one of my dad's old cigar boxes.

The last time I'd thought about this box was a few years ago when construction on this house ended and I'd moved in. I'd raked myself over the coals for keeping it that long but even then I hadn't been able to let it go. I'd never been able to let her go.

My phone vibrated in my pocket and I tucked the box under my arm to answer. "What?" I growled.

"Welcome home. We got some goats on the loose," Bones said. "The wind is really slapping our asses today. It took out fencing all over the property. We got most of the goats back in but it looks like two are pulling an REO Speedwagon taking it on the run. We've got some guys patching up the fence but we're also dealing with a few fallen trees behind the farm stand so we're shorthanded." He cleared his throat. "Any chance you want to fetch some goats before the skies open up?"

I ran a hand down my face. "Motherfuck," I groaned.

"That's the kind of enthusiasm I like to hear."

"Any idea where these goats are headed?"

"Goats don't announce their plans," he said with a cackle. "They're probably tearing up whatever is left of the pumpkin patches."

"I don't have time for this today," I grumbled. "Catch me on the radio if these goats figure out what's good for them and go home before I find them."

"Unlikely, but I'll do it," he said.

I ended the call and slapped a sticky note on the cigar box, scrawling a quick message for my wife, the woman who didn't see family birthdays and fresh bread, and ice cream scoopers sent to organize her classroom and general contractors sent to overhaul her farm as evidence of my love for her. As bottomless devotion. Just as soon as I rounded up these goats, we'd have a good long talk about the real reason—the only reason—I married her.

The shower was running when I climbed the stairs. It was better this way. I didn't think I could pull together the appropriate words to explain this box or why I'd held on to the contents all these years. I needed Shay to figure it out for herself. I needed her to remember and maybe then she'd understand. Then she'd believe me. Then she'd have all the proof she could ever want.

I stepped into her room. The mountains were exactly where I'd left them. Sweaters and jeans on one side, sundresses and shorts on the other. I set the cigar box on her bed, the hot pink note on top screaming for attention. I paused for a minute, the weight of all the vulnerabilities contained in that box pulling me back. If this didn't work, we'd never recover. I'd never recover.

With that realization heavy in my chest, I walked down the stairs and out into the storm. November afternoons had a way of turning into night in the blink of an eye, and the storm clouds only intensified the darkness overhead. Rain was spitting down sideways and the wind was howling. Any late season apples we had left were likely to fall tonight.

I found Gennie hurrying out of the shed, the cats watching her as they paced near the door. "There's no rain on me," she called.

That was not true but I didn't care. "I have to check on some fencing," I said, intentionally avoiding all mention of her goat friends. "Stay inside. Play with your iPad. I'll be back soon."

"Is it okay if I read a book?"

"What?" I peered at her, certain I'd misheard in the roar of the wind.

"Can I read a book in my room instead of playing on the iPad?"

"Yeah, of course. Why would you need permission to do that?"

"You said I should use the iPad but I want to read instead and I didn't want to blow off your directions." She shrugged before skipping off toward the house.

"Who is that kid and what the actual fuck is happening to my life?" I muttered as I settled behind the wheel of my ATV.

When I started up the machine, I realized I hadn't grabbed my radio on my way out. I patted my pockets for my phone but didn't find that either. I probably left it on my desk in the den.

But I couldn't run back inside now. I'd have to deal with Gennie or Shay—who would want a ton of answers that I didn't have the time to give her. Instead, I drove down the hill, past the orchards and toward the pumpkin patch on the border of Twin Tulip land as rain and wind lashed me from all sides.

I was wet and tired when I spotted the first goat picking her way through the remaining gourds. The second goat came out of nowhere and darted across the beam of my headlights. I swerved around her—and promptly rolled the ATV into a stream.

chapter thirty-six

Shay

Students will be able to make wrong choices for all the right reasons.

THERE WAS a time when I believed I was free. I was *independent*. I was unencumbered by the gridlock of family expectations or tradition. I could invent myself in any way I wished and no one would know any different.

The problem with that level of freedom was that it was all sky and no earth. There was no one to prevent me from floating out into space. From being lost and forgotten. The only solution was tying a rope from my waist to someone's wrist and begging them to hold on to me.

Jaime held on to me. Audrey, Grace, and Emme too. They held on even when I'd been a wedding-crazed fiend and they held on when I was too busy grieving the life I'd almost had to be a good friend.

And Noah held on to me too.

And that was why everything hurt. It hurt from deep inside and also everywhere outside me, like the weight of gravity on my body was too much to endure. And everything was wrong. My words, my feelings, my thoughts—all wrong. Nothing came out right. Never the way I wanted.

I felt like a child running around with a butterfly net after dark, overeager and too imprecise to accomplish anything other than flailing until I tired myself out. A child too, because it seemed like I couldn't explain to Noah that I was trying to protect him. I was trying to spare him the trouble of one more burden on his shoulders. The best I could manage was to rip up my words like blades of grass and throw them at him, hoping he understood that I couldn't stay here and wait for him to realize he'd never truly wanted me to begin with.

And that was why I was crying in the shower when the bathroom door opened and I heard, "Hi, Shay. I'm home."

I pressed my fingers to my eyes and sucked in a breath. "Hey, Gennie. How was your trip?"

"I went swimming every day and Noah let me have baby carrots when we stopped for snacks in Transylvania."

I rested my forehead on the shower wall. I could do this. I could pull myself together and have a kid conversation. "Pennsylvania?"

"Mmm. That's what Noah said but I still think it's Transylvania. I like it better." Then she added, "Noah went out to check the fences."

I started to shave my legs. "Okay."

"My mom said she's happy you and Noah got married. She said, 'Why am I not surprised it's Shay What's-Her-Name from high school?'" Gennie belted out a laugh. "Shay What's-Her-Name. That's funny."

A sob threatened to break free and I had to work at breathing through it. "That is funny," I managed. "Can you give me a few minutes to finish up in here and put on some clothes? You can tell me everything then."

"Okay. I'm gonna go read in my room," she called, the door slamming behind her.

Since I knew she'd come looking for me in approximately three minutes, I hurried through the rest of my shower and dressed quickly. It wasn't until I went to call for Gennie that I noticed the small box sitting on my bed.

I pulled the sticky note off the top. In Noah's firm hand it read: *Here's your proof.*

When I opened the lid, I found pages of notebook paper folded into precise squares. I sifted through them, a gasp whooshing out of me as I recognized the sunflowers drawn all over the backs of those pages.

Those were *my* sunflowers. I'd drawn those.

My heart was thumping hard in my chest and my fingers didn't want to work and my eyes were having trouble seeing through a mist of tears as I tried to unfold one of the notes.

My dearest Blue Gray,

This is my second note of the day but Walker's government class is draining the life out of me and I need this distraction to stay awake. You saved my ass on that algebra exam. There's no way I didn't pass but it was hairy on a few questions. Seriously, Blue, I owe you for all your help studying yesterday. I promise I won't leave it to the last minute again.

I'm supposed to go to the daffodil festival with some people on Saturday but that sounds like a horrible idea now that I say it out loud. Here's what I want to know: Why is that a festival, Blue? And can this town go a month without a festival? Or is life here so boring that they needed to plant a bunch of yellow flowers around town and send people on a scavenger hunt to prevent everyone from dropping dead from boredom? Another question: Should I expect a tulip festival next month? And a grand May Day the month after, complete with virgins dancing unironically around poles? A better question: Does this town have any virgins left? Based on locker room chatter alone, I'd have to say the answer is no.

Write back soon and explain these things to me, please. I risk dropping dead of boredom without your insight.

All of my endless love,

I REACHED FOR ANOTHER, nearly ripping the old paper in two as I loosened the intricate folds.

My darling Blue Gray,

I know you've grown weary of my complaints on the topic of this provincial town but have we discussed the matter of wind chill? Because it is quite unpleasant and this is coming from someone who was recently evicted from Switzerland. At this rate, I'm going to end up stealing every single one of your hoodies before spring comes.

In regard to your question from yesterday, I do believe it is time we start plotting our Old Home Days return. Do you think next year is too soon? Can we saunter in, you reeking of Yale and old boys' clubs and me fresh off New York Fashion Week and whichever university my mother bribes to accept me? Or should we give it five years and let some anticipation build up?

I'm getting the eyeball from Williamson so I have to cut this short. Teachers are the worst. Why can't they just let me ignore them in peace?

Love forever,

AND THEN THE OTHERS.

Blue Gray, my moodiest of the moody,

Thanks for the save the other night. I don't love football enough to sit through an entire game but I really don't love it when everyone decides to get drunk and be idiots. I know that's what high school is about, especially high school in small-town America, but I've already been an idiot. I'm over it. Thanks for taking me home and being over it with me, even if you were in one hell of a grumbly mood that night.

Someday we'll hang out together and talk about all the fabulous things we're doing. No small-town drama for us. We'll meet somewhere in New York, of course, and tell stories about taking over the world. It will be perfect. We'll be perfect.

All my drama-proofed love,

The Bluest of Blue Grays,

Sometimes I wonder if my entire life is going to be a series of mistakes. One after another, and I don't see any of them coming until they fly over my head. I feel like everyone else has a built-in sensor to know when they're on the verge of fucking it all up and I just have to find out what happens when I fuck it up because I don't have that mechanism.

Promise me you'll stop me before I fuck everything up. You're my only hope.

Love eternal,

BG—

Thanks for the coffee this morning. It reminded me of home. Or something vaguely familiar as vague familiarity is my only threshold for considering something home.

I know I sound like a spoiled brat when I say I miss European coffee—but I miss European coffee. You made my day.

Lovingly caffeinated,

Blue Gray of the misty morning,

You bring up a great point and my answer is a simple one: I have no idea what happens next year. College is a vast, aqueous mystery. I'll probably get legacy-admission'ed into Boston College but I don't care. I don't have the first clue what I'll do there and I'll probably waste a few years figuring it out. As long as I don't embarrass my mother, it doesn't much matter.

I wish I loved something enough to know I wanted to spend my life doing it but loving stuff is scary. It's a goddamn danger to my health. These things that people love, they often turn around and destroy them. Just look at Picasso and the ear. Really! I don't think I want the risk of loving anything that could ruin my life in the process.

Love and mysteries,

BG,

I hope you didn't get in trouble. I'm sorry I kept you out late last night. I didn't realize we were so far past your curfew. I don't want to make things difficult for you at home. I really am sorry. Please blame me. Everyone already thinks I'm a problem child. Just tell them it was me and get yourself out of this mess.

Also: thank you for listening. I don't know why I was so upset. My mother hardly ever remembers my birthday. I should've expected this. I know better than to get my hopes up with her.

Thanks for letting me cry it out all over your shoulder. I needed that. And for the love of god, throw me under the bus for this.

Blue Gray,

Someday, I want to see you smile. Like, a real smile. Not that smile you give me when I say I'm going to ditch phys ed and get a decent lunch in town or when I sit next to you in English and steal your notes so I can get participation credit for once.

You're going to tell me why you're so blue and so gray and before you write me a five-paragraph essay on blue and gray being your personality, allow me to say: I know. I know. I know and I love it and I want to know how it came to be this way. I want to know everything about you, dear friend.

All my love and smiles,

My sweet, sweet BG,

I hope your mom is doing okay. I'm sorry you and your family are going through so much with her health. I don't know if there's anything I can do to help but I want you to tell me if there is. You know I'll do anything for you. Just say the word and I'm at your service.

Love you lots,

Blue Gray Bananapants,

No, I don't know what that means. I just like it.

Another thing I like: Lollie. I thought I was getting stuck with some mean old lady when my mother sent me here but Lollie is actually awesome. I wish I didn't have to pick up and move all the fucking time but I'm happy I moved here. I feel like I don't have to worry about everything when I'm at Twin Tulip and that's pretty cool.

I know you don't feel the same way about your family's farm and that's okay. We're coming at it from opposite directions. I'd probably hate it if I was riding your tractor.

(Is that a suitable substitution for "in your shoes" in this area? I have no clue.)

A bunch of people asked if I'm going to the harvest festival (???) this weekend. Can you explain this to me as if I'm an outsider who doesn't set a watch by the moons and such? Do I want to go to this thing? Will I be required to harvest anything?

All the bananapants love I have to give,

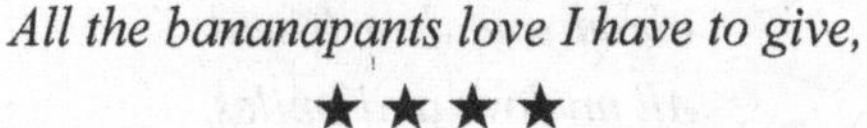

My once and future rescuer,

In case no one has ever told you this, you have the best heart in the whole world. Even when you're grouchy as fuck (see: the past two weeks straight), you do the sweetest things like taking me home when I'm stranded after the winter formal (thanks, Brett Schiveley, for leaving me at the dance because I didn't want to go to your uncle's lake house). I didn't think you were even going to the dance but there you were in your spiffy blue suit.

I never remember to plan my exits from these things but you never forget. For real, BG, you're my best friend. Never lose that sweet heart.

Someday, I'll rescue you.

Always,

I FLEW through the pages until the entire duvet was covered in blue ink sunflowers and my swirling teenage penmanship.

"The stars," I whispered to myself. "Oh my god. *Oh my god.*"

"What's that?"

I jumped out of my skin at the sound, one of the notes clutched to my chest as I whirled around to face Gennie. "I didn't hear you come in," I said, my heart going a hundred miles an hour.

She peered around me. "What's that?"

"Some old letters," I said, gathering them up.

She eyed one where I'd drawn a map of Twin Tulip on the back side. "They look like treasure maps."

"Nope, not treasure," I said, my words sounding as unsteady as I felt. "I know I said we'd talk but I need to make a phone call."

"That's okay." She bobbed her head, still angling for a look at the letters as I shuffled them back into the box. "I'm going to read a story to my toys."

Of course, these notes didn't fit now that I'd unfolded them, and I wasn't going to force them in there. These things were fifteen, sixteen years old. And he'd kept them for a reason, a reason I wasn't prepared to comprehend.

"Sounds good," I called after her.

Once Gennie was in her bedroom, I grabbed the box, the notes, and my laundry basket, and headed downstairs. I closed the basement door and crept down the stairs on tiptoe though I couldn't explain precisely why I was sneaking around. It didn't make sense but it felt extremely necessary.

Once I reached the bottom, I tapped Jaime's contact and held the phone out in front of me, waiting for her to pick up. When her face finally appeared on the screen, I blurted out, "Noah just told me that he loves me and I asked him for proof and I'm freaking out because I forgot all about the letters I wrote him in high school—which he kept—and all of this is too much. It's *too much*, Jaime."

She twisted her hair over her shoulder, saying, "Slow down, slow down. Why are we frazzled about this? I think I told you that he loved you when I was stuck in that tire swing of yours."

"Because he also said he's loved me for a really long time," I said, all the words rushing out at once. "Since we were teenagers. And then he left a bunch of notes I'd written back in high school and I realized I used to draw stars at the end instead of signing my name."

She blinked at me. "And?" I unfolded one of the notes, held it up to the screen. "Wait, wait, wait. There is no way. Holy bananas, doll. Did he…name his farm after you?"

"Maybe?" I scanned the note again. "I used to call him Blue Gray. Because he was sad and moody. And I was weird and thought I could read auras back then."

"You're still weird but we can't pretend it's a coincidence that his farm's logo is made up of the exact stars you drew on a blue-gray background."

"Why would he do that?"

She blinked at me. "Other than wanting a constant reminder of you?"

"He never said anything. I mean, we were friends but"—I sighed, rubbed my forehead—"but I never knew."

"It seems he's forgiven you for that oversight." When I didn't respond, Jaime hummed to herself for a second. "I'm going to miss the shit out of you."

"What?"

"I'll visit as much as I can. Long weekends, holidays, summers. You might have to pick me up—is there a train to Rhode Island? I'm not sure —but I'm going to visit. You're family to me. Just because you have your storybook town and your storybook husband doesn't mean you can blow off the chaotic bisexual friend."

"What the hell are you talking about?"

She rolled her eyes. "He *loves* you, Shay. He's loved you even longer than I have and he has the evidence to back it up. Add that to the fact he married you so you could get your granny's farm and he took down Xavier in the middle of the farmers market, and you know what comes next."

Tears filled my eyes as I said, "But I don't know."

"Yes, doll, you do. You let him love you. You live your happy life with your bizarre little tulip farm and his precious pirate niece. You take the job at that school—first grade so we can share plans, please—and you stay there. With the husband who loves you so much he wanted to see your little star drawing every single day, even before you came back to him."

"But what if—"

"Nope." She held up a hand. "No. We're not playing What If. We're playing Daddy Bread Baker Loves You. We're not spending our time looking for loose threads or sinkholes. We're not comparing him to the ex and his great many red flags. We're taking the incontrovertible proof that your husband provided you today—the proof you asked for—and believing in it."

"But what if he changes his mind?"

"You have a lot of practice at ignoring all the reasons a situation is wrong for you so it's going to take some time to recognize why it's right. You'll just have to trust me on this." She sighed. "You just don't see the way he looks at you. If you could, you'd know what I do, which is that he made up his mind a long, long time ago and he's been waiting on you to make up yours."

I stared across the basement for a minute. There were boxes stacked in one corner and some old furniture in the other. It was all precise and tidy, just as Noah would have it. Eventually, I said, "I don't know how to do this."

"Then tell him that."

"I just—I don't know—I know he's going to leave. Or he'll realize he wants to leave but can't because he's trapped in this thing with me or it would hurt Gennie or—"

"Tell him that too," she said. "Tell him you've road tested a whole lot of abandonment issues and the ex really topped that situation off. Especially when you met with him against my advice a few weeks ago. Tell him you're extra jumbled and mumbled from that, and you're trying to find your way through it. Tell him what's in your head right now."

"What if I don't live up to the fantasy he's been carrying around since high school?"

She snorted. "That's actually hilarious because it hasn't been a fantasy for months. You're married, doll. You live with him, you have lots of wild sex with him, and you sort of have a kid together. I think you can put those worries to bed—unless he's busy railing you in it."

"James."

"Speaking of which, *why* isn't he railing you right now? That sort of declaration requires the immediate removal of all clothes and inhibitions. You should have this convo naked. It would go much better."

"He went out to check on the fences," I said with a shrug. "But"—I frowned at the time on my screen, realizing I'd lost a full hour to those old notes—"it shouldn't take this long."

"The many joys of farm life," she murmured. "Go find your husband. Tell him you love him and you're not sure how to make it work but you want to try."

"Can I use those exact words?"

"Is there a guest room at your house and a seat around your holiday table for me?"

"Always," I said.

"Then yes, by all means, borrow all of my words." She grinned, adding, "I love you and I want the best things for you."

"I love you and I want the best things for you too."

"Okay. Enough of this." She sniffled and dabbed at her eyes. "I'm meeting some swingers for dinner and I need to put my face together.

You need to find your husband and give yourself permission to trust big, amazing, scary things. Maybe you also need to give him permission to love you the way he's always wanted. If he's felt like this since high school, maybe it's time for you to step up and do the hard work."

I nodded. If all of this meant what it seemed to mean then I didn't back Noah into a fake marriage corner any more than he needed me to defend against Christiane. He might've rescued me but he did it because he wanted to—because he wanted me.

I felt self-important and silly thinking that but a small piece of me recognized the truth and that piece shouted over all the other pieces playing the same old broken record of *no one wants you* and *they'll leave just like they always do*.

Noah wouldn't leave. Not even if I left him.

When the call ended, I sat there for a minute, searching for homes for all the new emotions filling my chest. I pulled in several deep breaths and pushed to my feet, the notes and laundry basket under my arm.

The kitchen was empty and the windows were streaked with rain. Noah's radio was still seated in its charging station and his phone was on the table. As I stepped into my tall rain boots, I called up the stairs, "Gennie, I'm running over to the shed for a minute. I'll be right back."

"Aye aye, captain," she shouted.

With my hood yanked over my head and my hands clutching the coat close to my chest, I jogged across the gravel drive toward the shed where Noah kept his four-wheelers. I figured I'd find him in here, messing around with his gear and generally avoiding me, but the shed was empty and his favorite vehicle was gone.

"I guess that leaves this one," I muttered to myself as I fired up the older vehicle. As I drove out of the shed, two other ATVs pulled up in front of the house. With the rain and all their weather gear, all I could make out were large, possibly male shapes. "Noah?"

"No, it's Tony," one of the drivers called. "Bones."

I came to a stop beside his vehicle, the rain whipping at the side of my face. "Have you seen Noah?"

"We came here looking for him," Bones said, gesturing to the farmhand in the other vehicle. "He's not coming through on the radio. He must've broken down out there."

"He left the radio inside. His phone too." I climbed out of the vehicle and headed for the steps. "Come on," I yelled to him. "I need you to stay here with Gennie while I look for him."

"You—oh, no. *No.* He'd kill me if I let you go out in the dark, in this weather. No, ma'am. We'll look for him."

"I'm going, and if he has a problem with it, he can work it out with me." I opened the kitchen door to find Gennie mixing a glass of pirate juice. "Mr. Bones is going to hang out with you for a few minutes while I help Noah with something. I'm sure he'd love some pirate juice."

A soaking wet Bones came up behind me, saying, "Your husband is going to kill me and then fire me and then dismember me for letting you take an ATV out in a storm. We take our ATV safety seriously around here, in case you hadn't noticed, ma'am."

"Pirates dismembered some of their prisoners," Gennie said.

I glanced between them. "Sounds like you have plenty to discuss."

With a great sigh, Bones said, "Go down the hill, past the orchards, near the marsh. There's a pumpkin patch down there, the one we use for wholesale pumpkins and squash. Not the pick-your-own patch up near the farm stand. It's flat but you have to watch out for streams. In this weather, they'll be running high. Don't try to cross them."

"Okay," I said, reciting those words over and over until they imprinted on me. "Okay. Thank you."

He grabbed the radio and pushed it toward me. "Take this. Stay on channel four. If I don't hear from you within twenty minutes, I'm calling for the cavalry. I mean it. I'm calling everyone. All-points bulletin. All hands on deck."

"Understood." I took the radio and tucked it into an interior pocket to keep it dry. To Gennie, I said, "You know what to do. I don't have to remind you."

She dropped two cherries into her glass. "Nope."

I wasn't an expert when it came to this land. I didn't know it the way Noah did, not even the way Gennie did, but I knew where that pumpkin patch was because it leaned up against the Twin Tulip border. I'd spotted a bunch of stray pumpkins when I went for a walk down there earlier in the week. Without that knowledge, I would've been driving blind.

I was about ten minutes from the house and clutching the wheel so hard my fingers were numb when I caught sight of white goat fur. I slowed to a roll, waiting for the goat to wander through the headlights again. But it wasn't a goat I saw next. It was muddy jeans.

Noah held a hand up to his face, shielding his eyes from the glare of the lights. There was blood running down his forehead and he had his other arm cradled against his abdomen in a way that said something wasn't right. A pair of goats milled around him. "Bones?" he called.

I turned off the vehicle and sprinted toward him. "Noah!"

"Shay? What the fuck are you doing out here?"

"Someone had to rescue you this time."

"You could've been hurt or killed out here," he roared.

"But I wasn't."

"Goddammit, Shay—"

"I love you too," I said. "And I'll love you as long as you'll let me if—"

"Don't finish that sentence," he called.

We could barely hear each other over the wind and rain but this had to be said and it had to be now. "I don't know how to do this. I don't know how to trust someone all the way and I don't know how to put myself in a position where I could get abandoned all over again."

"Shay—"

"But I think I want to do it anyway," I said. "I think I have to do it, even if it scares me. Even if I think it could fall apart or that you might change your mind, I have to stay here and I have to love you."

"I swear to you, I'm not changing my mind. I'm not letting you go. I couldn't. Not after all these years."

Right here, with goats nosing at my hand and a storm around us, everything shifted for me. It was a lot like being in my wedding dress and having the rug pulled out from underneath me again. My entire world flipped upside down. And just as I'd known then that all the fondness and affection I'd built for the ex was gone, I knew now that Noah loved me. He loved me and there was no way to force that into existence. Love like this couldn't be cornered, it couldn't be contrived. It was real and it wasn't about rescuing each other.

But I had to yell at my husband about cracking his head open first. "What are you standing over there for? We need to get that cut looked at and please explain what happened to your arm."

He trudged toward me. "I think I broke it when the ATV rolled."

"You *rolled* the ATV? What the hell were you thinking, coming out here in the dark, in a storm, on the ATV? Don't you have rules about this sort of thing? Don't you know better?"

"Yeah, I do." He caught a fistful of my coat and yanked me closer. "So, why don't you tell me what the hell *you* did the same thing, wife?"

"It was my turn to save you, husband."

He pressed his lips to mine and I *knew*. This was all the proof I needed.

AFTER BONES ASSURED us that he could stay with Gennie a little longer—and Gennie assured us there would be no escape attempts —we headed to the local emergency room. Noah grumbled the entire drive. He insisted his forehead wouldn't require stitches and that he didn't have time to deal with a broken arm and therefore it probably wasn't broken. Maybe a sprain, maybe a pulled muscle or a bad bone bruise. Nothing that would require a cast. He went so far as to explain this to the triage nurse, who promptly laughed her ass off and pointed us to the closest exam room while muttering "Farmers!"

Once we were alone, Noah scowled and grumbled about everything in the entire world until I pushed out of the metal chair and tucked myself in beside him on the gurney. "It makes sense now," I said.

"What's that?"

"All those times you said we were high school sweethearts."

"We were." He shrugged and then immediately winced. "You just didn't know it."

I asked, "Why didn't you tell me sooner?"

He brushed some dried mud off his wrist. "Sooner as in since you've been back, or sooner as in high school?"

"Let's start with high school and then we'll unpack our recent history."

He stared at the medical instruments on the wall. "Do you remember me in high school? Because I was shy and awkward and struggling through a ton of issues. I was tragically uncool and you were perfect."

"I wasn't perfect. You know I wasn't perfect. If those letters are proof of anything, it's that I was far from perfect."

"You were perfect," he said. "Fuck, Shay, you came here from *Switzerland*. Do you have any clue how that sounds to kids from this town? You'd lived in London and New York City. I couldn't compete with that. And I couldn't compete with everyone else. The popular crowd, the athletes, the rich kids. Everyone wanted you."

"I didn't need you to compete. I just wanted you to be my friend."

"I was amazed that you wanted that much from me," he said.

"And the notes." I dropped my palm to the center of his chest. "All those notes. I can't believe you kept them. You had them all this time."

"If you wanted me to die of embarrassment, you should've left me out there with the goats."

"I don't want you to die of embarrassment," I said with a laugh. "I'm trying to love you and you'd be making it really hard on me if you died right now. Please don't do that. But I do want to clear up a few suspicions that I have."

He wrapped his good arm around my waist, tugged me closer. "Whatever you're thinking, you're right."

"Tell me about Little Star."

An enormous sigh rattled out of him. "It's you," he whispered. "It had to be you."

"And those wonky stars?"

"Yours," he said. "I did use your intellectual property without proper permission though I'm hoping you'll forgive me for that."

I thumbed some blood off his cheek and kissed the corner of his mouth. "Forgiven." Then, "And the blue-gray?"

"There was no blue-gray without the wonky stars. They only ever existed together." He blew out another breath. "Every time you looked at my hat or the market tent or even the jam jars, I thought it would come back to you. That you'd remember and I'd be busted. You'd figure it out and I'd have to explain…everything."

"I think you wanted me to remember."

"Yes," he conceded, "but I wanted to find a way to make this work first. Make it work for real."

I smiled at my husband. There was an ugly bruise spreading from his forehead down around his left eye but I loved him and I knew he loved me too, and all of that scared the absolute shit out of me. "I want to try to make it work," I said, "if you want to try with me."

"Tell me all the things you want to try, wife."

I ducked my head, grinning into his neck. "I want a family."

"What does that mean to you?"

I lifted my shoulders. "It means you and me and Gennie, and Twin Tulip and this weird town that I love to hate but also kind of love."

"And Jaime," he added.

"Oh my god, Jaime. Yes. Don't tell her I forgot to include her in that list."

"Never," he whispered into my hair.

"I want to try making plans beyond the next few weeks, few months. I want to stay at Hope Elementary next year and I want us to make this wedding venue thing happen. And I want us to try being married. For real."

"I was wondering when you'd start taking this marriage seriously."

"I drove an ATV through a storm for you. At night," I added. "How's that for serious?"

"Sounds more like you need to be taken out to the barn again where I'll—"

"All right! It looks like someone here needs a few X-rays." We glanced up to find a nurse waiting in the doorway. He motioned to the wheelchair in front of him. "We're going for a ride," he said.

"I can walk," Noah said.

"No need when we've got wheels." Another pointed gesture to the chair. "Let's get this over with, big guy. The sooner we're done, the sooner we can get you patched up and out of here."

"Go on," I said to him. "I'll be right here."

He brushed a kiss over my lips. "I love you, wife."

"I love you too, husband." A smile forced its way across my face and tears pricked at my eyes as I spoke those words. I pressed my fingers to my mouth. "Wow. That's what it feels like."

Leaning close to my ear, he whispered, "Just imagine how much better it will feel when I'm inside you."

IT WAS ALMOST midnight when we returned home with a cast on Noah's arm and four stitches on his forehead. No concussion but a stern warning to take it easy for the next week. He was tired and sore all over, and even more grumbly than usual. I didn't think I'd ever loved his growling more than I did at that moment. It served as a fine distraction from the fact this accident could've been much, much worse.

When we stepped inside, we found Gennie seated at the kitchen table, her iPad playing *Pirates of the Caribbean* and every marker and colored pencil in the house spread out in front of her. "What happened? Are you okay?" she asked. "Did they have to amputate anything?"

"No amputations necessary," Noah said. "Just this boring old cast for a little while and these stitches."

Gennie beamed. "You're gonna have a badass scar."

"I guess that's the bright side of wrecking an ATV." He glanced around. "Wait. Why are you awake? And where's Bones?"

"I'm not tired and Mr. Bones is asleep," she said, still focused on her coloring.

"Isn't that wonderful," Noah said. "I'm going to kill that guy tomorrow. And then I'm going to fire him."

"No, you're not," I said. "None of those things are happening."

"And no dismemberment," Gennie added.

"Debatable," he muttered.

Gennie looked up from her coloring, glancing between us expectantly. "While you were gone, I decided we need some house rules."

"Is that so?" Noah asked as he opened the freezer.

"I made a list," she went on. "Do you want to hear it?"

As I retrieved Noah's prescriptions from my bag, I said, "Yeah, since we're all awake, go ahead and read it to us."

She held the paper up in front of her. "Number one, no more ATV driving at night."

"That lesson has been pounded into my head," Noah said. He grabbed a spoon before ducking into the pantry. "Actually and truly pounded. Won't make that mistake again."

"Number two, Shay and Noah have one date night every week." She looked up from the paper. "And I promise not to get into any trouble when you leave me with a babysitter."

"An important clause." Noah sat down at the table and made a small clearing in the art supplies. "Thank you for that addition."

"Adults are supposed to go on dates and do romantic shit so they can like each other," Gennie continued. "I think it's important for you and Shay to like each other."

I sat down between them and pressed a hand to Gennie's wrist. "We do like each other. You don't have to worry about that."

"But I want you to love each other and be happy." With a nod, she said, "One date night every week. No exceptions. I wrote a letter to Mrs. Castro to tell her I'm very sorry about scaring the shit out of her when I ran away with Bernie Sanders."

Noah wedged the pint of ice cream between his cast and his chest to wrench open the lid. I raised a brow. "I could've done that for you."

"I'm not so feeble that I need my wife to open my ice cream. Not yet." He wagged the spoon at Gennie. "Is there anything on your list about chores or kids not swearing all the time? Because that would be great."

She read over the page carefully. "Number three, we should have a pirate ship tree house." She glanced up. "That's all."

Noah shoved a large bite of coffee Oreo ice cream in his mouth as he studied Gennie. "I'm going to need some time to review these documents. Can we conference in a few days to negotiate terms?"

After a moment of consideration, she bobbed her head. "I'll agree to that."

"Can you also agree that it's far past your bedtime?"

Gennie shot a wide-eyed glance at the clock. "Maybe."

"It's time for me and Noah to go to bed," I said. "Why don't you come upstairs with us? Change into some jammies, brush your teeth, maybe hop into bed. What do you think?"

"What about Mr. Bones?" she asked.

"We're ignoring Mr. Bones right now," Noah said between bites of ice cream. Apparently, this was the effect painkillers had on him. "And he'll be out until dawn."

It took a few minutes and a lot of discussion but I got them both upstairs and into their bedrooms. Noah brought the ice cream along with him and I didn't protest. Despite her insistence that she wasn't tired, Gennie fell asleep sitting on her bed with her toothbrush in her mouth. I took care of that situation and tucked her in before making my way to Noah's room.

Was I supposed to call it *our* room? Was this *our* house? That would take me some time. Some adjustment. Some talking myself down every time I felt the doubt creeping back in.

I found him struggling to get out of his t-shirt. "It's a good thing I made you change out of all those wet, muddy clothes before going to the ER," I said as I freed his arm from the sleeve. I passed a hand over the scrapes and bruises dotting his torso. He needed a long, hot shower but it could wait until morning. "This would've been much worse with dried mud in the mix."

"You're sleeping in here now," he said, his arm around my shoulders.

I dropped my hands to his waist. "Is that a question?"

"I hope not." His gaze moved between my lips and my eyes. "But we can go as slow as you want. Just as long as we're going. That's all I need."

I unlatched his belt and drew down his zipper. His jeans hit the floor. "I think that all I need," I said, the words strange and unsteady as I formed them, "is you." I dragged my gaze up to meet his. "But you were in a rollover accident tonight and have multiple injuries. The only thing we're doing in this bed is sleeping."

He scowled with his whole face. "Can I lick your tits and tell you I love you when I wake up tomorrow?"

"I don't see why not."

"And the next day? Will you be here then?"

I grinned up at him, my chest feeling full and light at the same time. "The next day. The day after that. And the one after that too. Feel free to pencil me in through the new year."

That scowl broke when he laughed and I had no choice but to laugh along with him. "How do you feel about eating ice cream in bed and watching some reruns?" He dragged a finger along the neck of my sweater. "It's not nearly as interesting as what I'd like to do to you tonight, wife, but I have a feeling I'm going to crash pretty soon."

"Sounds great." I arched up on my toes and pressed a kiss to his mouth. "I guess that makes us an old married couple."

"There's nothing I'd rather be."

epilogue

Noah

Students will be able to make the right choices for the right reasons.

NEXT AUGUST

I DROPPED the papers on the kitchen table in front of Shay without explanation. She didn't glance away from her laptop which was not surprising seeing as she was sliding into back-to-school mode. Though she didn't admit it often, she was nervous about making the move to first grade permanent. "What's that?" she asked.

"It's a divorce filing."

She snapped her head up. "A *what*?"

I rested my hands on the back of the chair in front of me. "A divorce filing. Specifically, a filing to dissolve our marriage."

Shay rested her chin on her upturned fist. Her hair was back to strawberry blonde after letting it fade through the winter and spring. I couldn't explain why I liked the pale, subtle pink so much but every time I caught sight of it, I thought, *There's my girl.*

"And why do you want to dissolve our marriage, husband?"

It didn't matter how many times that word crossed her lips, it still hit me just as hard as the first time. "You don't need to be married anymore." I set another stack of documents on the table. "The title arrived yesterday. You're the owner of the Thomas Twins Farm now."

She paged through the documents. A grin pulled at her lips. Her face really was made for smiling. "I see."

"We don't need to keep doing this," I said, "if you don't want to."

"Hmm." She continued reading. "I know it sounds like you're doing me a favor but I'm also wondering if you're just itching to get my endless construction project off your books. Wash your hands of all things tulip and curse the day you attempted to bring my whimsical flower world under your reign?"

"If the past eight months have proven anything, it's that the whimsical flower world belongs to you and I have the privilege of pouring money into it indefinitely."

I couldn't call progress on the wedding venue slow. That would imply any amount of progress had occurred, and things hadn't gotten moving until the middle of May due to Twin Tulip's proximity to wetlands and new requirements for climatization and efficiency. We were rolling along now but our timeline was all kinds of fucked. We didn't have a date for a grand opening or a soft launch. We didn't even have a date for when we could safely assume most of the work would be complete.

It was a lot more than we'd bargained for but the interest was already overwhelming. The website for the Thomas House Gardens crashed the week we launched it. The marketing crew were up to their elbows in media requests and brides begging for bookings. We had to post signs at the turnoff for Twin Tulip announcing that the site wasn't open to visitors yet.

It was a nightmare but it wasn't a bad nightmare. Unsettling, maybe. Exhausting. *Expensive*. But it was the kind of nightmare that would work out for us in the end. If we could ever finish building the damn thing.

Gennie liked to refer to the project as a shitshow with flowers and I didn't want her to be right about that. She was doing better in school these days. It was still tough and there were times when she fell into her crusty old pirate ways, but she was making good progress in therapy and getting more specialized support for her ADHD. She was finally finding her way and it never stopped amazing me.

She gave field hockey a try this past spring. Who would've guessed she'd enjoy wielding a stick and running around in a mask while yelling her ass off? Shocking.

Gennie discovered a second passion in musical theater which also involved running around while yelling. Shay liked to remind me that the yelling was actually singing though I was still attuning myself to the difference. Gennie was a munchkin in the high school's winter production of *Wizard of Oz* and then an orphan in a middle school's spring production of *Annie*. She'd offered to clean the chicken coops indefinitely if it meant she could attend two four-week-long theater day camp sessions this summer. Last month, she was a stray dog in *The Aristocats* and tonight she was playing the role of a lifetime—one of Captain Hook's pirates in *Peter Pan*. This was the first time she had lines in addition to singing with the company, and she hadn't stopped reciting them to herself for weeks. Jaime, Grace, Emme, and Audrey—the unofficial aunties—were driving down from Boston to attend Gennie's opening night.

"Then you figured this would be a good time to end it?" she asked. "Clean break? The girls can just pick me up and take me home with them?"

I watched as she turned another page and ran her index finger over the words as she read. The strap of her sundress lolled down her shoulder, just begging for me to fix it. Her earrings were in the shape of pickles and they were completely ridiculous. I loved everything about them.

"I want to give you a choice," I said. "You didn't really have one the first time around."

"I had a choice," she said, her gaze still locked on the documents.

"City hall without any of our friends or family present? If you had it to do all over again, you'd choose that? A twine ring and a high five to seal the deal?"

"I'd include Gennie," she said. "I liked the ring. You know that." She gave a single shake of her head as she turned to the next page. "The lunch we had afterward was amazing. I'd do that again."

"I'll take you to lunch any time you'd like," I said. The school year was several weeks away and I already missed having her around during the day. "As I'm sure you're aware, wife."

"Bonus points if you wear a suit again. That did some nice things to me. It gave me some feelings." She pointed a finger toward her lap. "Some spicy feelings."

"Wearing a suit," I said, "gave you *spicy* feelings." I was half convinced she was fucking with me. She had to be fucking with me. There was nothing sexy—or spicy—about wearing a suit in the height of the summer heat. "I mean, if that's what you want, I'll do it but—"

"Noah." She folded her hands on the documents and looked up at me, her teacher stare firmly in place. "You could've told me to remove your tie with my teeth that day and I would've asked you where to put it when I was finished. You are devastating in a suit. Even more than you are in rolled-up sleeves and jeans that make me want to bite your bum."

I could feel the heat crawling up my neck and into my ears. I pointed at the document. "Decide if I'm divorcing you today. Okay? Thank you. We'll talk about what you can take off with your teeth later."

"Will I be doing it later or only talking about it?" She shrugged. "I just want to plan accordingly."

I fought the urge to roll my eyes. "What do you need to plan?"

"I don't know." She glanced to her phone. "Are you aiming for before Gennie gets home from camp or after her show tonight? Or in between? Do we need to sneak off somewhere? Will I need to protect my knees? Will I have to cover up beard rash later? These are the things I need to prepare for."

I shoved both hands through my hair. This wasn't going as I'd intended. "Read," I said, motioning to the document again.

"Someone has his bossypants on," she said under her breath.

"Shut up, Shay," I snapped.

"All right, all right." She twirled a lock of hair around her finger as she read.

A couple of months ago, her silence would've rattled me. I would've interpreted it as true consideration of the document I'd drawn up. But now I knew she was mine.

Strange, beaded earrings could be found on nearly every surface of our room, and her toys—plus a few additions—were housed in the middle drawer of my nightstand. We shared a home and a bed, and along with Gennie we learned how to be a family every day. I didn't believe I'd ever feel prepared to parent my niece to the level she required but now I didn't feel alone in that struggle.

As per Gennie's request, Shay and I went on dates just about every week though we didn't get too far. Thomas House had the exact number of beds we required and the ideal amount of privacy too. The complete lack of children down the hall was a powerful aphrodisiac. I couldn't think of any better date than allowing my wife to be as loud as she wanted and then taking her to the oyster bar for a drink and as many tiny appetizers as she could eat.

"I don't want another wedding," she said eventually. She turned over the final page and gathered the papers, tapping them against the table. "It wasn't perfect by any classical definition but it was perfect for us."

"Even the high five?"

She nodded. "I planned the perfect wedding once. I did everything right. Every last inch of it. But a perfect wedding does not translate to a perfect marriage—or even a good, healthy marriage." She pushed the divorce papers across the table. "Sorry, Noah. You're stuck with the high-five and twine-ring version of me. No divorces, no do-overs."

"Well, shit." I shoved my hands into my pockets and glanced around the kitchen. "What the hell am I going to do with this?" I set the small box on top of the divorce papers. "Since I'm not allowed a do-over."

She stared at the box for a long moment. "Noah," she whispered.

"Tell me, Shay. What should I do with it?"

Shocking the absolute fuck out of me, Shay stood up and walked out of the kitchen. This time, I was rattled. I didn't know where I'd made a wrong turn. I thought we were teasing each other, just snipping and poking the way we always did. But she'd *left*. Was I supposed to follow her? And say what—*Sorry about trying to replace the twine with a precious metal*? I didn't see how that was right.

As quickly as she'd exited, she was back—and she set a velvet box on the table beside the one I'd presented. "If I had it to do over again, I would've thought to bring something for you," she said. "I felt terrible that I didn't."

I brought a hand to the back of my neck. "You don't need to worry about—"

"But I do," she said. "That's my part of this deal. I'm the one who thinks about what you need while you're busy thinking about what everyone else needs." She nudged the box toward me. "Open it."

"You first," I said, nudging the other in response. "I'm not negotiating with you on that. Do it or I'll hold you down and do it for you."

"While that is a compelling offer—" The hinge creaked as she pushed back the lid. "Noah, how did you—" She glanced up at me. "How is this real?"

It was a slender bow of platinum studded with tiny diamonds. Though it wasn't an exact replica of the twine ring, it came damn close. "A local artist designed it from a photo I took of the original."

"Oh my god," she whispered. "I love it. I can't believe you did this for me."

I plucked the dainty ring from its box and slid it down her fourth finger. "It's only partially for you. I was tired of everyone in town asking when I was going to get you a ring."

"Anything to get the villagers off your back," she teased, reaching for the other box. My stomach hit the floor. She ran her thumb over the velvet before meeting my gaze. "I never expected this crazy plan of ours to go anywhere but I should've. I should've known from the start that it was the furthest thing in the world from fake. I'm so thankful that my life fell apart and sent me back here to get it right. To get you for good this time. So." She pried open the box, revealing a thick band with a thin rope detail around the middle. Just like twine. "I was going to give you this on our anniversary but since you want to divorce me—"

"All I want is for this to be your choice," I said. I grabbed her by the waist and sat her on the table, stepping between her legs. "I intend to keep you for all of your tomorrows but I don't want to keep this marriage unless it's the one you want. We can do it all over. Throw a party and invite all of our people. Or invite no one at all. We can end this and start fresh without the pressure of the estate and—and everything else that you went through. I want our marriage to be your choice and not a last resort."

She reached for my hand and settled the ring onto my finger. "You were never a last resort." She traced a finger over the band and a smile pushed at her lips. "Jaime would've been my last resort."

I dropped my head to her shoulder as laughter shook through me. "I love you so fucking much, wife."

"And I love you so fucking much, husband."

THANK YOU FOR READING! *I hope you loved Shay and Noah! If you'd like to read a bonus epilogue, get it here! (*https://geni.us/IAJbonuschapter)

*If you want more from Jaime, Audrey, Emme, and Grace, as well as the town of Friendship, Rhode Island, join my mailing list (*https://geni.us/officememos).

author's note

Friendship, Rhode Island isn't real but frozen lemonade, pirate ship playground structures, and milk delivery trucks painted like cows are real. Same with hills known for their very old windmill and towns with coves cutting them in half, daffodil festivals and Old Home Days. Coffee Oreo ice cream is real and so are tulip farms where you tromp through the muddy fields and pick flowers to take home. And goat yoga. Goat yoga is not a work of fiction.

While Friendship isn't a town you could find on a map of Rhode Island's Narragansett Bay, it draws inspiration from many real places. On the topic of Rhode Island's islands: there are about twenty-two of them, including Hope and Prudence. There's also Despair and Starve-goat, and a slightly sordid history of shipwrecks in Newport (Aquidneck Island) Harbor.

Another thing that is very real is the shortage of books in women's prisons. The Women's Prison Book Project puts books in the hands of prisoners around the United States. If you have gently used paperback books in need of a new home, please consider shipping them to this charitable organization.

also by kate canterbary

Vital Signs

Before Girl — Cal and Stella

The Worst Guy — Sebastian Stremmel and Sara Shapiro

The Walsh Series

Underneath It All – Matt and Lauren

The Space Between – Patrick and Andy

Necessary Restorations – Sam and Tiel

The Cornerstone – Shannon and Will

Restored — Sam and Tiel

The Spire — Erin and Nick

Preservation — Riley and Alexandra

Thresholds — The Walsh Family

Foundations — Matt and Lauren

The Santillian Triplets

The Magnolia Chronicles — Magnolia

Boss in the Bedsheets — Ash and Zelda

The Belle and the Beard — Linden and Jasper-Anne

Talbott's Cove

Fresh Catch — Owen and Cole

Hard Pressed — Jackson and Annette

Far Cry — Brooke and JJ

Rough Sketch — Gus and Neera

Benchmarks Series

Professional Development — Drew and Tara

Orientation — Jory and Max

Brothers In Arms

Missing In Action — Wes and Tom

Coastal Elite — Jordan and April

Get exclusive sneak previews of upcoming releases through Kate's newsletter and private reader group, The Canterbary Tales, on Facebook.

about kate

USA Today Bestseller Kate Canterbary writes smart, steamy contemporary romances loaded with heat, heart, and happy ever afters. Kate lives on the New England coast with her husband and daughter.

You can find Kate at www.katecanterbary.com

- facebook.com/kcanterbary
- twitter.com/kcanterbary
- instagram.com/katecanterbary
- amazon.com/Kate-Canterbary
- bookbub.com/authors/kate-canterbary
- goodreads.com/Kate_Canterbary
- pinterest.com/katecanterbary
- tiktok.com/@katecanterbary

CPSIA information can be obtained
at www.ICGtesting.com
Printed in the USA
LVHW090431081222
734762LV00001B/35